Secret of the
Dragon's Breath

"Here you enter the coils of the Dragon. Here my power was born. Here all things are possible and all things meet their opposite.

"I have awakened the Dragon. Can't you see all around you the Dragon's breath? A beast of such power that if you were to see it whole and all complete in a single glance, it would burn you to cinders. The Dragon is everywhere.

"The Dragon is everything. Its scales glisten in the bark of trees. Its roar is heard in the wind. And its forked tongue strikes like lightning.

"Do nothing. Be still. Sleep. Rest in the arms of the Dragon. Dream."

Merlin, the Magician, in *Excalibur, the Legend of King Arthur*

Secret of the Dragon's Breath

❖

Book Two

Derek Hart

iUniverse, Inc.
New York Lincoln Shanghai

Secret of the Dragon's Breath
Book Two

iUniverse books may be ordered through booksellers or by contacting:

iUniverse
2021 Pine Lake Road, Suite 100
Lincoln, NE 68512
www.iuniverse.com
1-800-Authors (1-800-288-4677)

Because of the dynamic nature of the Internet, any Web addresses
or links contained in this book may have changed
since publication and may no longer be valid.

This is a work of fiction. All of the characters, names, incidents, organizations, and dialogue in this novel are either the products of the author's imagination or are used fictitiously.

ISBN: 978-0-595-48095-1 (pbk)
ISBN: 978-0-595-60194-3 (ebk)

Printed in the United States of America

This book is dedicated to Emily Mari.
What a delightful girl, so full of life and good-natured!
She too loves imagining elves, fairies, dragons and the
world of make-believe.
Let's hope Emily always sees wondrous things through open eyes.

Contents

Foreword

Secret of the Dragon's Breath continues the adventures of Gavin Kane, Emily Scott, and Bunty Digby, thirteen-year-olds who continue to struggle with their daily lives, during the spring of 1941. While relatively safe on the north Cornish coast, the teens are well aware that England is under constant threat, as the Germans continue to bomb London and the surrounding industrial cities. While these friends have learned to cope with air raid sirens and strict rationing, they're soon faced with another sinister attempt to bring Britain to her knees. Yet with the addition of several new characters, the teenagers discover the true meaning of friendship from these unusual allies.

Secret of the Dragon's Breath also marks the return of that high-spirited dragon, Sir Thaddeus Osbert, who not only breathes fire, but also craves sugar. Faced with danger and intrigue, the teens call upon their dragon friend to help them battle the Nazis, who are determined to win the war, no matter what the cost. With a terrible new force threatening their beloved England, it's up to Gavin, Bunty, and Emily to seek out a magical solution. When their favorite dragon unleashes yet another secret power, you can be assured the outcome will not only be exciting, but full of long-lasting implications as well.

Preface

Throughout history, our beliefs have influenced our behavior. Perhaps the deadliest historical example of the impact of myth on belief comes from World War II, when Adolf Hitler drew upon ancient Germanic myths to help enthrall an entire nation. Hitler was deeply taken by composer Richard Wagner's operas, which drew vividly on the world of German heroic myths, pagan gods, heroes, demons, and dragons. Hitler intrinsically understood the deep emotional power of these symbols. Massive statues of ancient Germanic gods played a prominent role in the Nazi mass rallies at Nuremberg in the 1930's. Hitler grasped the visceral power, as well as the propaganda value, of a shared Teutonic myth in uniting the German people with the Aryan master race ideology.

Acknowledgements

First, to **Dave Hilburn,** who has established himself as a trustworthy and reliable advisor, while actively participating in the author's endeavors. Dave has made a difference on many fronts, but most of all as an honest and loyal friend, who believes.

A big thank you goes to **Harry Schwartz,** who has proven indispensable for a number of reasons. Harry enthusiastically provided critical assistance, willingly offered insights, which made the author's job easier, and has become a vital sounding board for Derek Hart's ideas. Harry is a consummate gentleman and a quality friend, who delivers on his promises. It is with great respect that the author acknowledges his contribution.

Also earning a place in the author's heart is **Katie Ashcraft**, who has proven a godsend in so many ways. Not only a dear friend and trusted financial advisor, Katie has quickly become a critical player in Derek Hart's success. Her positive nature and ready smile fills each day with possibilities. She also believes in the author and makes her impact felt.

Cover art by David M. Burke.

Introduction

The Breath of Dragons

Dragons once ruled
They formed alliances
They forged advances
Used by wizard and sage
Their lives numbered centuries
Filled pages in books
Jumped from every poem.

Where minstrels sang
Tales of knights and damsels
Battles with wings unfold
Brave deeds so bold
Yet tears were wept
Lives were shed
Loyal friends have bled.

Dragons once ruled
Magic touched every heart
Friendship kept faith alive
Carved in stone
Sacrificed in blood and sweat
Pain of flesh and bone
History witnessed deeds unknown.

Darkest evil invaded
Engulfed by the dragon's breath
Gentle races must survive
Love and trust will thrive

The call for justice rings
The voice of freedom sings
Saved by love.

Ian Lenthart
(Used with Permission)

1

Spring at Last

England's position was truly desperate. Civilian rations had been cut, cut again, and cut once more. The dreaded invasion had apparently been postponed, but was still a possibility. English cities were being bombed nightly. The Germans commanded a great arc of occupied land, stretching from Norway to the Spanish border, from which they could deploy their U-boats and Luftwaffe in an endless onslaught.

The year was 1941.

With Gavin by his side, Richard Kane stood on the heights of Hartland Point, overlooking the active ocean. Neither father nor son said anything for a long time, just enjoying each other's company.

"I'm sorry I won't be here for your birthday, Gavin," his father finally broke the silence.

"That's all right, Dad," the boy said. "It was fantastic you were able to get leave when you did. It was a splendid time."

"Yes, it was," Richard said. "I also believe you and Thaddeus are getting along famously?"

Gavin looked up at his father's face. "We do get along, it's true. He's a grand dragon and I have learned a great deal, but he can never replace you."

Suddenly the boy threw his arms around Richard's waist and squeezed him with all his might. "I shall miss you terribly."

"I'll miss you too, son," his father said. "Perhaps I'll get more time to come home, instead of it always being a national emergency."

"What makes your work so important?" Gavin asked.

"I think it was the Chief of the German General Staff, General Werner von Fritsch, who made a prophetic statement that the nation with the best photographic reconnaissance, would win the next war," Lt. Cmdr. Kane replied. "I'm trying to help win this war, by not letting any clue of what the Germans are up to get past our noses."

"You mean your eyes," his son corrected him.

They both laughed.

"Yes, my boy, you are correct," Richard said. "Sometimes I feel like my eyes are screwed up into my head they hurt so much."

"You should get Thaddeus to help you," Gavin suggested. "He's got incredible eyesight, you know."

His father was just about to shrug off the idea, when he had second thoughts. "That's not such an outlandish idea, my boy. A dragon has many lenses and perhaps the old boy might spot something we missed."

Richard pondered the possibilities for a few seconds more.

"How would that big clumsy dragon find a place to look at your photographs, without anyone knowing he was there?" Gavin asked.

His father replied, "I don't know, but I won't let that little detail stop me. Your suggestion has true merit and I would be crazy to pass up such an opportunity. I will have to noodle on this for awhile."

"Let's walk over to Boscastle, Dad," Gavin said. "I think you deserve a pint, don't you?"

"That sounds marvelous, son."

The pub they had in mind was located in a beautiful old building set on the hillside overlooking Boscastle. The *Napoleon Inn* had little rooms, and a quiet atmosphere, with a small car park across the road. All across England, in the rural towns and villages, the traditional country pub dispensed hand-pumped, cask-conditioned ales, decent wines, hearty home cooking, and local cheer.

Pubs traditionally were the focal point for villagers to meet with friends and wind down after a long day. The most popular drinks are draught beers, which meant they were pulled straight from the barrel. As each keg was delivered from the brewery and stored away from the bar in cellars until required, the beer was conditioned over time.

Beer wasn't rationed, but it was still in short supply. The beer drinking population soon got to know the delivery schedule of the various brewers. The *Cobweb Inn* received its supply on Monday, opened every weekday evening and sold out by Friday. On the other hand, the *Coombe Barton Inn* had its cellars re-stocked on Thursday, so had enough beer for the weekend drinkers, but Monday, Tuesday and Wednesday were usually dry. This meant the locals got plenty of exercise traveling between Crackington Haven and Boscastle.

Having something to eat at the local pub meant a packet of crisps, which were just plain cooked potato slices, with a pinch of salt, wrapped in a twist of blue paper inside a brown bag. After Gavin's father finished his one pint of ale, they started walking along the coast road, sharing a snack of fresh crisps.

"Where are we headed now?" the boy asked.

Richard smiled. "Before I report back to Medmenham, I thought we both should drop in to see Thaddeus."

"What a smashing idea!" Gavin exclaimed. "He'll be so glad to see you!"

At a leisurely pace, father and son headed for the little white cottage, which sat on a hill overlooking Tintagel Castle. Up the narrow path they traveled, to stand before an ancient ornate wooden door.

Gavin politely knocked and then opened the door.

Stepping inside, Richard had forgotten how tiny the hamlet really was. He smiled, however, when he saw the giant stone fireplace in the corner.

Swish.

It started coming apart, as each shaped stone shifted and moved through the air. Chunks and slabs sailed around the room, almost colliding, yet mysteriously always narrowly missing each other. This magical display of invisible levitation appeared random at first, but Gavin knew the rocks were coming together to form an entirely new shape.

What once had looked like ordinary fireplace stones, now glistened and sparkled with pulsating radiant colors, including bright sunrise yellow, burgundy red, burnished bronze, and ebony black.

Thaddeus Osbert appeared before them, his scales rippling with power.

"Greetings, Sir Osbert," Gavin's father said, bowing deeply.

The dragon had tears in his eyes when he replied, "You are most welcome here, Richard Kane."

"You are looking quite well," Richard stated.

Thaddeus grinned. "Even after fifteen hundred years, and far too many sweets, I have managed to keep up appearances."

Gavin's father became very serious then. "Thank you, from the bottom of my heart, for protecting Winifred and Gavin from the Germans, Thaddeus. There is nothing I can say or do to repay you for such service."

The dragon shook his head. "Oh, Richard, after all this time, you should know that my role doesn't revolve around debts. It is about loyalty and friendship, sacrifice and love. These traits are embodied in your son, as they are in you. Gavin has proven repeatedly that his heart is full of compassion and justice. For as long as the boy needs my council and protection, I will provide it willingly."

Richard put his hand on Gavin's shoulder and gave it a gentle squeeze. "I was remiss in my duties, Sir Osbert. I should have brought my son to you earlier."

Thaddeus shrugged. "Destiny is a difficult thing to gauge, Richard. Perhaps it was better that things developed as they did, for Gavin has come to truly appreciate his father's importance in his life, as well as his mother and friends. Life's lessons often occur when we least expect them, so their impact is well remembered."

Gavin's father felt better after listening to the dragon's words.

The boy had watched this exchange with fascination. A unique bond had developed amongst Thaddeus, Gavin, and Richard Kane, one fashioned by events and mutual respect. It became obvious to Gavin that this had been the dragon's intent all along and he loved the mighty creature even more than before. In response to these intense emotional ties, the teen reached out and took hold of his father's left hand, while scratching behind Sir Osbert's ear.

The dragon's throat rumbled with purrs of satisfaction and he chuckled with delight. "Your son has discovered how to tame the beast in me."

Richard grinned.

"Father must report back to duty tomorrow, Sir Osbert," Gavin said sadly.

The dragon frowned. "Please take care of yourself, Richard. My fellow dragons sense this war will go on for several more years to come."

"Did they share any other vision of the future?" the elder Kane asked.

"Only that the outcome is still in doubt," Thaddeus replied. "The forces of evil are powerful and committed to victory. Keep in mind, however, that it is always the darkest before the dawn."

"I must leave Gavin in your care once more, Sir Osbert," Richard said. "To protect him and his mother, I will do whatever I can to defend England."

"Don't forget Bunty and Emily," Gavin interjected.

Both the dragon and his father smiled.

"I promise not to forget your friends either," Richard Kane said.

"I shall look after them all, be rest assured," Thaddeus said. "Believe it or not, I am feeling quite useful again. I truly enjoy the time I spend with Gavin and his friends. Their youthful vigor has created the necessary jolt to awaken in me the lessons of old. I cherish this time, before they become adults."

Again, Gavin's father bowed deeply, but when he stood straight again, Richard scratched the dragon behind the other ear. It was his cue for departure. Father and son waved goodbye as they headed for the door.

"I will see you after school tomorrow, Sir Osbert," Gavin announced.

"I look forward to it," the dragon said.

For most of the journey back to Crackington Haven, Gavin and his father were unusually quiet, reflecting on their own concerns. Man-to-son, they were very close, but the heavy weight of responsibility made Richard's shoulders sag, while Gavin pondered how long it would be before he saw his father again.

When they arrived back home, instead of going straight inside, Richard took his son into the photography store. Strategically placed on the rear developing-table was a carefully wrapped bundle. Gavin's father handed the package over to the boy.

"I suspect you'll go out flying with Thaddeus now and again, so I picked up some proper equipment for your travels," his father said.

"Wow," Gavin reacted with delight, after pulling out the contents from a canvas carrying case.

There was a RAF Type C leather flying helmet, complete with accompanying MKVII flight goggles, binoculars and a cold weather tunic as well.

"So what do you think?" Richard asked.

"These are simply fantastic, Dad."

"I thought you would like them."

"Wherever did you get them?"

"Oh, one of the RAF boys is convinced he can fly without using an airplane, so before he soared off into the wild blue yonder, I convinced him to part with these," his father replied jokingly.

"Oh, Dad, you're so silly."

"I requisitioned them through normal channels," his father replied. "It took some doing, but when I made it clear they were for my son, the flight officer, Ian Warwick, became quite helpful."

Gavin tried them on. The flying helmet was a little big, but with some adjusting of the strap, Richard managed to secure it on the boy's head. The goggles pressed snugly against the teen's face, which were a perfect fit. In fact, it was a little disturbing to see how the gear and uniform jacket made Gavin look very much like a real RAF pilot.

"I don't want your mother to see you like this, so hide them until they're needed," Richard suggested.

"Yes, Father, I will," Gavin replied. "I know just the place where she'll never look."

They went into the house and as his father distracted Winifred with a few kisses, the boy hurried upstairs and hid the goggles and flight helmet inside his closet. When he came downstairs again, Bunty was in the kitchen, sampling tastes offered by Gavin's mother.

"Scrummy," the red-haired boy kept repeating.

"I hope so," Winifred said. "I want this supper to be special for Gavin's father."

"I'm switching on the wireless, boys," Richard called from the sitting room.

Gavin joined his father, but Bunty remained in the kitchen. His culinary skills were being honed by Winifred, who spotted a budding chef in the making.

The war news was bad, as usual, especially with the top story involving the withdrawal of British forces from Greece. When it became obvious the resistance of the Greek army to the German invasion was at an end, the Government of Greece requested the entire British contingent, who had been sent to help, should be withdrawn from Greece. Based on his father's reaction, Gavin knew the implications were serious.

"Time for supper," Winifred beckoned from the dining room.

Click.

Father and son hurried to take their seats and everyone bowed their heads.

"Lord God of infinite mercy, we humbly implore you to look down on the nations now engaged in war," Gavin's father prayed. "Do not count your people's sins against them, but grant them true repentance, that the evils of the human heart may be conquered by your spirit of gentleness and righteousness. Look in mercy on those immediately exposed to peril. Comfort the prisoners, relieve the sufferings of the wounded, and show mercy to the dying. According to your good and gracious will, remove the causes and occasions of this war, and restore peace among the nations, through Jesus Christ, our Lord. Amen."

"Amen," the others at the table repeated.

As a special treat, before Richard returned to **RAF Medmenham**, Winifred made Cornish pastries, which were hard pastry shells filled with real meat and vegetables.

"This sure is delicious, honey," her husband said after only a few bites. "I really do miss your cooking."

"Oh, you're just saying that," Winifred said, even though she loved hearing it.

"No, it's true," Richard insisted. "The food in the service is quite horrible."

"Oh, you poor dear," she cooed. "No wonder you're so skinny."

Her husband grinned and asked, "May I have another, please?"

She giggled and gave Richard a big kiss, before serving him another pastry.

After dinner, Gavin's mother and father retired early, but not before making certain the boys were ready for school and washed up. Once they said their bedtime prayers, Bunty and Gavin quickly fell asleep, exhausted from the day's events. Richard and Winifred enjoyed a hot cup of tea, sitting up in bed and chatting the night away.

The next morning, as they had done once before, when Richard Kane was first called up, Winifred and Gavin walked husband and father to the bus stop. This time they were joined by Bunty too.

"Goodbye, dearest," Richard said after kissing his wife. "I'll be home as soon as I can get leave again, I promise."

Winifred couldn't hold back her tears and she just blubbered.

"Come on, old girl," her husband teased a little.

She tried to smile, but instead gave him a big hug, burying her face against his chest as she sobbed hysterically. Gavin's father didn't attempt to rush things, but just let Winifred release her emotions.

Once she had a good cry, Gavin's mother wiped her eyes and stood bravely, hands on her son's shoulders. "Write often, Richard. The boys love it when I read your letters aloud."

Lieutenant Commander Kane waved as he stepped onto the bus, which had just arrived. "Be good, all of you. I'll be home soon, you'll see."

The driver waited for a few minutes, just in case there were other passengers. This gave Richard time to find a seat by the window and he waved again. It was very difficult to part from his family.

The bus pulled away.

Gavin shouted, "Take care, Dad!"

Standing right by his friend's side, Bunty waved enthusiastically.

"Time to head to school, boys," Winifred announced, wiping her eyes.

"Oh, bother," Bunty commented.

"You said it," Gavin added.

"No complaining now," Mrs. Kane said. "Off you go, so you won't be late."

The boys gathered up their books and things, hurrying to catch the morning bus to Launceston. They had memorized the journey, so they chattered the entire way.

"Learn a lot, you two," Winifred called after them, waving.

She suddenly felt very alone. Adjusting her apron and putting on a brave face, Mrs. Kane strolled confidently back into the house. It was all an act. Winifred just didn't want the villagers to see how vulnerable she really felt.

Back in the kitchen, Mrs. Kane cleaned the breakfast dishes and made ready for laundry day. Gathering up all the towels and sheets, she quickly discovered the dirty linens made quite a bundle. On top of that, by adding the boy's clothing, it meant she would be washing most of the day.

On her way to the washhouse, Winifred was joined by several other women. After all, it was Monday and British housewives were creatures of habit. All across the Isles, this scene was repeated and for the most part, the greetings were warm and genuine.

"Well, how are things with Richard gone again?" Carolyn Haversham asked while putting her hand on Winifred's shoulder.

Knowing her bloodshot eyes gave her away, Mrs. Kane merely replied, "Not as bad as it looks."

"At least we don't have to do bagwash, eh?" Samantha Cartwright pointed out.

"So true," Winifred agreed. "I can't imagine doing such a thing."

Bagwash was a system common in the bigger cities, where all the household washing was put into a large canvas bag marked with a personal code, tightly closed and taken to a local commercial laundry or to a collection point in a neighborhood shop in the morning. The bag was washed, unopened, in huge machines and delivered back to the collection point in the afternoon, damp dry.

That afternoon, when Winifred returned home with the clean laundry, she readjusted the cast-iron fire grate, which fit into the open fireplace. It was designed to hold coal and keep it burning. It was raised from the floor to allow a bottom draft. The upper portion fit into the lowest portion of the chimney and had a damper, with which to regulate the upward draft and hence the rate of burning. It produced a lot of heat, with just a little coal and was perfect for drying clothes.

Then she hung each damp item up to dry, on makeshift clotheslines, which crisscrossed the room. By the time this was done, the boys were home from school.

That night for dinner, there was quite a surprise for Bunty. Mrs. Kane had whipped up a batch of faggots, which was a working-class delicacy, something like a miniature haggis, made of liver and lights, herbs and onions, all wrapped in a piece of stomach membrane and cooked in a rich gravy.

The boys agreed they were simply scrumptious!

Winifred fluffed their hair and kissed them both, before shooing them out of the kitchen. Gavin and Bunty settled by the radio and waited for Mrs. Kane to switch it on for the nightly BBC war report.

This time, however, she decided there had been enough depressing news lately and the three of them would spend time playing card games. They sat around the breakfast table, two flickering candles casting enough light to see the cards, while seriously embroiled in round after round of gin rummy. The competition was fierce, but friendly and after several hours, Bunty was declared the champion. Then it was off to bed.

After Mrs. Kane had heard the boy's prayers and tucked them in, she went downstairs again to reread her husband's letters by candlelight as well. Winifred always read the latest one first, before working her way back through the stacks of envelopes. It was her way of keeping close to Richard and often spurred her to write a few notes of her own. More often than not, she would fall asleep on the sofa, a letter still clutched in her hand.

In far away London, an imposing red and white brick building sat on Victoria Embankment, overlooking the River Thames. It had been built specifically to be the new Metropolitan Police Headquarters, but was always known by the more familiar name of Scotland Yard. Surrounded by sandbags and bracketed with antiaircraft emplacements, the facility took on the look of a besieged castle. Yet the seven floors of offices were cramped and entirely inadequate under the strain of war.

The main structure was faced with granite quarried by prisoners from Dartmoor Prison and the impressive wrought-iron entrance gates were perhaps the only such metal barriers not confiscated during scrap drives throughout the city. New Scotland Yard was understaffed and overworked in their endeavors, but when the telephone number Whitehall 1212 rang, the department was always quick to respond.

Busy working in his fifth floor office, Inspector Peter Grimsby was busy rereading several files he had pulled from the records office. Grimsby had been assigned to investigate recent reports of espionage activity in Manchester. While most of these so-called spy cases turned out to be dead-ends, Scotland Yard was required to follow-up on every possible sighting, no matter how ridiculous they might seem at first.

Up on the seventh floor, where many of the rooms were full of filing cabinets and boxes of case files, the lights were off and blackout curtains permanently in place. People seldom had any reason to go up there and the cleaning staff was forbidden access, so the place was covered in dust and cobwebs. It was nicknamed *Sherlock's Attic*, after the famous fictional detective.

As the nightly sirens began to wail and all the Scotland Yard personnel prepared to take shelter if necessary, Inspector Grimsby wondered if he could still get a spot of tea. He peered out of the office, down the hall, and spotted one of the clerks.

"Oh, Miss Garver, is there any tea remaining, by chance?" Peter asked.

She smiled and waved. "I'll check the pot, Peter. Are you headed down to the shelter?"

"No, I think not tonight," he called out. "It's too much bother, really. I want to finish up and then see if I can get home for a change."

Daisy Garver understood exactly how he felt. She missed seeing her husband, as their lives seemed to be at cross-purposes and on different schedules. She stopped by the burner and the little kettle was still warm.

"There is some hot water, Peter," Miss Garver told him. "I'll fix you a cuppa."

"Bravo, lass," he said. "I'll be there in a moment."

As the two of them sat down across from each other to enjoy a cup of tea, an unidentified person slid two lengths of wire into the lock mechanism of the door leading onto the seventh floor. Carefully and quietly fiddling with the picks for awhile, the intruder patiently worked the calibrated teeth of the lock.

Click.

Smiling with satisfaction, the person slipped inside, closing the door before slowly making her way down the hallway. At the third door on the left, the woman gently touched the doorknob and gave it a slight turn. It opened, but only enough to allow the visitor to slip inside.

Out came a small penlight torch, the beam directed towards a series of big black filing cabinets. It appeared as if this person knew exactly what she was looking for and where to find it, because she headed directly for the drawer labeled **M**.

The intruder took a moment to put on gloves and produced a small oilcan, which she used to lubricate the cabinet lock. Then, once again, the mechanism was picked. Very slowly, an inch at a time, the drawer was pulled outwards, the tracks being oiled after every pull.

Fingers danced across the tabs of each folder, suddenly stopping over one specific manila file labeled—**Wilhelm Morz**.

The items in the accordion file had been numbered and cataloged. There was a pocket watch, handkerchief, shaving tube, studs, toothbrush, fountain pen, propelling pencil and compass, a box of matches, and certain toiletries. There was also a key.

This was apparently the only thing of interest to the thief, because the key was removed and the woman hurried away.

Down on the fifth floor, Inspector Grimsby and Miss Garver were oblivious to the break-in. As the nightly air raid progressed, they changed their minds and took shelter in the basement of Scotland Yard, along with certain prisoners in their cells.

It was a good thing too. Not but twenty minutes later, several bombs struck the commissioner's and special branch offices, as well as demolishing much of the file room on the seventh floor. No one was injured, but only because everyone had sought safety in the basement.

In Crackington Haven, it was well past midnight when Gavin tiptoed down the hall into Bunty's room.

"Are you awake?" he whispered after closing the door behind him.

"Yup," came a reply from under the covers.

"Are you sketching?"

"Yup."

"May I see?"

"Yup."

Gavin grinned and crawled under the makeshift tent Bunty had created using his blankets. His torch was positioned at just the right angle to cast a beam of light on the pad of paper.

"Wow," Gavin commented. "That's really good."

"Thanks," Bunty whispered. "It was in my dream last night, so I thought I'd try to draw what I remembered."

With pencil and ink, the red-haired boy had sketched a creepy and eerie castle, surrounded by pine trees and shrouds of mist. There was a definite foreboding about the structure, as if haunted or possessed.

A shiver ran up Gavin's spine. "It looks so real."

Bunty shrugged. "I think this castle really exists, somewhere."

"I hope not," Gavin whispered. "It's too scary."

Bunty stopped drawing and studied his artwork for a moment. He too was struck with a powerful sensation, which left goosebumps all over his skin. Suddenly, without warning, he ripped out the page and tore it into little pieces.

Gavin was shocked. "Why did you do that?"

Bunty closed his eyes and sighed. When he spoke, it was just above a whisper. "It may have been a simple drawing, Gavin, but there was something wicked about the place. I think I had that dream for a reason. When we see Thaddeus again, I'll tell him about it."

Gavin looked down at the bits of paper scattered all around. "You should have kept your drawing until then. Now you don't have anything to show him."

Bunty shook his head. "Don't worry, chum. I won't ever forget that castle."

2

Fortress of Fear

Clear across conquered Europe, in Germany's Alma Valley, a striking castle overlooked the picture-postcard scenery that stretched in every direction. Jutting majestically above tall green pine trees and bathed in mist-shrouded moonlight, it looked more like something out of a fairytale, rather than the headquarters of the dreaded Nazi SS. Sadly, Schloss Wewelsburg had become irretrievably intertwined with the insanity and cruelty at the very heart of the Third Reich.

Equidistant between Hamm and Paderborn, Wewelsburg Castle overlooked the great valley that housed both of these strategic cities. The structure was not old, as German castles go, for it dated from the Renaissance period, while some parts of it were added even later. It was neither large nor powerful, but had been decaying for a long time. The castle's crumbling walls were in the shape of a triangle, where a round tower stood at the top, a lineal descendant of the early-medieval donjon. From this tower two wings stretched southward, connected at the basis by a third wing. In consequence, the inner courtyard also had the form of a triangle.

The castle was situated at the northern end of the flat top of a steep hill. The plateau contained one other building of significance, a Roman Catholic Church. At the foot of the hill was the village of Wewelsburg, with 900 inhabitants, almost all of them devout Catholics.

Schloss Wewelsburg had originally been constructed between 1603 and 1609. It was intended to serve as a second residence for the Prince Bishop of Paderborn. It was erected on the site of an earlier Saxon stronghold, where archeologists discovered a Stone Age burial pit containing dozens of human remains. Nearby excavations also uncovered Neanderthal skulls, as well as items of Bronze Age jewelry and other signs of early human habitation.

During the 17th Century, the castle played a key role in the witchcraft trials sweeping across Europe. The persecution of witches had been particularly ferocious in Germany, especially in territories presided over by the Catholic Prince

Bishop. Some estimates place the number of accused witches, who perished at the stake, as high as 100,000. In Westphalia, local women accused of witchcraft were held in Wewelsburg's dungeons and confessions were extracted under torture in an adjoining courtroom. Many of them were subsequently executed before the castle gates, including the legendary witch named Agnes Olmanns, who was burned at the stake. The beautiful young woman was rumored to be the leader of a nefarious moot of black magic.

The surrounding area was similarly rich in historical significance. Nearby was the Teutoburg Forest, widely believed to have been the site of the legendary battle in which the united Germanic tribes defeated the Roman legions of Varus, forever establishing the border between the Roman Empire and Germania. Also, just miles away, was Externsteine, a distinctive natural rock formation, which was used as a place of habitation and pre-Christian worship since Neolithic times. Archeologists excavated the site, unsuccessfully attempting to prove it had been a religious center of immense importance to an advanced prehistoric German civilization. However, during these Nazi-sanctioned digs, the bones of strange prehistoric creatures were unearthed. It was rumored amongst the locals that the remains of dragons had been discovered.

It was Reichsführer Heinrich Himmler, considered by some to be the second most powerful man in all of Germany, who selected the stronghold, because he was told it lay on a nexus of strange occult energies. The castle's north tower became a storehouse for powerful magical icons and artifacts stolen from the occupied countries throughout Europe. Prisoners from the Saxonia and Niederhagen concentration camps were used as laborers to perform much of the restoration work on the old dilapidated buildings.

Himmler was a small man, balding, who looked more like a college professor than anything else. Contrary to his appearance, he had become the most sinister and feared man in Nazi Germany. Uncomfortable in the company of men he considered superior to him, Himmler was nonetheless an extremely organized and crafty individual, qualities that served him well in his pursuit of power. Himmler had formally joined the ranks of the SS, originally created as a personal bodyguard for Adolf Hitler.

Himmler was also deeply affected by the old sagas brought to dramatic life by the composer Richard Wagner. The torch-lit secret initiation ceremonies of the SS, which took place every year all over Germany, were held at midnight on April 20, the Führer's birthday. These gatherings were dominated by not-so-subtle references to ancient Germanic myths, incorporating a great deal of Wagnerian music and dramatic stagecraft.

The combination of historical significance and mythic resonance held an obvious appeal for the Reichsführer, who entertained a lavish fantasy life, in stark contrast to his public image of a prim and clerkish bureaucrat.

Himmler borrowed from both ancient German and ancient Nordic mythology to supply the SS with its symbols, oaths, and rituals. The castle rooms, where their secret meetings were held, were decorated with runes or prehistoric markings, which were said to give the power of prophecy to anyone who knew how to read them. The symbol of the Schutzstaffel itself, the twin twisted lightning bolts resembling ϟϟ, was a runic symbol for dragonheads.

Heinrich Himmler had studied all sorts of esoteric teachings and he preferred the magic as dark as possible. He was especially interested in rune-power. Within the SS hierarchy, all the occult knowledge of the Third Reich was gathered in one place. The SS was ruled by black magic and their rituals were borrowed from other similar orders. The highest-ranking SS priests were the 13 members of the Dragon Knight's Great Council, which was ruled by Grandmaster Heinrich Himmler himself.

With all his heart, Himmler believed in the Aryan racial theories and manifestations of Nazism. He was a rabid fanatic, who suffered from constant psychosomatic illnesses, like stomach pain, headaches and other unidentified maladies and diseases. His undying passion for control over others was enormous and his favorite word was *merciless*.

Himmler saw his soldiers as the reincarnation of Teutonic knights. He arranged elaborate parades in the streets, with his favorite men dressed in full armor, as living symbols of ancient power.

The focal point of the Wewelsburg complex was the stone-lined chamber in the North Tower, in which Himmler had installed an oaken Arthurian-type round table. To enter the chamber, a guest was required to descend a stone staircase and traverse the inner hall through a small door. The interior was mathematically circular. Himmler had the tower restored copying a Mycenaean dome-shaped tomb he once visited. Acoustically the tower was the exact opposite of a whispering gallery.

To understand a speaker in the middle of the hall, it was necessary for people to press themselves to the wall in order to hear the words. It only required one step forward and it was impossible to understand anything at all, because of the reverberation and the echoes. A huge swastika, with SS-runes at the four ends, was prominently displayed in the top of the cupola crowning this unusual room.

Situated perpendicularly under this SS-swastika, sat a table in the form of a giant dish. A flame was always burning in the dish, a symbol of the eternal fire in the heart of the earth. Set high up in the walls were four windows. They had been designed to allow sunbeams to radiate into the interior. The four shafts of light crossed each other just above the dish. The placement of the dish signified the exact center of the earth.

Elsewhere throughout the castle, Himmler had the builders create many cryptic and strange meeting rooms, all with their own unique purpose, but guarded by secrecy. For instance, the design of floor mosaic laid in the Marble Hall was known as the Black Sun or *Schwarze Sonne*, while another location was dubbed the Himmler Crypt.

Himmler's plans included making the castle the center of a new world order, completely controlled by Germany following the final victory. He also imagined the castle as a rebirth of the Teutonic Knights and appointed twelve handpicked SS officers as his followers, who would gather within the various rooms and perform unknown rites.

Himmler always wore black. He had a thing about black leather, with tall shiny black boots, a long black leather coat, and black leather gloves.

The Reichsführer walked down a long, winding flight of steps, down into the dark recesses of the castle. There, under strict secrecy and armed guards, his chosen scientists, doctors, and hack intellectuals all gathered on a daily basis. They were under orders to study and perfect the use of black magic. Their leader was Dieter Gortz, a sadistic and evil lout, who relished in suffering and pain, but was also an accomplished scientist.

In fact, he was perfect for the job Himmler had assigned.

Unfortunately, a serious miscalculation occured after certain experiments began.

It seems that *Herr Gortz* had gone missing a few days earlier, presumably too busy with his concoctions and formulas, to let anyone know what he was up to. As it turned out, it was far more complicated than that, because Dieter Gortz had lost control of his experiments. In fact, after drinking one foul mixture after another, he was no longer even human.

Himmler stopped outside the lab.

"Is everything ready yet?" Himmler impatiently asked one of Gortz's aides. "Did Dieter succeed with his experiments?"

"*Jawohl, Herr Reichsführer,*" the inept hack lied.

"Where is *Herr Gortz?*" Himmler asked.

The man in the white lab coat shrugged. "We do not know, *Herr Reichsführer.*"

Himmler was dumbfounded. "What do you mean you do not know?"

"*Doktor Gortz* has vanished, *Herr Reichsführer*," the man replied, suddenly cowering. "We do not know where he has gone, but his experiment succeeded."

Dieter Gortz had been a very powerful and evil Nazi party leader. Unknown to Himmler or his cohorts, the man's wickedness was repaid in kind, because Gortz dabbled once too often in dark sorcery and black magic, accidentally turning himself into a creature of foul myth and darkest legend. The potion Dieter drank forever entombed him inside the most dangerous of all mystical beasts, a black dragon. Never before appreciating human kindness, Gortz now faced the unquenchable urge to kill anything he encountered.

To complicate matters even more, the quack scientists working at the castle were convinced that Gortz had somehow given life to a real dragon, when nothing could be further from the truth. With their inaccurate conclusions and worthless evaluations, the bogus physicians and fraudulent lab technicians had stubbled upon Gortz's archaic formulas, which fell far outside their limited experience. To cover for their lack of scientific methodology, the charlatans were able to convince Himmler they had been a part of the creation of this bloodthirsty and vicious dragon.

"Let me see it," Himmler commanded with barely contained impatience. He twittered like an anxious schoolchild. "I must see this dragon you speak of."

Ten SS soldiers guarded an enormous covered cage. The black-uniformed and heavily armed men stepped aside, revealing the secret that lay beneath the dark cloth. Himmler's eyes widened at the sight. There before him, sitting crouched in one corner of the pen, was a creature that only existed in legends, fables, and Wagnerian operas.

The newborn dragon weighed over 180 pounds and was already well past ten feet in length. The wyrmling was able to see and hear, with a full set of razor sharp teeth. However, the creature's wings were too small and weak to fly yet and the tiny scales covering his body were still very soft, although they would harden within the year.

Himmler was smart enough and patient enough to wait for the right opportunity to unleash this abomination. Until then, the Reichsführer would bide his time.

"In the name of the *Führer*, I hereby christen this dragon, *Schwarzer Flügel*, or *Black Wing*," Himmler proclaimed. "He will be trained to fly faster than our finest fighter planes and destroy all British aircraft, thereby gaining supremacy in the skies. He will bring terror to our enemies and fulfill the prophecies of Nazi Germany. This dragon will represent the Third Reich in all her Aryan glory. *Sieg Heil!*"

All those gathered raised their right hands in the traditional Nazi salute and repeated, "*Sieg Heil!*"

As a result of this event, further darkness swept over the continent, pushing aside any glimmer of hope. Himmler had ventured into the bottomless pit of forbidden evil, from which there was no return. By doing so, unspeakable horrors had been released from the depths of the abyss, ripping open the space-time continuum.

The next afternoon, Reichsführer Himmler welcomed Reinhard Heydrich to Wewelsburg Castle. Earlier that month, Heydrich crashed his ME109 during take-off and was injured. For a short time, Reinhard had been flying patrols over Northern Germany and the Netherlands. Heydrich's fighter-plane had an ancient Germanic runic character ≤ painted on the side of the fuselage.

To prevent any further incidents, Himmler forbid any more flying and instead ordered Heydrich to accompany the Reichsführer wherever he went. Himmler was becoming very wary of Heydrich, as his evil cohort was rapidly developing into his nemesis. By keeping his rival close, the Reichsführer was certain he could maintain control of Heydrich's activities and whereabouts.

It was actually during this meeting that Heydrich wrote the first draft regarding the extermination of all Jews in conquered Europe. Surrounded by the evil aura of Wewelsburg, it was little wonder that this wretched man could imagine the murder of millions of innocent people. Yet Heydrich had fallen under the spell of a malignant creature that no human could fathom, much less understand. Deep underground, hidden for eons beneath the stone palisades of the castle, resided a throbbing and pulsating entity beyond description. This life form thrived on misery and suffering, death and destruction, growing stronger with each passing barbaric act of the Third Reich. Soon it would rise from the depths and consume everything.

Reinhard Heydrich was the unwitting connection, a portal from one plane to another. With this representative promoting the expansion of evil, it was only a matter of time before a gap in the space-time continuum would be wide enough to allow the creature's escape.

Meanwhile, in an icy valley in central Iceland, members of the dragon clans had gathered from all around the world. This meeting was in direct response to the growing threat created by the war currently being waged between humans. While the nations of men rallied to propaganda, causes and flags, fighting bitterly over lands and ideals, Draconia had no such delusions. After so many previous failings, dragons had learned to put aside their differences and protect the basic right of survival for the species.

Erupting geysers, bubbling spots, and hot springs surrounded their secret meeting place, effectively keeping any curious explorers away. Massive waterfalls plunged into vast and untamed landscapes, untouched by human intervention. The sky stretched out forever and seemed to hover as rolling clouds peacefully glided past, intermittently broken by rays of brilliant sunlight.

Smocza Jama, or Dragon's Cave, was located at the base of a gigantic glacial hill. It was here, by special decree, that dragon clans formed ranks to discuss current events.

In an effort to understand the latest human conflict, the Council of Dragons had summoned Sir Thaddeus Osbert to attend an emergency meeting. They hoped his close-knit ties to humanity might shed some light on their dilemma.

"Thank you for responding to our invitation, Thaddeus," spoke Drasius Fly-lander, the president of the current elected council. "This meeting of the clans is called to order. The issue at hand is the human war that now rages around us and threatens to engulf all living things. There are many indications that this conflict may lead to the final extermination of all life on this planet and certain members have approached the Council to request a ruling. Therefore, an open forum has been arranged, so that dragonkind may have a voice in our future."

The fervent rumble of low growls and roars traveled amongst the hundreds of dragons gathered on the icy slopes. They were unanimous regarding the inherent dangers, but quite divided regarding possible solutions.

"Thaddeus Osbert, you have resided with humans for centuries," Drasius opened the proceedings. "Is there any hope that this war can be resolved quickly, or are these humans bent on destroying everything, including themselves?"

Thaddeus spoke candidly, his draconian words floating above the gathered throng like strange music. "If some of my brothers and sisters have formed the opinion that understanding human motivations is important, because with such knowledge we can kill them easier, then I must protest. Yes, humans are prone to war, but our species was not innocent of such barbaric pursuits in our own past. I am here as an ambassador of goodwill. I believe peace is possible, but the human race must discover how to live with each other on their own, without our intervention."

A magnificent purple dragon, by the name of Korban Vex, spread his wings with the talons fully exposed. It was a sign he was highly agitated. However, Korban was well respected and when he spoke, every dragon listened.

"We have proof the Aryans have somehow created a black dragon of their own," Korban said in a booming voice. "They have flaunted forbidden magical powers, casting spells as the wicked wizards did in the olden days. Such behavior proves the humans are without regard for the laws that bind the universe. We must exterminate the species before they can create more havoc."

Many voices were lifted in praise to echo Korban's words.

Another brilliantly colored dragon, with dramatic hues of reds, oranges and yellows, was allowed to practice his oratory skills next. Wasabi Watanabe was an Eastern dragon, with a very long tail and many legs. He had been selected by his allies to represent the feelings of the Asian contingent.

"We have tolerated humans for centuries," Wasabi said. "They have done nothing but destroy each other and lay waste to this planet. I hate all of mankind with a passion and lobby this Council to initiate their immediate destruction, once and for all!"

This statement instantly galvanized the membership to take sides. The uproar of raised growls drowned out any attempt by Drasius to regain order. He patiently waited for all the excitement and emotional discussions to follow their natural course. Once the furor died down, the Council president recognized Sir Osbert again.

"It hurts me greatly when a dragon takes a stance that condones hating others," Thaddeus said. "We really have much in common with humans. There are so many things we could teach each other, while mutually benefiting from such a bond. Do we not revel in their music, their art, their books, and their inventions?"

One of the elder dragons stepped forward, clearing his throat. Silence swept through the ranks, for reverence was not only expected, but had also been earned.

"I, for one, am most pleased that Thaddeus Osbert has returned to offer his wisdom," said Growlius Tilius. "Certainly it is not our intention to sabotage his efforts in this regard. We have met challenges before and we will do so again, but not by exterminating the life of another species. No such act can ever be condoned."

Next to speak was Brianna, her scales reflecting prisms of countless shades of blues, shimmering with waves of silver and white. She was an ice dragon and seldom did her kind ever communicate openly, much less in front of other dragons. Therefore, when she stepped forward to voice her opinion, a gasp of surprise swept through the crowd.

"I don't hate humans, but I do hate stupidity," Brianna hissed quietly. "There is a big difference. I dislike stupid people, because they're stupid, not because they're humans. You should all acknowledge that dragons are just as capable of such insipid and mindless behavior. We have always judged the other creatures of this planet on their capabilities as a whole and there is no reason to change that process now. Surely my fellow dragons do not think humans are of lesser value than orcs?"

This brought a crescendo of laughter.

Brianna smiled with embarrassment, for she shied away from accolades or attention of any kind. Still, what she believed was important and the ice dragon felt compelled to express it. "Be careful, my brethren, for you must not make judgments based on race alone."

While her soft-spoken delivery was lost on some, the tide seemed to shift with her message. There was a favorable murmuring and many scaled heads nodded in agreement.

"The Council recognizes the dragon from Mazeland," Drasius announced.

"The winds cry in wordless lament," said Vortex Puzzler, who spoke only in riddles and verse. "A life born of fire will end in ash. What Merlin's spells and Arthur's sword could not defeat, only the hourglass will vanquish. The foul beast will enter the coils of the dragon and be consumed!"

"Thank you for your insight," the president responded, perhaps one of the few in attendance who could translate the full meaning of Puzzler's opinion.

Sir Osbert patiently listened as each of his fellow dragons state their various viewpoints. When it appeared as if everyone had taken the opportunity to speak, he raised his paw and was allowed to make a closing statement.

"I believe in dragons," Thaddeus said. "I also believe in humans and their potential to do wondrous things. I believe that one day we will live together in harmony, but hatred will never be the answer. Only through love, patience, and understanding will we be able to inhabit this planet as partners."

The ensuing applause was thunderous indeed. Hundreds of dragons stomped their feet or pounded paws together and the ice valley shook with the sounds of approval.

Except for some.

"We shall see," Korban Vex whispered to himself. "We shall see."

In fact, more than one dragon didn't see eye-to-eye with Sir Osbert's summation. Wasabi Watanabe was also not pleased at how things had developed. He angrily stormed off, returning to distant Asia through a labyrinth of subterranean tunnels that wound their way through the center of the earth to the other side.

Korban Vex was still a law-abiding member of the dragon council and while deeply concerned over the conduct of humanity, he did not intend to foment rebellion. Instead, the giant firedrake arranged an impromptu meeting with Thaddeus.

"I am pleased you agreed to this little chat," Vex said as Sir Osbert joined him by several frozen geysers.

"I am honored that you wished to speak to me, Korban," Thaddeus replied.

"You are still a consummate speaker, my old friend," Vex went on. "I am convinced your oratory skills turned the tide in your favor."

"Perhaps," Thaddeus said.

"Never mind, for that is not why I requested this meeting," Vex said.

"Please, continue," Osbert said.

"There is a serious breach in the continuum."

"I have felt it as well."

"Evil pervades amongst the Aryan leaders."

"Yes."

"They must be stopped."

"I imagine that's why there's a war going on."

Vex shook his head. "The humans may not be able to prevent what they have unleashed. Even now, there are men experimenting with the building blocks of the universe, splitting atoms and releasing power they don't understand. They have no concept of what horror they might accidentally create."

Thaddeus nodded. "It is true, Korban. I can only hope mankind survives long enough to learn from their mistakes."

Vex did not back down. "You must exercise caution, Thaddeus. I know you have great love for humanity, but they are failing in their responsibilities to every other creature on this planet. If the rift becomes wide enough, unspeakable terror will consume us all. I won't allow such an event to occur."

The emotion and anger in Korban's voice was impossible to mistake.

"What are your intentions?" Osbert inquired.

"I wish to guide the hand of the humans who are fighting this evil," Vex replied.

"What guidance do you offer?"

"They must kill a German officer named Reinhard Heydrich, by any means possible," Vex stated firmly. "It is imperative that this human not be allowed to live, or his unholy alliance will consume all living things."

Thaddeus contemplated what he had heard.

"No action on your part will be considered a violation of our laws, Thaddeus," Vex added. "If you feel that you must pass this responsibility along for men to handle, I understand. However, it must be accomplished soon!"

"Then it shall be done, Korban Vex," Thaddeus finally said. "I shall make arrangements for Reinhard Heydrich's death, or I will do it myself. In either case, if such action will stop the widening hole in the continuum, then it must succeed."

Vex smiled grimly. "Thank you, Sir Osbert. I am greatly relieved. I worried that our meeting would turn into one of our old chess matches."

Thaddeus managed to chuckle. "Now that would have been most unfortunate. Some of those games lasted for years."

"Yes, but they were magnificent contests, even if I always won," Vex commented.

Thaddeus held his tongue.

"Fair thee well, friend," Korban said as he walked away. "The future of humanity may well rest upon your shoulders."

After Vex was gone, Thaddeus mumbled to himself, "Bloody marvelous. Just what I need is more responsibility for the fate of mankind! Does anybody remember what happened last time?"

None of the other dragons heard Thaddeus complaining, which was a good thing. He grumbled a little more, wished he had some sugar to sweeten his mood, and then took wing for the flight back to England.

As the dragon passed over the North Sea, he looked fondly down on Ireland and then Scotland. Britain had been his home for hundreds of years, but he never tired of seeing the towering mountains, sparkling lochs, magical castles, and misty isles, not to mention certain luxuries, such as tea, scones with strawberry jam, and rare roast beef.

Of all of the countries of Europe, the British Isles were most exposed to the varying weather and Thaddeus marveled at how brilliant the sunshine shown over Wales, while a mass of clouds obscured his view of the Channel.

Suddenly he heard the distant grinding sound of many airplane engines.

Several miles away, a line of black specks emerged from the cloud cover and came ever nearer. German bombers were approaching in tight formation, but above them was another group of little dots, which were the escorting fighters.

From the opposite direction raced a group of British Spitfire and Hurricane fighters on the attack. They went straight for the enemy bombers. Seconds later, the Messerschmitts came zooming down.

Thaddeus turned in time to watch two German fighters pass by his tail. To avoid a possible collision, the dragon dove to his left, but was suddenly surrounded by airplanes darting left and right. While Thaddeus was invisible, he posed a real danger to any of those fighters if they flew into him.

One Me109 went by, the noise of his eight guns echoing in the dragon's ears. Right behind him was a Spitfire, hot on his tail. The British fighter let loose a long burst. A sudden flash of brilliant flame, followed by a cloud of smoke, before a piece of the wing flew off and the German fighter went down.

More German fighters pursued the lone Spitfire. The British pilot tried to evade into some low clouds, but they chased him into the puffy whiteness. The Spitfire was hit repeatedly and went into a spin. The pilot managed to straighten the plane out and maneuvered past several barrage balloons, which probably saved his life. The Germans broke off their pursuit and the Spitfire managed to crash-land in a field.

Thaddeus soared past and sighed with relief when he saw the pilot scramble free. As the dragon returned to Tintagel, he shook his head sadly, because he knew there would be many more people killed in this terrible war.

3

Birthday Plans

All streetlights and illuminated signs in Britain had been extinguished for the duration of the war. All windows and doors had to be curtained, so that no chink of light escaped to guide enemy aircraft. Torches and vehicle lights had to be shielded, so no light escaped upwards. Traffic lights were covered, so that only a small cross of color showed. The windows of trains, buses and trams were buttoned up with material, which prevented the glass from shattering, with a small diamond left open in the center so a person could see where they were. Most commuters were forced to rely on the driver to tell them which stop was coming up next. The interior lights of vehicles were disabled in every town and heavily dimmed in long-distance trains.

Yet life went on, no matter the hardship.

Emily Scott and her fellow girls attended Truro County Girls School, but shared the building with the grammar school pupils. The younger children attended in the morning and the older students went in the afternoon and Saturday mornings as well. Each morning the girls queued up before a guard hut, to go past a soldier who checked their identities. The classrooms weren't heated anymore and some mornings the ink was frozen in the wells. Sometimes Emily was so cold that she did her lessons in her overcoat and hat. Along with her friends, they became especially fond of a restaurant in town, whose kind owner allowed the girls to sit inside where it was warm, to eat their sandwiches at lunchtime.

When school was dismissed that day, instead of taking the bus ride back to Boscastle, Emily decided to stay aboard until reaching the Crackington Haven stop instead. She really needed to talk to Mrs. Kane about Gavin's upcoming thirteenth birthday.

Emily knocked on the front door of the Kane residence. After a few moments waiting, the door opened and she was greeted by a friendly smile and warm hug.

"You're just in time for tea," Mrs. Kane said.

Emily was delighted. She stepped inside and followed Gavin's mother into the kitchen, where the pot was just about to whistle.

"We girls just love to have a spot of tea and chitchat," Winifred commented.

"My mother says a hot cuppa tea soothes the nerves and relaxes the mind," the teenaged girl added.

"Just like the wicked boys sometimes say, we'll have a bloody good moan over this and that," Winifred whispered.

Emily was shocked at Mrs. Kane's off-color candor, but giggled just the same.

They sat together on the sofa, over tea and homegrown cucumber sandwiches. Gavin's mother provided entertaining conversation, while pouring out two cups of real Earl Gray. Emily nibbled on the little squares and sipped politely.

Winifred sighed with satisfaction. "A cuppa tea makes the world seem right."

Emily closed her eyes and said, "Hot tea, fresh scones, strawberry jam and clotted cream, you know, the unbelievably rich, super thick cream that you apply with a trowel."

They both said, "Yummy" at the exact same time.

This was followed by giggles.

So anxious were the British to protect their precious tea stocks from German bombs, the government stored emergency tea supplies in 500 secret stashes around the countryside, guarded by some of England's finest troops.

"What shall we do about Gavin's thirteenth, Mrs. Kane?" Emily asked.

Winifred's shoulders sagged. "Oh, Emmy, I'm so frustrated. There's hardly enough sugar to do anything with and eggs are scarce, even out here. Thankfully, Gavin's father already gave the boy a gift, because we don't have enough money to purchase anything of note."

The depressing lack of certain foodstuffs, made more glaring by increased and even more stringent rationing, really put a damper on any birthday plans. Emily and Winifred did agree to meet once again before Gavin's official birthday, to see if they could come up with some ideas. After tea, Emily went home to Boscastle, but there was no doubt she was disappointed by the prospects.

While his mother was preparing dinner, Gavin began to tell her the list of friends he wanted to invite to his birthday party. After all, he would be a teenager and that was a monumental event.

"I'm sorry, honey," she said. "I'm afraid you can't have a party this year, because there just aren't enough ingredients to make a cake."

At that very moment, Aunt Mabel came into the kitchen. "You want a party, my boy?" she asked after giving Gavin a big hug and fluffing Bunty's hair. "Then you shall have one. Auntie will fix it for you."

"Dearest sister," Winifred protested. "We haven't got any margarine to spare and there haven't been any fresh eggs for weeks."

"We'll manage," said Gavin's aunt. "Old Auntie will make her favorite nephew a cake with thirteen candles, and we'll have red and green jelly too."

"I'm your only nephew, Auntie," the boy laughed.

"That's not important, you silly child," she countered, kissing him until he turned red with embarrassment.

Still, it was a pretty rash promise his aunt had made.

"But Mabel, we can't afford ..." objected Mrs. Kane.

"No more fussing. Where there's a will, there's a way!"

With the discussion closed for the time being, Aunt Mabel hurried back to the post office, where she prepared for the late afternoon pickup. She planned to come back for supper.

Birthday plans were not discussed over the meal, but for some reason Gavin felt secure that his auntie would come through. Once the dishes were cleared, the two boys scampered upstairs, because rain prevented going outside to play. They sat in Bunty's room and quietly read.

The next afternoon, Gavin arrived home from school to be greeted by thumps and crashes from the kitchen. His mother was vigorously attacking something in a brown paper bag with a rolling pin. It turned out she had filled the bag with a week's ration of ordinary granulated sugar, and was pounding it into icing sugar.

Aunt Mabel managed to get two bottles of soda pop, one red and one green. She was dissolving a chunk of gelatin into a pan of hot water. Gavin's dear auntie was attempting to make fizzy jelly. However, the smell wasn't too promising.

On the kitchen table were thirteen candles, which were made from gas tapers cut into three-inch lengths and with the wax scraped off to form wicks. Mrs. Kane had dyed them rainbow colors, using all sorts of inventive methods. Winifred had even managed to squander two ounces of margarine to make an egg-less sponge cake, stuck together with the universal plum jam.

The day of Gavin's birthday arrived at last, which was Sunday, May 4, 1941. Not only was the cake resplendent on a silver cake-stand and arranged on a homemade doily, but the fizzy jelly tasted a lot better, once it had set. Winifred had put together a few jam tarts from the sliver of margarine left over from the cake, and chocolate powder sandwiches as well. Auntie Mabel and Mrs. Kane must have used a week's supply of rations to feed the children invited to the party.

Just after 1:00 in the afternoon, five well-behaved teens arrived, each bearing a present, or a shilling, or maybe a sixpence, and a greeting card made from bits and scraps. There was Emily Scott, of course, with Niles Pemberton, Colin Baker, Ian Norton, and Nora Tilsey, all joining Bunty for the celebration.

They weren't too old to play blind-man's-bluff and musical chairs, with Gavin's mother at the piano. Laughing hysterically after each the game, the exhausted guests finally collapsed at the table to eat every little crumb of the feast so lovingly prepared.

"Mum, this was simply grand," Gavin voiced his opinion for all to hear.

The others agreed unanimously. It had been a splendid party.

Once Gavin's other birthday guests had departed, he and Bunty went down to the beach to play. It was a beautiful afternoon and they thoroughly enjoyed themselves making sandcastles, and then pretending Thaddeus came along and crushed each one.

In spite of all the desserts and snacks the boys had indulged in at the party, the two of them came home quite hungry.

"Are you two feeling peckish?" Mrs. Kane asked as they burst into the kitchen.

Winifred had been cooking while they were gone and the menu was obviously full of tasty birthday delights, including crisps, bangers, and runner beans.

"That food looks scrummy, Mum," Gavin said.

After dinner, the three of them gathered around the wireless. Gavin's mother wanted to listen to a special broadcast from North America. A major BBC affiliate station in Canada had arranged a radio link-up, so children overseas could speak to their parents back home in Britain.

"Here in Ottawa we have little Molly and James Milford, aged eight and ten," the announcer began. "Now ... come in Mrs. Milford and say hello ..."

"Hello, Molly!"

"Hello, Mummy!"

"How are you?"

"Alright, thank you!"

"This is the nicest thing that's happened to me since you went away—a sort of extra birthday present, isn't it?"

"Yes."

"Tell me about yourself. What have you got on?"

"I've got on my favorite party dress."

"What does it look like?"

"The blue one with white spots."

"Oh yes, that's a very pretty one, isn't it? How are you getting on with your piano lessons?"

"Alright, thank you."

"You enjoy them?"

"Yes."

"That's fine. Are you learning French?"

"Yes."

"Oh, that's fine. I'm so pleased, because it's a grand chance to learn, isn't it?"

"Yes."

"We sure do miss you two."

"We miss you too, Mummy."

"Here's Daddy. I'm sure he wants to talk to you too."

"Hello, old girl."

"Hello, Daddy!"

"How's your brother behaving?"

"Oh, he's been very good."

"Really?"

The girl giggled. "Yes, Daddy, Jimmy has been very nice."

"Hello, James."

"Hello, Father."

"How are your studies?"

"Just fine, sir. I'm especially enjoying history."

"That's grand, my boy."

Molly interrupted. "Do you think we'll be coming home soon?"

Her mother answered. "Not yet, sweetheart. It's still very dangerous here."

The announcer cut in. "Well, that's all we have time for today. Everybody say goodbye."

"Goodbye Mummy and Daddy," Molly sniffled, the sound of tears quite evident.

"Goodbye Mother and Father," Jimmy added.

"Goodbye, children," Mr. and Mrs. Milford said simultaneously.

"Thank you all," the announcer added. "Now back to your regular BBC news programming."

Mrs. Kane wiped her eyes and held out her hands to both of the boys. Bunty scrambled to one side, while Gavin went to the other. They received great big squeezie hugs and kisses. "I sure am lucky to have you boys here with me. I don't know what I'd do without you."

Sunday was also the first day of Double Summer Time, which the government had continued into 1941, to extend the productivity of each day. The boys were allowed to stay up later than usual, as an additional birthday present. They didn't venture very far away, however, content to play in the backyard.

After school on Monday, Bunty, Gavin, and Emily agreed they would go visit Thaddeus Osbert. They tried not to be pests too often, constantly interrupting the dragon during whatever he was doing, but they missed him terribly.

Bunty always knocked on the door first.

"Come in, children," Thaddeus said cheerfully.

The trio scrambled inside, thrilled to see their dragon.

"Sit here," Thaddeus said. "What shall we talk about today?"

"When's your birthday, Thaddeus?" Emily asked.

"Dragons celebrate birthdays by the lunar cycle," the dragon explained. "Each time thirteen full moons pass, a dragon marks another year gone by, nothing more."

"When was the last time you celebrated your birthday?" she asked.

Thaddeus didn't reply right away, because he couldn't recall anyone ever acknowledging his birth date before. Instead, he just shrugged.

"That's what I thought," Emily said. "It's not right for a fine old gentleman like you to go without a few celebrations in life. We will plan a birthday party for you, the likes of which you could never imagine."

Thaddeus grinned. He was always so amazed at Emily's bubbling personality, which varied between feisty and angelic. "Thank you, lass. I'll look forward to it."

"When should we plan on having this gay event?" Gavin asked.

"As soon as possible, I should think," Bunty offered. "Sir Osbert isn't getting any younger, you know."

The dragon roared with laughter. "So true, so true."

"That's settled then," Emily took charge. "We'll have a birthday party next Saturday, right here in the cottage."

"I could nick a keg of beer," Bunty said.

Emily punched him in the arm.

"Ouch!" Bunty groaned.

"Dragons don't drink beer, but we do love wine," Thaddeus said.

Scooting a safe distance from Emily, Bunty said, "Then I'll pinch a bottle or two, late at night, when the customers are all asleep."

"A proper drinking man never, ever falls asleep in a pub," the dragon said.

"Oh, bother," was Bunty's reaction.

Emily crossed her arms and gave Bunty a wicked glare. Then she huffed and puffed, saying, "I was thinking we could make some paper hats and bring some of the decorations from Gavin's party and have a simple celebration, with punch and sweets."

"Oh, all right," Bunty agreed, even though he was pouting.

Gavin just laughed at their antics.

However, in nearby hidden hamlets and secret cottages, the little people of Briton had felt the reverberations of some new unidentified evil unleashed across the seas. As this darkness rumbled up from the depths, it rattled their gentle nature and disturbed their daily lives. Fairies, dwarves, pixies, and elves all gathered in their special meeting places, troubled by the messages of warning carried on the wind. Destruction and suffering had always been the curse of man, but now a horrible threat had been reborn.

Suddenly Thaddeus stood up.

His sudden movement shocked all the children.

"What's wrong, Thaddeus?" Gavin asked, his voice shaking. He had never seen the dragon look so alarmed.

Sir Osbert's eye narrowed to mere slits and his teeth were bared in a silent growl. The dragon took a guarded stance, as if danger was near.

"You must go home, children," Thaddeus said in a low voice.

The three of them knew better than to argue. Quickly they headed for the door.

"Go, quickly now," the dragon added.

"Yes, Sir Osbert," they agreed in unison, but still hesitating.

"Go," Thaddeus said more sternly.

Gavin took Emily's hand and out they went. As soon as they were outside the cottage, there was an eerie cold wind swirling about them, which chilled their bones. Suddenly frightened, the teens took off on the run, heading straight for Boscastle.

"What do you think was wrong?" Emily asked after they had gone a few kilometers.

Gavin shrugged. "Whatever it was, Thaddeus wanted us to leave."

Back inside the cottage, the dragon was greatly disturbed. There were many haunting voices carried on the icy breeze and they were filled with terror. Something horrific was about to happen.

Gavin and Bunty made certain Emily was safely inside her house, before they hurried home to Crackington Haven. The boys seemed to have forgotten their sense of foreboding as soon as the marched in the front door.

"We're home, Mum," Gavin announced.

"I'm in the kitchen, boys," his mother called out.

"May we have a snack, Mum?" Gavin asked as they joined her.

"Do you mind running over to see Mr. Cooper first?" his mother asked. "He has a package for me.

"No, Mum, of course not," Gavin replied. "I'll be back in a flash."

Out the door he went.

Now as Sub-lieutenant John Mobley entered Crackington Haven, he was wearing the zigzag gold stripe of the Royal Navy Volunteer Reserve and his new wings. Born in Kelso, Scotland, John had volunteered for flight school with the outbreak of the war. He was originally sent to *RAF Sydenham*, outside Belfast, Ireland, where he learned to fly. Then in 1940, Mobley was sent to No. 1 Flying Training School at *RAF Netheravon*, which was home to a new torpedo-bomber squadron, where Mobley learned to fly advanced open-cockpit aircraft.

John and his crew were on their way to the Naval Air Station in St. Merryn, known as *HMS Vulture*, but decided to stop long enough to see a bit of the Cornish countryside, especially the northern coastal regions. Mobley couldn't resist visiting Boscastle and Tintagel, since they were so steeped in Arthurian legends.

"Not much to speak of," observed Michael "Squaddie" Watkins, Mobley's observer.

"There's a pub, so it can't be too bad," commented Virgil "Chips" Radcliff, Mobley's gunner.

The three of them had been together from the beginning, so a solid friendship had been formed, not to mention a camaraderie that reflected in their exemplary performance. Teamwork and compassion had formed a bond that was airtight.

"Let's nip in and have a round," Radcliff suggested.

"Sounds good to me," Mobley agreed.

The trio entered the *Coombe Barton Inn* and went straight to the bar.

"What's your pleasure, gents?" asked Davey, the gruff daytime barman. His tone was never very hospitable.

"Three pints of your best ale," Watkins ordered.

"Out of ale," the bartender replied.

"Then three pints of your bitters," Watkins countered.

"Out of that too."

"What have you got?" Radcliff wondered.

"Not much, I'm afraid."

"Where's the bog, mate?" John impatiently asked the barkeep.

"Are you referring to the toilet?"

"Well, I imagine it's the smallest room in this place."

"There's a closet behind me."

"True, but I might have been asking for the bathroom."

"We reserve that term for the room upstairs, which actually contains the bath."

"Next time I'll ask for directions to the khazi!"

"Don't go bleedin' Cockney on me."

"Well, I don't need the tub, mind you, just the loo."

"Keep your knickers on. It's down the hall, towards the kitchen, on the left."

Mobley followed the directions, mumbling every step of the way.

"Bloody foreigners," Davey grumbled.

Once John was finished doing his business, he decided to forego another round of snappy bantering with the local proprietor. Mobley slipped out a side door, knowing his men would take care of themselves.

Crackington Haven seemed like a nice little village, ignoring the grumpy old fart in the pub. The people seemed friendly enough. There was a strange sense of adventure in the air, even though Mobley didn't have the slightest idea why. He decided to go for a walk, just to meander here-and-there.

Suddenly, as Gavin Kane dashed out the front door of his house, he ran smack dab into Mobley coming down the lane.

After the collision, John helped the boy to his feet.

Gavin was quite embarrassed.

"Greetings to you, lad," Mobley said, dusting Gavin off. "Are you all right?"

"I'm so sorry I ran into you, sir," Gavin apologized profusely. "I'm afraid I wasn't looking where I was going."

"No bother," John said. "I was young once too."

It was then that Gavin recognized the uniform. "You're in the Royal Navy."

"Yes, I am."

"My father is a lieutenant commander," Gavin stated proudly.

Mobley took a step back and saluted. "Yes, sir."

Gavin waved him off. "Not me, my father."

"Oh," John said. "I thought you looked like an officer."

Gavin laughed and checked John's rank. "You're a sub-lieutenant, right?"

"Quite so. Sub-lieutenant John Mobley at your service. And you are?"

"Gavin Kane," the boy replied. "It's a pleasure to meet you."

"Likewise," Mobley said.

"What brings you to Crackington Haven, sir?" Gavin asked politely.

"Just stopped for a sip of suds," John replied. "My men and I hoped to tour Tintagel Castle this afternoon. This is Cornwall and I want to see where King Arthur and his Knights of the Round Table bandied about."

There was something passionate in the way the officer had answered Gavin's question, which made the boy take to the man straight off. Gavin wondered if

Mobley believed in dragons too. Unfortunately, he didn't have time to find out, because his mother had sent him on an errand.

However, Gavin was suddenly struck with a brilliant idea.

"If you and your men would like a guide for touring Tintagel Castle, I'm the one," the teen proposed. "For a few bob, I'd be happy to show you the haunts of King Arthur's fortress and even Merlin's Cave."

Mobley grinned. "Sounds like a grand idea, lad."

"Let me finish gathering Mr. Cooper's package for me mum, and then I'll be right back," Gavin said.

"We'll meet you outside the inn," John told him.

Gavin waved and scurried off to the shop, where he handed the proprietor several ration tickets. "Here's me mum's stubs, Mr. Cooper. You have something for her?"

"Indeed I do, young Gavin," the owner said. "Here's her tea."

The boy was excited too, because he knew how much his mother loved her tea. "Thank you, sir. She'll be most pleased."

He hurried back to his house, handed off the packet, and charged right back outside again, before anyone could stop him. Gavin only stopped running when he came to a stop in front of the *Coombe Barton Inn*.

Three men in uniform soon joined the teen.

"This is Gavin Kane, our intrepid guide," Mobley introduced the boy.

Radcliff and Watkins looked Gavin over.

In unison they said, "He'll do."

"Good, then pay him," John instructed with an exaggerated smile.

Gavin held out his hand expectantly.

Two shillings dropped into his palm.

"Right this way, gents," Gavin said.

With the Kane boy in the lead, the three men had to hustle to keep up, as they headed along the coast road. They were immediately entertained by Gavin's theatrics.

"While all of Cornwall is steeped in legend and tradition," the boy began his dissertation. "It's Boscastle and Tintagel that guard the most wondrous tales of King Arthur and his knights. In fact, Boscastle is where Arthur was born."

In a highly animated style, Gavin shared his wealth of knowledge about the area. He answered questions and pointed out scores of interesting historical and mythical facts.

Tintagel Castle was set on a dramatic and picturesque headland that was virtually an island, connected to the mainland by a slim finger of land. Over the centuries much of the castle had fallen into the sea and very little remained, but for the three men, it was worth the steep climb up the steps to either part of the castle for the setting alone.

"This area has been linked with the tales of King Arthur since 1136," Gavin explained. "Stories told of how Arthur lived at Tintagel, but there is no direct evidence to connect him with the area. However, the remains of a large fifth and sixth century settlement and the quantity of imported luxury goods found, suggest that this may have been a stronghold of a kingdom comprising Cornwall, Devon and parts of Somerset. During this time a large defensive ditch was dug, effectively cutting off access to the headland, and helping give Tintagel its name, Din Tagell, which means Fortress of the Narrow Entrance."

"How do you know all this, lad?" Watkins asked.

"My love of English history, sir," Gavin replied.

"Most unusual, I do say," Radcliff said. "Carry on."

Gavin concluded his tour with a quick peek at Merlin's Cave, but the tide was in, so they couldn't actually go exploring. Standing by the side of the road again, the three naval officers seemed pleased at how things turned out.

Mobley gave Gavin another shilling as a tip. "Thank you again, young man. It was most fortunate that we ran into each other, literally."

Gavin laughed.

"I must be going home now, before me mum worries," Gavin said, heading back towards Crackington Haven. "Good luck to you all and remember to give Hitler one for me."

"Gladly, my boy," Watkins called out, waving.

Radcliff was distracted by the quaint little white cottage on the hill, which appeared to have a magnificent view of Tintagel Castle. "Excuse me, but before moving on, shall we go up there and take a look around?"

The others agreed.

Up the trail they went.

The surface of the ancient front door was carved with ornate runes and unusual symbols. The three men stood hesitantly, not certain what to do.

Watkins reached out to grab the door handle, when suddenly …

4

Conflicting Agendas

In his private office deep within the Reich Chancellery, Adolf Hitler selected several records to be played on the phonograph. Listening to the music of Richard Wagner was commonplace for the leader of the Third Reich. After setting the needle down, the sound crackled for a moment, before he heard the overture to *Parsifal*. The Führer remarked to his aide, "I have built up my religion out of *Parsifal*. Divine worship should be in solemn form, without pretenses of humility. One can serve the gods only in the garb of the hero."

Wagner had become the unofficial court composer of the Third Reich. The Führer was quoted as saying, "Whoever wants to understand National Socialistic Germany must know Wagner." The composer was a cultural hero for Hitler and his Nazis. The strains of Wagner had played during the Nazi book-burning ceremonies and now accompanied concentration camp prisoners about to be put to death. Germany's main defensive fortification was dubbed the Siegfried Line, named after the mythical hero in Wagner's *Ring of the Nibelung*.

Wagner's music had great influence on the Führer and his cronies, even though the composer died in 1883, 50 years before Hitler became Reich Chancellor. Wagner perpetuated the Aryan myth, expressed through music and as such, everyone presently in power embraced it. The music instilled pride and honor, stirring darker emotions too.

The records continued to play. The next selection was the funeral march from *Götterdämmerung*. Hitler closed his eyes and focused on listening, his thoughts known only to him. Once that arrangement had concluded, another was selected. This time it was the third opera of Wagner's famous Ring trilogy.

To the Führer, opera was all about telling a heroic story, and Wagner took a larger-than-life story and set it to equally gigantic music. The Wagnerian dragon had a deadly stinger on his tail and poisonous breath, which Hitler viewed as symbolism for Communism. Dispatching this beast required strength and ambition, but fortunately, the German hero Siegfried possessed more than enough of both.

So Hitler dreamed of creating a nation of dragon slayers. He became obsessed with this mission and as his visions evolved into nightmares, so followed Germany. Perhaps the people went willingly, perhaps not, but all the while headed towards utter destruction. At the forefront was a little man, with a silly mustache and beady black eyes, whose sole purpose in life was to lead Nazi Germany to its former glory, no matter what the cost.

He gathered around him men of questionable intelligence, but ruthless in their pursuit of power and conquest. Thieves and scoundrels all, Hitler's cabinet consisted of Herman Göring, Joseph Goebbels, Rudolf Hess, Erich Raeder, Franz Schlegelberger, and Wilhelm Keitel, with Heinrich Himmler and Reinhard Heydrich sitting in the wings, rapidly gaining favor. Each member was constantly jockeying for more power, even at the expense of Germany's strategic advantage.

In fact, for Hitler's birthday, several leading German industrialists, with the financial assistance of Heinrich Himmler, presented the Führer with a case containing the original scores of some of Richard Wagner's music. They had paid nearly one million Reichmarks for the collection. Hitler was elated and promised to keep them in a safe place. The manuscripts included the scores of *Die Feen, Die Liebesverbot, Reinzi, Das Reingold, Die Valkure* and the orchestral sketch of *Der Fliegende Hollander.*

What was incredibly ironic about the entire scenario was how polarized Himmler and Hitler truly were. While the supreme leader of Nazi Germany was waging war to slay the dragons of his enemies, his most powerful ally, the man dressed in black, had supported the creation of a living dragon. While Hitler spoke in images of propaganda and symbolism, Himmler surrounded himself with sorcery and black magic.

Hitler commented to his aide, "How fortunate for me the masses do not think."

Perhaps it was a darker destiny that would eventually force these two ideals to collide, plunging Europe into a quagmire of horrible death and destruction. When darkness was forced to wage war against darkness, the only possible outcome was even greater darkness.

At that very moment in England, the Allied Central Interpretation Unit, based at **RAF Medmenham**, was headquarters for photographic intelligence gathering. Photo-interpreters played a key role in identifying enemy movements, as well as locations singled out as potential targets. No attack, whether a bombing raid, the landing of a few men on a beach, or massive fleet movements, was possible without the preparation of material by these interpreters. Innovative photographic techniques made it possible for the interpreters to view the enemy's activities in three-dimensional clarity, thereby allowing them to prepare highly detailed Interpretation Reports.

Already by this time in 1941, hundreds of thousands of aerial reconnaissance images had been accumulated at **RAF Medmenham**. Heading up this force of eagle-eyed volunteers was Lieutenant Commander Richard Kane. His dedicated staff had already proved themselves invaluable on countless occasions. However, as the commanding officer of this skilled team of men and women interpreters, Kane also was quick to acknowledge the sacrifices of the RAF pilots who went on the photographic reconnaissance missions in the first place.

One of Lieutenant Commander Kane's favorite pilots was Wing Commander Ian Warwick, who believed the mission wasn't a success until the film was returned home and properly processed. To this end, Warwick always managed to come back with quality pictures.

When the weather was too poor for flying, Ian also went around and took photographs of downed German aircraft. On one particular excursion, a German Heinkel bomber had been on the receiving end of a British Hawker Hurricane's machineguns. The He111 had gone straight into the ground, creating a crater with mangled bits of aircraft and dead airmen scattered all around.

Warwick had seen more than his fair share of death and destruction, so while the sight of the wreckage wasn't pleasant, it really didn't affect him. Ian took his pictures and started to look around the area at some of the bits and pieces, because maybe he would find a suitable souvenir.

Something made Warwick go toward a patch of long grass, a little ways from the crater. He immediately noticed a small leather case and after opening it, discovered an expensive 35mm Leica camera.

After Ian completed his photographic duties, he set about examining his newly obtained piece of German technology. Warwick could tell there was film still in it, so he rewound it and later processed the film. The only photograph was a snapshot of three grinning young Luftwaffe aviators in their early twenties. Based on the evidence gathered at the crash site, the German airplane was on a reconnaissance mission of its own when it was shot down.

Wing Commander Warwick was deeply disturbed by this image and from that day forward, he had the snapshot wedged up under the lip of one of the gauge housings, inside his Spitfire. As part of a new personal ritual, Ian would study the picture before every take-off and landing.

On Warwick's Spitfire, cameras were mounted facing down, with electrical remote controls and heating coils to counter the intense cold at great heights, which could freeze oil or frost over the lens. Ways had been devised to achieve exactly the desired overlap between one picture and the next, so the resulting prints could be stuck together in a row to give a continuous series along the aircraft's track. Warwick's Supermarine Spitfire had been modified to take camera equipment in each wing, along with additional fuel and oil in a small streamlined pod.

Spitfires were used for most missions, especially low-level work. They were unarmed, and relied on their extra speed to escape interception. Their greatest danger lay in the appearance of vapor trails, which alerted the enemy to their presence. Warwick's Spitfire was camouflaged to blend with the sky. Ian could fly at 42,000 feet, where few enemy aircraft would venture, but anti-aircraft fire was always a danger.

Ian's aircraft was fitted with pressurized cockpit, but at those heights, it imposed a severe physical strain on him. The aircraft was almost at its maximum altitude and any clumsy movement could cause the aircraft to stall. There was also the problem of oxygen failure.

The engine itself, which was practically in his lap, only made a sort of ticking noise like a clock. The cold, the low pressure and the immobilizing effect of the elaborate equipment and bulky clothing in the tiny cockpit, all had the effect of damping down and subduing all the senses, except the sense of sight. On a clear day, Warwick could see an immense distance, whole countries at a time. Below him, a scrap was going on, the fighters glinting as they circled in the sun. He felt like a man looking down into a pool, watching minnows playing near the bottom.

Outside the aircraft, the temperature was 60 degrees below zero and if the cockpit heating failed, the cold was agonizing. Everything inside became covered with frost and long icicles grew from the Warwick's mask. Most alarming of all, the entire windscreen and blister hood was liable to frost over, making it impossible to see out.

Of course, it was at times like this the sky would fill with Messerschmitts. Still, the wing commander returned from another mission, unscathed, but exhausted. He was leisurely strolling across the runway and thinking about several days' worth of sleep, when one of the messengers intercepted him.

"Lieutenant Commander Kane would like to request the pleasure of your company at the *Olde Dog*, sir," the young man said after saluting.

"Oh, isn't that special," Warwick replied. "I could do with a pint or two. On my way, laddie."

Ye Olde Dog & Badger was the local pub in the nearby village of Medmenham. On the very rare occasions when Richard was allowed a few hours away from the base, he would meet some of the off-duty RAF pilots there for pints of lager and friendly conversation. However, since it was a senior officer who requested this meeting, Ian figured the talk would be more focused on war.

Warwick spotted Lt. Cmdr. Kane sitting by the dark frosted windows. Ian stopped at the bar to grab a pint of bitters, and then went to join Richard. Warm handshakes started the gathering on a high note.

"Have a seat, Wing Commander," Kane said as he sat down again.

"Thank you, sir," Warwick replied.

They both took big swallows of beer.

"So what's the occasion, sir?" Ian asked straight away.

"Well, there's a nagging issue distracting my staff and I wanted to discuss it with you straight away," Richard replied candidly.

"Very well, let's have it."

"Well, the ladies in my unit want to know how you're able to grow such a very handsome mustache?" Kane asked with a straight face.

Warwick almost spit out his mouthful of beer. "Damn."

Lieutenant Commander Kane burst into laughter.

"That was bloody unsporting of you, old man," Ian sputtered.

"Sorry, chum, but you had that coming," Kane said.

Warwick was busy wiping spilled beer and mumbling under his breath.

"Would you care for some help?"

"Not bloody likely."

"You must admit the growth under your nose is quite impressive."

The pilot rolled his eyes.

"My staff agrees you are a handsome old boy," Richard went on.

"That's enough, sir," Warwick protested.

Lt. Cmdr. Kane shrugged. "I don't know, Ian. I think you should reconsider. I'm sure all that flying makes you lonely for company and several of the Wrens are quite good looking. If that handlebar mustache gets you a date, how can you complain?"

Warwick held up his hands in surrender. "Very well, sir. I'll stop by and have a chat with the girls. Anything to get you to cease this silly banter."

"All right, then," Kane said.

Warwick changed the subject. "How did your son like the helmet and goggles?"

"He loved them, thanks," Richard replied, smiling at the memory of Gavin's elated reaction. "They'll come to good use, believe me."

"You're a grand old father, that's clear to see," Ian commented.

"I try," Kane said quietly. "I'd rather be home being a father, than staring at photographs all day. Sometimes it's difficult to see how we're making any difference."

Inside the little white cottage on the hill, Sir Thaddeus Osbert was clearly not in the mood for uninvited guests. He was exhausted from his long flight to Iceland and then the grueling discussions before the Dragon Council. The dragon wished the humans would just go away.

As Watkins was about to open the ancient door, Thaddeus opened his mouth and let out a rumbling roar, "Grrrrrrr."

The hamlet shook from his mighty growl.

Watkins fell over backwards and Radcliff retreated, trembling with fear.

Mobley, on the other hand, skirted past them and fearlessly pushed open the door.

"Don't go in there," Radcliff managed to shout.

"Why not?" John asked.

"Because there's some wild beast inside, waiting to attack you," Watkins replied, as if the answer was so incredibly obvious.

"Oh, nonsense," John said. "It was just the sound of the wind."

Mobley bravely stepped inside.

The cottage was empty, except for a lone stool sitting in the middle of the earthen floor. Against one wall was a magnificent flagstone fireplace, which by the looks of it, hadn't been used for a fire in a very long time.

John was a bit disappointed. He had expected so much more.

"Well, what is it?" called Radcliff from outside.

"Nothing at all, like I said," Mobley replied.

However, if he had really looked closely at the fireplace, he might have noticed two large eyes staring at him. Thaddeus didn't feel threatened by the British airmen, but neither did he feel like entertaining anyone today. The dragon closed his eyes and waited for the intruders to depart.

Mobley had no intention of leaving just yet. There was something fascinating and historical about the cottage and John could sense its importance. He just wasn't sure why he felt this way.

"Stop acting like a pair of old ladies," Mobley scolded his crewmates.

Yet no amount of cajoling could make his crew come inside the hamlet, so John had a look around by himself. What fascinated him the most was the grand stone fireplace, which looked out of place in such a tiny cottage. As he ran his fingers over the surface, Mobley was astounded at how smooth each stone felt, polished to a glossy sheen. It was almost as if the stones were alive.

Thaddeus had to stifle his chuckle, because the human's touch tickled him right under the chin. It suddenly struck the dragon that perhaps this specific man was in the cottage for a specific reason, perhaps to make initial contact. Sir Osbert was wise enough to know that things seldom happened by chance or coincidence. He made a point to memorize Mobley's features and stance, just in case.

John was satisfied that he had seen enough of the little white cottage and he rejoined his crew outside. He pooh-poohed their childish behavior and they made their way back to Boscastle, where the men arranged for transportation to the Royal Navy Air Station at nearby St. Merryn.

5

Caves and Secrets

Cornwall was famous for its standing stones, stone circles, burial chambers, and the scattered remains of prehistoric villages. Many ancient relics were still in remarkably good condition and provided Gavin, Bunty, and Emily an intriguing insight into the customs, culture, and rituals of their predecessors.

These historic sites could be found across the county, in fields, on the moor, or by the roadsides. Gavin and Emily knew right where to look, having explored the countryside for miles and miles in every direction. Although some of the ancient sites were located in the middle of nowhere and necessitated long treks to get to them, they were ideal for imaginative minds. Likewise, the coast of Cornwall was one of the most picturesque in the world. Giant cliffs were occasionally broken into strange shapes by the action of the waves and weird formations added to the unusual landscape.

This was especially true near the legendary Tintagel Castle, which had been constructed in such a way to incorporate the sheer cliffs for defensive advantage. Potential attackers could neither storm the compound en masse, nor navigate a ship past the rocky perimeter. Perched several hundred feet above sea level, this locale not only afforded a spectacular view of everything around it, but also the entrance to two shoreline caves that ran beneath the isle itself. The larger of the two was dubbed "Merlin's Cave" and was believed to be the hiding place where the wily wizard sequestered the newborn Arthur from potential harm by enemies of the Pendragon crown.

Only one cave ran completely under Tintagel, but both caverns were well worth exploring. At high tide, however, the sea intervened between the island and the land, and rendered a visit to the caves impossible. Gale force winds were not uncommon there as well, so sometimes the ocean was calm and tranquil, while at other times the waves rushed in and dashed in fury against the cliffs. Therefore, to enter the caves, access to the pebble-strewn beach was only possible during low tide.

On their first visit of the day, the children used the traditional route of climbing down over a few boulders and walking along the beach for a few hundred yards to Merlin's Cave. They entered through a large opening and immediately heard the roar of the ocean coming through from the far end of the cave. This unnerved them enough that a hasty retreat was in order.

The next day they returned, but it was high tide and the beach was completely underwater. Not to be deterred, Gavin managed to climb over the fence and scramble down to a different area below, from where he led the way into Merlin's Cave once again. Bunty and Emily walked carefully over the rocks, avoiding the water and examining the sides of the cave for signs of secret passages. The lighting was quite poor and may have contributed to the fact that they didn't find a trace of any hidden corridors. Tradition hinted there was a hidden door leading to the wizard's secret chamber somewhere in the interior of this huge rock. This visit was also shortened by the rising tide, which rapidly cut off their exit from the cave. Scurrying out, the trio made it to safety, just in time.

This unsuccessful challenge spurred Gavin to announce his intention to explore other spots along the entire Cornish coastline, until he discovered the fabled wrecker's hideaway. Rumors and legends suggested a fabulous treasure was hidden near the banks of the Helford River. So once again, right after school, the three of them headed for the cliffs near St. Keverne.

There was a cave in the cliffside that was of some extent, which in old days was a hiding-place for smugglers, who were rather abundant in this wave-washed county. The inlets and coves held an evil reputation of being the abodes of wreckers. There were many smuggler caves or eddy holes scattered up and down the coast.

A pathway down the hill brought the children to a hollow, which divided the lofty crags from the wild crashing waves, very near some fishermen's dwellings. The village also has a fogou, the Cornish word for man-made cave, which was really an underground passage stretching far underneath the massive cliffs.

Within a few yards of the land rose a rocky pyramid, and in front of the glen was an island, and to the left a range of cliffs of exquisite serpentine, a species of rock found only in Cornwall, Wales, and Scotland, but nowhere else in England. To be the first to enter such a place was an experience unlikely to be forgotten. The caves under the cliffs, gnawed out by the sea, extended deeper and deeper into the earth. The children hesitated taking such a risk.

Since almost all of the coastal towns and villages on the Cornish coast had some kind of connection with smuggling, it wasn't always wise to go snooping around. With rationing hard-felt by the locals, the black market had replaced traditional smuggling. Once again, ordinary folk and clergymen alike dabbled in a spot of contraband goods to supplement their income. Unfortunately, most of the caves and secret passages used in the old days had long since been blocked up, but the legacy of Cornish smugglers lived on as part of the coastline's heritage.

For the teens, the intriguing possibilities were too enticing to ignore. On yet another return trip, Gavin had outfitted his friends with flashlights pilfered from his father's inventory. While mucking about, their torches cast eerie light throughout the seaward cave entrances, scaring them half-to-death. Bravely overcoming their jitters, the trio went onward, deeper into the creepy confines.

"Look over there," Bunty blurted, pointing with a shaking finger.

"What do you see?" Emily quivered, her eyes closed.

"It looks like bones again, Emmy," Gavin called out in delight.

"Pirate's treasure!" Bunty exclaimed. "We'll be bloody rich."

"Don't get your hopes up yet, chum," Gavin said. "More likely they once belonged to some poor bloke who stubbled on smuggler's goods and met an untimely end."

Gavin's guess had been pretty close to the truth, as they looked down on yet another skeleton, this one green and crumbling with age, stretched out beside three kegs of unidentified contents.

"What should we do?" Emily asked as she stared at the remains.

"Whoever he was, he still deserves a proper burial," Gavin said. "We'll come back for him later."

"Not before we hide them barrels," Bunty stated. "They must be worth a lot of lolly, believe me."

"That's illegal," Emily protested.

Gavin was perplexed. The barrels, especially if the contents inside was still good, could fetch a handsome price, or at least promise a sizeable bunch of ration tickets in exchange. Likewise, several local pubs could benefit directly from a free shipment of spirits, regardless of the source, as long as it wasn't stolen. After all, it wasn't as if they had pilfered the kegs or something. They found them abandoned in a cave and that meant the finders had title to the property.

"I think Bunty is right, Emmy," Gavin said after making up his mind. "We won't try to profit too much from these barrels, but we found them and I think there's gain to be had."

"Bravo," Bunty reacted.

"If you think it's the right thing to do, Gavin, then I'll go along with it," Emily reluctantly relinquished.

"Right, now that that's settled, give us a hand," Bunty suggested.

The teens carried the three kegs out of the cave and hid them by the road, so each of them could carry a barrel back to Boscastle, which was the closest town. Gavin wasn't finished exploring yet, so they went back inside the cave.

Past the old bones, they ventured, deeper and deeper into the blackness, only their torches giving any light to their path. The cave continued to narrow and shrink, until the three of them were forced to scoot sideways. Steep walls on either side of the passage reinforced the feeling they were walking through a narrow canyon or valley.

Then, quite unexpectedly, the passageway opened up into a large cavern.

The sound of rushing water greeted them as they wound their way along the wet, slippery shore of a subterranean pool of trapped seawater. Mysterious twinkling lights give the water a soft greenish cast. As the teens proceeded further, the sound of rushing wind whipped past their ears. Air currents, created by changes in barometric pressure, produced the flow as the wind entered and exited the cave via a series of vents to the outside.

An unbroken sheet of flowstone, deposited over the eons as sheets of water washed over the cavern floor, gave a polished look to the base of the next attached domed chamber. A series of granite columns against one wall gave the impression of a pipe organ. Making their way along steep inclines and difficult traverses, the trio finally came to a section of the cave that showed signs of human improvements. A wooden barricade blocked any further progress, but steps cut into the stone led upwards.

While waiting for Gavin to decide what they would do next, Bunty spotted a piece of crystal sparkling under the water. He retrieved it, but as soon as the stone was plucked from the small eddy pool, it lost its luster. The red-haired boy decided to keep it anyway, because the crystal was good-sized and polished smooth. In his pocket it went.

"We're very near Porthleven," Gavin said finally. "I wonder if this cave leads to the town's local, *The Ship Inn*, which legend claims was a hive of smuggling activity and intrigue throughout the 18th century and supposedly had smuggling tunnels in the basement."

"That might explain those kegs," Bunty chimed in. "Smugglers loot, I tell yee."

Emily rolled her eyes. "They're probably so tainted by saltwater that whatever was inside is no good anymore. Let's get away from here. This place gives me the willies."

"What's this?" Bunty asked, flashing the torch beam to shine up on the cave wall.

"Now what?" Emily demanded.

"Come look, please?" the red-haired boy insisted.

Gavin and Emily joined Bunty and looked up.

There was an inscription intricately carved into the rock, but none of them could translate the strange characters.

Ωιτηιν Τηισ Χαϖε Λιεσ Τηε Σεχρετ Οφ Τηε Δραγονσ Βρεατη

"Let's write this down and see if Thaddeus can decipher it," Gavin suggested.

Emily, of course, had a pencil nub and piece of paper in her pocket. She never went anywhere without them. Carefully transcribing the symbols, it took her a long time to make certain they were accurate.

After that, the children hurried out of the cave and trundled the kegs back to Boscastle, where Gavin delivered them to the owner of the *Napoleon Inn*, a fine pub known for fairness and good will.

The next day, right after school, the teens met again outside Boscastle and made their way to the little white cottage on the hill. The door was already open, for Thaddeus was apparently expecting them.

Sure enough, the dragon was curled up in the corner, but he appeared to be asleep. Tiptoeing inside, they didn't want to disturb him, but couldn't help their giggles after hearing his snoring, which sounded like two train engines rumbling down the tracks.

Suddenly, one eyelid lifted.

The huge eye focused on them, the catlike lens narrowing to mere slits.

"What's so funny?" Thaddeus grumbled.

"Hello," Gavin said, trying not to snicker.

The dragon lifted his head and suddenly yawned. Without exception, the teens were amazed at how many teeth Sir Osbert's mouth could hold, every one of them razor sharp. Especially impressive were his fangs, which glistened with dangerous intent.

"We're sorry we woke you from your nap, Thaddeus," Emily apologized.

"No need," the dragon said. "I always enjoy your visits."

"We had something specific to ask you today," Bunty volunteered.

"Oh, and what might that be?" Thaddeus wondered, his curiosity piqued.

Emily stepped forward and pulled the slip of notepaper from her pocket. Holding it up high, she asked, "Are you able to read what I've written on this piece of paper?"

Thaddeus changed lenses to magnifying power and looked at the girl's fine printing. "Yes, child, I can read the symbols. Where did you find such runes?"

"In one of the caves on the coast," Gavin explained.

Thaddeus scratched his chin with one extended claw. "Hmmm."

"What does it say, Sir Osbert?" asked Bunty.

"Beware of the Dragon's Breath," Thaddeus stated matter-of-factly.

"What does it mean?" Bunty wondered.

The dragon shrugged. "Don't ask me. I know my breath can be most foul at times, but I didn't think it was that bad."

The children all laughed.

Thaddeus grinned. He so enjoyed entertaining them. Of course, what he was really trying to do was distract them from their discovery, for it was neither the time, nor the place, to discuss the repercussions of the cryptic carvings. The dragon was well aware what the riddle meant, but some secrets were better left undisclosed, at least temporarily.

Meanwhile, Lieutenant Commander Kane's dedicated Photo Reconnaissance Unit at **RAF Medmenham** was firmly established, which meant they could handle the subsequent processing, plotting and interpretation of more than 5,000 exposures a week. This steady flow of photographs translated into long workdays, sore eyes, and the consumption of lots of coffee. It also meant that certain trends were quickly recognized, as Richard's people began noticing certain enemy habits.

Already subjected to aerial bombardment, the Germans tried to develop serious camouflage and decoy methods. Many of these measures were unsuccessful, not necessarily because they were too simplistic or too childish, but because the various tricks and illusions employed were not able to withstand the sophisticated search procedures of the British photo analysis experts based at **RAF Medmenham**.

Track activity was the biggest telltale giveaway of all. Kane's staff had learned that disturbed areas of grass or soil would show up on photographs, much lighter in tone than the surroundings, and those areas depressed by feet or vehicles deflected light back to the camera at a different angle, thus causing this phenomenon. It turned out that track activity was almost impossible to conceal.

This rule-of-thumb became more commonplace as the interpreters got more used to what they should be looking for. One day, just after Richard came on duty, one of the new Wrens came to him with a set of photographs. Kane looked with his magnifying glass first.

"All four emplacements of this coastal battery are occupied and nicely toned down to blend into the surrounding ground," the Wren named Polly Knightly pointed out. "Shelters have been skillfully camouflaged, but track activity from men walking to mess, latrines, and transportation give the site away. Dummy positions, like other decoys, are given away by a lack of activity, such as no vehicles, tracks and associated objects."

Richard smiled. "Well done, Miss Knightly. You've certainly got an eye for footprints, now don't you?"

The Wren smiled in return. "Thank you, sir. I try."

"Lieutenant Commander?" called out another analyst from her viewing station.

"Yes, Miss Fairborne, I'll be right there," Kane replied. He looked back at Knightly. "Keep up the good work, Polly. You'll do just fine."

When Richard reached Sally Fairborne, he was greeted with another set of photographs to look at. He peered through the optical lens at the images, which stood out in three-dimensional clarity.

"The awkward construction of branches and netting are more suitable to children's games, then to men whose lives are at stake," she commented as Kane looked through the stereoscope.

The Lieutenant Commander looked up at her. "Did they do this on purpose, just to throw us off?"

"Perhaps," Sally replied. "I've never seen such a poor attempt at camouflage before. It must be a dummy installation."

"Or it's real and they're trying to convince us otherwise."

"Possibly."

"But you don't think so?"

"No, I don't."

"Why not?"

"It's too obvious, in either case."

"So what do your instincts tell you?"

"Well, perhaps there's something really important nearby, so this rather obvious emplacement draws our attention away from it?"

Miss Fairborne pulled out the other photographs from the same series. Sally went over to the long viewing table in the center of the room and placed each snapshot end-to-end, to create a flow. Richard joined her and they looked at each of them, one-at-a-time, walking along slowly, evaluating the potential of each shot, back-and-forth, and to-and-fro.

"What's this, then?" Kane said as he picked up a photograph almost in the middle of the series.

He slid that print, and the one after it, together under the stereoscope, squinting to get the right angle. For a long time, he said nothing, but chewed his lip in concentration.

"These photos were taken over Germany?" the lieutenant commander asked after awhile.

"Yes, sir," Miss Fairborne replied. "A long-range Wellington took these while following one of our bomber sorties."

"Where, exactly?"

"The Alma Valley, near the village of Wewelsburg," she answered after looking at her notes. "Do you see something?"

Kane rubbed his eyes for a moment. "I don't know. There's a castle on the promontory overlooking the village and there seems to be a fair amount of traffic leading to a truck park below the castle. There are structures which are military in nature, I guess, but fairly recently constructed, based on the earth-moving equipment nearby."

"Could it be possible that the poorly erected camouflage was designed to pull attention away from that area?" Miss Fairborne wondered.

"It's possible, of course," Richard agreed. "But the question is why? What might they be hiding?"

"Should we request another sortie?"

Richard nodded. "Yes, I think this merits another pass. Let's recommend Wing Commander Warwick be sent this time."

"Very well, Lieutenant Commander," Sally obeyed. "I'll get the paperwork together after my break."

Kane looked at his watch. Time always seemed to go by so quickly. "Pardon me, Miss Fairborne. Is it morning or afternoon?"

She smiled with pity. "Just about perfect for my morning cup of tea, sir."

He shook his head in wonder. "Where does the time go? Carry on."

Sally patted him on the forearm. "Would you care to join me for a cuppa?"

He grinned. "Sounds wonderful."

After they fixed their cups of warm tea, they sat in the tiny base cafeteria for a short break. After a few sips, Miss Fairborne started up a conversation.

"Have you heard from your wife and son lately?" she asked.

He nodded. "Another letter came in the post yesterday. They're getting by, of course, but I miss them terribly."

"I'm sure you do, sir," Sally said. "How is your son?"

"Gavin is a great lad, strong, active, and full of healthy mischief. He is not a bit shy and makes friends easily."

"He sounds wonderful."

"Well, I'm off to make my rounds," Kane suddenly announced, hoping to hide the emotion welling up inside. "Send someone to look for me if you find anything interesting."

"I will, sir," she said.

Richard quickly strolled out of the photographic section and made his way towards Modeling, where miniature models were constructed to aid military planning. Kane's people provided most of the photographs used to construct the detailed mock-ups and he checked twice a day to see how the projects were progressing.

In between buildings, however, Richard pulled out the most recent letter from Winifred and stopped to read it again.

Dearest Richard,

Your letter took four weeks to come and arrived just before Gavin and Bunty got home from school on Tuesday last. I was busy doing some sewing, and bottling fruit for the winter, so didn't have much time for writing. I have been showing Emily Scott how to bottle fruit without sugar and she has become so keen on it, she says she will end up by having far too much.

We have enough sugar for ordinary use and some extra for jam, but not enough for all the fruit, hence the craze for bottling has arisen and incidentally, of course, the price of bottles! Your dear son managed to discover a dozen jars abandoned in an old dilapidated barn. This is always what happens when there is a run on anything, we start scrounging.

There was a very large crop of strawberries and lectures on how to preserve fruit are often given over the wireless, but people are afraid to tackle it unless they have also seen it done. Most fruit grown in the back garden has been made into jams and jellies, but that will soon be impossible too, now that sugar is rationed.

The boys miss you and so do I. Gavin is doing fine in school, in spite of the constant interruptions. Bunty has natural artistic talent and he should

pursue the gifts God gave him. I shall speak to his father soon, perchance to help this process along.

Love,
Wini

Richard smiled and read it again. Letters came regularly, but they were never enough to replace the void he felt being away from his wife and son. Still, it was better than nothing.

He also had another passing thought. Perhaps the increasing shortage of sugar in Britain was not solely the result of constant bomber raids over the London docks. It was just possible, while somewhat unlikely, that a certain dragon with a sweet tooth might have something to do with the diminishing supplies.

Richard chuckled. When he had an opportunity, he would write Gavin and request that Thaddeus find another source of sugar, even if that meant flying all the way to America. Such a thought made Kane laugh again. Wouldn't the Yanks be shocked if all of sudden their sugarcane and sugar beet stocks simply started vanishing?

"Come to think of it, I don't recall ever hearing Thaddeus mention visiting the United States," Richard said to himself. "I wonder if he's ever been there before?"

That night, while asleep, Kane dreamt that Thaddeus had found a sugar-processing plant in the southern United States. Covered in sugar, from head to spiny tale, the dragon was in seventh heaven, slurping up vast quantities of the sweet white powder.

When the lieutenant commander awoke several hours later, he remembered every detail and marveled at how real the dream had seemed. Richard also recalled how often the dreams of his youth had come to pass. Thaddeus had made it clear that dreams were often messages sent from another time and place. It was up to the receiver to decipher the true meaning.

In Berlin, the steady clomping sound of Heinrich Muëller's boots echoed throughout the hallways of the Reich Chancellery. It was past midnight, but he was on his way to meet with Reinhard Heydrich. Politely he knocked on the door of an office tucked away in a dark corner of the third floor.

"*Kommen Sie herein,*" a voice called out from behind the door.

Muëller entered, clicked his heels together and said, "*Heil Hitler!*"

"Good morning, Heinrich," Heydrich said.

"Good morning, *Herr Heydrich,*" Muëller said.

"What have you discovered?" Reinhard asked.

Müeller was instantly uncomfortable and he did not answer immediately.

"*Report, bitte*," the Nazi demanded.

"The *Reichsführer* has summoned his closest SS officers to Schloss Wewels-burg," Müeller reported. "They are to meet there by the week's end."

Heydrich's lips were tightly drawn. He stared at Müeller for a moment. "I have received no such invitation."

Poor Müeller didn't know what to say.

"That will be all, Heinrich," Heydrich said in a low threatening voice, dismissing the man with an impatient gesture.

After coming to attention and clicking his boots, Müeller moved to exit, but before his hand touched the handle, Heydrich was standing beside him.

"*Was ist falsch?*" Müeller asked what was wrong.

"Have you chosen sides, Müeller?" Heydrich demanded.

"Sides?" his aide asked. "I do not understand."

Heydrich vigorously rubbed his chin for a moment, as he considered his suspicions. He was well aware that Reichsführer Himmler was a scheming and treacherous man, but that didn't mean Müeller was party to such behavior. In fact, Heydrich's aide had always been exceedingly loyal.

"I am sorry I questioned your intentions, *Herr Müeller*," Heydrich said. "You may continue with your duties."

"*Jawohl, Herr Heydrich*," Müeller obeyed. He quickly departed.

Heydrich knew Himmler was always conniving, plotting, conspiring, and manipulating his way into the good graces of Adolf Hitler. Therefore, Reinhard was forced to be unusually careful about everything he said and did, because he too had an insatiable greed for power and was a cold, calculating manipulator without human compassion.

Therefore, it was only a matter of time before these two men would come in direct conflict with each other. Heydrich had every intention of coming out on top. It was time to put into motion a desperate plan to eliminate Reichsführer Himmler. Everything might hinge on a certain key, which was somewhere in England. Heydrich had arranged for a special envoy to retrieve the key, but as of yet no word had come as to her success.

6

Love at First Crash

Tabitha Bixley had enlisted in the Women's Royal Navy Service (WRNS), affectionately nicknamed Wrens, to get away from her mother's overly protective nature. Tabitha wanted to join the service as a driver, because she had lots of experience driving her uncle's delivery van. There was no doubt she hoped to land an undemanding job carting important naval officers back and forth.

However, things seldom turn out as planned and Miss Bixley was instead assigned responsibility for the emergency equipment used at the Royal Navy Air Station at St. Merryn, or **HMS Vulture.** This meant she had to know how to operate everything from fire trucks to ambulances. Fortunately, Tabitha was quite gifted in this regard and was quickly promoted.

HMS Vulture was a front-line training establishment for carrier-borne aircraft and crews. Royal Navy shore bases and naval air stations were traditionally named in the same manner as seagoing ships. St. Merryn was used by many combat-ready naval squadrons for flying, armament, air-to-air and ground attack training, as well as aircraft storage and workshops.

Before reporting to **HMS Ark Royal**, Sub-lieutenant John Mobley and his men had been ordered to detour to **HMS Vulture**, for a final series of training exercises, including launching live torpedoes at moving target buoys. After hitching a lift from Tintagel to St. Merryn, the three men stood outside the base entrance, hands in pants pockets, looking over the possibilities.

It was unanimous. They were unimpressed.

"Why did we get sent here, of all places?" Watkins wondered.

"John must have flirted with the admiral's wife," Radcliff suggested.

Mobley chuckled. "More likely it was to keep the two of you away from the admiral's lovely twin daughters."

After presenting identification discs and copies of their orders to the front gate guards, the men were permitted to enter the airbase. There were at least fifteen

Swordfish torpedo bombers lined up in a huge revetment near one of two concrete runways.

"Seems we've come to the right place," Watkins said.

Mobley licked his index finger and held it up, gauging the air direction. "Let's check in with the base commander and get ourselves acclimated."

After reporting to Squadron Leader Bernie Talbot, Sub-lieutenant Mobley received permission to take one of the Swordfish up on a late afternoon flight. While heading out to his assigned trainer, John dropped a bit of a bombshell on his cohorts.

"I want to take the old *Stringbag* up alone," Mobley informed them.

"What's this then?" Radcliff asked.

"Are you sure you don't want us to tag along, sir?" Watkins wondered.

Mobley shook his head. "It's nothing personal, chaps, you know that. I guess I'm not feeling very confident about flying off the deck just yet, so I thought I'd go up and have a turn with a few touch-and-go exercises. No need for you two to go along."

Watkins patted John on the shoulder. "Don't worry, chum, we'll be here when you get back. Just make sure you don't attract any passing Jerries, what."

They all laughed.

"I promise," Mobley said. "I'll just go up for an hour or two, and then we'll go grab a pint at the local."

John slipped into his flying boots and buttoned up his battledress tunic. His crewmates walked with him all the way out to the waiting Swordfish. While pulling on his flight gloves, they stopped to admire the torpedo bomber they had come to know and love.

It was a big, unsophisticated biplane, slow and cumbersome. It looked antiquated, because it was. Nicknamed *Stringbag*, the Swordfish was large, but because of its single engine, it tended to look deceptively small from a distance. Its fabric-covered metal construction was sturdy and reliable, but lacked refinement. The biplane wing had ailerons on both lower and upper planes, and leading edge slats on the upper wing. For the take-off, the ailerons could be drooped eight degrees to increase lift.

Mobley climbed into the open cockpit and started up the engine. As John lowered his goggles into place, his crew waved, and held their thumbs up.

Rolling and bumping along down the uneven runway surface, the Swordfish lifted off slowly. The control tower signaled clearance for Mobley to make a few practice landing approaches, as well as runs on the torpedo gates. John complied, swinging the biplane around for his first landing dry run.

The flying instruments on the Swordfish were pretty basic. All the pilot had to guide him was a turn-and-bank indicator, and some red mercury in a small thermometer tube, to tell him whether he was flying nose-up or nose-down.

Landing on a pitching aircraft carrier was not going to be easy. The Swordfish had a Bristol Pegasus radial engine, which obscured both the flight deck and the ship, in the very last stages of a deck landing. Normally, by approaching in a gentle turn to port, right down to the deck, it was possible to keep the carrier in sight until straightening up. Then it was necessary to look between the engine cylinders to line up the flight lines. This was fine by day, but at night the cylinders were always red-hot and the glow obscured even more of the view.

Mobley headed out to sea, to try his hand on a few practice drops.

There were no refinements to bother with either, such as flaps or a variable pitch airscrew, and the undercarriage could not be retracted. The aircraft had one very special asset, however, which, like everything else on the machine, was simple and very effective. Its torpedo sight was foolproof, if used with care. Mobley was convinced that whoever designed it was a genius. Two rods, one on either side of the front cockpit, fixed to the trailing edge of the top mainframe, displayed a neat little row of electric light bulbs, spaced equally apart. The distance between each bulb and the next represented five knots of enemy speed.

Bonk.

John was startled. He'd never heard that noise before.

Zip, bonk, bonk, bonk.

Clang!

The engine sputtered and revved on its own.

"Stop that!" Mobley shouted at the airplane, patting the instrument panel with his gloved hand. "You behave!"

John suddenly decided to abort his practice torpedo run on the floating targets, because the Swordfish continued acting strangely, the engine repeatedly misfiring. Not wanting to take any chances, he turned around and headed back for **HMS Vulture**.

Blam!

This time the engine coughed a burst of flame, which actually ignited part of the lower wing canvas. The wind fanned the fire for a moment, before it extinguished.

Now Mobley knew he had a serious problem.

Blam!

Once more, the engine spewed flame, which again scorched the canvas, this time on the upper wing.

Pow!

Bang, bang, bang ... zip!

Instinctively, Mobley ducked and it was a good thing too, because part of the engine just broke apart, pieces flying past him like bullets.

Smoke began billowing out.

At the **HMS Vulture** control tower, the men on duty reacted immediately.

"Swordfish 8369 in trouble!" one of the spotters announced.

"Ring up the emergency crew," Squadron Leader Talbot commanded. It was his air station and his responsibility to safeguard not only the permanent personnel, but also the pilots and crewmembers that rotated through the base for training.

The alarm whistle sounded and bells clanged.

Tabitha Bixley, who was the only senior Wren presently on duty, struggled to squirm into her asbestos suit and scurried out to the runway to await the incoming flight. The cumbersome gear was hot and she was quite uncomfortable.

Mobley's Swordfish now had one wing on fire, there was engine damage, and the controls were becoming increasingly sluggish. Trailing ragged fabric streamers and with gaping holes in virtually every part of its wings, fuselage, and tail, John tried to prevent it from stalling. In fact, he was determined to get back to **HMS Vulture** in one piece, even if the Swordfish fell apart on the way.

Putt-putt-putt ... sputter, pop.

Then there was complete silence.

The engine just conked out.

Mobley really concentrated then, fighting the stick and keeping his eye on the edge of the oncoming cliff. If he could make it that far, John could set it down, hoping the Swordfish would take the strain of impact.

One hundred feet and closing.

Fifty feet.

Almost there.

Bump.

John didn't exactly want to close his eyes, but with parts of the biplane breaking off all around him, it was only natural to cower a little. The Swordfish bounced, careened, and shuddered, until the undercarriage snapped off.

Crack.

"Bloody hell," Mobley shouted. "Don't fail me now."

The biplane skidded along, tearing up a huge swath behind it, before slamming to an abrupt stop.

John grunted with the impact, his head jolting forward, but the harness held fast. He sighed and thanked God for his good fortune.

Tabitha ran forward and jumped up onto what was left of the right wing. It was her duty to quickly get the pilot out of the crumpled fuselage. Luckily, the Swordfish didn't catch fire, but as the Wren attempted to yank the pilot free, she almost dislocated his shoulder.

"Argh," Mobley groaned in pain. "Easy there, chap. I still have need of both of my arms."

"Oh, I'm so sorry," she spoke from behind her fogged mask.

Sub-Lieutenant Mobley was pleasantly surprised to hear a woman's voice. "No bother, lass. Just help me unbuckle this bloody great harness and I'll wiggle out like a worm."

His sense of humor made Tabitha giggle. She reached down to pry open the jammed buckle, but it would not budge. "Oh, bother, I'm afraid I can't do a thing."

Now able to move his right arm and purely by instinct, Mobley lifted off the heavy mask from her head. He was startled by her beauty, for he had been expecting some old hag instead. She was simply gorgeous, an auburn-haired beauty with an ethereal visage John couldn't look at without thinking of an angel. Her feisty emerald-green eyes seemed to change colors in dangerous and alluring patterns.

With a casual flick of her head, Tabitha shook the locks of hair from her face. Mobley merely sighed.

"Are you all right, sir?" the Wren asked worriedly.

He shook his head. "No, I must be dead. Since there's an angel right here before me, I must be in heaven."

Tabitha gasped and plopped him right on the forehead with her palm. "Oh, you spoiled rotten lout. You had me all upset, worrying you might be injured, but instead you turn out to be …"

Mobley didn't let her continue. He boldly lifted his lips to hers and kissed her.

Tabitha should have resisted, but instead she kissed him back.

However, her temporary weakness only lasted for a few seconds. The clang-clang-clang of the approaching fire engine brought her back to her senses. With a powerful punch of her hand, the Wren slapped the buckle on Mobley's harness and it sprung open.

With her finger now wagging dangerously close to his nose, John had to listen to her passionate tirade. "Now you stop misbehaving right now, sir. Get out of the plane!"

Sub-lieutenant Mobley obeyed immediately. He vaulted out of the open cock-pit, scrambled over the side and down the wing, to land in the dirt. Amazingly, even with the bulky fire-fighting suit, the Wren had followed him just as quickly.

"I should put you on report for such behavior," Tabitha scolded him.

"Yes, you should, Miss," John agreed. "But I hope you won't."

"Why shouldn't I?"

"Because it would be such a terrible start to a wonderful romance."

"Oh!" she fumed. "You're impossible."

With that, the Wren stormed off towards the control tower.

John watched her walk away, with a huge smile on his face.

While the crashed Swordfish was pretty much a total write-off, John Mobley had managed to get back to **HMS Vulture** without any serious injury, except maybe his pride. Even though he was already assigned to **HMS Ark Royal**, he naturally wondered if this incident would somehow end his flying career with the Royal Navy.

Suddenly his two comrades arrived, wide-eyed and full of concern.

"Are you all right, sir?" Watkins asked.

"Do you need to go to hospital, sir?" Radcliff added.

Mobley grinned and said, "Settle down, chaps. I'm just fine."

Tabitha, however, had stomped along the entire trip back to the control tower. She was fuming over the pilot's arrogance and self-confidence. Sure, he was remotely handsome, but then what man in uniform didn't look sharp?

"Is the pilot all right, Miss Bixley?" Squadron Leader Talbot inquired.

"Who cares?" she snapped.

"Begging your pardon, Miss?" the commander asked with surprise.

Tabitha instantly realized her behavior was quite unprofessional. "Excuse my rudeness, Squadron Leader. I was just a little put off by his cocky attitude, that's all."

Squadron Leader Talbot shook his head in wonder. "Perhaps the pilot had good reason to act out-of-sorts, Miss Bixley. His Swordfish's engine decided to conk out on him while he was still out-to-sea. With the biplane falling apart around him, Sub-lieutenant Mobley managed to get back here, landing without power. Did you stop to consider what shape that airplane was in when you helped the pilot to safety?"

She shook her head, suddenly ashamed.

"If the boy was flirting with you, I can hardly blame him, since you are a very attractive young woman," Talbot continued his little fatherly lecture. "However, I don't think he was trying to be too forward, but was merely blowing off steam."

"Yes, Squadron Leader," Tabitha said.

"I think you should cut him a little slack, Miss Bixley, all things considered."

"Yes, Squadron Leader."

"Dismissed."

While this was transpiring, Mobley had aimlessly walked off the base, leaving his open-mouthed buddies behind. John wandered out the gate and down the main road into the village of St. Merryn, his legs still a little wobbly. It was taking longer than he expected to calm down his nerves.

"What I need is a bit of foam," Mobley announced to himself.

Looking up and down the road, John was hoping to find someone who could direct him to the nearest pub.

"Pardon me, kind sir," Mobley spoke to the first local he spotted. "Is there a pub hereabouts?"

"*The Cornish Arms*," the citizen replied, pointing. "Good beer, mighty fine chips."

"Much obliged, chap," John said. "Good day to ya."

"Bloody foreigners," the man mumbled to himself.

St. Merryn was a lively little village with a cluster of gray slate cottages, two pubs, three good fish-and-chip restaurants, various shops, a post office, and a bakery. This was mainly a farming parish and there were seventeen farms in the immediate area, many of which have been tilled and harvested by the same families for countless generations.

The thought of living in such a village greatly appealed to John.

Just as he was about to step inside *The Cornish Arms*, Mobley spotted a familiar face. It belonged to the attractive young Wren who had rescued him.

John stepped out onto the road and waved, hoping she would notice him.

Which she did.

Much to his surprise, the Wren immediately crossed over. She acted a bit sheepish, but smiled just the same.

"It's good to see you again, Miss," John said after taking off his hat. "I must apologize for my behavior earlier. I'm afraid my nerves were a bit rattled after that rough landing and all. That's no excuse for acting like a cad, but I do hope you'll forgive me."

She reached out and touched his right wrist. "It is I who should apologize, sir. I shouldn't have treated you so harshly. Squadron Leader Talbot was quite upset with me. He told me what a spot of bother you had with your Swordfish."

John smiled and lifted her chin with his index finger, to look into her big green sparkling eyes. "Then we're friends?"

She smiled too and nodded.

He held out his hand. "I'm Sub-lieutenant John Mobley."

She took his hand and said, "I'm Senior Wren Officer Tabitha Bixley."

"Jolly good," he spouted with an exaggerated British accent. "Then let's duck in here and grab a pint or two. Then I'll be on my way."

Tabitha hesitated.

"Come now, lass, you have nothing to fear from me," John said.

She thought about it for another second, before leading him into *The Cornish Arms*. The military presence became even more obvious once they were inside the pub. The place was full of flyer types. However, being a pilot himself, Sub-lieutenant Mobley didn't feel out of place at all. He waved to the others, while holding a chair for the Wren. There were no obnoxious comments or whistles and the couple sat down to spend a pleasant evening comparing notes over a few beers.

"The obvious first question is how you came to be a Wren?" Mobley asked.

"I don't know why I wanted to be a Wren," she replied. "I think it was because everyone thought it was the best service, and I knew some fellas who had gone in the Navy. It seemed glamorous at the time!"

John laughed heartily. "You fell for these uniforms and the stories about good food, didn't you?"

Tabitha nodded. "The work enthralls me. The Wren quarters were only round the corner from the Royal Naval Barracks, so most of us walked to our watches, raids permitting. I often used to wander along the shore, especially before or after night watch. I remember the cool, damp air, the gray slabs of the promenade, and the high barricades of barbed wire dividing it from the heavily mined beaches. Beyond the wire, the lapping and crashing of the waves, gray and white, cold and cruel in the darkness, simply fascinated me. I would feel part of our vital convoys creeping along, which were frequently lit by the flashes of guns and torpedoes and bombs, pursued by packs of E-Boats, or overhead from relentless German bombers. It was thrilling to see our magnificent little MGB's and MTB's waiting near Lowestoft, ready to pounce."

Tabitha paused.

"Thank you," John said.

"For what?" she wondered.

"For being so honest with me," Mobley said. "When was the last time you told anyone how you felt that night?"

She shook her head. "Never. You're the first."

John smiled warmly. "So, again, thank you."

"You're welcome."

"What brought you to this heavenly little spot?" he asked.

"After general training in the ways of the Navy and being kitted out, I was told that I would be assigned to the Fleet Air Arm as an Emergency Equipment Driver," she answered.

"Well, I owe the Navy a great deal of thanks, because if it wasn't for you, I might not be here enjoying this ale," John said.

"Oh, don't be silly," Tabitha reacted with a giggle. She looked at her watch.

"One more pint before we head our separate ways?" Mobley suggested.

Tabitha smiled.

When John returned with their glasses of frothy ale, the conversation picked up right where it left off, as if the two of them had known each other their entire lives.

"One night, when I was on duty, our Barracks received a direct hit," Tabitha recounted. "As usual the OPS and plotting rooms were well protected below ground, so none of us were badly hurt. After being buried in the dark and dust for some considerable time, the first gulp of fresh air coming through a gap in the ceiling and the first mug of tea, were something I will never forget."

"Were you frightened?" he asked.

She nodded. "Dreadfully so, I'm afraid."

John gently patted her wrist and said, "Nothing to be ashamed of, old girl. You and I share a common desire to stay alive through all this."

Tabitha took a sip of beer, but did not move her hand. John's presence made her feel quite safe, even from the Germans.

Once their second round was polished off, Mobley suggested they be on their way. It was a beautiful clear moonlit night, so they were able to see for miles, which was quite a change from stumbling about in the blackout, when there was no moon to light up the sky. Both Tabitha and John were well aware that such conditions would mean the German planes would come over again, but bombing runs happened so often, that just about everybody took them in stride and carried on.

"Would you mind if I walked you home?" John asked hesitantly.

"No, of course not," she replied. "I'd like that."

Tabitha's residence was one of a row of several small, but warm and sturdy brick cottages fronting directly onto the main street, and lit by oil lamps, because many of the units didn't have electricity yet. There was a single hand-pump that supplied water for the row of cottages, located in the back yard, as were the toilets in their wooden out-houses.

Tabitha was paying two shillings and sixpence a week for rent, but she had electricity. The constant noise from *HMS Vulture* would have made sleeping difficult for the locals. The torpedo bombers and fighters continuously circled the village, obviously practicing their circuits and bumps.

"Goodnight, Tabitha," John said at the front steps. "Thank you again for a wonderful evening. I hope to see you again."

"You are a dear," she said. "Please take care of yourself."

"I promise. You too."

She nodded.

He turned to leave, but before he took another step, Tabitha leaned forward and gave him a quick kiss on the cheek.

John touched the spot and said, "I shall never forget you, Tabitha Bixley."

Then the young man headed off toward the barracks, disappearing in the fog.

It was very late, or very early, depending on one's point-of-view. In either case, Tabitha was painfully aware that her duty shift was about to start again. Instead of trying to grab a few hours sleep, the Wren decided to visit the base canteen.

She managed to get a mug of hot tea, which tasted like nectar. Then it was off to the control tower once again. Tabitha was happy thinking about John Mobley and what a good sport he turned out to be.

Several days after John and his crew had safely departed St. Merryn, *HMS Vulture* was bombed by low-flying German aircraft. There was some structural damage and Mobley's wrecked Swordfish was completely obliterated, while four cottages burned down. Fortunately, Tabitha's little bungalow was undamaged and no one in the village was killed or injured.

That evening, Tabitha managed to place a call through the trunk exchange. Callers had to dial trunk lines for calls outside London. She waited for the connection to her father, who lived in Piddlehinton, a tiny village in Dorchester, Dorset, with a population of less than 300. Dr. Dymchurch Bixley operated the local *Thimble Inn* and she loved him dearly.

"Your party is connected," said the operator.

Crackles … static … buzz.

"It's Tabitha, Father," she had to shout, because of the bad connection.

"Are you all right, child?" her father yelled back.

"Aye, Dad, I'm just fine," she replied, pushing her index finger into the other ear to help her hear. "The Germans couldn't hit a barn painted bright red."

Dymchurch laughed. "It's good to hear your voice, lass."

"Aye, Father, you too. How is Mum?"

"Just fine," he said. "Do you want me to go get her?"

"No, Dad, that isn't necessary," she said. "I called to talk to you."

"Oh, what's got you worried?"

"Nothing. I need a favor. One that calls on your particular talents."

There was a long pause.

"Dad, are you still there?" Tabitha called out.

"Yes, I'm here. What is this little favor, if you don't mind me asking?"

"I've met a wonderful man, Father," Tabitha said.

"That's grand, child."

"I want you to use your network to keep a watchful eye over him," she said.

Another pause.

"Father?"

"Yes, child, I'm thinking. What's the lad's name?"

"Sub-lieutenant John Mobley, Father. He's in the Royal Navy."

"No, imagine that."

"Stop teasing," Tabitha said, giggling.

"Do you love him, child?"

Tabitha hadn't thought about that possibility. "I just met him, Father. But I do like him very much."

"Consider it done," Dymchurch assured her. "I will inform our people to make certain Sub-lieutenant John Mobley is well looked after."

"Thank you, Father," Tabitha said. "I love you."

"We love you too, daughter," he said.

"Goodbye."

"Cheerio."

Click.

Tabitha hung up the phone. Before departing, she paid the operator for the call. As Miss Bixley stepped from the telephone exchange, out onto the street, she felt a great sense of relief.

Near Tintagel Castle, the sounds of a celebration drifted out from the little white cottage on the hill. There was laughter and singing, with the occasional whistle blowing for good measure.

"Happy Birthday, Thaddeus," three teens shouted in unison.

To the casual observer, a gigantic red dragon wearing a party hat might have looked a bit absurd, but such was not the case. Besides, no one would have taken the risk to comment on it in the first place.

Thaddeus grinned, showing his teeth. "This is grand. Thank you, one and all!"

"We put some spare coins together and purchased as many sweets as possible," Bunty announced. "It's not much, we know, because you're a very big dragon, but perhaps it will satisfy your cravings for a wee bit."

"You children are very thoughtful," Sir Osbert said. "I shall enjoy whatever you have brought for me."

"So, exactly how old are you, Thaddeus?" Gavin asked.

The dragon replied, "Fifteen hundred and thirty-two years."

"Wow, that's old," Bunty reacted.

"No, it's not," Emily protested. "It's just a number. I don't think you look a year over eight hundred."

They all laughed, the dragon the loudest by far.

Emily had managed to get her hands on some parsnips, peeled them, and sliced them through like bananas. Then she soaked them in banana essence and served them up as bananas and custard. Her concoction was actually quite tasty.

The boys had used some pilfered ration tickets for candy bars and Gavin had borrowed a tiny portion of sugar from the secret stash. He prayed his mother wouldn't notice. With everything combined, it wasn't even a swallow for the dragon, but he smacked his lips accordingly.

"Um, delicious," Thaddeus said.

Emily volunteered to read a story, which was about a dragon, of course, and the boys sat on the dragon's paws, listening intently. It was a splendid tale, full of action, romance, and adventure, with a dragon as the main hero. Once Emily reached the end, she was greeted with enthusiastic applause.

"Oh, bravo!" Thaddeus said. "Did you write that story yourself?"

Emily smiled shyly and replied, "Yes, did you really like it?"

Both Bunty and Gavin added their praise.

"It was fantastic, Emmy," Gavin said. "I wish I could write like that."

"He's right, Emmy," Bunty said. "You have a real knack for making the story seem real. I felt like I was watching it take place right here in the hamlet."

Thaddeus agreed. "The story was very entertaining, Emmy. You have been blessed with natural talent. Perhaps when this war is over, you should get it published."

Emily was convinced they were just being nice. "Oh, I don't think it's that good."

"We do!" Gavin said.

"It's important for you to pursue your passion, Emily Scott," the dragon said. "We can see it in your eyes and hear it in your voice. You love to tell stories and be entertaining. It makes you happy. So take some advice from someone who's been around for centuries. Follow your heart."

Emmy smiled and said, "I will, Thaddeus. Thank you."

"The three of you should run along home now," Sir Osbert suggested. "It's getting late and you need to help your mothers with your chores."

They didn't want to leave, but there was no point in arguing with a six-ton dragon. After Thaddeus received big hugs and even a gentle kiss from Emily, they said goodbye. The trio headed for Boscastle, of course, but their conversation was a bit stilted, which was highly unusual.

"Will I see you tomorrow?" Emily asked outside her door.

"Of course, Emmy," Gavin replied.

The girl went inside, but there was no mistaking the sad look on her face.

"What's wrong with Emmy?" Bunty asked.

"I don't know," Gavin replied. "Something's troubling her, there's no doubt of that. I just don't know what it is."

"Girls," Bunty said with exasperation. "I just can't figure them out."

Gavin grinned, but he just tugged on his friend's sleeve. "Come on, let's head straight home."

The boys took off on the run, racing each other up the hill to the coast road. Then it was off again, following a well-traveled shortcut along the cliffs overlooking the sea. They didn't take time to stop at their favorite lookout spots, but kept up a rapid pace.

Cars had all but disappeared from Crackington Haven's streets, because ordinary people weren't allowed to buy petrol any more. Milk, bread, and coal were delivered solely by horse and cart. Gavin and Bunty were sent out with the coal shovel to scoop up anything the horses left behind, to fertilize the garden with fresh manure.

Supper was very light fare, for the ration tickets were almost all gone and Mrs. Kane wanted to scrimp until the next book arrived. The conversation around the table was subdued as well, reminding Gavin of Emily's earlier mood. There was certainly something in the air that seemed to affect everyone in the same fashion.

That night, when the rumbling of airplanes overhead rattled him too much, Gavin climbed into the big bed with his mother. Almost asleep again, they heard something thump on the roof and roll down to the gutter.

Gavin leaped out of bed.

Bunty met Gavin in the hallway and they raced downstairs to see what it was.

"You be careful!" Mrs. Kane called out after them.

Just as the boys reached the front door, the local air-raid warden arrived with a ladder. Mr. Hawkins whipped it up against the gutters, scurried up the rungs with a bucket and coal shovel, scooped the incendiary bomb into the bucket, slid back down the ladder and dumped the contents of a sandbag on it before it could set fire to anything.

Gavin and Bunty applauded with delight.

Mr. Hawkins grinned and bowed.

It had been a dangerous form of entertainment, but thoroughly satisfying too.

7

Lessons of Strategy

The enormous fireplace broke apart, each shaped stone shifting and moving through the air. Chunks and slabs sailed about the room, almost colliding, yet mysteriously always narrowly missing each other. This magical display of levitation no longer appeared random, for Gavin knew the rocks always came together to form the distinctive and recognizable shape of a dragon.

What had looked like ordinary fireplace stones, now glistened and sparkled with pulsating radiant colors, including vibrant sunset yellow, ruby red, penny-bright copper, and coal black. The scales undulated with life and vitality. In a blink, Thaddeus Osbert had reappeared, his body rippling with power and definitely not of this world.

"Greetings, my boy," the dragon said cheerfully.

"Hello, Sir Osbert," said Gavin. "It's so good to see you again."

"I am pleased you have come today," Thaddeus said.

"Why's that?" the boy wondered.

"Do you play chess?" the dragon asked.

"Just a little," Gavin replied. "My father was starting to teach me the rules and basic moves before he was called up."

"Well then, I think it's time we continued your mastering of this most noble and strategic game," the dragon stated.

"All right," Gavin agreed. "I'm ready when you are."

Right before the boy's eyes, a chessboard suddenly appeared, suspended in midair between them, all the pieces already in place.

"Remember, seldom does the dragon lose," Thaddeus stated with a chuckle.

Gavin took to the challenge, studying his scaly opponent's every move and asking lots of questions. The boy was seriously determined to learn the intricacies of chess, while expanding his knowledge of the possible opening moves.

For his part, Thaddeus was thrilled to have someone to play with, as well as a student so willing to embrace the dragon's vast experience. The first goal was just to play, to have fun, and get comfortable with the basic moves. Then, as Gavin progressed, Sir Osbert added more difficult tactics and advance thinking.

The "Osbert Variation" soon became one of the key chess battlegrounds between Thaddeus and Gavin. The dragon always chose black and he developed the movement of his pieces to maximize his strategic impulses.

If Gavin was to have any chance of ever defeating the dragon, it required direct attacks, which often led to ferocious battles. White would try to checkmate the black king, while black sought to counterplay on the long diagonal.

Thaddeus quickly discovered using his Rxc3 exchange sacrifice particularly important. Black often possessed a swathe of mobile pawns in return for an exchange, a piece, or even a whole rook. Their tactics were brilliant and tested the capabilities of each opponent to the limit. Thaddeus never lost sight of his obligation to teach Gavin both the intrinsic joys of chess, combined with the strategic planning necessary to think as many moves ahead as possible.

The center of the chessboard was focused on an algebraic notation, which was signified by squares d4, e4, d5, and e5. Gavin decided that by controlling those squares, directly or indirectly, it would mean controlling the most active part of the game. From the center, he had the most space to control the rest of the chessboard.

Most chess pieces moved through the center for attacking or defending. By being in the center, all of Gavin's pieces had more squares to attack or defend.

Gavin made certain his white knight reached the center first, where it had eight squares covered. Sir Osbert's black knight sat on the edge of the board and only had four squares covered and if the knight was then in a corner, it only had two squares in could cover. Likewise, a bishop could cover 13 squares in the center, but only 7 squares in the corner.

Gavin tried to develop his pieces to control the center. He accomplished this directly, by placing pawns on d4 and e4, or indirectly with his bishops to the b2 or g2 squares and controlling the long diagonal.

Center control gave Gavin greater piece mobility, with better chances for attacking or defending. By losing the center, Thaddeus was forced into a cramped and restricted game. By controlling the center in the opening move, the boy started winning matches, much to the dragon's satisfaction.

Thaddeus was very pleased. "Well done, lad. You're getting the hang of this straight on. I have found a worthy opponent at last, what."

Gavin laughed, for he so loved it when the dragon assumed his exaggerated English accent. It just sounded so preposterous for Sir Osbert to talk in such a way.

"It's time for you to be on your way, young man," the dragon suddenly announced. "It's getting late and I don't want your mother worrying about where you are."

"Yes, Thaddeus," Gavin obeyed. "I'll see you later."

"I'm looking forward to it, son."

Gavin departed and hurried down the path to the coast road. He ran most of the way to Boscastle, where he wanted to stop by and say hello to Emily. However, before he reached her house, the proprietor of the *Napoleon Inn* intercepted the boy with a very friendly wave.

"There you are, lad," Mr. Winchester said.

"Yes, sir, have you been looking for me?" Gavin asked hesitantly, a little worried that he was in trouble.

"Indeed I have, young man," the barkeep replied. "Those three kegs turned out to be full of premium whiskey. I owe you a small fortune, I do."

Gavin considered the windfall. "My friends Emily and Bunty are owed equal shares of the credit, sir."

"Very well," Mr. Winchester said. "What with the war and all, I'll be forced to pay you over a lengthy period of time, if that's all right with you."

Gavin smiled and held out his hand. "Of course it is, Mr. Winchester. In fact, please pay us for only two kegs. Consider the third keg as our gift."

The pub owner was stunned by Gavin's generosity. He patted the boy on the shoulder and said, "Thank you, lad. Now run along and I'll make sure your share gets to your Mum."

Gavin initially frowned at this revelation, but then decided the funds would be truly appreciated by his mother, who was struggling to provide food for the family, as well as make ends meet.

So off he went, waving goodbye and heading straight to Emily's house.

Emmy's mother came to the door, but informed Gavin that Winifred had called looking for him, so instead of having time to play with his best friend in the whole world, he had to hurry home.

It was early evening by the time Gavin stepped through the front door. His mother didn't scold him, but made sure he washed up before supper and helped Bunty set the table.

Mrs. Kane had come home earlier with a new menu book printed by the *Ministry of Food*. It included 24 different ways to serve cod and potatoes, with another 26 new recipes for spam.

Gavin was not impressed.

Not surprisingly, the dinner fare that night included spam, which was enthusiastically devoured by Bunty.

Gavin, however, made no comment.

After supper, they gathered around the wireless to listen to the nightly BBC War Report. All throughout Britain people were doing the same, ears glued to the radio to hear the latest events of a world at war. Only America seemed immune to the conflict, but many folks wondered how long their isolation would last.

"Here is the news, and this is Alvar Lidell reading it," the announcer opened with his all-too-familiar introduction. *"I can see practically the whole of London spread round me, the whole of the skyline to the south lit up with a ruddy glow, the flames are leaping up in the air now, the dome of St. Paul's Cathedral is silhouetted blackly against it, it's almost like the Day of Judgment."*

Gavin looked over at Bunty, wondering how the description might affect his friend. Even though it had been almost a year since Bunty had left Plymouth, the tragic memories must still have been pretty clear.

Now as for Gavin, he had actually been to London during a bombing raid. So as the reporter described what was going on all around him, Gavin could remember what such a raid smelled like, what falling incendiary bombs sounded like and how fear actually tasted.

Alvar Liddell continued, *"As I walked along the streets it was almost impossible to believe that these fires could be subdued. I was walking between solid walls of fire. Shops and office buildings came down with a roaring crash, panes of glass were cracking everywhere from the heat, and every street was criss-crossed with innumerable lengths of hose. Men were fighting the fires from the top of tall ladders, shot up from the street, while others were pushing their way into the burning buildings, taking the water to the core of the fire. Sparks were driving down the street like a heavy snowstorm."*

"It doesn't seem possible that anyone could survive all that," Mrs. Kane commented. "What horrible things must they endure?"

"Obviously small children couldn't walk across to the station in this and so some of us went backwards and forwards carrying them in our arms," Alvar Liddell went on. *"I took off my Macintosh and covered them up completely with it. It must have been rather frightening for them to be carried across by someone they didn't know and not being able to see anything, but it was the only way to protect them from those sparks. By the time we got the last one across, we should have had to do it anyway, because the building above the station was on fire. Luckily the station escaped and they were all moved off in trains to get food and drink."*

Click.

Gavin and Bunty both looked up in surprise.

"I'm sorry, boys, but I just can't listen to another word," Winifred said, tears streaming down her face. "I just can't."

"It's all right, Mum," Gavin said as he stood up and put his arms around her waist.

Bunty wanted a hug too, but didn't think it was right to muscle his way in. However, Winifred was sensitive enough to respond to the boy's unspoken needs.

"Come here," she beckoned to the red-haired lad.

Bunty scrambled to his feet and relished the attention.

Mrs. Kane just held them for a while, trying to reassure the boys that love would make a difference in the end. She firmly believed it and wanted them to believe it too.

"It may be hard to accept right now, but someday this war will be over," Winifred said. "Until then, we must remember the sacrifices so many people are making to protect our dear England."

Although the times were grim, Gavin's mother did everything in her power to keep a positive attitude. Working at the *Bude Cinema* helped, of course, because she and the boys could see every film that came to town. There were heroic naval epics and films starring George Formby or Gracie Fields, while Winifred looked forward to seeing her favorite singers, Bing Crosby and Frank Sinatra.

Big band music and crooners were all the rage. Vera Lynn sang *We'll Meet Again* and *White Cliffs of Dover*, or swing played in the background, while Mrs. Kane worked in the kitchen. Without the wireless, Gavin wasn't sure how his mother would have made it through these difficult times.

The next day Gavin returned to the little white cottage, to begin anew his chess lessons. Thaddeus was waiting patiently, the chessboard already hovering in the air between them.

"It's your move, as I recall," the dragon said.

"Good afternoon to you too," Gavin quipped.

Thaddeus grunted.

"Oh, so I see you're in a fine mood," the boy reacted.

Thaddeus grunted again.

Gavin sat down on the stool and studied the board to familiarize himself with the current situation, while planning at least ten moves ahead.

"Today's lesson will revolve around the application of strategy and tactics," the dragon said quietly.

"What's the difference?" Gavin asked.

"Tactics is the art of using available resources to win each battle," Thaddeus replied. "Strategy is the art of using each battle to assure overall victory."

"Chess must be a combination," Gavin surmised.

The dragon nodded. "The relationship between chess and military strategy is profound. Each time we play, your moves create my counter-moves, and so on. The lessons you learn here will impact your outlook in the future."

"Do most dragons play chess?" Gavin wondered.

Thaddeus replied, "There are six hundred and eighty-three dragons still living on this planet and each one of them is unique. This diversity is true on every level, including their hobbies and politics. While dragon society doesn't mirror human culture exactly, there are certain similarities."

Gavin shook his head. "That was fascinating, Sir Osbert, but you didn't answer my question."

"No, I didn't, did I?" Thaddeus said. "Yes, there is one other dragon that practices the intelligent art of chess."

"Do you ever play him?"

"Yes."

"Do you win?"

"Seldom."

"Who is this chess master?"

"He goes by the name of Korban Vex, if you must know."

"You don't like him, do you?"

"Whatever makes you say that?"

"By the look in your eyes."

"What look was that?"

"You couldn't hide your true feelings."

"Nonsense."

"My father says the eyes are the gateway to the soul."

Thaddeus sighed. "Your father is a wise man."

"So I gather you are not very fond of this Korban Vex?" Gavin asked.

The dragon blinked, to shield his eyes.

"Oh, that won't work with me," Gavin said. "I'm wise to your ways."

Thaddeus shrugged and said, "Korban and I have been competitors for hundreds of years. Sometimes it developed into serious arguments over petty issues. He grates on my nerves and I probably do the same to him. We'll never see eye-to-eye, but Korban is a great dragon and knows that there are certain obligations he must adhere to."

"Is it difficult being a dragon, Thaddeus?" Gavin asked.

"At times, I suppose," Sir Osbert replied. "I really don't have anything to compare it with. However, based on some species on this planet, we have it relatively easy. I'd hate to be a domesticated cat, for instance."

"Why?"

"Well, if I tell you, you'll never look at a tabby the same way again."

"Please, Thaddeus, I want to know."

"All right then, but don't say I didn't warn you."

Gavin was not only intrigued, but he squirmed with anticipation.

The dragon chuckled. "Have you ever wondered why some humans adore kittens and some people just can't stand cats at all?"

The boy nodded.

"Cats know this and immediately go straight towards people who don't like them, and then jump on their laps and upset them," Thaddeus pointed out. "However, cats don't hate people. Cats are wonderful animals, which have been brutally domesticated by ignorant humanity. Still, it's the humans who have been fooled, because cats know they are in charge."

"I like cats," Gavin volunteered.

"Of course you do, because you like dragons and we befriend cats very easily," Thaddeus said. "Due to their curiosity and need to understand and investigate everything they come across, cats are also exceptionally smart creatures."

"Just like dragons," Gavin blurted.

Thaddeus laughed. "Certain humans, too."

Gavin waved him off.

"No, Gavin, it's true," the dragon insisted. "You are very bright. I think your father once described you as dangerously intelligent."

"I like the sound of that," the boy said.

"Don't get too caught up in yourself, my boy," Thaddeus warned. "Your brainpower should always be directed with finding solutions to humanity's problems, not adding to them."

Gavin vehemently shook his head. "I would never do anything really bad, Sir Osbert. I love our talks and your lessons have taught me much."

"I also enjoy our philosophical discussions," Thaddeus said. "Most humans don't like to believe there are creatures that are smarter than they are, or better suited to look after the planet. Man is the most egotistical creature in the universe and someday will suffer for his arrogance. I am pleased you are different in so many ways."

Unexpectedly, a sneeze erupted from Thaddeus, throwing him backwards and causing a miniature tornado of swirling dust. A puff of blue smoke curled up from the dragon's nostrils.

"Bless you!" Gavin exclaimed, covering his face in self-defense.

"Thank you, son," the dragon said

The boy pointed to dissipating vapors. "I've never seen blue smoke before."

Thaddeus cleared his throat and said, "I must be catching a bit of a cold."

"I didn't know dragons caught colds."

"They're not like human ailments, that's true, but I still get a stuffy head."

That response seemed to satisfy Gavin, even though it was far from the truth. The dragon hated not telling the boy the truth, but there were things better left a mystery, if only for the time being.

"Would you care for a snack?" the dragon asked.

Gavin's eyes lit up with delight. "Oh, yes."

A wonderful tea setting appeared before them from nowhere. There were cucumber sandwiches, scones, fresh marmalade and a pot of hot tea, of course.

"I'll play mother," Thaddeus announced.

Gavin watched in amazement as the gigantic dragon carefully selected several sugar cubes for each cup, then picked up the pot of tea with two talons.

"You are exceedingly gifted, Sir Osbert," the boy said. "Your manners are impeccable."

"Dragons have a formidable reputation when it comes to table manners," Thaddeus stated proudly. "There's no substitute for good manners, except fast reflexes."

The two of them enjoyed a wonderful afternoon tea, before Gavin had to go home. That evening was one of the rare occasions when the boys had homework. Once supper was over, they settled down to write their essays about how the war was affecting their lives.

Bunty wrote:

Being British, being proud to be British, isn't simply about going through the bombing with our heads held high. Hitler's blitz will not sap British will, but will unify it against him.

When I was living in Plymouth, whenever a bombing raid took place, I would make for the nearest shelter, but I did not like using them myself. The stench was unbearable. The smell was so bad, I couldn't figure out why people didn't die from suffocation. There were so many people and no fresh air.

My mother built an Anderson shelter for us in the backyard. Each time a bomb hit, you felt the next bang would be your last and it was very frightening. My Mum was a very religious person and she would say her prayers. She was also an air-raid warden and had to leave me alone sometimes. When I was with her, I always felt safe, no matter how many bombs fell. Then one night, the Germans killed Mum and life changed forever.

Here I am in Cornwall, living with Gavin Kane and his mum. They are very nice and I have learned a lot since joining them. My Dad is fighting the war from the aircraft carrier *HMS Ark Royal.* I miss him, but he is taking the war to Hitler.

Life has changed and I miss Mum. Still, there is a lot of life ahead of me.

Gavin wrote:

The strangest sensation was my first air raid of the war, which was, of course, a false alarm. The Germans came to Crackington Haven on a lovely autumn evening. The siren wailed just before supper and my mother and I hurried down into the cellar and hid under the stairs. The German planes rumbled overhead, their engines grinding. Then it was absolutely still, for no bombs dropped. The Germans were heading elsewhere and didn't bother with our little village.

I'm not too proud to say I was frightened. I still am, every single time a German airplane flies overhead. They have upset our peaceful lives, but taught us many valuable lessons. I appreciate everything my mother does to make our lives more comfortable. I pray for my father, who is away months on end. I have learned how to save water, sugar and so many other rationed items.

Perhaps this isn't truly hardship, but I am thankful for the smallest token of kindness. I love to read, to listen to the wireless, and to help anyone who needs something. We British should vow to end all wars forever.

My friends are the most important gifts in the world, including my mother and father, Bunty, Emily and Uncle Thaddeus. Most of all, I love our freedom.

As it turned out, Bunty and Gavin were both asked to read their essays aloud in class. While most of their mates felt the words were quite patriotic, ex-Londoner Reginald Sands took exception.

"What blithering nonsense," Reginald commented to his friends sitting nearby, in his upper crust, three-farthing British accent. "What would they know about being English?"

While he was indeed the offspring of some very wealthy Londoners, Reginald had been relocated to Cornwall for his personal safety, living in one of the manor houses outside of Launceston. Both mocked and envied by his peers, the boy had bribed several local lads into becoming his allies. Sands had perfected the whole clenched-jaw routine and spoke with infinite clarity. He carried himself properly, with excessive politeness, impeccable manners and possessed a practiced dry wit. Still, the boy was petty and shallow, without much substance and surprisingly, not very bright.

Reginald's comments were immediately echoed by laughter from several of his lackeys, who directed their ridicule at the local Cornish boys.

"Well, Duke of Argyll, I guess you wouldn't know what we're fighting for, now would yee?" Gavin fired back, using Reginald's hated nickname.

"Quite the show old boy," the Sands boy spouted. "If one believes one's station is above the chattering classes, one is always careful of one's reputation."

The teacher was just about to put a stop to this bickering, when it escalated.

"Call us names if you must, Duke of Argyll, but everyone knows you're still a snooty nob, sloany pony, willie and a prat!" Bunty shouted as he stood up. "The bloody Germans don't give a bunch of thingamujiggies about who they drop their bloody bombs on. Everyone's English when we're dying."

"That's why you're in Cornwall, you bloody fool," Gavin added, also on his feet. "Your parents sent you away from the bombing, to be safe, among us common blokes. So why don't you show a little respect and shut your bloody mouth!"

Even the teacher was stunned to silence by their combined outburst.

Then, quite unexpectedly, most of the students started to applaud.

The clapping increased, until it was a thunderous round of approval. Everyone in the class was cheering, all gathering around Gavin and Bunty.

The teacher did nothing to settle them down, because she was clapping herself.

Poor Reginald Sands sat completely dejected, quite aware he had been snubbed.

After school, Bunty and Gavin went to see a dragon, of course.

To their mutual disappointment, however, Thaddeus was not at home.

8

Commando School

Royal Army Major Traber Vickers was suffering from a serious headache. He was almost overwhelmed by everything that needed to be done and with a shortage of staff at that. Ever since his promotion and transfer to the Commando School at Dartmoor, Vickers was in constant demand. Of course, it probably had something to do with the Prime Minister's splendid recommendation for advancement, after the much-denied German infiltration incident at Crackington Haven.

Still, Vickers could do with a little less fuss. He had just been doing his job, taking into account certain irregularities, what with that dragon character and the children being involved. In the end, everything had turned out all right, but it had been a sticky wicket for a time.

During Traber's present assignment, potential commandos were given physical and mental tests designed to examine their endurance and their desire to "stick with it." The course was built around a series of field exercises on the vast expanses of Dartmoor in southwest England. Dartmoor was a desolate area of rocky hills, bogs, and marshes, while Vickers was convinced the area had some of the worst weather in all of England.

The subjects covered in training were focused on conditioning the men to handle all sorts of challenges. This included obstacle courses, with bayonet, grenade, and hand-to-hand fighting methods, use of the compass, map reading, military sketching, message writing, aerial photographic analysis, mine laying techniques, demolitions, knots and lashings, crossing barbed wire and beach obstacles, operating and disabling motor vehicles and weapons, preparation of personnel for commando raids, reconnaissance patrol techniques, booby traps, operation of personnel at night, techniques of rubber boat operation, techniques of embarking and debarking from landing craft, boat formations, interrogation of prisoners, planning for and conducting raids, and practical work in the form of night raids to secure information and destroy hostile installations.

The forces were made up of volunteers only, but the washout rate was very high, leaving only a small percentage of successful graduates. The demand for elite forces was staggering, so Vickers had to make certain the commandos weren't snatched away from their intended destinations. However, things apparently were changing.

Vickers looked at the roster once again. There was another incoming bunch of recruits, though this time they were all foreign nationals. These candidates didn't have the luxury of failing the course, for it had been deemed necessary to teach them everything, in the shortest amount of time possible, and hope they would survive long enough behind enemy lines to account for something.

"Bah!" Vickers scoffed. "What typical nonsense."

The major took more time to scrutinize the list.

"More Poles, I see," he said to himself. "Not to mention Norwegians, Belgians, Frenchies, and even some poor souls from Czechoslovakia. What in blazes am I supposed to do with all these refugees?"

In frustration, Traber threw his pencil clear across the room.

There was an untimely knock on the door.

"Enter," Vickers called out.

He immediately jumped to his feet as several high-ranking officers stepped inside. Snapping to attention, Major Vickers certainly looked the part of a polished British officer.

"Stand easy, Major," one of his superiors said.

"Thank you, sir," Traber said.

"Sorry to disturb you, but this is rather important," the same officer continued.

"Of course, Colonel Clark, please continue," Vickers replied.

"There are three gentlemen arriving today for your next session, Major," Clark said. "They are Czechoslovakian, but should be considered as critical to the war effort. I've come to ask you to pay special attention to their schooling and give them the very best you have. Understood?"

"Yes, sir, Colonel, sir," Vickers said.

"Good. Now, since that's settled, would you care to join us for refreshments?" Clark inquired politely.

"I'd be honored, Colonel," Traber said. "Thank you."

The officers all filed out, Vickers bringing up the rear.

In the Officer's Mess, they gathered for a neat spot of gin and noncommittal conversation. Nothing of importance was discussed and even less achieved. Still, it was good to be seen with such officers, for Traber's career and for his peace of mind. As long as his superiors relied on him to turn out capable commandos, then he was satisfied.

With the arrival of a new class of students, tents were erected for accommodation and equipment. The cookhouse and stores were located on the shore of a lake, but the living quarters were located about three hundred metres up a steep bank overlooking the water. Running up and down the bank several times a day, combined with icy swims in the mornings, soon whipped the students into tip-top shape. Training was continuous, seven days a week.

Just as promised, three Czechoslovakian men had also arrived at the training camp. They were all in their mid-twenties and seemed in pretty good physical shape. One thing was obvious from the start. They were certainly eager enough.

All the students learned wireless operation, small arms, demolition, unarmed combat, silent kill, sabotage and attaching limpet mines to vessels. The Czechs were taught additional survival techniques, propaganda, photography, and ambush planning and execution. Toward the end of the prescribed training program, the Czechs were sent out on practice raids against military and industrial installations, before their specialized instruction on assassination techniques began.

"Assassination is the deliberate killing of an important person, usually a political figure or other strategically important individual," Vickers taught the three Czechs. "It usually requires split-second timing and you won't get a second chance."

"Do you recommend using explosives or a close-up attack?" Jan Kubis asked.

"A combination, actually," Vickers replied. "Hand grenades and automatic weapons leave little doubt."

Kubis made a point to remember this advice.

"Some of you will go on to serve in elite covert units," Vickers said in his closing comments before graduation. "Others will be singled out and sent on top-secret missions. I hope you'll never forget what you've learned here. It might just save your life."

A variety of people from all social classes and pre-war occupations served in the field for the British. In most cases, the primary quality required was a deep knowledge of the country in which the agent was to operate, and especially its language, if the agent was to pass as a native of the country. Dual nationality was often a prized attribute.

In other cases, a lesser degree of fluency was required, as the resistance groups concerned were already in open rebellion and a clandestine existence was unnecessary. A flair for diplomacy combined with a taste for rough soldiering was more necessary.

An agent working clandestinely in the field obviously required clothing, documents and so on, which would not arouse suspicion. Vickers maintained centers, which specialized in producing foreign clothing, forging identity cards and ration cards, even to the extent of manufacturing cigarettes, which would pass as the local product.

The major's men had developed a wide range of explosive devices for sabotage, such as limpet mines, shaped charges and time fuses. These were already in use by commando units. Other, more subtle sabotage methods included lubricants laced with grinding materials, incendiaries disguised as innocuous objects and so on.

After the subdued graduation ceremonies, Major Vickers retired to his billet and changed uniforms. He strolled out the gate and headed directly for the village local, of course, where a bit of refreshment seemed very appealing at the time. Traber ordered a pint and picked out a table in the corner, where he hoped to be left alone.

"Be with ya in a minute, Luv," the barmaid called out.

Vickers waved his understanding.

"Whatcha have, Luv?" she asked after a few minutes.

"Bitters, please," he replied.

The full mug clunked down before him.

"Thanks," he said.

He maneuvered through the crowd to find an unoccupied table, where he quickly sat down. Vickers leaned back and took a long, slow swallow of his beer. He closed his eyes and tried to relax. The noise of the pub ebbed in and out of his subconscious mind, creating a low buzz. Traber couldn't help but remember some troubling images that had plagued him ever since the incident near Crackington Haven.

'I wish I had that dragon for just one day,' he said to himself. 'Then I'd fly to Berlin and take care of Herr Hitler.'

Swallowing another gulp of suds, the Major realized he was no longer alone.

Standing before him were the three Czech operatives, who had graduated from the commando school with excellent results. They were dedicated and serious, which bode well for their future success.

"Good evening, gentlemen," Vickers said, sitting up straight. "Would you care to join me?"

"No, Major, thank you," Joseph Gabcik replied with a thick accent. "We only wished to thank you again for our most excellent training."

"It was my duty," Vickers replied. "I give every candidate the same attention."

"Still, we feel it necessary to thank you very much for this training," Jan Kubis added. "It is good to know how we may punish the Germans for their atrocities."

Without saying another word, the three men turned and walked away, passing through the entrance door and exiting outside.

"Time gentlemen, please," a voice rang out from behind the bar. "If you can't drink them, leave them, if you can't leave them, drink them—time gentlemen, please!"

It was closing time.

The incident with the Czechs left Vickers unsettled and he was unable to stop the feeling that something profound had just happened. No matter how hard he tried to shake the sensation, Traber was convinced those three Czechs operatives would someday make a difference in the war. As a result, the major was no longer interested in enjoying his beer, but suddenly decided he needed a change of scenery to calm his nerves.

Once outside, however, he started to feel foolish. Was it just his imagination, or was something else behind his erratic behavior? Vickers was convinced he needed a distraction, something to do. After a few minutes weighing his options, the major drove to Bristol to see a movie. Once he arrived within the town limits, Traber parked his vehicle behind the Broadmead Hotel. According to accepted military procedure, he immobilized the automobile by removing four spark-plug wires, because it was impossible to reach and remove the rotor-arm, due to the location of the engine.

High security measures were in place in Bristol, because its docks and aero-engine factories were heavily bombed. This was also due to the anticipated German invasion, which by now was unlikely, but still possible. The major handed the ticket-girl his ten bob and went inside the cinema. Traber sat down and thoroughly enjoyed Abbott and Costello in *Buck Privates*, laughing hysterically at their silly antics.

Returning to the hotel after the movie, Vickers was horrified to find his transportation had gone missing. The major immediately reported the stolen vehicle to the local Home Guard commander, implying that a German spy must have absconded with it. Major Vickers was directed to notify the nearest British military police station, and was promptly informed that they had driven his vehicle to their compound.

On his arrival at their office, Military Police Sergeant Dithers released the vehicle to Vickers, but informed the major that there would be a hefty fine for improper immobilization methods.

"You're joking?" Vickers asked incredulously.

"No, Major, I'm sorry, sir, but you know the regulations and you failed to properly immobilize your vehicle, thereby creating a serious security risk," replied the Sergeant.

Vickers eyes narrowed and he countered with a low voice, "And I am charging you with the misuse of a Royal Army officer's vehicle, possibly causing harm to it by driving it a considerable distance on only four cylinders!"

The sergeant swallowed and said, "Have a good evening, sir."

"Not bloody likely, Sergeant," Vickers said as he exited to the car park.

Once again finding himself in a foul mood, there was no way that Traber intended to return to the training camp. Instead, completely against regulations, the major started driving to the north coast of Cornwall. There was a certain young man he had to see, no matter what the repercussions. It was a long drive to Crackington Haven, but Major Vickers was determined to talk to Gavin Kane.

Rumors circulated through Crackington Haven that a Lancaster bomber had crash-landed at night in a field near Bude. The next morning, Bunty and Gavin furiously cycled over and were pleased to discover that indeed there was a Lancaster with its wheels in mud up to the axles and missing the left wing. The pilot had done an amazing job landing the damaged plane, but two oak trees at the edge of the field were a little closer together than the wingspan. By the time the boys arrived at the scene, the aircrew had already been picked up and the aircraft was being guarded by an RAF corporal. Bunty found the left landing light some distance away and persuaded the corporal to let him keep it. The reflector was crushed by the impact, but the bulb with filament looked as if it still worked.

"I can't wait to show the lads at school this little beauty," Bunty announced.

By this time, Bunty had acquired an impressive collection of shell fragments, incendiary bomb fins, and several pieces of the metal skin from German aircraft. He was often the talk of school and beamed with pride whenever asked to show off his latest acquisitions. With Gavin's help, Bunty's collection of bomb fragments and dud incendiary bombs, were secreted inside Richard Kane's garden tool shed. Some of the unexploded incendiaries even had notes inside, apparently written by conscripted workers, who endured forced labor and risked their lives to make sure the bombs wouldn't go off.

Outside of London, Plymouth was one of the worst bombed cities in England, with almost nightly raids leaving the city a smoldering ruin. In fact, Bunty was forbidden to go there, because Mrs. Kane was so worried for his safety. Sometimes Gavin would find his chum standing on a high hill, staring off in the direction of his hometown, watching the glow from the continuous burning fires.

They didn't talk about Bunty's past very much, because Gavin didn't want to make his friend sad.

Then, with a shrug and a sigh, Bunty would regain his smile and the lads would scamper off to play. Strangely enough, the war often provided great entertainment for boys all across Cornwall, because they were so far removed from the actual death and destruction. They could watch dogfights and later collect souvenirs that fell from the sky. There was always something to do, such as pretending they were casualties, in ruins that stood in for bombed-out buildings, for rescue teams to find, acting as bike messengers for the ARP, playing make-believe soldiers training to repel the Nazi invasion, or listening to the BBC every night to hear the daily score of German planes shot down.

For Gavin, though, being a teenager and able-bodied, was a frustrating situation. There must be something for him to do, which would make a difference in the outcome. The adults told him he was too young for this and not old enough for that, but those off-handed comments certainly didn't help his frustration.

That evening, instead of listening to the nightly BBC War Report, Winifred decided to turn the dial in search of CBS Radio. She hoped to find the American newscaster, Edward R. Murrow, who broadcast every night from London.

"*This ... is London,*" spoke Murrow, his distinctive voice crackling over the airwaves from a city in the midst of another terrible bombing. "*For three hours after the night attack got going, I shivered in a sandbag crow's-nest atop a tall building near the Thames. It was one of the many fire-observation posts. There was an old gun barrel mounted above a round table marked off like a compass. A stick of incendiaries bounced off rooftops about three miles away. The observer took a sight on a point where the first one fell, swung his gun-sight along the line of bombs, and took another reading at the end of the line of fire.*

"*Then he picked up his telephone and shouted above the half gale that was blowing up there. Five minutes later a German bomber came boring down the river. We could see his exhaust trail like a pale ribbon stretched straight across the sky. Half a mile downstream, there were two eruptions and then a third, close together. The first two looked as though some giant had thrown a huge basket of flaming golden oranges high in the air. The third was just a balloon of fire enclosed in black smoke above the housetops. The observer didn't bother with his gun-sight and indicator for that one. He just reached for his night glasses, took one quick look, picked up his telephone, and named the street where they had fallen.*

"*There was a small fire going off to our left. Suddenly sparks showered up from it as though someone had punched the middle of a huge campfire with a tree trunk.*

Again, the gun sight swung around, the bearing was read, and the report went down the telephone lines.

"There was peace and quite inside for twenty minutes. Then a shower of incendiaries came down far in the distance. They didn't fall in a line. It looked like flashes from an electric train on a wet night, only the engineer was drunk and driving his train in circles through the streets. Half an hour later, a string of firebombs fell right beside the Thames. Their white glare was reflected in the black, lazy water near the banks and faded out in midstream where the moon cut a golden swathe broken only by the arches of famous bridges.

We could see little men shoveling those firebombs into the river. One burned for a few minutes like a beacon right in the middle of a bridge. Finally, those white flames all went out. No one bothers about the white light, it's only when it turns yellow that a real fire has started.

I must have seen well over a hundred firebombs come down and only three small fires were started. The incendiaries aren't so bad if there is someone there to deal with them, but those oil bombs present more difficulties.

As I watched those white fires flame up and die down, watched the yellow blazes grow dull and disappear, I thought, what a puny effort is this to burn a great city."

The report ended and Winifred turned off the wireless.

"He's right, you know," Bunty spoke up.

"Right about what, dearest?" Gavin's mother asked.

"The Germans aren't so tough," the red-haired boy replied. "They've been at this bombing stuff for over a year now and we haven't surrendered yet. I think it's time they just gave up."

"That's right, ol' chap," Gavin chimed in, exaggerating his stiff upper-lip delivery, copying classmate Reginald Sands. "Let's show Jerry what we're made of, what."

The boys broke into fits of laughter, right along with Mrs. Kane. It was good to laugh, even faced with such diversity. They readily shared their doubts, worries, and fears, so Winifred thought it only made sense to likewise share their hopes, dreams, and aspirations. With this in mind, she made a valiant attempt to lighten the mood as often as possible. She kept up appearances, even when the war news was especially bad, while looking for the bright side of things and made sure the boys kept a positive outlook on life.

Mrs. Kane exemplified the British down-to-earth viewpoint of the world and seldom lost this touch with reality. While most of the countries in Europe were under Nazi rule, she maintained her own conservative ideals. Through all the turmoil, she was never inclined to trust anyone or anything, which offered an ideal solution. Winifred was not skeptical, but pragmatic. Life must go on, as she aimed for making small improvements.

"My positive outlook might not solve every problem, but it makes the journey a more pleasant experience," she told Gavin one afternoon. "I do what I enjoy and I make a positive contribution to the world by looking after my family. With the world torn apart by this senseless war, I can only offer peace under this roof."

"Mum, you should run for office," Gavin proclaimed. "You're bloody marvelous!"

His mother was just about to scold him for his profanity, when she decided to let it go. Beaming, Winifred gave him a big kiss. "Oh, don't be silly. Your father would throw a wobbler!"

Her use of British slang caught her son by surprise, but then he burst into laughter.

Mother and son enjoyed their time together in the kitchen and warmly greeted Bunty when he wandered in to join them. In fact, Mrs. Kane was in such a splendid mood, she fixed some toast, intending to treat everyone with real butter and sprinkled sugar.

However, the sugar bowl was empty.

Before the negative impact soured the festive mood, Bunty interrupted, saying, "Did you hear the joke about the American chap who went into a London shop to order a cup of coffee?"

"No," Gavin's mother said.

"It goes like this," Bunty replied. "The waitress looks out the window and says it looks like rain. Then the American tells her the coffee tastes like it too and says, bring me some of your bloody English tea instead!"

Silence.

Then Winifred started laughing hysterically. The boys looked at each other and burst into laughter too. The more she laughed, the more they did. It took almost fifteen minutes for them to settle down, but they all felt better afterwards.

9

Never Trust a Grinning Dragon

In the very early stages of yet another bombing raid over London, a stick of high explosive bombs struck one of the riverside distilleries and fired a warehouse containing about three million gallons of whiskey. A tremendous conflagration was almost immediately generated, and from this time on, the area was systematically bombed, many neighboring premises being set on fire as well. The fire-fighting services were powerless to control the initial fires, under such circumstances, and the situation rapidly deteriorated as adjoining buildings burst into flames.

At the Surrey Docks, 250 acres of cut timber were set alight by incendiary bombs. North of the river, rows of warehouses were full of sugar, rum, paint, and spirits, which all caught fire. Blazing rivers of molten liquid poured out onto the quaysides and into the water itself. Flames leaped into the sky and huge clouds of dense black smoke billowed over the entire East End. To many observing the catastrophe, the scene looked like something from hell.

Sugar, it seemed, burned well in liquid form, as it floated on the water in the dockland basins, or seeped along the streets and gutters. The first line of sugar warehouses was ablaze from end to end, creating a syrupy nightmare.

Rowntree's original North Street candy factory was an early casualty, for it too was packed full of sugar and burned with intense heat. Fortunately, because of the nearness of the river, an adequate supply of water was available to fight the fires.

Communications in the city were completely disrupted. The Royal Albert, Victoria, and King George V Docks were all badly damaged. Countless warehouses were set alight, docked freighters were damaged, and the industrial areas of Custom House, Silvertown, and Canning Town were still on fire the next day, as raw materials and chemicals added fuel to the burning buildings. Places like *John Knight's Soapworks*, the *Tate & Lyle Sugar Refinery* and the *Silvertown Rubber Works* were among the factories badly hit.

In fact, government authorities noticed almost immediately that sugar had apparently been a target of the German bombers, which seemed very odd, since almost every storage bin, warehouse, and refinery in the city had been damaged or destroyed.

On the other hand, had this merely been coincidence?

Unbeknownst to fire fighters and air-raid wardens alike, there was actually an invisible dragon trailing along behind the path of destruction left by the enemy bombers. With each sortie, as the incendiaries and high explosives were erupting, Thaddeus Osbert was gorging himself on vast quantities of melted sugar and volumes of floating ash.

The dragon didn't dare endanger any human life with his voracious eating habits and in fact saved a number of trapped individuals, who never did figure out how they escaped the flames and falling debris. Thaddeus would plop down in the middle of a raging inferno and simply lap up the liquid torrents of melted sugar. The syrupy and sticky mess covered the dragon's face and he spent hours licking away the residue, even after he had returned to the little white cottage on the hill. However, he missed a few spots.

That very afternoon, right after school, Gavin made a beeline to Tintagel.

The boy knocked on the door. "It's me, Thaddeus."

Sir Osbert looked around desperately for something he could use to wipe his face. He even considered becoming invisible, but before he could do so, Gavin let himself in and quickly ran up to see his favorite dragon.

"Hello, Thaddeus," Gavin called out, waving.

"Greetings, young man," the dragon said.

The boy stopped suddenly, looking at the dragon with curiosity.

Thaddeus tried to act nonchalant.

"Thaddeus, what have you been up to?" Gavin asked.

"Oh, nothing," the dragon replied. "Why?"

"Because you have sticky gooey stuff on your ears and whiskers," the boy said, laughing. "Have you been out stealing sugar again?"

Gavin made a point of retrieving a large burlap bag that was wedged in between two of the dragon's spines on his tail. The words, **Westburn Sugar Refinery**, were printed plainly on the material.

Sir Osbert nodded sheepishly. "I'm sorry, Gavin. I know you try to satiate my sweet tooth with your generous presents of pastries and candy, but my cravings get the better of me sometimes. I only consumed a few hundred tons."

The boy was aghast. "A few hundred tons? No wonder there's a shortage."

Thaddeus shook his head. "The sugar warehouses were destroyed by German bombers. I just made sure that nothing went to waste."

Gavin's eyes narrowed as he grinned. "You didn't by chance help any of those fires along, did you?"

It was the dragon's turn to be incensed. "I most certainly did not!"

"It's all right, Thaddeus, I was just teasing."

The chessboard appeared again, the pieces still in the positions from where the players had progressed during the previous game.

"Now, where were we?" Thaddeus asked.

"I was about to checkmate you, as I recall," Gavin quipped.

"Ah, such confidence is good, lad," the dragon reacted. "Have at it, if you dare?"

They set about another round of intense tactical maneuvering and subtle subterfuge, all the while having a marvelous time. While the competition was fierce, dragon and boy were once gain proving how solid there friendship had become.

The next day, Gavin fancied purchasing a candy bar for Thaddeus. He climbed up on a chair and took sixpence out of his mother's purse, from her shopping basket on top of the kitchen cabinet. The boy quietly slipped out of the house, heading straight for the general shop and newsagent.

"Where's your coupon?" asked Mr. Cooper from behind the cash register.

Not to be thwarted, Gavin returned home, climbed up again for the ration book and sped back to the shop, feeling triumphant.

He got his candy bar, but he should have had the sense to hide it before returning home, for Mrs. Kane had observed all this activity and it was confiscated forthwith!

Feeling defeated, Gavin went back to the store, where Mr. Cooper took pity on the boy and let him read *The Beano Dandy* or any other comics they had in the shop.

The introduction of sweet rationing during the war was a major trauma in the lives of children Gavin's age, who could still remember the good old days of readily available sweets, such as chocolate, ice cream and Easter eggs, only to have them snatched from their grasp by the insensitive government.

Gavin wondered if Winston Churchill was ever denied his choice of sweets.

Somehow, he didn't think so.

In fact, because of his vivid memories, Gavin attempted to make his own ice cream, by mixing a bowl of dried milk with saccharine and water. Instead, he was left with a gooey paste, which he then placed outside, hoping it would miraculously turn into ice cream. This attempt failed miserably, of course, and the concoction tasted like sugary sawdust! Further attempts to make chocolate, using a mixture of dried milk, saccharine and cocoa, resulted in a paste that stuck to his tongue and throat like glue.

"Hello," a familiar voice spoke from behind Gavin.

The boy turned around to see Major Vickers. "Hello."

"Having a rough go of it?" Traber asked.

Gavin frowned and looked at his messy fingers. "I have discovered there is no substitute for genuine English sweets."

Vickers chuckled. "Well, I just happen to have some candy in the boot. Would you like a few pieces?"

Gavin was about to agree enthusiastically, when he was struck by a thought of warning. "Just what do I have to do to earn such a treat?"

Vickers acted wounded. "I have no ulterior motive, young man. I just thought you'd like some chocolate, real chocolate." With that, he continued walking to his car, which had been running quite poorly since he picked it up at the military police station.

Gavin followed the major and was pleased to discover the selection of candies was quite enticing. He chose two pieces.

"You can take more," Vickers offered.

Gavin shook his head. "No thank you, sir. Two is enough."

Vickers also plucked one piece from the box and plopped it into his mouth, enjoying the flavor immensely. The two of them chewed quietly, while leaning back against the major's car, as if they were loitering from school.

"What brings you to Crackington Haven, Major?" Gavin asked after finishing his second piece of chocolate.

Vickers hesitated answering, but finally replied, "Oh, my same old problem. I never imagined one particular incident in this war would cause me so much grief. However, seeing a real dragon with my very own eyes changed my entire perspective on life."

Gavin nodded and said, "I know what you mean."

"I have no right to ask you this, Gavin Kane, but do you think it would ever be possible to meet your dragon friend?" Vickers asked.

The boy smiled. "Just like I told the PM, all I can do is ask him. It's up to Thaddeus who he reveals himself to."

"So that's his name?" the major reacted. "Thaddeus?"

"Actually, it's Sir Thaddeus Osbert, if you must know," Gavin said. "He's from a long line of dragons who have watched over England for centuries."

Vickers was truly captivated by their discussion. "Where did he come from originally?"

"Iceland, although they have a different name for it," Gavin answered. "Thaddeus was born in a volcano and he's over fifteen hundred years old."

"Wow, that's incredible," Vickers said.

"Yes, it is."

"Are there more like him?"

"Yes."

"Many more?"

"Hundreds."

"What does this Thaddeus do all day, other than rescue children kidnapped by German raiders?"

Gavin grinned. "He thinks great thoughts, wonders why humans are so determined to kill each other, plays chess, and consumes vast quantities of sugar."

"Sugar?"

"He has a sweet tooth."

"Like us?"

"Indeed."

Vickers held out the box again. "Have another."

Gavin hesitated.

"Go on," Vickers coaxed. "I won't tell your mother."

Gavin took a piece from the corner of the box, the biggest chunk of chocolate remaining. He would save it until later.

Traber offered his hand and after they shook hands, he said, "I appreciate having this talk with you, Gavin. I must be getting back to the base."

"I hope you will sleep better now," the boy said sincerely.

"I imagine I will," Vickers said. "Thank you."

Then Vickers handed Gavin the entire box of sweets. "Here, keep it. You've earned it. I'm extremely grateful you willingly answered all my nagging questions."

Gavin took the box of chocolates as if it was full of gold. "Thank you, Major Vickers."

"You're welcome, young man."

"How should I get word to you if Thaddeus agrees to meet you?"

"Don't worry about that right now, lad," Vickers chuckled. "I think I'll know the answer, somehow. Take care of yourself and mind your studies in school. England's future relies on her young people, so your education is vital."

"Yes, sir," Gavin said.

Major Vickers shifted the auto into low gear and headed up the coast road. He was in a wonderful mood and felt vindicated in his quest to seek out this dragon, this Thaddeus Osbert.

Evening was approaching, but Vickers enjoyed the sunset's colors and the rustic beauty all around him. The Cornish coast was not only scenic, its ruggedness added a sense of timeless historical significance. He would like to retire here someday.

While driving past Tintagel Castle, the engine suddenly conked out.

"Damn," Vickers cursed, as he pulled over to the side of the road. Climbing out, Traber viciously kicked one of the tires and sighed with frustration.

A curious thing happened just then. A frisky cold wind swirled around him and swept his cap away. The hat floated and danced on the breeze, carried up the hill, until it landed in front of a little white cottage. As Major Vickers walked up the path to retrieve his cap, he recognized the hamlet. This is where the children had been playing the day after Traber had witnessed the dramatic dragon rescue.

The major picked up his cap and brushed it off. He couldn't help but notice the door was slightly ajar. Curious, Vickers pushed it open and peered inside. The single room was empty, except for a small wooden stool sitting before the massive stone fireplace. The dirt floor had seen a lot of traffic recently, evidence that the children came here often. Hat in hand, the army officer stepped inside and studied the interior.

His senses tingled.

Rumble … rumble … rumble.

Right before his eyes, the fireplace started falling apart, as each shaped stone shifted and moved. Chunks and slabs tumbled around the room, almost colliding, yet mysteriously always narrowly missing each other. This unexplained display of controlled levitation appeared random at first, but Vickers suddenly realized the rocks were coming together to form an entirely new shape.

What once had looked like ordinary fireplace stones, now glistened and sparkled with pulsating radiant colors, including blinding yellow, blazing fiery red, brilliant bronze, and blackest black. Once inanimate objects now undulated with massive power and incredible strength. Before he could swallow, Traber was looking directly into the eyes of a gigantic dragon.

The major wiped cold sweat from his brow. "I assume I'm in the presence of Sir Thaddeus Osbert?"

"You assume correctly, Major Traber Vickers," the dragon said, his voice thundering all around them.

The officer came to attention and said, "It's indeed an honor to meet you, sir."

It was true Thaddeus was intrigued by this army officer. There was something about the young major that spoke well of his upbringing, as well as Traber's belief in such things as dragons.

There was an uncomfortable moment of silence, as Vickers battled his initial emotional reaction about actually meeting a real live dragon. As he reflected on the implications, Thaddeus remained respectfully quiet, to allow this realization to sink in.

"I would like to ask for a favor, Major Vickers," the dragon suddenly spoke up.

"What?" Traber was startled. "Yes, but of course."

"Splendid," Thaddeus said. "Then I must insist that you cease your constant blithering about dragons. You know bloody well we don't really exist. There's just no point in continuing this line of reasoning. To do so will only hurt your career in the Royal Army and I think England would suffer dearly with your absence."

Vickers stared open-mouthed. "But you do exist. You're sitting right before me!"

"Am I?" Thaddeus asked. "How do you know it wasn't something you ate, or perhaps you drank one beer too many? You're not a boozer, are you?"

"No, of course not," Vickers objected.

"But you do see my point, now don't you?" the dragon pressed.

The major started to protest again, but stopped in mid-argument. He frowned.

"I thought you might," Thaddeus said sympathetically.

"Oh, bother," Vickers huffed.

The dragon chuckled as he remembered Bunty's common use of the phrase.

"Don't let this revelation interfere with your duties, Major," Thaddeus said. "I am available for counsel, if you think that would be of some use. However, I will not directly intercede on your behalf. The affairs of men are not in my domain."

"But you killed those German soldiers," Vickers quickly pointed out.

"Only to protect the children," Thaddeus responded. "I am Gavin Kane's guardian, while his father is away fighting this war. The Germans were threatening my charges and I responded in kind."

"I'll say you did."

"I did not find pleasure in killing, but under similar circumstances, I would do so again."

Vickers took a moment to consider all he had heard. "How do you survive?"

Thaddeus grinned. "Over the years I have learned how to get by. It's all a matter of timing and avoiding detection."

"Do you hunt?" Vickers asked.

"Seldom any more," the dragon answered. "I manage to satiate my hunger in more sedate ways now. Lately, however, the Germans have provided sustenance with their constant bombing, for the ash fills the air."

"Don't dragons have a taste for salt and charred meat?" Vickers asked.

"Actually, I crave sugar!" Thaddeus said. "I can't go for a day without having it."

"Sugar," Vickers repeated. "I never imagined such a thing."

"Dragons are mammals and like humans, prefer sugar and fat," Sir Osbert tried to explain. "Such nutrients were once crucial for our survival. Fat and sugar were so rare that when they were available, we gorged ourselves."

Major Vickers looked at his watch. "I really must be going, Sir Osbert. I have thoroughly enjoyed this meeting and must thank you for your time. I feel honored."

"Before you leave, Major Vickers, there is one more issue we must discuss, which is far more serious in nature," Thaddeus said.

"Of course, please, what is it?" Vickers asked.

"Does the name Reinhard Heydrich mean anything to you?" the dragon asked.

The major was shocked. "Why yes, of course. He is one of Himmler's top officers, closely associated with the SS, and implicated in certain unverified atrocities. Why?"

Thaddeus hesitated. "He must be assassinated."

Vickers was even more surprised. "Assassinated. You're asking me to kill a high-ranking German officer?"

The dragon nodded slowly.

The major took of his cap and slowly ran his fingers through his hair. "I'm sure you have your reasons."

"Reinhard Heydrich is the single most evil man on the planet, Major," Thaddeus said. "I'm sure the PM is convinced it's Hitler, but he's only a pawn in a more complicated game. Heydrich is the link between powerful forces humans couldn't begin to understand, much less accept. If Reinhard is allowed to live, he will eventually make it possible for all life to be destroyed."

Vickers could hear the conviction in the dragon's voice.

"Why can't your own dragons kill him?" the major naturally asked.

"We will, if and when it becomes necessary," Thaddeus replied sternly. "It would be better if dragons remained on the sidelines of this conflict, for a number of complicated reasons."

"Why are you bringing this issue to me?"

The dragon tilted his head to one side with a look of mild disdain. "Please, Major, you must be joking? You are currently the head instructor at a top-secret school for commandos and secret agents. Within the ranks of the most recent graduates, there must be a few men or women who would be capable of pulling off such an operation?"

"How do you know that?" the major asked.

Thaddeus grinned. "I have my sources."

Vickers immediately thought of the three Czech men who had been extremely keen to learn assassination techniques. Traber's expression must have disclosed this fact.

"Ah, I thought so," Thaddeus said.

"I do have some Czech agents in mind, Sir Osbert, but such policy decisions are not up to me," Vickers pointed out. "Such an attack would have to be approved on the highest military and political level."

The dragon was well aware of that. "Leave the political and diplomatic intricacies to me, Major. I have a few connections with members of Parliament and even an insider at Whitehall."

"Why doesn't that surprise me?" Vickers commented sarcastically. "It would seem that for a dragon, you're certainly well-connected."

"Indeed," the dragon said. "So, do we have an agreement?"

The major put his hat back on, came to attention, and snapped off a proper salute. "Yes, sir! I'll see to it immediately."

"Thank you, Major Vickers," Thaddeus said, assuming his own rendition of proper posture, which meant trying to make his tail hold still. "Carry on, then."

Traber headed for the door. When he looked back over his shoulder, the dragon was gone, replaced once again with a grand stone fireplace. The officer wondered if he had been hallucinating all along.

"I'll be here if you need me," Thaddeus spoke from nowhere.

Vickers blinked, shook his head, and hurried outside, not slowing his pace until he reached his vehicle. This time the automobile engine kicked right over and Traber drove away, heading back to Dartmoor.

Major Vickers contemplated everything he had seen and heard. Perhaps he should have questioned his sanity once again, after apparently having a dialogue with a dragon, but such was not the case. Instead, Traber wondered how he was going to convince his superiors to commit men, money, and material to an operation, which was really nothing more than murder.

Then, just like being hit by a lightning bolt, Major Vickers had an outlandish idea. He would arrange a visit with Dr. Edvard Beneš, the Czechoslovakian President-in-exile, who had established his headquarters in London. It was common knowledge that Beneš was considered a close personal friend of Winston Churchill.

In fact, the Prime Minster and President Beneš had met that very afternoon to enjoy high tea at Ditchley Park near Oxford, which was closely surrounded by a stand of mature trees and much less conspicuous from the air, even if the Luftwaffe had known Churchill was going to be there. This previously scheduled meeting had been organized by British intelligence to allow the two leaders time to discuss the current situation in Czechoslovakia. Winston Churchill hoped to convince Beneš that his country needed to take a more active role in resisting Nazi rule.

Once in Dartmoor, Major Vickers applied for permission to meet with Dr. Edvard Beneš, to surreptitiously promote recruiting more refugee Czechoslovakians for service with the British Army. In reality, Traber intended to suggest that Beneš seriously consider an assassination attempt on senior SS officer Heinrich Heydrich.

10

Trouble at School

Although letter-writing was a duty, Bunty's letters revealed a lonely little boy who wrote willingly, never missed sending special letters to pick up his father's spirits, reported every detail of the movies he saw with Gavin, promised he was reciting all his nightly prayers, never failed to send love to his mother up in heaven, and signed each and every note with several kisses. He was determined to hang onto his boyhood the only way he knew how, by sharing his life with the only person who was important, outside of Gavin, Emily, and Mrs. Kane, of course. It didn't matter that his mother was dead and his father was far away on the aircraft carrier ***HMS Ark Royal***.

For amongst all the sorrow and loneliness, Bunty had rediscovered one very important trait. The boy had regained his sense of hope. This was the result of Winifred Kane's loving support and his genuine friendship with Gavin Kane. Yet there was also a certain fire-breathing dragon that made a huge difference.

This was because, if Thaddeus Osbert could exist in this crazy, war-torn world, then anything was possible. Thinking of that silly sugar-eating dragon put a huge smile on Bunty's face. The possibilities were endless. Retrieving his memory book from underneath the bed, the red-haired boy sketched yet another rendition of the fantastic dragon he once never believed truly existed.

"You really are quite talented, do you know that?" Winifred asked from the doorway.

"What?" Bunty asked, startled by her presence. He quickly closed the journal.

"I'm sorry I startled you," she said. "I didn't mean to interrupt your drawing."

"Oh, no bother, Mrs. Kane," Bunty said. "I was just doodling. It wasn't anything important, really."

"Your dragon looks very realistic, Bunty, as if you had really seen one," Winifred commented, hoping to build his confidence.

The red-haired boy retrieved his art. "Do you really think so?"

"Yes, I do," she said after studying the sketch in more detail. "You have a gift, which is drawing with pen and pencil. This dragon comes alive with how you've drawn the scales and even the expression on the creature's face. I've very impressed."

"Thank you, Mrs. Kane. I do like to draw."

"It shows. Perhaps when you get older, you should enroll in an art school."

Bunty shook his head. "No, I don't think so."

"Why not?" Winifred asked.

"My pa would never think such a thing was wise," the boy replied. "Throwing away money, don't ya know. Good steady work is all that counts in his world."

Gavin's mother was sensitive enough not to dwell on such discussions while Bunty was still a teenager, but she vowed to have a word with CPO Charles Digby, if she ever had the opportunity to meet him in person. Until then, Winifred was convinced her purpose in life was to nurture and council Gavin, so it might as well include Bunty too.

"Well, let's not worry about that right now," she said. "You're still young and there's plenty of time to decide what you want to be when you grow up. For now, keep drawing and keep learning at school."

"Yes, Mrs. Kane, I will," the boy said.

Bunty never felt his school days were particularly productive. He wasn't stupid and he could read and write, but there always seemed to be one or two handicaps, which put him on the wrong side of the Headmaster, who nicknamed the red-haired boy "Leprechaun." While the teasing never seemed to bother him on the outside, Gavin knew his friend didn't appreciate the mocking from other students.

Sometimes, however, Bunty would prove to the peers that he was perfectly capable of quick-thinking solutions too.

After several weeks of reading poetry aloud, Bunty was selected to memorize a poem to present to the entire school. The boy told Mrs. Kane about his choice of a poem—*A Night in Bethlehem*. Winifred remembered she had learned the same verse as a girl and mentioned a bit of doggerel that her generation had substituted for certain choice phrases. It was probably a mistake to teach Bunty the replacement lines, but Gavin's mother really didn't see any harm at the time, because it was an effective memory tool.

The next day the teacher decided to showcase her students' skills and called on Bunty to recite his selection. After all, the boy had proven he could project his voice quite effectively and his memorization skills were really quite impressive.

Well, as Bunty was doing superbly, he suddenly couldn't remember a certain stanza, but quickly substituted the lines Mrs. Kane had shared with him.

Instead of, "while shepherds watched their flocks at night," it came out as, "while shepherds *washed* their *socks* at night."

The entire classroom erupted into fits of raucous laughter, but poor Bunty was made to explain where he had learned such a thing. The boy didn't want to tell a lie, so he sheepishly replied, "Gavin Kane's mother taught me, so I wouldn't forget the right words."

The teacher sighed and glared at Gavin, who was slinking down in his chair, trying to disappear. Then, with a haughty air, Miss Bentley declared, "Well, that's just what one might expect from Methodists."

Bunty didn't go out of his way to make waves, but it was often the result of his actions, as innocent as they were. One day in particular, the boy from Plymouth made quite an impression on his fellow students and teachers.

All over Britain, after many air raids, children would come to school with bits of bombs they picked up along the way. Such was the case when German bombers dropped their leftover payload on hapless Truro. The very next day, Bunty arrived at school carrying a completely intact incendiary bomb, which had not yet ignited.

After an incredibly harsh scolding, the device was rapidly confiscated by the teacher and turned over to the bomb disposal squad! Poor Bunty was required to stay after school, where he was not only required to write, "*I will not pick up unexploded bombs*, 200 times on the blackboard, but he was also repeatedly admonished by the headmaster.

"What were you thinking, boy?" Mr. Washburne kept asking.

"I thought everybody would like to see what the Nazis were dropping on us," Bunty replied innocently. "I thought that if they could actually touch one of those nasty things, they'd realize that England is tougher than any old stinking bomb."

The boy began to cry.

The headmaster didn't know what to say just then. It was obvious that Bunty meant no harm and his motives were in the right place. The boy had just failed to consider the inherent dangers of bringing an explosive device into a crowded school, even if the bomb turned out to be a dud.

"There, there, lad, don't go on so," Mr. Washburne said. "I think the lesson was learned. In the future, if you find something like that again, please note the location and come tell me."

"Yes, Headmaster," Bunty sniffled.

"Promise?"

"Yes, sir."

"All right then, off you go."

When Bunty was finally released from his torture, he was surprised to discover Gavin was standing just outside the main gate.

"You didn't have to wait for me, sport," Bunty said, but smiling anyway.

"No bother, old chum," Gavin replied.

They fell into step on their journey home.

"I thought bringing that incendiary was simply smashing, you know," Gavin offered. "I didn't even know you had found it."

"It was supposed to be a surprise," Bunty said.

"Bloody right it was," Gavin exclaimed, laughing loudly. "You surprised the life out of everybody."

The boys burst into hearty cackling and took off on the run, hoping to make up some of the time they had lost with Bunty's after-school punishment.

Gasping for breath, they slowed down the pace. They walked along silently for some distance. It was a beautiful day and they were enjoying the weather.

"I heard Colin Baker telling Winslow Spears that a Stirling bomber had crashed near the road to Camelford," Bunty blurted after awhile.

"Well then, I think we should hurry home and then head off in that direction," Gavin stated in a most exaggerated and pompous accent. "Cheerio."

The boys broke into a run again, over hills and across fields, hoping their sense of direction would not lead them astray. Gavin decided their secret shortcut was the only sensible route to reach Crackington Haven without any further delay. They didn't inform Mrs. Kane of their arrival, but slipped quietly into the garage instead.

Gavin and Bunty bicycled to the wreckage site of the crashed Stirling airplane. The bomber had come down in a small wood and was minus its wings. It wasn't completely destroyed, so the boys played inside, climbing through bulkheads and hatches, up and down the length of the fuselage. They also found a few bits and bobs to take as souvenirs.

On the way home, Bunty was elated to find a piece of dried lemon rind in the middle of the road. He hadn't seen a lemon for years, but vaguely remembered his mother squeezing them on pancakes before the war. Bunty took the peel with him, then washed and re-dried it. He soon discovered that if he broke off a small piece and sucked it long enough, the flavor of lemon would eventually come back.

That evening, just before they sat down for dinner, the air raid siren went off. It had been awhile since the eerie and haunting wailing had sounded, so everyone reacted quickly, figuring it wasn't just a warning. Once inside the basement shelter, Winifred still managed to serve a light supper.

Between bites, they could hear the deep rumbling of distant explosions. Gavin looked at Bunty's face, because they knew that Plymouth was the target again. The *All Clear* didn't come for hours and once it did, it was time for bed.

Oil lamps were the main source of lighting in Crackington Haven, with candles reserved for the bedrooms. Now most of the nearby farms didn't have main lines of any sort, not for water, electricity, or gas. The cooking was done on a day-to-day basis, with paraffin stoves and the oven was only lit on baking days. Drinking water was pumped from a well, while rainwater was piped from a large tank for washing and bathing.

While Gavin and Bunty sometimes complained of hardships, they had it pretty good, overall. After saying their prayers, the boys peered out past the blackout curtains, to gaze at the orange glow in the sky, which they knew was Plymouth burning, almost 35 miles away.

Gavin could only guess, but Bunty was truly thankful to be away from the constant bombing, which reduced his birthplace to nothing more than ruins. Afterwards he went to his room, where Bunty hid under his blanket and wrote a short note to his dad.

Dear Pa,

The Kane house is big and Mrs. Kane is very nice. She's a splendid cook.
   I'm doing well in school, but I hid the headmaster's spectacles.
   Not even Hitler's armies could find them.
   Only Gavin and I know where they are. We'll give them back tomorrow.
   Hurry up and defeat Hitler, so you can come back home. Watch out for those nasty old U-boats. A bit of sweets would be nice.

                                                                          Bunty

The wailing started up again.

Bunty always got a churning knot in his stomach whenever the air raid siren sounded. He would never forget that fateful evening when he lost his mother.

Bunty quickly joined Gavin and Mrs. Kane as they went down into the cellar and scooted into the Morrison shelter.

For light, Winifred had a lantern covered with green baize, and the boys enjoyed the smell of the warm cloth. Of course, blackout regulations were always in effect, so they couldn't have much light, even tucked away in the shelter. Yet Bunty felt safe and protected in their hide-away. When the **All Clear** siren sounded, it was such a relief. The three of them would pile out and Gavin's mother would put the kettle on, to make a cup of Earl Gray for each of them.

They quietly sipped and savored every drop. Winifred usually was able to find something sweet to go along with their tea, unless the sugar had run out. There always seemed to be a shortage, no matter how they scrimped and saved.

Of course, the boys knew where the powdery white stuff was going.

"Mums the word," Bunty whispered.

Gavin crossed his heart.

Then it was back to sleep for everybody.

The next morning, Major Traber Vickers was shown into an impressive wood-paneled library to meet Dr. Edvard Beneš. Their discussion was private and brief, but because of the major's conviction, his suggestion to assassinate Heydrich was greeted with cautious agreement. It was just a matter of planning, timing, and recruiting the men necessary to pull off such a mission.

"All in a day's work, sir," Vickers assured Beneš.

11

Teenage Concerns

"I prefer my rashers limp and fried slowly in the frying pan, if that wouldn't be too much a bother, please?" Bunty requested of Mrs. Kane.

"Isn't it wonderful to have bacon again," Winifred chirped, lifting out pieces to sit on a piece of newspaper. She would use the pan drippings later in a recipe.

Gavin's mouth watered, for his mother had also made fresh bread.

There was jam too.

Sugar was stored in the sideboard cupboard, which was a closely guarded family secret. Gavin and Bunty would bicycle out to the countryside and pick black currants, so Mrs. Kane could make blackcurrant jam with the saved sugar.

When they were finished eating, the boys hurried off to school. Even with the bus ride, it was a long hike and with each daily trip burning off calories, it was little wonder that Gavin looked skinny. Even Bunty, who had come to Crackington Haven a little on the plump side, was now noticeably thinner.

At school, it proved very difficult to learn anything, as there were about 60 children in one class. Bunty was convinced that school consisted only of singing lessons, with mostly patriotic songs and reciting useless poetry. They also did a lot of marching around the playground, for the Cornish headmaster had been a major in the First World War.

After school, the two boys took their time going home, as if there was something tedious awaiting their arrival. This feeling did not abate itself and without understanding why, Bunty and Gavin made a wide detour in the direction of Tintagel. It was as if a magnet was pulling them to the little white cottage.

At the base of the hill, Bunty stopped Gavin with an outstretched arm to block his path. "Do you think we should be here?"

"I want to see Thaddeus," Gavin said.

Bunty was troubled. Then, with his mind made up, the red-haired boy stated, "He wants to talk to only you."

"How do you know that?" Gavin asked.

Bunty shrugged. "It's just a feeling I have."

"Are you sure you're okay?"

"Of course. Now go inside and talk to Thaddeus."

Gavin did so. However, it was immediately apparent that the dragon was not his usual self. Thaddeus looked quite troubled. His teeth flashed and he snorted as if threatened again by unseen forces.

"What's troubling you so, Sir Osbert?" Gavin asked timidly.

"Oh, nothing," the dragon replied, though not very convincingly.

No matter what the dragon said, it was obvious to see that Thaddeus was disturbed by something. Gavin just wasn't sure if he should pry. He studied Sir Osbert's expression and decided to offer his friendship as a possible solution.

"What is it, old friend?" Gavin inquired again. "Perhaps I can help."

The dragon looked down at the boy, evaluating both Gavin's inherent compassion and sense of justice, while comparing those qualities with the possible dangers that lay ahead. Was it fair for him to ask the boy to commit to such an undertaking?

"I have been contacted by an old friend," Thaddeus finally said. "He's asked me to do him a favor, which involves a lot of flying. I'm concerned that so much time away will interfere with your chess lessons."

Gavin thought about what the dragon wasn't saying. "You can still teach me the moves while I'm sitting on your shoulders."

The dragon chuckled. "Oh, so you think if I'm distracted, I'll slip up, do you?"

Gavin grinned. "Not me."

"Then we will continue your lessons, even when airborne."

The next day, at the Truro County School for Girls, Emily was doing her matriculation exam, which was a combination of assessments testing reading, writing, and mathematic skills, when the air raid siren went off. All the girls gathered up their examination sheets, their pencils and erasers, then hurry in silence down to the basement, where long tables had been set up in case of such an interruption. Emily was filled with pride at the self-discipline of her fellow students.

Even with the interruptions, Emily received high marks on her test. There was no doubt she was an excellent student and all the teachers recognized the fact she was quite bright. Unfortunately, it just wasn't enough for Emily. Something was missing in her life and no amount of good grades or praise filled the void. The spirit of adventure ran through her veins and her daydreams often revolved around exploring the world one day.

That same urge to seek excitement often distracted Gavin in the middle of lecture, but he was usually successful in camouflaging his true thoughts from the teachers. He couldn't help but doodle, while gazing out the window and daydreaming of flying around the world on a dragon's shoulders.

"Gavin Kane?" a voice jolted him to consciousness again.

"Yes, Miss Drew," he replied, pretending to be fully aware of what was going on.

"Which monarch unsuccessfully tried to stop William Gladstone from becoming Prime Minister?" the teacher inquired in a wicked and impatient tone, convinced she had caught the boy not paying attention.

Without logical explanation, the answer suddenly appeared scrawled on one of the classroom windowpanes, written by an invisible hand, or more accurately, a claw.

QUEEN VICTORIA

"That would be Queen Victoria, Miss Drew," Gavin answered confidently.

The teacher was unprepared for Gavin's correct answer. She stuttered for a moment, before admitting, "That is correct. Well done."

With a pronounced sigh of relief, Gavin smiled, while a bead of sweat dribbled down his back. When the moment was right, he faced the window again and mouthed the words, "Thank you, Thaddeus."

For a brief flickering instant, the dragon appeared, wagging a talon as a reminder to pay better attention to his schoolwork. Gavin nodded his understanding and sat up straighter, focusing on the lesson at hand.

"Nice recovery there, sport," Bunty whispered from behind.

Gavin ignored him, but smiled anyway.

After school, the boys headed straight to Boscastle's beaches, where they collected mussels and cockles from the sandbanks, which were exposed at low tide. Gavin gathered winkles, or sea snails, while Bunty looked for cockles. Later they would take the winkles home, where Winifred would boil them and when cooled, Bunty and Gavin would travel to Plymouth on the weekend to sell them to the local children at one penny a bag, including a pin for extracting the winkle from its shell. Whenever the boys had winkles to sell, they were very popular, because sweets were in such short supply and winkles made a passable substitute.

During their excursion along the beach, Gavin spotted the wreckage of a crashed German Me109 lying on the sand banks. Running over to take a closer look, they were surprised to discover unused bombs and bullets lying everywhere.

Only a few yards from the partially submerged fighter, lay the body of the dead pilot.

"It's sad to think he saw this sand bank and thought it was a suitable place to land his damaged aircraft," Gavin said softly. "Only to discover that with the return of the tide, the seawater would rise quickly."

Bunty said nothing, only staring at the bloated remains.

Many aviators on both sides escaped being killed in aerial combat, only to drown while trying to walk ashore. Their bodies would often be picked up by fishermen, who received a bounty for the recovery of these tragic souls.

Boscastle was the nearest village, so with the grim task of dragging the body to higher ground, Bunty and Gavin each took hold of the pilot's harness. It was a depressing task, but neither did they want to leave the poor man to the elements. Fortunately, they were relieved of this morbid duty by two Royal Navy sailors who saw them from the harbor docks.

"There you go, lads, we'll take him from here," one of the uniformed men said. "He'll receive a right and proper burial now, thanks to you."

Gavin shoved his hands in his pockets and watched silently as they carried the enemy pilot away with deep reverence. No words could express what the boys were feeling at that moment.

"Come on, chum," Bunty said, trying to sound cheerful. "Let's go nick some apples or something."

Gavin shook his head. "I'm not in the mood, I'm afraid."

"Me neither," Bunty agreed.

"When will this all end?" Gavin asked.

Bunty only shrugged.

They faced each other.

"It won't be long before you and I get called up, you know?" Gavin stated.

His friend nodded. "Yes, I know."

"It's for God, King, and Country, but I really don't feel like putting on a uniform and going off to fight Germans," Gavin stated.

"Or the Italians," Bunty said.

"So we have to do something."

"Yes, but what?"

"I don't know. I just know we have to do something to end this war!"

"It's too bad you had to return that magical sword."

Gavin sat down on the end of the dock, his legs swinging back and forth over the water. Bunty plopped down beside him, fiddling with a section of rotting planking. They silently watched their reflections in the lapping waves.

"Thaddeus might have the answer," Bunty offered. "He's very wise, I think."

For a long time Gavin had been considering confiding in the dragon about his reservations, but there never seemed to be the right time for such discussions. Besides, there were bigger issues at stake, including England's survival.

Instead, Gavin merely shrugged.

Lost in their own thoughts, neither boy realized that Thaddeus Osbert was sitting right behind them, his face etched with concern. While invisible, the dragon often kept a close eye on his charges, as he had promised Richard Kane he would do. Thaddeus too was deeply troubled by how the war was progressing and it sometimes seemed that darkness might prevail after all.

Sir Osbert just couldn't allow that to happen.

It was the dragon's great secret that all he really wanted was love, friendship, and affection. Gavin Kane, Emily Scott, and Bunty Digby certainly provided those basic requirements and because of this, Thaddeus had dedicated his life to protecting them. He was already determined to end this war as soon as possible, even if that meant direct intervention. He had been exiled once before from the dragon kingdom for meddling in human affairs, but this current situation was far more serious.

"Everything seemed simpler when I was a kid," Bunty said.

"That's for sure," Gavin agreed.

"Peter Pan had the right idea," Bunty said. "We should have run away at ten and headed straight for Neverland."

They both laughed.

"I just don't know if I want to be an adult?" Gavin wondered.

"Not if it's going to get us killed," Bunty said.

"Countries have fought each other for centuries, everyone claiming they would make the world a peaceful place," Gavin complained. "My father told me the last war was supposed to be the war to end all wars."

They fell silent again.

Then, very slowly, Gavin put his arm around Bunty's shoulder and said, "We're pals, right?"

"Of course."

"I never would have known you, if it wasn't for this rotten war."

"I'd still like to have me Mum, I would," Bunty said quietly.

"I know," Gavin said.

The boys tossed a few more pebbles into the sea, before they got up and strolled along the shore, heading home in a roundabout manner.

"Do you ever wonder what will become of us?" Bunty asked.

"Of course," Gavin replied. "I especially wonder when Thaddeus will leave us."

Bunty stopped and frowned. "I hope he never goes anywhere. Life wouldn't be the same without that dragon."

Gavin couldn't argue with that. Still, there was some unspoken understanding between Thaddeus and Gavin's father that troubled the Kane boy. He had seen the signs while witnessing their reunion.

It was as if they were saying goodbye to each other.

Forever.

With these thoughts crowding Gavin's mind, he had trouble deciding what to think about first. Everything seemed to jumble together, adding to his confusion.

When the boys walked into the kitchen, Gavin suddenly ran to his mother and threw his arms around her waist. Winifred was the recipient of a huge squeezie hug.

"What's this, then?" she asked, giving him kisses on both cheeks.

"I love you, that's all," he replied.

"I love you too, Gavin, very much," she said, tears welling up in her eyes.

"I know," her son said.

Mrs. Kane held out her hand and pulled Bunty to her other side. Hugging the boys, she knelt down on the kitchen floor and they stayed that way for several minutes, very close and very emotional.

The dinner conversation was a bit subdued, but the three of them still ate heartily. All week long Winifred had saved bits and scraps, until there was enough to make soup. The concoction was delicious and the boys asked for several refills. With some biscuits and raspberry preserves, it was another satisfying meal, compliments of Mrs. Kane's long hours in the kitchen.

The next day, right after getting off the bus from Launceston, Gavin ran practically the entire way to Boscastle. He came over the hill just as Emily stepped off her bus home from Truro.

"Emmy!" Gavin called out, waving frantically.

Emily was surprised and pleased to see him, for their after-school meetings had recently become far and few between.

To her complete surprise, when Gavin reached her, he threw his arms around her waist and kissed her on the cheek.

Emily blushed. "What was that for?"

"Because I haven't seen you for days, because you're my best friend in the whole world, and because I wanted you to know that I wouldn't know what I'd do without you!" Gavin replied in one sentence without a breath.

Emily took his hand and said, "Thank you, Gavin. That was very sweet and I feel the same way about you."

They decided to go for a stroll along the coast road.

"Do you remember the first time I met Thaddeus?" she asked.

"Yes, I do," he said.

"I thought you were just making him up."

"Well, that makes sense. I do, after all, make lots of things up."

"But Thaddeus is real. That makes it so much more earth-shattering."

"Why do you say that?"

Emily stopped. "Don't you realize what it means?"

The boy shook his head.

"Gavin, we know a real dragon," she said loudly, her hands gesturing. "The implications are far beyond our little existence in this world. I bet there aren't a hundred people on this planet who have met a live dragon."

"Not that would admit it, that's for sure," Gavin said.

"Exactly," Emily agreed. "Dragons just don't go around talking to anybody. Thaddeus picked you to reveal himself to. You're very special, even if you don't realize it yet. My best friend is the modern-day King Arthur."

"I am not," Gavin angrily protested.

Emily was hurt by his reaction. "Gavin, what's wrong?"

"I am not King Arthur!" the boy shouted. "I'm just Gavin Kane and I happen to know a dragon. That's special, I admit, but there's nothing more to it. I'm supposed to keep my eye on a certain lake, like all the other Kanes before me and then pass this obligation along to my son, whenever that is."

Emily shook her head. "Oh, Gavin, you're so much more than that. Don't you get it? You were given the sword to protect England in her hour of need."

Gavin stuck his hands in his pockets and blew out an angry gust of air. "Bah!"

"How can you say that?"

"Because I didn't do anything," he replied. "Thaddeus saved us, remember?"

"But ..."

"But nothing," Gavin interrupted her. "Oh, Emmy, it isn't as exciting as it seems. There's no great mystical and magical adventure. This is reality. There's a war going on and England's in trouble, but Thaddeus would never let anything terrible happen. If the Germans defeat us, then the dragons will come and wipe them out. They don't need me."

Emily was disappointed by his comments. She didn't know what to say, so instead, she flopped down on the side of the road and began to cry.

Poor Gavin.

Now he really was at a loss.

The teenaged boy sat down next to her and put his arm around her shoulder. "Don't cry, Emmy. I'm sorry. I didn't mean to make you upset."

She kept right on sobbing, tears rolling down her cheeks to splash on her bare knees. Gavin wished he had his handkerchief, but he had used it as a sail for his wooden sailboat and it disappeared in the surf weeks ago. If his mother ever found out, he would be in trouble for sure.

Emily wiped her eyes with the back of her hand and sniffled. "I think you're very important, Gavin. I think Thaddeus knows the fate of England rests with you. It won't be because of some great heroic battle or epic search for some silly cup. It will come down to something you believe and hold dear. Your name won't show up in any history books or be announced over the BBC, but you will make a difference. I believe that and so should you. It's your destiny!"

Gavin looked into her bloodshot eyes and smiled. "Okay, Emmy. I'll believe in what you say, but only because it's you."

She smiled. "You'll see. You will make a difference."

12

Emily's New Friend

Several days later, while Emily was playing in one of the fields outside Boscastle, she heard machine-gun fire and an engine roaring behind her. Turning around, the girl saw a German Heinkel 111 emerge suddenly from behind a fluffy white cumulus cloud, jet-black smoke pouring from one of the engines. The plane was diving straight towards her. Emily was terrified, convinced she was going to be machine-gunned. The girl partly jumped and partly fell from the fence, but then froze with fright as the plane, screaming above her head, crashed into the next field over, about 200 yards away.

Kaboom!

The Heinkel disintegrated in a terrific explosion of flame and smoke.

Emily's mother was pulling weeds in the backyard and saw the plane crash. Harriet Scott was convinced it had come down in the field where her daughter was playing. She ran up the road to the field, to find Emily crying hysterically, trying to climb over the gate to escape the horror of what she had just witnessed.

Several members of the Home Guard, along with the local member of the Air Raid Precaution Service, went to look at the wreckage to see if there were any survivors. Mrs. Scott spent several minutes trying to help Emily calm down. The girl cowered behind the hedge, still sobbing, while the men approached the smoldering plane.

Two of the German aircrew had bailed out before the crash and villagers from Boscastle, armed with shotguns and pitchforks, arrested one of them. Several miles away, one of the nearby farmers managed to apprehend the other.

Eventually everyone left the crash site to return to Boscastle. Emily knew that the local villagers had found the remains of the pilot and co-pilot. They passed around a wallet containing a photo of one of the Germans with his wife and young child.

When Emily looked at the picture, she quickly realized that the little girl in the photograph was probably the same age as her. This revelation made her very sad.

All alone again, Emily decided to venture closer to the smoldering wreckage. At the time, she didn't understand the powerful magnetic draw the crash held over her.

Inching closer still, Emily shivered with uncertainty. It was as if the enemy aircraft was alive, calling to her to come closer.

Closer.

Closer still.

"Help!" called out a pitiful little voice from somewhere underneath a piece of the airplane's tail section.

Emily jumped from surprise and fear.

"Who said that?" her voice cracked.

"I'm trapped," the person answered. It distinctly sounded like a female voice.

Emily tripped in her hurry to free the unfortunate soul and slammed painfully into the blackened fuselage. Realizing her injury wasn't serious, the girl lifted up the stabilizer section, but almost fainted with surprise.

Sprawled underneath was a little girl, perhaps five or six years old at the most. Emily offered her hand and pulled the child safely away from the wreckage. Apparently uninjured, the girl bowed slightly.

"*Acheyla*," the girl said quietly.

Emily shook her head. "I'm sorry. I don't speak Welsh."

The unidentified child brushed the dirt off her clothes and struggled to speak in English. "Thank you for rescuing me."

"How ever did you get under there?" Emily asked.

The girl frowned and replied, "This monster tried to eat me."

Emily giggled, not because what the other girl said was funny, but because she had been terrified by the same airplane, for much the same reason. It reaction, she reached out and gently patted the girl on the forearm. "I was very frightened by this wretched beast too!"

The little girl was wearing a splendid robe, made of luxurious colored fabric of white, silver, yellow, and gold, adorned with silver and mithril thread. She had very pale skin and silver hair, along with sparkling violet eyes and the most mischievous smile Emily had ever witnessed. There was something very odd about her, but whatever it was, it wasn't readily obvious at the time.

"I will take you home now," Emily offered. "Where do you live?"

"Oh, that won't be necessary," the other girl said, now distracted.

"Are you looking for something?" Emily asked.

"Yes," the girl answered. "I seem to have misplaced my *parma*."

"What's a *parma*?"

The silver-haired child seemed perplexed by the question, but after a few seconds of thinking hard, she blurted, "Book."

"Oh, delightful," Emily reacted. "I love books. I will help you look for it. What does your book look like?"

The strange little girl scratched her head and in so doing, knocked off her cap. Emily suddenly spotted the girl's exposed ears. They were very pointed.

"Oh!" Emily exclaimed.

With silver locks spinning around, a small glimmering spear instantly appeared in the girl's tiny hand. "What did you see? Is there an orc nearby?"

Emily stared, which she knew was exceedingly rude, but she couldn't help herself.

The other girl looked back at Emily with confusion written all over her face. "I do not understand. What did you see?"

Swallowing, Emily slowly regained her poise and whispered, "Are you an elf?"

"Of course I'm an elf," the pixyish girl replied. "What did you think I was?"

Emily shrugged and said, "A girl like me, of course."

The elf giggled and emphatically shook her head. "No offense to thee, but a human I do no wish to be."

"I am Emily Angelina Scott," Emily introduced herself with a curtsy. "My friends all call me Emmy."

"I am Kitto Bideven," the elf reciprocated. "My friends must still call me Kitto."

Emily grinned and said, "It is my pleasure to meet you, Kitto."

The elf bowed deeply and when she stood straight again, Emily had an opportunity to really observe her new acquaintance.

Emily thought Kitto was unusually tall for an elf, but she was also more thinly built, lacking the strength and agility of her male counterparts. However, living in the mountains had accustomed Kitto to harsh climates, and as such, she was more enduring than common elves. Besides, this female elf had been blessed with a quick brain and she knew how to use it. Gray elves were among the smartest of elvenkind, and this was probably what contributed to their somewhat aloof behavior, including their relations with other elven races.

"Were you reading your book when the monster attacked?" Emily asked, pointing at the crashed airplane.

"No, I was looking for clues," Kitto replied.

"Clues to what?"

"Why you humans are fighting a war again."

"Oh, that," Emily said. "That's easy. It's because we're stupid."

Kitto's mouth opened in shock, but then she giggled. "Are all humans so quick with their tongues?"

"Just me, I think. Oh, and perhaps my friend Gavin."

The elf's eyes widened. "Do you speak of Sir Gavin Kane?"

Nodding, Emily was equally surprised. "Do you know Gavin?"

Kitto shook her head. "I have never met him, but his name is spoken with great awe and respect in our village. He was chosen by Vivienne to protect all of Briton with a magical sword."

Emily knew this was true.

"I would like to meet him one day," the elf announced.

"And meet him you shall," Emily assured her.

Kitto smiled. "You are very nice Emmy, for a human."

"Why thank you, Kitto," Emily said. "I think you are a very nice elf."

They both giggled.

"What is it like being an elf?" Emily asked.

"We are the most noble and reclusive of the gentle races," Kitto whispered. "My fellow elves are protectors of justice in the shadow world."

"Why did you venture from your village, Kitto?" Emily asked. "It's so dangerous out here amongst us humans."

"I am a scout."

"I see."

"There is a great stirring amongst the hidden people," the elf added, sensing she needed to explain. "Elf, faerie, and dwarf alike have gathered to discuss the coming of darkest evil."

"Is this evil, human, by chance?"

Kitto nodded. "From across the seas."

"The Germans, I bet," Emily surmised.

Kitto shrugged, because she didn't know what the term meant.

Emily pondered how she might describe the enemy, when an idea popped into her head. She picked up a stick and scratched a crude swastika in the dirt.

"This is their emblem."

Kitto recoiled. "It is the Black Sun. Where have you seen this?"

"Our enemy uses this symbol on their flags."

Kitto seemed deeply troubled. "Used by humans in such a manner is horrible."

"What will you do?"

"Prepare for the inevitable, I'm afraid."

"We could certainly use your help against the Germans," Emily said.

Kitto shook her head. "Our kind hasn't come to the aid of humans for ages."

"Why not?"

"Mankind had no further use for us, or so I've been told," Kitto replied.

"Well, as I said earlier, men are pretty stupid when it comes to things like this."

"I must go," Kitto said impatiently. "I will deliver this information to my elders."

"Will I see you again?" Emily asked.

"Of course."

Emily waved.

"*Ceshar*," Kitto said slowly. "It means goodbye."

"*Ceshar*," Emily repeated.

Poof.

Suddenly the elf was gone, vanished into thin air.

Emily was sad, but also excited that she had actually met a real elf. She wondered if she should keep the secret to herself for awhile, just in case it had all been a dream. While walking home, Emily whistled with happiness and skipped the rest of the way to her house.

Most houses in Britain had a letter slot or letterbox in the front door, rather than a mailbox at the gate. While her mother was busy in the kitchen, Emily went to gather the mail. She was surprised to find an envelope addressed to her.

The letter turned out to be from her father, the first she had received since he went away to fight in the war. Opening it very carefully, Emily read it aloud to herself.

Dearest Emmy,

Now that I have a few minutes to spare, I thought you might like to get a letter from your dear papa.

How are you old girl?

Things in Bomber Command are a bit dicey, but I'm getting by.

Hope you are doing well in school. Your mother says you are very bright and your marks are quite high. Good show.

After the latest bombing raid, the dust and debris was floating in the air for hours. Then it slowly descended and covered my uniform with a fine white ash. I looked like it had been snowing.

Some day it will end, I suppose, but we may have to endure more yet. Folks are brave, but the strain is telling on them.

Love,

Pa

Emily's school welcomed many girls who had come to Cornwall, either with their parents or to live with relations. Some of these girls stayed only a short time, others went right through the school. For some time they had, in the school, six girls who were pre-war refugees from Nazi Europe. They very soon settled into school life and did very well indeed. Early in 1941, the girls were asked to make room for 120 more girls from West Ham High School, together with their Headmistress and some of her staff. By using every available space, even the dining room and part of a corridor, as classrooms, they managed to squeeze them in, as the Truro County School numbers were then only about two hundred and fifty.

A partition of green blackout material screened the balcony from the auditorium and made a little room for teaching staff. The material was lightweight and certainly wasn't soundproof, and the occupants longed for peace and quiet, but were amazingly tolerant and good-tempered. The girls proved to be cooperative hosts. Hardly had they settled into a pattern juggling their crowded existence, when severe air raids on Plymouth began. Shortly after one devastating bombing attack, it was announced that a large part of Stoke Damerel High School was coming to Truro and would need to use the building too. For three schools to study simultaneously, in one building, was quite impossible, so the students had to go to classes in shifts.

During the year, Emily was able to see brief glimpses of a world of gaiety, too soon snatched from her eager heart by the depressing news of war. By choice, the original students became isolated from the constantly rotating mistresses, as female teachers in Britain were labeled, using their own entrance, their own cloakroom, and eating their meals in private. In their isolation, apart from the rest of the school, the girls developed a fierce spirit of independence. Emily didn't mean to be troublesome, but somehow she always did the wrong thing and everyone was cross with her.

Earlier that spring, Emily was denied her passing marks in Biology, which was also her favorite subject. More than ever before, she was determined to do her best, to prove the faith in her hadn't been misplaced. Even with the constant distraction of Gavin, Bunty, and that wonderfully fascinating dragon, Emily redoubled her focus on her studies.

Finding useable paper, or being in the right place at the right time, was something of a nightmare. Mistresses strove to teach the girls how to make cakes with little or no fat, ice them with dried milk, use eggs that came in packets, and even flour was a luxury to be hoarded. Sewing continued to be a challenge, with the necessity of clothing coupons forcing each girl to decide between material for a new coat or a new nightdress.

However, the flower arrangement competition was Emily's favorite event and many of her fellow classmates wondered how she was able to obtain such beautiful flowers in the first place. While it seemed a mystery to the entire student body, Gavin knew that his best friend had received the assistance from Thaddeus himself, who flew up to Iceland to pick her rare and exotic samples. Surprising as it seemed, the dragon had quite a knack for picking out wonderful combinations of colors.

Icelandic Poppies ranged from white to cream, and orange to yellow, while among them were alpine and meadow flowers of all colors. Buttercup, saxifrage, roses, and daisies were also common, while millions of little purple and blue blossoms sprung up from the grasslands all along the coast.

Upon his return, the dragon presented the girl with an armful of choices, which covered the spectrum of the rainbow and made an impressive arrangement in anyone's eyes. Emily slowly sat down on the stool, at a loss for words.

"The whole of Iceland sits atop a giant volcano," Thaddeus informed her. "With moss and feisty pink flowers digging into its hardened lava surface to hide the churning power that lies underneath."

"They are so beautiful, Sir Osbert," Emily said. "However may I repay you?"

"There is no need to do so, Emmy," Thaddeus replied affectionately. "I can see the gratitude in your eyes and hear the thrill in your voice. I need no other payment to prove to me that you are pleased."

The day of the festival, Emily brought a huge bouquet of flowers to school. The one blossom Emily loved most was lupine, which became her centerpiece arrangement, surrounded by blossoms of red, white, purple, orange, and yellow. The other girls just gawked, but quickly complimented their fellow classmate on her handiwork.

Little did she know, but an invisible dragon sat crouched outside the window, watching Emily display her arrangement for all to see. He smiled with intense pride and savored Emmy's feelings of joy and accomplishment. It came as no great surprise that Emily Scott won first Place.

At the end of a long day at school, Emily usually found escape and solace in reading. New books were becoming very scarce, what with paper shortages, but Gavin managed to keep a steady flow of old books coming her way. He borrowed volumes from his father's library, with his mother's permission, of course, and lent them to her. As if the pages were made from butterfly wings, Emily treated them with great care and respect.

It was about this time in her life that the teenaged girl made up her mind to become a published writer as soon as the war was over. There were so many strange and wonderful things happening in her life, which would amaze and entertain other people. To see the words come together on paper was becoming her driving passion. Emily intended to seriously pursue a writing career.

13

Unexpected Visitor

When not ushering at the *Bude Cinema* or helping the rare customer at her husband's photography studio, Gavin's mother was always knitting. She knitted socks, mittens, balaclavas and thick blanket squares for the soldiers and sailors fighting overseas. While Vera Lynn was singing for them, Mrs. Winifred Kane was knitting them everything else.

The boys listened to their favorite programs on the crackly old radio, which Bunty called the Static Box. First, they finished with their daily chores, while Gavin's mother was knitting. Bags of wool would appear at the side of her chair and she would put her knitting down only to do other essential chores.

Earlier that afternoon, Gavin and Bunty were sent out with jars for blackberries, trekking for miles over the local fields to gather mushrooms and blue-stales, as well as kindling and fallen logs for the fireplace. They collected rose hips and elderberries too. Emily took the rose hips to the local chemist and he sometimes gave her a penny, but more often, he rewarded the girl with a special treat, such as licorice-root or a little bag of lemon sherbet, with a hollow licorice tube to suck the sherbet through!

Sometimes late at night, after the sun went down, the boys would sneak out to knock walnuts off huge trees, but they had to be careful, or they would be caught. Bunty became quite skilled at scrumping, which was slang for pilfering apples, pears and plums from the nearby farms. Winifred didn't ask any questions, especially when food was sometimes scarce and Richard's Royal Navy pay-stub hadn't come through yet, which happened with monotonous regularity.

Mrs. Kane often took time to visit the outlying families, sometimes to trade foodstuffs, but more often than not, just to be friendly. It did her heart good to be busy and if there was anything Winifred could do to help someone else, then she was thrilled.

Most of the neighboring farms were purely dairy operations, with a dozen or so cows, a few pigs, some sheep, and many hens. There was usually one horse too, with a few noisy dogs and varying populations of cats. The *Ministry of Food* had asked all the farms to grow wheat and potatoes to help the war effort.

Winifred decided to barter her ration tickets for potatoes, a staple that really pleased the boys, no matter how they were prepared. In fact, Bunty constantly asked about boiled peelers and whenever she cooked a batch, he would devour several helpings. Mrs. Kane also discovered that her knitting was in demand with several farmers' wives, who were more than willing to trade food for her patchwork quilts. This developed into something of a side business, much to Winifred's satisfaction.

Then one day, unannounced, Bunty's father just showed up at the front door. Chief Petty Officer Digby barely had enough leave to take one day getting to Crackington Haven, two days wondering what his son was turning into, and another day to get back to **HMS Ark Royal** in Scapa Flow.

While not very culturally refined, Bunty's father was still quite generous and brought gifts, including wooden toy Spitfires for the boys and a stick of butter for Mrs. Kane. Winifred had the good sense not to ask where it came from, since it was either black market or pilfered from Navy supplies.

That night the four of them sat down for dinner.

"My boy tells me you can cook, Mrs. Kane," Charles Bunty said as he pulled up a chair. "My Marilyn was a wizard in the kitchen, so I'll be a tough sell."

Winifred smiled and looked right at Bunty. "Oh, I can't compete with your Mum's cooking. I do my best to make things scrummy, what with this rationing and all."

While meat was severely rationed, the use of offal, which applied to things like brains, kidneys, liver and other internal organs, was left to the discretion of the local butcher. Mrs. Kane had become one of Mr. Timley's favorite customers and proudly presented her latest recipe for dinner.

There were no objections to eating the strange stew.

"This makes a nice change from fish-head soup," Gavin commented after a taste.

From then on, until the meal was consumed, very little was said. They were all hungry and since Winifred had prepared a large pot, everyone partook of seconds. When finished, the boys helped Gavin's mother clear the dishes, as CPO Digby retired to the sitting room. He switched on the wireless set and the BBC War Report was heard all the way into the kitchen.

What they didn't know, however, was that Bunty's father, like so many other servicemen, enjoyed his daily glass of beer, so he had popped over to the *Coombe Barton Inn* for a pint. Even though Bunty wanted to skip school to spend more time with his dad, Winifred wouldn't allow it. Gavin never said anything disparaging to Bunty about his father, but it didn't really seem like CPO Digby had come to Cornwall to visit his son, but rather was more interested in sampling all the local brews at the neighboring pubs.

At least Bunty always knew where to look for his father. It was just a matter of finding the right pub. When he wasn't at the *Coombe Barton Inn*, it probably meant Charles Digby had ventured down the road to Boscastle or Tintagel, or even as far away as Bude.

At the top of Boscastle's steep corkscrew hill, high above *The Wellington Hotel*, stood *The Napoleon Inn*. It was said the inn served as a recruiting office during the Napoleonic Wars, but the sympathies and interests of many Cornish smugglers were more attached to their French suppliers, then with King and Country. Legends claimed that the *Napoleon Inn* was so named, because it was actually used to recruit volunteers for the enemy.

On CPO Digby's last day of leave, Bunty found his father sitting at a corner table inside the *Napoleon Inn*, nursing a full pint of bitters.

"Over here, boy," the senior Digby waved him over.

Bunty joined him.

"I wanted to see you before you went back," the boy said.

"Aye, that's a good lad."

"How do you like the **Ark Royal**, Dad?"

"She's a bit of a cow," the chief replied. "Makes a fat target for U-boats."

"Do you like bein' in the Royal Navy?"

"A lot of water has flowed past the bows to make me a chief petty officer," his father replied proudly. "Service makes a man outta ya, that's fer sure."

The conversation became stilted then, because they really didn't have much in common and even less to talk about. However, Bunty managed to snooker his old man into buying him a glass of grape fizzy, which was delicious.

In the end, when it was time for his father to leave, Bunty wasn't happy to see him go, but neither was he sad to see him go. The boy figured he could finally settle back into his normal routine.

As Chief Petty Officer Digby headed up the road, Bunty called after him.

"When will you get leave again?" the boy asked.

"That all depends on Hitler," Charles Digby replied.

"Well, give him a punch in the jaw from me!"

"That's the spirit, lad."

Then his father disappeared over the hill.

As Bunty wandered back into Crackington Haven, he spotted Gavin playing down by the seashore. They waved to each other. Nothing was said at first, but instead they just laughed and scampered through the surf, skipping rocks and being teenaged boys.

"I wish I had a dragon friend like yours," Bunty suddenly blurted.

"He's your friend too, chum," Gavin said.

"No, Thaddeus is partial to you, anyone can see that."

"He cares just as much about you and Emmy."

"Maybe. I wish I had believed in him sooner."

"I don't think Thaddeus minds. I'm sure he understood your hesitation. In the end, when it counted most, you came through."

"Let's go visit Thaddeus," Bunty suggested. "I miss him."

Not wanting to exclude Emily, they boys cut overland to Boscastle.

They were in luck, because the girl was in the front yard picking berries with her mother.

"May Emmy come play with us?" Gavin asked her mother.

"Of course, Gavin," Harriet replied. "Don't stay out too late."

"We won't, Ma," Emily assured her. "We're just going up to the old cottage on the hill."

"You dears sure do like that old hamlet," her mother commented.

"It's the view, Mrs. Scott," Gavin said. "We can see Tintagel Castle and the entire coast from up there."

"Have fun," Harriet said, waving.

The teens hurried off.

Thaddeus must have known they were coming, because as the trio stepped into the cottage, the dragon was already uncloaked.

"Good afternoon, Sir Osbert," Bunty cheerfully called out.

"Greetings to you all," Thaddeus said. "What do I owe the honor of this visit?"

"We just wanted to see you, that's all," Gavin said.

"You're always welcome. Sit her on my paws."

They did so.

"What shall we talk about today?" the dragon asked.

"I'd like to know what you do all day, especially when we're not around to entertain you?" Emily asked.

"Sleep."

"When do you eat?" Bunty asked. "I've never seen you eat anything but sweets."

Thaddeus hesitated for a moment, but then said, "I go out at night, when humans are asleep."

"Do you hunt?" Bunty asked.

The dragon nodded, but said nothing more.

As if it had been timed, Sir Osbert's stomach grumbled.

It sounded like miniature explosions tucked inside his stomach.

"Pardon me," Thaddeus said.

"Are you hungry?" Bunty seemed to ask the obvious.

"No, not at all, actually," the dragon replied. "I recently swallowed several rocks and they're settling to the bottom of my stomach."

"You eat rocks?" Bunty was bewildered.

"Dragons will occasionally swallow small rocks to aid in their digestion," Thaddeus informed him.

"Just like chickens," Emily was quick to point out.

Considering his frown, it was obvious that Thaddeus didn't appreciate the comparison. "Anyway, in the wild, when we hunt our food, and wolf it down on the run, these stones act like rear molars and help grind up the more solid bits, like bone and armor."

The teens looked at each other in surprise.

"Did you say armor?" Bunty had the courage to ask.

Thaddeus grinned with mischievous delight. "Well, not recently, of course. It has been several hundred years since I last swallowed a knight in shining armor."

His laugh boomed around them.

Suddenly aware that his sense of humor was sometimes lost on these teenagers, the dragon cleared his throat and continued the discussion.

"Seriously, in these civilized times, I seldom hunt in the wild, nor do I need to devour my meals so quickly," the dragon said. "I am able to enjoy a wide variety of delicacies."

"Besides sugar, what else do you like to eat?" Emily asked.

"Just about anything sweet, such as pastries, pies, candy, ice cream," Thaddeus replied. "For protein I'm partial to sheep or goat. It's an acquired taste, but I consider lamb the best meat charbroiled."

"Can we change the subject?" Bunty blurted. "All this talk of food is making my stomach growl now."

Everyone laughed, including the dragon.

"I have a question about something that has intrigued me since I first met you, Sir Osbert," said Gavin.

"Yes, my boy, what is it?" Thaddeus coaxed him to continue.

"Your scales are so dazzling and seem strong enough to resist any weapon man has devised," Gavin began. "How do you keep them that way?"

"The natural color of a dragon is a dark, dusky gray," Thaddeus answered. "To change the colors of my scales, I must eat certain metals or minerals. By actually ingesting and adsorbing such materials, unique compounds circulate throughout my digestive and circulatory system in solution form, eventually being deposited in the scales. This not only increases their strength, but also makes them glossy, shiny, and healthy."

"So you actually eat copper to get that tint?" Bunty asked.

"That's correct."

"Where do you find enough copper to keep them glowing?" Emily wondered.

"I swallow a penny a day," the dragon quipped.

"I've heard an apple a day keeps the doctor away, but never anything about a penny before," Bunty said.

"Copper does the same for me," Thaddeus explained. "I eat all sorts of things that would be indigestible or dangerous for humans."

"May we watch you and Gavin play a game of chess?" Emily asked.

The chessboard magically appeared and once again, the dragon and boy faced off. Over the next hour, however, the combatants only moved twice, so Bunty and Emily were seriously bored by the entire thing.

The girl yawned.

"I think that's enough for today," Thaddeus announced. "Hurry home now, before it gets too late and your mothers begin to worry."

The teens reluctantly departed, first to Boscastle to drop off Emily, before the boys raced over the hills to Crackington Haven. Gavin and Bunty had become the best of pals and were almost inseparable. This fact pleased Mrs. Kane greatly and she sometimes wished she could adopt the Digby boy and raise him as her own. Still, Bunty had a father and Winifred wasn't about to meddle in someone else's affairs, especially when it came to parenting.

14

Elfish Mischief

Much to Gavin's surprise, when he opened the red postal box in front of his house, he discovered a food parcel all the way from Canada. He brought it into the kitchen for everyone to see. It turned out to be a canned ham and the instructions for cooking were in French, which Emily was able to translate. To celebrate this culinary windfall, Winifred immediately announced they would eat the ham that very evening. She got on the telephone and called Emily's mother Harriet, who squealed with delight at the news and promised to bring something special to round out the meal. The teens were so excited and chipped right in to help Gavin's mother make preparations. They were giddy and with such high spirits, the chores were finished in no time.

Everyone sat down for a splendid dinner, which was simply delicious.

"I wonder who sent us this wonderful ham?" Gavin asked after a few bites. "It's simply scrummy."

"Better than bubble and squeak, though I do fancy some potatoes 'bout now," Bunty chimed in.

"I could see an ice lolly after this feast," Emily wished.

All three teenagers wistfully imagined their favorite flavor.

Winifred and Harriet chuckled, before getting up to clear the dishes.

"Go out and play now," Emily's mother suggested. "We'll scrounge up some bread and jam later, while we listen to the wireless."

The trio raced outside and ran up the hill behind Gavin's home, to flop in the tall grass. They were stuffed, too full to play strenuously. Laying back and gazing up at the passing clouds, all three of them were uncharacteristically quiet.

"Hello, Emmy," a childlike voice spoke out from behind them.

Emily sprang to her feet and was delighted to see it was Kitto Bideven. "Oh, how wonderful to see you again!"

The elf smiled broadly.

"Kitto, I'd like you to meet Gavin Kane and Bunty Digby," Emily introduced her friends.

The female elf's mouth dropped open, her eyes wide with awe. "The most wonderful Gavin Kane?"

Of course, poor Gavin was very uncomfortable with such instant adoration. He backed away, not certain of what he should say or do.

However, instead of escaping Kitto's admiration, he bumped into Bunty. Both Bunty and Emily laughed, but the elf came running forward to make sure Gavin wouldn't retreat any farther.

"Do not be shaky leaf," the elf said reassuringly. "I not hurt thee."

"I'm fine," Gavin replied.

Kitto swept off her cap and bowed. "My great honor to step on you. Your name is vomited through our land, with mighty sword to tickle enemy dead."

While Kitto's words were quite confusing, Gavin and Bunty were far more amazed by the girl's very pronounced pointed ears. There was no mistaking the conclusion both boys reached, at exactly the same moment.

"She's an elf!" they proclaimed in unison.

Kitto held her index finger to her lips and hissed, "Shhhhhhhhhhhhhhhh!"

It sounded like escaping gas.

Gavin recovered some of his poise and shyly said, "It's a pleasure to meet you."

Bunty nodded. "Kitto, wasn't it?"

The elf looked over her shoulder at Emily and shook her head. It appeared the boys were not making a favorable first impression.

"Head full of walnuts and spice," Kitto chattered. "No brains."

"Do all elves talk in gobbledygook?" Bunty wondered.

Kitto frowned. "You smell and borrowed us gold."

"Doesn't is seem strange she uses such bad grammar?" Gavin asked pointedly.

"Perhaps she should take lessons from a dragon we know," Bunty suggested.

Kitto giggled. "Dragons belch nonsense."

"Just how many dragons do you know?" Bunty demanded.

"Stick finger up nose," the elf replied defiantly, gesturing.

"What?" Bunty reacted.

Emily started giggling, because she knew that Kitto was capable of speaking perfectly correct King's English. It was obvious, based on the reaction of the boys, that the elf was teasing them. However, before it got out of hand, Emily quickly stepped in as peacemaker.

"No harm done, now. We're all friends here."

The elf sneered and Bunty stuck out his tongue.

Not seeing Kitto's act of escalation, Emily wagged her finger at Bunty. "Stop acting like a child."

Bunty huffed and puffed, but said nothing in his defense. Instead, the red-haired boy retreated to stand behind Gavin, as if for protection.

Kitto suddenly decided the bad-grammar game should end. "*Urulooke* is the elven word for dragon."

"*Urulooke*," Emily repeated for everyone's behalf.

"Most of the time our dragon speaks proper English," Gavin informed the elf with a grin, for he too realized Kitto had merely been playing with them. "He occasionally uses a smattering of bloody-this and bloody-that, with a snippet of Cockney slang, and some stiff upper-lip blithering thrown in for good measure."

"Does he have many teeth?" Kitto wondered. "Is he fierce?"

"Thaddeus is only fierce when he doesn't get his sugar," Bunty answered.

Kitto made a snarling face, exaggerating her curled lips and bared teeth.

"What are you doing?" Bunty demanded.

"Looking fierce," she replied.

"I don't think so," the red-haired boy said. "You couldn't scare a butterfly."

Kitto folded her arms across her chest, jutted her head forward and said, "Even our weakest warriors would frighten you to death!"

"Bah!" Bunty scoffed, folding his arms in the identical fashion.

"When preparing for battle, elven warriors don shimmering suits of hand-made plate or chainmail, and protect their heads with distinctive winged helms," Emily tried to distract their bickering, remembering a passage she had read in one of Gavin's books. "Mounted fighters ride gryphons or hippogriffs into battle, swooping down on the enemy with deadly perfection."

"Now that's something I'd like to see," Bunty said.

"Not you, smelly one," Kitto quipped.

"I do not smell!" Bunty objected loudly.

The elf skittered away. "Stinky and putrid, rotten and foul."

Bunty's face turned bright red with anger.

Gavin leaned over and whispered, "I think Kitto likes you."

Bunty was aghast. "What? Are you crazy?"

"Hey, don't get mad at me," Gavin said defensively. "I can't help it if she's acting just like some of the girls in the playground. Next thing you know, Kitto will try to steal a kiss."

Bunty made fists. "She better not!"

Emily and Gavin both laughed.

Kitto peeked out from behind a tree and her smile was sparkling.

"See, she does like you," Gavin teased.

Bunty merely sneered in return.

Emily, however, dispensed with any further discussion, noting, "Elven kisses are rarely bestowed in public, Bunty, so I wouldn't worry too much. After all, Kitto will come to her senses soon and forget the whole silly idea."

"How do you suddenly know so much about elves?" Bunty demanded.

"I read a lot, which is something you should try to do more often," Emily sniped.

"I read plenty, Miss Know-it-all!" Bunty retaliated, sticking his tongue out for good measure.

"Come on, that's enough," Gavin scolded. "We're friends here, remember? Let's not let a little elf spoil everything."

Kitto joined them again, but looked very sad. "I am sorry. I did not mean to make friends mad at each other."

"It's okay, Kitto," Emily said. "Bunty's just being difficult."

Before he could say anything, Gavin clapped his hand over Bunty's mouth. "There, there, old chap, none of that."

Kitto took Emily's hand. "We must all go cause mischief."

"Must we?" Emily wondered.

"Oh, yes, it is what elves do."

"You go ahead and play," Gavin said. "I'm not in the mood."

Bunty looked at Emily and they both winked at each other. They knew Gavin wanted to head up to the white cottage on the hill, to be alone with Thaddeus for awhile.

"You go on, then," Bunty said. "We'll catch up to you later."

Gavin smiled. "Thanks."

When Gavin reached the hamlet overlooking Tintagel Castle, he was surprised to find the front door ajar. He also heard the sounds of someone crying from inside. Fearing the worst, Gavin charged into the cottage, not knowing what to expect.

There, curled up in the corner where the fireplace usually stood, crouched Thaddeus, his expression very sad and tears rolling down his cheeks.

"Goodness gracious, Thaddeus, why are you crying?" Gavin asked.

"Just look at this," the dragon sniffled.

He held out a copy of the Times of London for Gavin to see.

The headline read:

U-boat Sinks *SS Spencer*—12,000 Bags of Sugar Lost!

"Now do you understand why I'm so upset?" Thaddeus asked.

Gavin tried not to snicker, but he couldn't help himself. "Yes, Sir Osbert, it's quite understandable. After all, that much sugar would satisfy your cravings for at least a few days." Then he burst into uncontrolled fits of laughter.

Thaddeus was shocked. "I don't think this tragedy is at all humorous."

The big beast blew his nose into a giant handkerchief.

"I'm sorry, Sir Osbert," Gavin said, wiping tears of mirth from his own eyes. "You should see yourself, a big dragon like you, crying over some sunken sugar."

The boy burst into laughter again.

Thaddeus crossed his front paws and frowned, patiently waiting for Gavin to cease his cackling. When the boy had stopped, the dragon cleared his throat and said, "Now that you're quite finished with all that guffawing, perhaps you have a suggestion how I'm going to find enough sugar to replace what went down with that ship?"

Gavin shrugged. "I dunno, Thaddeus."

The dragon mimicked the boy, shrugging and repeating, "I dunno. What kind of answer is that? Besides, what atrocious English is that? I dunno? Bah!"

Gavin stepped forward and scratched Thaddeus behind one ear. "You are exceedingly grumpy today, my friend."

The dragon sighed heavily. "Yes, I am."

"You have become too dependent on sugar, Sir Osbert."

"Perhaps."

"Maybe it's time to switch to saccharin?"

"Never!"

"Don't be so stubborn."

"Ghastly invention, I tell you. Sugar substitute? Why, it's preposterous!"

Gavin grinned. "Now don't get yourself all in a tizzy over this."

The dragon grunted and pouted. "No, unacceptable! I won't do it."

Sugar rationing had suddenly provided a unique opportunity for the growth of sugar substitutes, especially saccharin. According to government rationing controls, sugar bowls were removed from tables in all the restaurants, hotels, boarding houses, and institutions across England. Sugar came in sacks and had to be weighed into one and two pound bags. People would stand in queues for hours with their ration coupons, hoping to get a chance to purchase the maximum limit of sugar allowed.

Even during these difficult times, people waited their turn to be served, strictly in order of their arrival in the line. Anyone who tried to jump queues without a good reason were very roughly dealt with, but that was seldom necessary. Expectant mothers, the elderly or injured veterans were always spontaneously given priority by other people in line.

Yet because sugar was such an important part of everyone's diet, British citizens tried just about anything to supplement their collective sweet tooth. The fact that someone had a ration ticket did not guarantee sugar would be available. Various substitutes were used whenever possible and Karo Syrup was in great demand.

The sugar shortage meant putting less sugar in drinks and foods or finding substitutes. Honey was another popular replacement and after a number of beehives were reportedly stolen, the British Army had to assign guards to protect honey production. Coconut kisses sweetened with honey and molasses replaced chocolate kisses, while restaurants asked customers to limit sugar use. People bought more goods from bakeries to avoid depleting their own sugar supplies at home.

Later that week, Gavin actually had an opportunity to sample Saccharin, which tasted about 300 times as sweet as sucrose. Unfortunately, he was also quick to discover it had an unpleasant bitter or metallic aftertaste.

"I guess I'll drop my plans to convince Thaddeus to give saccharin a try," Gavin said to himself after making a face. "This stuff tastes good for about ten seconds, then yuck!"

One morning, after discovering there was not enough sugar to make a new batch of strawberry preserves, Gavin refused to eat breakfast. No matter how sweetly Winifred cajoled, the boy shook his head.

When Bunty came into the kitchen, he greeted everyone with, "Smashing morning."

"What's so blood …?" Gavin started to ask, before his mother's wicked glare interrupted him.

"I'm afraid we're out of sugar, Bunty," Mrs. Kane informed him.

"Oh, no bother," Bunty said cheerfully. "Could you pass the marmite, please?"

Winifred handed over the jar, her nose scrunching up a bit.

With the consistency and visual appeal of old axle grease, marmite was a yeast extract used predominately on breakfast toast. Bunty slathered it on with zeal.

"Oh, how can you stand that stuff?" Gavin demanded.

"It's an acquired taste," Bunty replied.

Gavin rolled his eyes and fumed. He started mumbling.

"What did you say, dearest?" his mother asked.

With a huff, Gavin headed for the door. "I said I'm going to have a few choice words with a dragon I know."

Winifred looked at Bunty, who shrugged.

"You better hurry and catch up with him," Mrs. Kane suggested. "You don't want to walk all the way to Launceston."

Bunty snatched his piece of toast and marmite, before scurrying out the back door. Running as fast as he could, the red-haired boy reached Gavin's side just as his friend was boarding the bus.

"Weren't you going to wait for me?"

"I guess so."

"You guess so?"

"That's right. If you weren't so bloody slow all the time, then I might now have to wait for you."

Bunty hadn't expected a tongue-lashing. He refused to sit beside Gavin on the trip to Launceston and they didn't speak to each other at school. However, when they waited to board the bus again for the trip back to Crackington Haven, Gavin was the first to offer an olive branch.

"I'm sorry about what I said, chum," Gavin said. "It wasn't right."

"No bother, sport," Bunty said cheerfully. "All is forgiven."

That quickly they were friends again.

At the crossroads, the boys exited the bus at the Tintagel stop, heading up to the little white cottage on the hill. By the time Thaddeus appeared, they were cheerful again.

"I'm tired of doing without sugar too!" Gavin announced to the dragon.

Sir Osbert was surprised by the teen's vehement statement, but said, "Then I shall share some of my supply with you."

His generous offer immediately shamed Gavin, who replied, "No, that isn't necessary, Thaddeus. You're a big dragon and need sugar more than we do. Besides, without a steady intake of sweetness, you are an exceedingly grumpy creature."

Both Bunty and Gavin bust into laughter.

15

Photographic Evidence

The year had already seen a steady parade of military disasters for England and her Commonwealth. German forces had smashed through the Balkans, conquering Greece and Yugoslavia in three weeks. A British relief force was driven into the sea and took refuge on Crete. A new German general named Erwin Rommel took command in North Africa and swept aside British forces, while driving them back into Egypt, trapping over twenty thousand British troops in a Libyan port called Tobruk.

Convoys attempting to relieve Malta were repeatedly smashed from the air. London was bombed in the deadliest raid of the war so far, as hundreds were killed. Westminster Abbey, the House of Commons, and the British Museum were all hit and damaged. In the North Atlantic, U-boats were sinking ships almost at will, attacking convoys with apparent impunity.

In the first five months of 1941, British civilian casualties from German bombing raids amounted to 18,007 killed and 20,744 injured. April and May saw the heaviest death toll, with 11,459 killed and 12,107 injured.

Even with these setbacks, there was no serious talk of surrender or conciliation, and even a negotiated peace was out of the question. Hitler would be fought and beaten, no matter how long it took or whatever the cost. No British citizen doubted that the tradition of Nelson resided at 10 Downing Street, as well as the spirit of Drake. Perhaps there was even a little of King Arthur too. Nevertheless, the people needed more than tradition, spirit, and legend to survive.

What they needed was a miracle.

Without a doubt, every political and military leader in the world would vehemently argue against anyone suggesting that a dragon might have something to do with the outcome. Such a possibility was ridiculous and absurd. However, underground in the subterranean depths of the War Room, Winston Churchill was thinking just that.

He chomped viciously on his cigar and impatiently drummed his fingers on both arms of his comfortable plush chair. In fact, his ring finger was making a noticeable impression on the soft wood. Winston was painfully aware that he couldn't come out and actually tell anyone that his faith was first in God, and then the British Empire, and finally in a bloody great dragon named Thaddeus Osbert!

"Mr. Prime Minster, I do not see the benefit of keeping the fleet bottled up in Scapa Flow," said Admiral of the Fleet and First Sea Lord, Sir Dudley Pound, who always spoke his mind to Churchill directly.

Churchill's uneasy relationship with his military leaders stemmed, in large part, from his willingness to pick commanders who disagreed with him. He considered this a vital part of innovation and preferred aggressive action over any other option.

"The fleet must remain in Scapa Flow, because their primary duty is convoy protection," Churchill stated. "If the Germans do venture forth with their battleships, we'll have plenty of firepower to match theirs."

At **RAF Medmenham**, Lieutenant Commander Richard Kane was busy directing the ongoing efforts of his photographic analysis team. The first phase of interpretation on newly arrived reconnaissance photographs was conducted by available Wren section officers. A stereoscope was used to examine two consecutive photographs of the same object, to achieve a three-dimensional effect. Anything of interest was set aside for examination by a different set of eyes.

The correct interpretation of any snapshot depended not only on the expertise of the interpreter, but also on the resolution of the photo and on the sharpness of its focus, on the quality of the cameras, films, and the photographing technique. Stereoscopy effected great improvements in air photo interpretation. In this technique, two photos of the same area were taken in rapid succession. Due to the motion of the airplane, the angle at which the photos are taken changed somewhat in that brief time. If those two slightly different photos were then viewed through a stereoscope, one picture with each eye, the result was a three-dimensional effect that allowed for the easy differentiation between raised and flat objects on the ground.

Most of Richard's staff was female and despite the stress, monotony, lack of privacy, and long hours, the women in the photographic analysis section really performed their duties admirably. He was truly impressed with their attention to detail and made a point of mentioning their exemplary work in his daily reports.

Life was not always easy for the women. Shift work duties interrupted regular sleeping and eating habits, which led to health related problems. Women working the midnight shift found it difficult to sleep, while their barrack-mates conducted normal daytime activities. Lack of sleep often led to irritability and even open arguments, which tested the lieutenant commander's patience, but he managed to keep morale relatively high. In fact, it was after Richard turned to his wife for suggestions that things improved dramatically.

Dearest Wini,

I need your help. Most of the staff here is female and the Wrens are doing a marvelous job. However, the present workload and changing shift schedules play havoc with the women's health. Do you have any constructive ideas to help alleviate the stress?

**Love,
Richard**

Several days later, Lieutenant Commander Kane received his answer.

Oh, you poor dear,

The solution is really quite simple. Chocolate, flowers, real stockings and some time off, so the Wrens can take a hot bath. If you put these steps into place, I guarantee a significant improvement in their health and morale.

**Love,
Wini**

PostScript—I could do with a few of those things too, so if you have anything left over, send it home to me!

One bleak morning in late May, orders were issued from Coastal Command to send Wing Commander Ian Warwick out on a high-priority mission over Norway. In fact, the top-notch reconnaissance pilot had been specially selected to seek out the dreaded German battleship *Bismarck*.

To enhance the element of surprise, the mission was to be flown just above sea level, from the English coast to the target area. By doing so, the aircraft would be safely below all enemy radar surveillance and subject to minimum detection. The tradeoff achieved from cloudless conditions would more than make up for the amount of distortion experienced from the oblique photography taken at such extreme low altitudes at speeds of 300 miles-per-hour or more. Warwick's Spitfire was retrofitted with the installation of right and left side-angled cameras, equipped to run continuously with the nose camera, also installed in the oblique position.

However, before Ian reached the Norwegian coast, he ran into a random German fighter patrol, so he rapidly gained altitude to escape pursuit. This maneuver proved to be fortuitous, because when Warwick burst through the clouds, he immediately spotted what the air patrols had been protecting. The wing commander successfully identified and photographed two large German warships in the Korsfjord, from an altitude of 26,200 feet and then returned to Scotland, where he landed at *RAF Wick Airfield*.

As soon as the aircraft rolled to a stop for refueling, the film was removed from the cameras and new film installed. It took less than an hour to develop the film and process prints, which were then flown down to *RAF Medmenham*. While this was going on, Ian and the other line mechanics checked the Spitfire for anything needing immediate attention and the plane was given a thorough check-over. Warwick was ready to go up again if necessary.

Several very clear photographs were developed. Warwick's Spitfire had snapped a series of shots with *Bismarck* at anchor in the Grimstadfjord, with three resupply merchant ships. Various steamers were anchored nearby, to serve as torpedo shields in case of enemy attack.

Meanwhile, in the little white cottage on the hill, Thaddeus had received a mysterious communiqué warning the dragon that something monumental was about to occur out to sea. He was about to take flight, when Gavin Kane arrived unexpectedly.

"Hello," the boy said glumly upon entering the cottage.

"Right now is not a good time, lad," the dragon hesitated saying. "I was just leaving."

Gavin thought he knew what Thaddeus was up to and scolded him, "Now don't you go on one of your sugar warehouse raids, Sir Osbert. England is suffering from a serious shortage as it is, without compounding it with a certain voracious dragon I know."

Thaddeus was insulted and roared, "I was not going out to steal sugar, young man. I have duties to perform and will not have you lecturing me. Is that understood?"

Gavin cringed under the dragon's harsh tongue and Thaddeus immediately felt guilty for losing his temper.

"I'm sorry, lad. I didn't mean to growl in your face."

"That's okay, Thaddeus. I didn't mean to accuse you of anything."

The big dragon lifted his wings, preparing to launch himself into the air. He waited until the roof of the hamlet parted wide enough to make room for his exit.

"May I go with you, please?" Gavin asked.

"No, it's far too dangerous this time," Thaddeus replied.

"For you or for me?" Gavin countered. "I thought we were partners, or was all that stuff you told me just exaggeration?"

The dragon spun around, his teeth bared. "How dare you insinuate such a thing!"

The force of the creature's breath whipped the boy's hair from his face.

Yet Gavin didn't retreat, standing his ground. "I cannot safeguard what is truly important to England, if I let something terrible befall you, Sir Thaddeus Osbert. If I am the true protector of the Kane legacy, then perhaps I have earned the right to accompany you wherever you travel, with or without that bloody great sword."

"Wha …?" Thaddeus pulled back his head in shock.

The young man said nothing more, but with his hands on his hips, he painted the picture of defiance and confidence, all rolled into one. It was impossible to ignore, but at only the age of thirteen, as Gavin Stuart Kane stood before the dragon, it was obvious he was growing into a man.

Thaddeus nodded his understanding. "I'm not too proud, nor am I too stupid to turn down your help, Sir Kane. Climb up here on my shoulders and we'll do this together."

Gavin ran forward and scrambled up the dragon's tail, taking his usual place on the creature's broad shoulders. Once the boy's legs were draped to either side of the beast's neck and the scales were lifted as protection, he patted Thaddeus on the ear.

"Ready when you are, Thaddeus."

With a mighty leap, the dragon hurled himself high into the air, his wings unfolding and flapping with powerful downward beats. It was not as graceful a take-off as he had executed in the past, but still sufficient to get him airborne. With a gust of wind to aid his flight, Thaddeus headed upwards towards the clouds.

"Would you mind awfully, if we made a slight detour to my house, Thaddeus?" Gavin inquired.

"What for, old chap?" the dragon asked in an exaggerated British accent.

"I want to pick up my flying helmet and goggles."

"Right-oh then, here we go." The dragon engaged his invisibility cloaking.

Thaddeus swooped down over Crackington Haven and dropped Gavin off on the roof of the Kane house. The boy scrambled along the tiles and slipped through his open bedroom window, where he grabbed his flying gear. Then, without a moment to waste, he climbed back up and jumped on the dragon's back.

They were off!

"Thanks, chum," Gavin shouted over the wind whistling past his head.

"No bother," Thaddeus replied.

"So where are we headed?" Gavin asked.

"We're looking for the German battleship *Bismarck*," Thaddeus replied.

"Bloody marvelous," Gavin reacted. "How come?"

"It's a complicated story," the dragon shouted over the wind. "Let's just say I feel the need to watch over certain events as they unfold."

Gavin hugged Thaddeus and called out, "You are a compassionate and caring dragon. Perhaps you and I can make a difference in this war after all, and save lives while we're at it."

Thaddeus merely nodded. He was often amazed by the boy's sense of duty to a greater good, rather than merely victory and honor. Gavin truly cared about people and that trait probably would make a difference in the final outcome.

However, no amount of defending England would justify the dragon's direct interference in the course of the war. Thaddeus could observe and advise, he could even offer transport, but in no way could he participate in any direct military action. Such a violation would once again get him in serious trouble with the Dragon High Council.

This time, no matter how serious the temptation, Sir Osbert swore he would remain a bystander.

No matter what.

Still, based on past history, that might be easier said than done.

Gavin looked down at his hands and realized his knuckles were white from gripping the dragon's scales so tightly. Very slowly, he released his hold and flexed his fingers to relieve the stiffness.

Thaddeus chuckled. "I was wondering how long it would take you to trust my flying skills. We dragons were born to fly."

"I'm sorry," the boy apologized. "Flying may be natural for you, but I'm still not used to being on your back."

The dragon shouted, "Hang on, boy, because I'm going to pick up the speed. We must reach our destination by a certain moment in time?"

Gavin's hand instinctively shot back towards the scale he had been holding. He didn't care if such an act was a sign of weakness. It made more sense not to fall off.

"Do you know where you're heading?" Gavin asked as the coastline disappeared behind them.

"Of course," replied Thaddeus. "Are you questioning my navigational skills?"

"I wouldn't think of it," the teen said as he shook his head.

Thaddeus tucked his wings, which instantly propelled him faster and faster. Everything below grew smaller and smaller, until the world shrunk to tiny dots moving across a vast green carpet.

The dragon gazed up into the sky, his breath forming clouds of crystallized vapor. From this height, Gavin could see for almost fifty miles in every direction. Thaddeus checked to make sure the boy was secure as he gently shifted the teen's weight on his neck. The dark line of an advancing storm closed on them from the northwest and the dragon worried he might not be able to outrun it. While invisible to the human eye, Thaddeus cast strange shadows on the surface below and in the waning light, his scales reflected a muted red.

To aid his flight-plan, the dragon switched lenses, projecting a golden-white beam of light, which cut through the encroaching darkness like searchlights. He continuously scanned the stillness of the dark forest and rock beneath him.

The wind whipped past his scales with a powerful and continuous flow.

It was then that Thaddeus heard Gavin laugh out loud.

"Yippee!" the boy shouted, lifted his arms over his head. "Whoopee, this is fantastic. Go, Thaddeus, go."

The dragon grinned and shared in his passenger's delight. To be able to fly was the one true indication that he was still alive, free to soar above the clouds. He snapped his wings out to their fullest extension and felt the wind tug against the surface of the membranes, gaining every inch of lift. Thaddeus flipped down a different set of outer protective lids over his eyes, and the landscape below became three-dimensional in detail. Sir Osbert swooped lower and with an extra burst of speed, headed straight for the Scottish Highlands.

At the last minute, Thaddeus veered away from the jutting mountains, twisted his wings while pumping frantically, and gained altitude almost vertically. The powerful muscles along the dragon's neck strained as he propelled himself higher and higher.

The change in altitude made Gavin light-headed for a moment, but before it became a problem, Thaddeus was heading back down to earth. The dragon straightened his wings and coasted. As the trees sped past beneath them, the boy realized the dragon was just skimming the pointy tops of the evergreen trees.

Then, without warning, it began to rain.

In sheets it came, a torrential downpour that drenched both dragon and rider in seconds. Gavin could no longer see the familiar treetops, only walls of water coming down almost sideways.

A jagged bolt of lightning crackled and exploded so close that it lit up the sky all around them. Thaddeus struggled against the swirling howling winds, using his wings to shield his passenger as much as possible, without losing flight integrity. As the dragon lifted his head higher, water cascaded down and entered his horned ears.

Gavin flinched again when another flash of lightning ripped the sky apart and he ducked down behind the raised scales, which briefly drown out the wind's incredible roar.

To the dragon, this inclement weather didn't make any sense.

There had been no red sky in the morning to give warning. Thaddeus was perfectly capable of translating the clues regarding the weather and thunderstorms were not part of his forecast.

So how could he have been so mistaken?

Something wasn't right. The dragon was suddenly convinced that a malignant power was behind the squalls and gale-force winds. It was as if the weather was being wielded like a weapon.

Thaddeus flew ahead of the storm, along the leading edge. With no moon or stars to direct him, he depended on the startling glow of crackling lightning to illuminate the path ahead. Towering black thunderheads coiled and twisted, boiling up and ripping the surface off the sea with a howling roar.

"It's like being caught on a giant chessboard," Gavin shouted his observation.

Thaddeus smiled grimly and pushed on.

16

Brazen Breakout

The 41,673-ton **Bismarck** was the largest battleship in the German fleet, and the pride of the German Navy. Newly commissioned on August 24, 1940, she subsequently sailed to port in Gotenhafen, in occupied Poland. On May 19, 1941, after finishing work and sea trails, Bismarck left Gotenhafen, accompanied by the eight-inched gunned cruiser **Prinz Eugen**, to begin *Operation Rhine*. Their mission was to attack British shipping, mainly convoys between Halifax and the British Isles. The British were aware of this new titan-of-the-seas and **Bismarck** had been spotted by Ian Warwick's RAF Spitfire, just two days out of port on her maiden voyage.

That very afternoon Winston Churchill cabled the US President, Franklin D. Roosevelt. His message read:

Yesterday, twenty-first, **Bismarck**, **Prinz Eugen** and eight merchant ships located
in Bergen. Low clouds prevented air attack. Tonight we discovered they have
sailed. We have reason to believe that a formidable Atlantic raid is intended.
Should we fail to catch them going out, your Navy should surely be able to mark
them down for us. **King George V**, **Prince of Wales**, **Hood**, **Repulse,** and aircraft
carrier **Victorious**, with auxiliary vessels will be on their track. Give us the news
and we will finish the job.

Horror distracted the Allied forces when **Bismarck** and her consort sailed from the Kors Fjord, near Bergen, Norway. There were eleven convoys at sea and one, which was bound for the Middle East, was loaded with troops. The battle-cruiser **HMS Hood** and the battleship **HMS Prince of Wales** put to sea from Scapa Flow and made for the Denmark Straits, the 80-mile-wide passage between Greenland and Iceland.

This was where the cruisers **Suffolk** and **Norfolk** had sighted the German ships and broadcast the alarm. **Bismarck** turned and opened fire, hurling several salvoes at her tormentors. Unharmed and continuing to broadcast sighting signals, the cruisers turned away and began shadowing *Bismarck*, remaining just out of range and concealed by the constant swirling fog. *Hood* and *Prince of Wales*, skirting the Greenland ice, charged in to make the kill. They turned line abreast and began the naval battle of the century.

May 24 turned out to be a day that rocked the British Navy, shattering the world's confidence and depressing an entire nation. At a range of 25,000 yards, the furious action began. Exchanging salvo after salvo, *Hood* and *Prince of Wales* concentrated their fire on *Bismarck*.

In response, *Bismarck* and *Prinz Eugen* returned full broadsides, but targeted their rounds solely on *HMS Hood*. Those first shots bracketed both British ships, sending geysers of water towering into the air.

The opening salvo was far too close for comfort.

Baboom!

Bismarck's mighty guns roared.

Exactly eight minutes after the action began, one of *Bismarck's* shells penetrated *Hood's* main deck and plunged into her vulnerable magazines.

Kaboom!

As if struck by a comet, the sky was suddenly filled with a bright light, immediately followed by the thunderclap reverberations of an incredible explosion. The entire bow of the *Hood* was hurled up out of the sea, before the fore part of the ship began to sink. A giant cloud of black smoke hovered over the scene, temporarily masking the location of the calamity.

When it cleared, the *Hood* had completely vanished.

HMS Hood had blown up and sank immediately.

Several escort destroyers circled the area, searching for any survivors. The rescue teams were terribly shocked by the sight of so many bodies being dragged from the sea.

There were only three survivors out of the *Hood's* complement of 1,418 men.

The *Prince of Wales*, with two of her turrets completely out of action and spewing forth dense brown smoke, desperately turned away, but not before hitting *Bismarck* with two of her own fourteen-inch shells. One of them crashed through the German battleship's bow and started a leak in the fuel bunkers. Losing oil, *Bismarck* turned south, assuming a new course and heading for St. Nazaire in France. In the confusion, *Prinz Eugen* was able to break away undetected, steaming off to the north to carry out her own style of commerce raiding.

On the following day, things continued to go badly for the British. That morning, *Norfolk*, *Suffolk*, and the *Prince of Wales* lost track of *Bismarck* in the dense fog. Even worse, believing that *Bismarck* was returning to her base by making for the Iceland-Faeroes gap, *King George V*, *Rodney*, *Repulse*, and *Victorious* turned to the northeast, actually away from the German battleship's true destination.

However, later that afternoon *Bismarck's* commanding officer foolishly sent a long, thirty-minute message boasting of the victory over the *Hood*. It was picked up by radio directional finders, and fresh coordinates were sent to the English fleet. The ships reversed course and closed in. Unfortunately, *Bismarck* was now 110 miles ahead of her pursuers. Nothing short of a miracle would stop her from reaching the safety of the French port.

Adding more insult to injury, the British were running low on fuel too.

The *Prince of Wales* broke off and headed for Iceland to replenish her supply, while *Repulse* made for Newfoundland, with her tanks nearly dry.

The British Admiralty announced the loss of *HMS Hood* in the form of a simple communiqué, which read:

British naval forces intercepted early this morning off the coast of Greenland German naval forces including the battleship *Bismarck*.

The enemy were attacked, and during the ensuing action *H.M.S. Hood* (Major R. Kerr, C.B.E., R.N.) wearing the flag of Vice-Admiral L.F. Holland, C.B., received an unlucky hit in the magazine and blew up.

The *Bismarck* has received damage and the pursuit of the enemy continues. It is feared there will be few survivors from *H.M.S. Hood*.

The Times of London carried the story matter-of-factly on page 4, calling it, *the heaviest blow the navy has received in the war* and an editorial characterized it as a *heavy calamity*.

The loss of *HMS Hood* shocked all of England and the free world. The feelings of horror and anger were something no words could describe.

The German communiqués refrained from their typical gloating, simply stating that *HMS Hood* had been sunk in a five-minute engagement between a German flotilla and heavy English naval forces, and that the Germans had received no damage worthy of mention in return.

The chase for the *Bismarck* instantly became electrically tense, where no one and nothing was spared. Throughout the Royal Navy, the call went out and in no uncertain terms, Winston Churchill gave orders to, "Sink the *Bismarck*!"

As it happened, a few hours earlier, two Coastal Command Catalina flying boats had taken off from the RAF base in Castle Archdale, on Lough Erne, Northern Ireland, hoping to discover the whereabouts of the elusive *Bismarck*.

United States Navy Ensign Leonard "Tuck" Smith was sitting in the copilot's seat, with RAF Flying Officer Dennis Briggs in command.

Yet this was May 1941 and the United States of America was still officially neutral. Secretly the young ensign was on loan to the British from the US Navy, in order to check out the pilots who would fly the Catalinas loaned by the United States to the RAF, under the Lend-Lease program. The big seaplanes could fly for ten to twelve hours, and were particularly suited to the Atlantic coastal patrols so essential to the protection of British merchant ships.

Two hundred miles to the south, but closing rapidly, a dragon named Thaddeus Osbert was racing with the wind at his tail. Sitting on his shoulder was Gavin Kane and together they were also seeking the **Bismarck**. The boy was quite certain that his dragon friend would have no difficulty in tracking down the vaunted German behemoth.

One Catalina PBY headed due north and the other turned in a southeasterly direction. In either case, on their present course and heading, both reconnaissance airplanes would miss spotting the elusive battleship.

Severe stormy weather over the North Sea was not uncommon. Extremely strong winds were sending active waves toward the European continent, while the violent seas churned up clouds of sediment, staining the water with a brownish-green hue.

While the clouds of war encompassed all of Europe, massive black thunderheads darkened the skies over most of the Atlantic Ocean. Driving this threatening weather were powerful updrafts and downdrafts. Looking like marshmallow castles, there were spectacular bands and whorls of swirling clouds, punctuated by lightning strikes, strong winds, and lashing rain.

Flying through this mess presented quite a challenge for the dragon, but not as a test of his airborne skills, but rather keeping his passenger firmly situated on his neck. Thaddeus was traveling at spectacular speeds, zipping into clouds and back out again.

By its very nature, the dragon was the master of tempests, able to tame the wind and subdue lightning. As Sir Osbert tucked his wings and put on another burst of speed, a haunting sound cut through the storm's roar.

"What is that?" Gavin shouted.

Thaddeus knew what it was, but he was unwilling to admit it. Instead, he called out, "Hold on, Gavin. We're going to get closer to the sea, away from all this turbulence."

"Whatever you say, Thaddeus," the boy cried. "My eyes are closed."

The dragon smiled.

Then he heard that sound again.

It was the echo of mighty wings flapping, but not his own.

Was that possible?

Could it be?

If so, why was another dragon following them?

17

Gentle Nudge

At that very moment, Thaddeus was speeding northeast, with Gavin holding on tightly. The dragon was flying as fast as he dare with a passenger aboard.

"Will we make it ahead of this?" the boy shouted over the wind and thunder of an encroaching storm that had been chasing them the entire way.

"I hope so," the dragon roared.

The weather was dark and ominous, with thick clouds and heavy rain. Thaddeus was flying without any navigational aides. Rain was beating down on Gavin's head and fogged up his new flying goggles, badly obscuring his vision as well. The dragon thought he could climb above the clouds, but quickly discovered he was wrong. Thaddeus made it to 8,000 feet, looking for a break in the clouds, but there was none. He could go no further without endangering Gavin, who was having difficult breathing as it was.

Suddenly, the dragon lost control of his wings and began to spiral downward. He struggled to regain control, but to no avail. Thaddeus could speed up or slow down, but he could not stop the spin.

Gavin closed his eyes and held on his all his might.

Thaddeus was unsure of his location, but knew he was falling rapidly and might smash into one of the Scottish mountains before coming out of the overcast skies. Everything around them became darker, and the clouds were turning a strange yellowish-brown. The rain came down even heavier. There was something unnatural about the storm, as if some unearthly power was behind it.

At two hundred feet and still spiraling downward, Thaddeus began to see a bit of daylight through the murky gloom, but his descent toward seemingly inevitable death was far from over. Struggling to regain the strength in his wings seemed fruitless, but he had to try.

The dragon came hurtling earthward at over 150 miles per hour. Thaddeus emerged from the clouds, coming out directly over rotating waters, which he recognized as the Firth of Forth. Yet he was still falling. Directly before him rose a stone seawall, with a path, road, and railings on top of it. The road seemed to be slowly curving from left to right. The fog and mist swirled before him, down to barely forty feet above the ground. The dragon was now just twenty feet from colliding with the cliffs and within an instant of tragedy.

Gavin opened his eyes again, just in time to see a young girl with a baby carriage running through the pouring rain.

"Look out!" the boy shouted.

The girl looked up at the sound of a voice overhead, but could see nothing, since the dragon and his passenger were invisible. However, feeling a rush of hot air, she ducked her head and barely avoided being clipped by the dragon's wingtip. Thaddeus succeeded in leveling out after that. He barely missed striking the water, after clearing the seawall by only a few inches.

The dragon was skimming only feet above the stony beach. Fog and rain obscured practically all visibility, but Thaddeus somehow regained his bearings. Then the downpour became a deluge, the sky growing dark once again, and Gavin was badly shaken.

A bolt of lightning lashed out violently and struck Thaddeus in the tail. However, instead of this being a bad thing, the charge of electricity instantly cleared the dragon's wings of ice and he could fly once again.

Regaining altitude quickly, Thaddeus headed out over the North Sea.

"That was close," Gavin found the strength to say.

"Too close," the creature agreed. "Something evil tainted that storm."

Gavin didn't know how to react to the dragon's observation, so instead he focused on their mission, which had been interrupted by the horrible weather.

"How will you find the **Bismarck**?" Gavin asked.

"All things man-made give off a spectral signature," the dragon tried to explain. "I have special lenses that can locate the heat of life. I'm scanning the ocean looking for a collection of human bodies encased in a large metal container."

Gavin was impressed. "Wow, you dragons sure can do a lot of neat things."

An hour later, the boy gave a start, as a dark shape appeared on the far horizon. Gavin's heart furiously banged against his chest and he was suddenly incapable of swallowing. With trembling fingers, he made fine adjustments to the focusing knob, before pressing the binoculars against his eyes.

There was dark smoke billowing up from a funnel.

It looked like a ship hull down.

In an instant, time held still and Gavin could see everything with brilliant clarity.

There was a great mast and the tip of a single raked stack, with massive upper works. The closer they went, the bigger its silhouette became, looming up before them.

No doubt about it, it was a capital ship.

"There it is, Thaddeus," Gavin exclaimed. "That must be the *Bismarck*!"

The dragon nodded his agreement and tucked his wings close to his body, dropping down out of the clouds like a bullet. Thaddeus skirted around a thick bank of fog and slowed his approach. They were about 700 kilometers from the coast of Northern France. The vessel matched the description of the German battleship, so the dragon intensified his chemical invisibility, before going down to take a closer look.

Thaddeus coasted over the battleship, soaring just above the mainmast.

They were so close to *Bismarck* that Gavin could see every detail, such as her forward director turned toward him, the emerging sun reflecting from the glass on the bridge, life rafts hanging from the superstructure, searchlights mounted on her upper works and past the signature single-raked stack, with silver-gray funnel cowling. As Thaddeus zoomed over *Bismarck*, Gavin could almost touch her rigging, antennas, and even the battle ensign whipping from her mainmast. Her 15-inch guns seemed to be pointed up at them, but he quickly remembered that Thaddeus was invisible to the human eye.

Bismarck carried at great height above it, a flying bridge between turret mast and funnel, which accommodated the supports for the ship's cranes. It was here the dragon landed, sitting like a giant bird overlooking the great battleship.

The North Atlantic was gray and brooding, swirling mists and banks of fog obscuring the early morning sun and lending a leaden hue to the surging swell. Chains of atmospheric depressions swept across the frigid waters with gale-force winds, building sea upon sea, unchecked rollers sweeping implacably across the length of the ocean like an endless procession of gray hills.

Sweeping his eyes before him like the great predator he was, the dragon grunted in frustration, as time-and-again his lenses fogged over with swirls of frosty mist. Far below, the sea was as hard and cold as slate, while on the eastern horizon, where occasional shafts of feeble sunlight broke through, it appeared like molten chrome. To the north, towering clouds massed and rolled across the horizon, lightning flashing as if doing battle. Giant thunderheads collided, blended, and darkened the horizon, unleashing solid sheets of rain.

The cold was bitter, born on the brunt of Arctic winds that whistled past the dragon's scales and ripped the tops from the ocean whitecaps in gray-white sheets. The shock of the frozen air whipped Gavin's breath away in solid banners of vapor, causing him to gasp. Tears streamed from his eyes and across his cheeks, the icy spray scoring his face like frozen sand and coating his lips with salt. The boy tried to contract his body into his coat and cinched his muffler until it almost strangled him. Nevertheless, the cold found its way between his gloves and sleeves, seeping in around the scarf as if it were full of holes. Down below, the sea was very active, with white foam from breaking waves blowing in streaks across *Bismarck's* bow.

Bismarck was 823 feet long, with the unusually wide beam of 118 feet, and she was armed with a main battery of eight 15-inch guns, while capable of thirty knots. She was intricately compartmented and would be hard to sink. Yet the ship's design left her rudders and steering gear poorly protected, and her communications and data-transmitting systems vulnerable. Worse, because her fifteen-inch ammunition was poorly fused, many of her shells would not explode. However, *Bismarck* was a convoy killer with massive secondary batteries including twelve 150-millimeter guns, sixteen 105-millimeter guns, sixteen 37-millimeter guns and twelve 20-millimeter guns.

"What should we do, Sir Osbert?" the boy shouted over the howling winds. "We must stop *Bismarck* from destroying England's convoys."

"I cannot attack the ship directly, Gavin," Thaddeus replied. "Such an act would be yet another violation of the dragon code. I am just getting used to my freedom again."

"Is there anything we can do?"

The dragon pondered the boy's question, when he suddenly saw the reflection of something glittering in the distant clouds, heading the wrong way.

"Hang on, lad. I've got an idea."

Thaddeus launched himself into the air and took off in the opposite direction the battleship was sailing. He was chasing after a specific target, something his acute hearing and keen eyesight had picked out of all the sounds of the storm around them.

It was the grinding rumble of airplane engines, heading away.

Coastal Command Catalina Z was flying high in search of the battleship *Bismarck*. However, the airplane was heading in the opposite direction from where the enemy ship actually steered. The aircrew of ten, including pilot, an American co-pilot, bow turret gunner, flight mechanic, radioman, navigator, two waist gunners, and tail gunner, were all looking for the German battleship, but without success. The aircraft's parasol wing and large waist blisters allowed for a great deal of visibility, which combined with its long range and endurance, made it well suited for the task.

Thaddeus raced ahead on an intercept course.

Catalina Z was commanded by Flying Officer Dennis Briggs, who was flying in a northwesterly direction, while everyone on board was trying to scan the seas below. The conditions were certainly unfavorable and the crew was becoming despondent.

Unbeknownst to them, outside the airplane and out of sight behind a cloud, a dragon was positioning himself to interfere with the Catalina's flight plan.

"Please be careful, Sir Osbert," Gavin cautioned.

"Yes, Gavin Kane, I will be," the dragon replied.

Thaddeus closed the distance, closer and closer, until he was almost alongside the Catalina. Then, with a carefully timed bump of his wing, the dragon nudged the airplane in an entirely new direction.

"There, perhaps that will make a difference," Thaddeus said.

Gavin patted the dragon on his neck and scratched the beast behind his ears. "I think they'll see the **Bismarck** now."

The flight-crew reacted to the unexpected jolt.

"Whoa!" Flying Officer Briggs exclaimed, fighting with the controls.

"That was some turbulence," US Navy Ensign Tuck Smith called out.

Briggs looked at the controls. "Now we're on a completely new heading."

"That's not possible," Ensign Smith said. "Is it?"

Briggs shrugged. "No matter. I'll get us back on the original heading."

Without understanding why he did so, Ensign Smith looked down through the fog and saw a great battleship directly below them.

Pointing, Smith shouted, "Gee, we were sent out to look for it, there it is!"

Briggs first looked down, and then over at Smith. They both shared silly grins.

"Let's take a closer look, shall we?" Briggs suggested.

The Catalina quickly dropped altitude, coming out of the thick cloud cover. The German battleship immediately began blasting away with very accurate anti-aircraft fire.

The pilot took evasive action after the fuselage was holed by shrapnel.

"Jettison those depth charges!" Briggs commanded.

Free of the extra weight, the PBY was able to evade the enemy fire and returned to the relative safety of the clouds.

The Catalina flying boat headed up into the clouds to elude the anti-aircraft shells coming from Germany's greatest battleship. Sitting in the copilot's seat was Tuck Smith, a young US ensign having the adventure of his life, even though he was not supposed to be there. Ensign Smith had spotted the **Bismarck**. They would stick with her until the Royal Air Force and the Royal Navy were able to converge.

"We'll shadow her for as long as possible," Briggs informed the crew.

Flying Officer Briggs immediately reported to Coastal Command, sending the message, "Have sighted enemy battleship, bearing 240 degrees, distance 5 miles, and course 150 degrees. My position is 49 degrees 33' North, 21 degrees 47' West."

The **Bismarck** had finally been located, with a little help from a dragon.

18

Sink the Bismarck!

After more than 31 hours since contact was broken, the **Bismarck** had been located again. Unfortunately, for the British, however, Admiral Tovey's ships were too far away from the German battleship. The **King George V** was 135 miles to the north, and the **Rodney** was 125 miles to the northeast. They would never catch up with the **Bismarck**, unless her speed could be seriously reduced.

Only Force H, sailing from Gibraltar, had a chance to intercept **Bismarck**. The battlecruiser **Renown** was in the best position, but having lost the **Hood** only two days earlier, the British Admiralty wouldn't permit **Renown** to engage the **Bismarck**. The best hope for the British was to launch an air strike from the carrier **Ark Royal**. The **Ark Royal** had already launched 10 Swordfish to try finding the **Bismarck**, and once the report of the Catalina sighting arrived, the two closest Swordfish altered course to intercept. Swordfish 2H located the German battleship too, followed seven minutes later by 2F. Shortly afterwards two more Swordfish, fitted with long-range tanks, were launched to relieve 2H and 2F and keep in touch with **Bismarck**.

Later, fifteen Swordfish took off from the **Ark Royal** to attack the **Bismarck**. They obtained radar contact with a ship and dived to attack. The attack, however, turned out to be a failure, because the ship sighted was actually the light cruiser **HMS Sheffield**, which had been detached from Force H to make contact with the **Bismarck**. Luckily, for the British, the **Sheffield** was not hit by any of the 11 torpedoes launched, because they had magnetic detonators, which were hopelessly unreliable. Two torpedoes exploded upon hitting the water and three blew up after crossing the cruiser's wake, as **Sheffield** maneuvered wildly in the rough seas, to escape unscathed. The Swordfish returned to the **Ark Royal** to be re-armed and the **Sheffield** again obtained visual contact with the **Bismarck**. There was no time for recriminations and the fiasco proved valuable.

The British put every effort into one last attack. It would be dark soon, and they knew this was their last real chance to stop, or at least slow down, the **Bis-**

marck. If they failed again, **Bismarck** would reach the French coast on the next day, since another attack late at night was unlikely to succeed. Late in the day, another group comprised of fifteen Swordfish, mostly the same used in the previous attack, took off from the **Ark Royal**, and this time their torpedoes were armed with contact detonators.

The Fairey Swordfish engine started easily, being warm from the previous flight. Raindrops rippled the puddles on the aircraft carrier **HMS Ark Royal's** flight deck. Sub-Lieutenant John Mobley was wearing his leather flight-jacket, leather helmet, and silk scarf as he mounted up, belted in, and pulled the release for the tail rope. Past experience had shown the prop blast tended to keep rain away from the open cockpit. It seemed to work as he slowly taxied ahead.

The Swordfish received the *Stringbag* nickname, not because of its construction, but because of the seemingly endless variety of stores and equipment the aircraft was cleared to carry. Crews likened the aircraft to a housewife's shopping bag, which was common at the time and, due to its having no fixed shape, could adjust to hold any size or number of packages. Like the shopping bag, flight crews thought the Swordfish *could carry just about anything*.

When Mobley pulled his goggles down, they were covered with raindrops. He wiped them with the back of his glove, only to be rewarded with smears. His handkerchief was out of reach and his scarf was tightly wrapped around his neck. John gave it a minute or so to clear, while he waited for the signal to take off.

Timing was everything, and the deck officer was crucial, because he knew how the ship rolled and when the planes could depart safely. Reggie "Bats" Cortland was brilliant, but because of the gale, he had to be tied to the deck. When Cortland signaled it was time to go, Mobley knew it was time to go.

Taking off from the deck of the carrier in a Force-9 gale was quite something, but Mobley was able to climb up to the proper altitude without too much effort. He was still blind up forward. The droplets flowed up the windshield, piling up at the top. Occasionally, a large drop would flip past the rim and plummet toward his knees. The droplets didn't go straight up the windshield, due to the prop blast, but Mobley could wiggle the tracks with a little rudder pressure.

The Fairey Swordfish biplanes took off in formations of three. Sub-Lieutenant John Mobley was the wingman flying beside the Commanding Officer, Lieutenant Tommy Crackston. They flew just below cloud level, until they spotted **HMS Sheffield**, which signaled with an Aldis lamp, giving them the bearing and the distance to the **Bismarck**. The CO gave everyone a hand signal to show that they had to climb up into the clouds to over 6,000 feet. Mobley's observer and navigator was Squaddie Watkins, who did his best to call out conditions and keep an eye on the flight leader's messages, while Radcliff would drive off any German fighters with his swivel machinegun.

As the speed increased, the windshield got blurrier. By the time they circled around **HMS Ark Royal**, forward visibility was gone. The view to either side was great, but the rain completely obscured the windshield. The conditions were appalling.

Kicking the rudder from side to side, Mobley could see forward occasionally. A little bit of yaw let him look past the windshield almost straight ahead, and he kept a gentle serpentine path to clear the area along his anticipated track.

The Swordfish had an open cockpit, which was brutal when operating in the North Sea, it didn't have radar, and lacked a sensitive altimeter, which was a crucial bit of equipment since the temperamental torpedoes had to be dropped from a height of 60 feet, no more and no less.

Overall, Mobley wasn't too uncomfortable. His flight-jacket handled the freezing temperature, while his flight suit and boots were well out of the wind. When the rain hit his flying helmet, none of it soaked through.

The rain thundered down on the wings of the biplane like millions of tiny pellets, and visibility was so bad that the wing tips were not visible and the surface of the ocean was completely blotted out. It was like flying from day into night, and in the semi-darkness, the luminous instruments glowed an eerie green from the dashboard.

Very soon, the open cockpit was almost flooded, and Mobley's flying-suit wet through. It was distinctly unpleasant flying blind at such altitude. The engine gave an occasional splutter, but then regained its steady roar, and he marveled how it kept going in the deluge. Through a break in the clouds, Mobley suddenly saw the dark blur of the ocean beneath him, whitecaps visible.

Then the **Bismarck** spotted them on radar and opened up with its big 15-inch guns. The #3 Swordfish got clipped on the wings, but carried on. Then Crackston gave the order to go line astern.

The CO signaled for them to dive.

John Mobley did so.

His fellow companions followed.

Mobley couldn't see where he was going, because he was just diving through the clouds. He got to about 600 feet above the sea, and was diving at a 45-degree angle.

Mobley thought, "How the hell am I going to pull out of this in time?"

Then he burst through the clouds and pulled out of the dive. They were about 100 feet above the sea. It was then that Mobley saw the **Bismarck**. It was on his right, a massive thing, about two miles away. CO Crackston, to his front, turned towards it.

Boom!

Bismarck's big guns fired.

The battleship fired different kinds of shells, which exploded in front of them, sending up great sheets of water.

How they got through them, Mobley just didn't know.

Then the ***Bismarck's*** smaller guns erupted. The bullets were coming at them like hail. Mobley thought the closer he was to the water, the better chance they had of surviving, so he dropped down to 50 feet above the waves. It must have worked, because instead of all that hot stuff battering them to death, the bullets just went right through the canvas covering on the Swordfish.

They were about 1,000 yards away now. All Mobley thought about was keeping the plane down, because when he let go of the torpedo, the release of the weight made the plane bounce up, and he had to offset that. Mobley couldn't bank and turn, because that would show the belly of the aircraft and make them a bigger target, so he did a flat turn, which meant he skidded around, as if he was skiing.

Right on his tail, but slightly to the left, Thaddeus maintained shadowing the torpedo bomber. He too was only feet above the active waves.

"Is there anything we can do to help them?" Gavin shouted.

The dragon growled and dropped even lower, his giant belly just inches from hitting the water. The air turbulence caused by Sir Osbert's mighty wings pushed the Swordfish even faster.

Watkins turned around to see if he could figure out where the wicked tailwinds were suddenly coming from. Yet there was nothing there, except the parting clouds. There didn't seem to be a readily acceptable explanation or even a low pressure current. It didn't make any sense why their Swordfish was traveling faster than any other.

To deliver the torpedo, which weighed 1,610 pounds, Mobley initiated his attack from a steep dive, at a speed of 180 knots. Then he straightened out to fly at a mere 90 knots.

Mobley made his approach to the dropping range of about 2,000 yards. He had a calibrated bar in front of him that calculated the speed of the target and the distance. For some unexplained reason he decided to ignore accepted procedures and relied on his senses instead. The ***Bismarck*** was coming straight towards them at about a 30 degrees angle, showing its starboard side, so Mobley thought the torpedo was bound to hit somewhere.

Watkins shouted, "Not yet! Not yet!"

Radcliff was no longer firing his gun, but was hanging over the side of the plane, with his backside up in the air. He had realized the sea was so rough, and the waves were so high, that if Mobley put the torpedo down too early, it would go into the sea at too steep an angle and would simply dive to the bottom and be wasted.

All of this was happening in split seconds, but to Mobley it felt like years. Quite unexpectedly, John suddenly thought of the Wren, Tabitha Bixley. She was such a lovely girl and they got along quite famously.

The Swordfish got closer and closer.

Squaddie shouted, "Let it go!"

His hand on the control, Mobley yanked the release handle.

He let it go.

On the late evening of May 26, 1941, while flying a fragile Swordfish biplane, bouncing fifty feet above the waves in a force-nine Atlantic gale, Sub-Lieutenant John Mobley released his single torpedo.

Splash!

"Now, Thaddeus, now!" called out Gavin.

In that instant, the dragon opened his mouth and sent a stream of liquid fire out over the ocean waves just ahead of the torpedo's path. The intense heat stabilized the barometric pressure in the immediate area, instantly calming the waves. Racing before the churning torpedo, Thaddeus maintained his fiery breath, which actually masked the trail of the racing high-explosive charge with a wall of rising steam.

The torpedo ploughed through the sea.

Just above the water, Mobley headed away as fast as he could. John looked back over his shoulder and watched the *Bismarck*, which instead of turning towards the torpedo, as it should have done, was turning away, exposing its vulnerable stern.

Mobley's delivery hit the rudder and the ensuing explosion instantly put the battleship's steering out of action. The *Bismarck*, with its rudder now disabled, was mortally wounded. Unable to maneuver, it was at the mercy of the pursuing British ships.

All Squaddie could say was, "By God, that was something!"

Radcliff was stunned to silence. He had spotted something very strange out ahead of the torpedo, something that didn't make any sense. Had he really seen flames?

Mobley flew straight back to **HMS Ark Royal**, still disbelieving how things had turned out. When he made his first approach, the aircraft carrier temporarily disappeared behind the Swordfish's obscured windscreen. He brought the airplane in a little high, before kicking into a steep slip. The raindrops flew sideways off the windscreen and the flight deck's white line emerged to one side of the translucent panels.

As the Swordfish didn't respond to gentle nudging, it was eventually necessary to kick it straight. By this time, most of the **Ark Royal** was in sight and the approach to the carrier deck was made at a staggeringly low speed, yet the response of the controls remained firm and insistent. Mobley was thankful he was flying the Swordfish on a dark and stormy night, with the carrier pitching up to the height of a house.

Mobley landed successfully and taxied to the far end of the carrier.

During the course of the attack, the **Bismarck** received at least two torpedo hits. One torpedo hit the port side amidships, and another struck the stern in the starboard side. The first hit did not cause any significant damage, but the second jammed both rudders at 12 degrees to port. The **Bismarck** made a circle and involuntarily began to steer northwest into the wind. None of the Swordfish were shot down, although some were hit several times by the wicked anti-aircraft fire.

The damage to the **Bismarck** was so serious that German Admiral Lütjens sent an emergency message, which read:

Ship unable to maneuver. We will fight to the last shell. Long live the Führer.

The mists pulled back as the sun finally broke through the haze and fog. Gavin could see the upper works of the German battleship quite clearly. Obviously not in control, the Bismarck was creeping along on a meandering course. She was still quite capable of putting up a fight, her eight fifteen-inch guns trained to port.

Bismarck was trying to make port at Brest, France, but her progress was fatally slow. Alone and without air support, **Bismarck** found herself boxed-in by opposing forces.

On the morning of May 27, 1941 **Bismarck** was surrounded by British forces consisting of battleships **King George V**, with ten 14-inch guns and **Rodney**, with nine 16-inch guns, battlecruiser **Renown**, with six 15-inch guns, aircraft carrier **Ark Royal**, heavy cruisers **Norfolk** and **Dorsetshire**, cruiser **Sheffield** and nine destroyers.

Even from that distance, Gavin could hear the speaker blaring from the British battleship *KG V*, as she was nicknamed. Orders were issued by confident voices, which echoed across the waves.

"Starboard fifteen."

"Starboard fifteen, sir. Fifteen of starboard wheel on, sir."

"Steer one-two-five."

"Steering one-two-five, sir."

"Midships."

"Rudder is amidships. Steady on one-two-five now, sir."

"Very well. Full ahead together. Give me revolutions for twenty-nine knots."

There was a clang of bells as the four great Parsons turbine engines delivered incredible horsepower to the four propellers. The ship was charging straight in.

HMS Rodney was bearing down on the enemy in a reckless head-on approach, unmasking all nine of her forward-mounted sixteen-inch guns. *King George V* was rapidly closing the range as well.

Yet the enemy did not alter her course.

Bismarck must have been seriously damaged by those torpedoes.

King George V turned toward the great German battleship, reducing the range, but also cutting down on **X** turret's firing arcs. An unnatural and deadly silence settled over the waves, as if each side was incapable of making the first move. With blowers secured and vents closed, *King George V* seemed to be waiting for something to happen.

"Guns loaded," the turret captains called out.

"On target, on target," replied the trainers and layers. "Bloody hell, on target!"

Gavin jumped as a commanding voice shouted through the speaker, "Shoot!"

There followed the sound of a high-pitched chime, floating on the wind. It sounded melodious and innocent, but actually signaled the gunners to open fire.

Despite clinging to the dragon's neck, Gavin was staggered by one massive concussion. Six 14-inch guns fired as one, brilliant orange flames leaping from the muzzles, filling the air with cordite fumes and thick, swirling brown smoke.

HMS Rodney had opened fire!

The volcanic eruption reflected off the ocean surface and lit up the clouds above with a hellish combination of reds, oranges, and yellows. The battleship jerked, sending visible shockwaves reverberating through the water.

Although Gavin had clapped his hands over his ears, the great thundering sounds of the mighty guns assaulted his ears. The boy screamed in fear and awe. He couldn't help it, because the intensity of each blast pummeled him, as if he was surrounded by a thousand thunderstorms.

The battle was engaged.

Fortunately, Thaddeus withdrew to a safer distance.

Then *King George V's* six 16-inch guns roared with a single gigantic orange-yellow flash, followed by billowing clouds of black smoke.

Simultaneously, Gavin witnessed a scene that frightened him even more, as it sent shivers racing up and down his spine. *Bismarck*, looming out of the mist, had finally opened fire, the flash of her main armament lighting up scattered patches of fog and low clouds. With his glasses pointed directly at the muzzles, the blast leapt at Gavin with a glare that nearly blinded him.

The boy was staring directly into the flames of hell.

He dropped his binoculars, cowering again behind the dragon's lifted scales. It was the most frightening sight he would ever see in his life. Eight 15-inch shells were actually visible, arcing slowly in the clear blue of the morning sky and dropping down directly toward him.

Bismarck's opening salvo hit at least 200 yards short, as eight great geysers of water towered hundreds of feet high, rising majestically into the air.

The British ships closed on the enemy, coming to point-blank range. *Norfolk*, *Dorsetshire*, and the escorting destroyers scurried out of the line of fire. This was a fight for the big boys.

The great ships were built to duel at ranges exceeding twenty miles. However, the British commander rushed in, near enough to fire over open sights. It would be a stand-up fight, toe-to-toe, where the battleships could pound each other to pieces.

HMS Rodney was the first to draw blood, lofting a 16-inch shell between *Bismarck's* two forward gun turrets, knocking out four of her eight 15-inch heavy guns. The battle raged on, and after shelling from *Rodney, King George V,* and the *Norfolk*, which had joined the battle, the *Bismarck's* fate was sealed.

HMS Rodney veered to the south across *Bismarck's* bow to keep her firing arcs open and to stand clear of *King George V's* fire. Repeatedly *KG V* fired her big guns. Fourteen, fifteen, and sixteen-inch shells poured in, weakening the German armor.

Bismarck's A Turret was flung into the sky, one barrel breaking off like a twig. The main director was hurled into the sea and the mainmast tilted over to touch the main deck, before it toppled and plunged into the water, trapping every man and drowning her lookouts. Slammed by a dozen direct hits, the bridge disintegrated in a shower of shattered plate and deadly fragments of flying glass.

Bodies and body parts rained down into the water. The battleship's stack exploded, followed by wild flames leaping high, as black smoke billowed over the horrific scene of destruction. Wreckage, bodies, and secondary turrets shot into the air, as ammunition began to explode on her main deck. *Bismarck* began to wallow in the swells. **Y** turret continued firing defiantly, until a full salvo blew it off its barrette and it skidded across the fantail and toppled overboard.

Gavin Kane shuddered. The exhilaration of battle faded quickly. Men were dying horribly, blown to pieces or trapped in flooding compartments. The boy tried desperately to remind himself that they were the enemy, bent on England's destruction. The *Bismarck* was just a ship, like any other ship. Could he forget what had happened to the **Hood**? Yet his binoculars visually took him aboard the burning wreck. Gavin witnessed men being killed, blown high into the air. He looked away, closing his eyes and praying the sights and sounds would fade one day.

Bismarck's guns ceased firing after a 90-minute battle, but she would not sink, even though the British fleet had put at least 400 rounds into her. *Bismarck* was dead in the water, guns silent, burning from a dozen fires. Although she was down by the head, she appeared in no danger of sinking. Her superb compartmentalization and excellent damage-control parties were keeping her afloat. Admitting there was no hope of assistance and realizing their demise was imminent, the remaining crew set off explosive charges to scuttle the ship.

However, the British cruiser *HMS Dorsetshire* was ordered to finish off *Bismarck*, which by then was nothing more than a burning wreck. Scores of men were jumping overboard into the very rough ocean.

HMS Dorsetshire fired three torpedoes and *Bismarck* turned slowly over and bottom up, showing her newly painted underside. Gavin witnessed this terrible scene from the safe vantage point on the dragon's shoulder. The boy watched, as the once mighty battleship poured out volumes of dense black smoke as it heeled over, spilling the crew into the sea.

Many German sailors were scrambling to hold onto the steel plating.

Even though the enemy had lost, there was very little celebration on the British ships. No man who had sailed for very long, ever took pleasure watching any ship sink, no matter what had transpired before.

The British cruiser started the dangerous task of picking up survivors. With the ship stopped in the water, they were inviting attack from any U-boat in the area. Even with that in mind, boat-ropes were thrown over the side and the survivors hung on as best they could. Many crewmen on *HMS Dorsetshire* began to pull them up the big sides of the cruiser, but the ropes were very slippery and often the German sailors fell back into the sea.

As the ***Bismarck*** went down, a half-drowned cat was plucked from the waves by the Royal Navy and joined the Allies as official ship's cat on the destroyer ***HMS Cossack***. The tabby was quickly named Oscar and was pampered with supplies from the galley.

"Periscope!" shouted an officer on the bridge of ***HMS Dorsetshire***.

There were still hundreds of men in the water, but no one could be certain the U-boat would allow the British cruiser to continue with the rescue operation.

HMS Dorsetshire's captain had no alternative but to push off. German survivors were still trying to get on board as the ship started to move away.

Gavin watched in horror. The cries and screams of those poor abandoned souls was heartbreaking. The teen covered his ears and cried with despair. More than 2,000 men perished that morning, with only 115 survivors.

Thaddeus wished the lesson hadn't been so harsh, but the boy needed to learn that the Germans were human beings too. As Sir Osbert flew back to Cornwall, the dragon kept looking over his shoulder. For some reason he couldn't shake the uneasy sense they were still being followed.

Gavin sighed and tried not to think of what had happened.

The ***Bismarck*** had been sunk, with a little assistance from a dragon.

19

Intriguing Questions

Only twenty minutes after the firing stopped, Winston Churchill updated the House of Commons regarding naval operations against the ***Bismarck***.

"This morning, shortly after day-break," the Prime Minister began. "The ***Bismarck*** virtually immobilized, without help, was attacked by British battleships that pursued her. I don't know the result of this action. It seems however, that ***Bismarck*** was not sunk by gunfire, and now will be sunk by torpedoes. It is believed that this is happening right now. Great as is our loss in the ***Hood***, the ***Bismarck*** must be regarded as the most powerful enemy battleship, as she is the newest enemy battleship and the striking of her from the German Navy is a very definite simplification of the task of maintaining effective mastery of the Northern sea and maintenance of the Northern blockade."

Churchill had just sat down, when he was given a note.

The Prime Minister rose again and said, "I have just received news that the ***Bismarck*** is sunk."

The cheers were loud and enthusiastic, yet somehow missing the true passion of victory. Everyone knew the war would drag on and such battles carried with them a hollow sense of accomplishment. For in fact, war was such a waste.

Churchill took time to receive each and every handshake, quite aware that morale had been very low and with the sinking of the ***Bismarck***, England's confidence would soar. The battle had been costly, but it also proved that the British Royal Navy still ruled the waves.

The Prime Minister bid farewell to the members of Parliament and climbed into the back of a black automobile. Whisked away, Churchill was driven to 10 Downing Street, only long enough to pick up a few personal items, before heading deep underground again to the War Rooms.

Much to the Prime Minister's surprise, Professor Frederick Lindemann was waiting inside Churchill's private subterranean study.

"Well, good afternoon, old chum," the Prime Minister greeted him warmly.

"I should say it is," Lindemann replied. "Right forward job on the ***Bismarck***, Winston. Well done."

"Indeed," Churchill agreed. "We had some good fortune, mixed with brave men and women."

"Quite so," Lindemann said, with a certain sarcastic tone in his voice.

Churchill didn't especially like the way his friend had said it, but neither did he feel like pursuing the possible implications. Winston lit up a cigar and flopped into his big armchair, drumming impatiently on the arm with his ring finger.

"What brings you my way?" the Prime Minister asked suspiciously. "I don't recall summoning you?"

"I was wondering if you've had any time to consider just how much good luck was involved in this ***Bismarck*** situation?" Lindemann asked.

"I don't believe in luck, Frederick, you know that," Churchill replied.

"Well, based on some of the reports I've been allowed to read, I think you should consider how much good fortune had to do with it," Lindemann began to clarify his earlier statement. "For instance, the Catalina pilots who spotted the ***Bismarck*** reported that a massive turbulence knocked them onto a new course and heading, thereby presenting them with the opportunity to spot the German battleship. Later, the Swordfish attack group reported an unnatural calming of the seas just ahead of them, at the very moment they launched their torpedoes."

"What exactly are you implying, Professor?" Churchill demanded, leaning forward, his forehead creased with wrinkles. He poured them both a cup of tea.

Lindemann shrugged. "These facts seem more than coincidental."

"I don't believe in coincidence either."

"No, I didn't think so."

"So, do *you* have an explanation?"

Lindemann shook his head as he picked up his cup. Then he said, "Perhaps young Gavin Kane's dragon had a hand in all this."

Churchill's eyes narrowed considerably. "The ***Bismarck*** was sunk by the incredible fortitude and tenacity of the Royal Navy and Fleet Air Arm, with the ***HMS Dorchester***, ***Rodney***, and ***KG V*** in on the kill."

"I'm not suggesting otherwise, Winston," Lindemann said.

"When the signal came through that the ***Bismarck*** was sunk, I somehow expected to feel a great surge of poetic justice, but it did not come," Churchill reflected aloud. "The rage and hatred that followed the loss of ***HMS Hood*** seemed to dim with that signal. Many heads were bowed, but I know my tears were not the only ones."

Lindemann sighed. "All I could think of since the **Hood** was destroyed, was the thousand men dying with her and the countless tears of those who loved them. With the news today regarding **Bismarck**, I felt the same horror again, only this time there will be countless German tears."

There followed a long period of silence, as both men reflected on what had transpired. Unbeknownst to Lindemann, however, the Prime Minster was actually considering the possibility that a certain dragon *was* somehow involved.

Churchill puffed on his Havana and watched the white smoke swirl up to the ceiling. There were always a great many things on his mind, crowding each other for primary attention.

"I suppose it is possible," Churchill said quietly.

"What's possible?" Lindemann asked.

"That a dragon really does exist," the Prime Minister said.

Lindemann didn't finish his sip of lukewarm tea. He looked over the rim and studied his friend, who at the time also happened to be the most powerful and influential man in all of Britain. "Winston, you're not serious?"

Churchill shrugged. "I don't know, maybe I am. Stranger things have happened. Who am I to say that such things don't exist?"

"I thought you were just humoring the boy," Lindemann protested.

"I was, I guess."

"Winston."

"What?"

"Were you, or were you not humoring Gavin Kane?"

"Perhaps."

"Oh, you infernal Conservatives!"

Churchill grinned and took another puff.

Lindemann downed the remaining tea and headed for the door.

"Frederick, what is really bothering you?" the Prime Minister asked. "The chance that there might actually be a dragon or that there might not be one?"

Lindemann stopped with his hand on the doorknob. He turned to look at Churchill and said, "Neither, Winston. I am far more worried about how you will use that poor bloody dragon to your own ends, whether he exists or not!"

With that, Churchill's most trusted aide walked out.

The Prime Minister continued reflecting, white smoke obscuring him from any casual observer that might come through the door. Churchill had one other factor to consider. Major Traber Vickers had sworn he saw a dragon that night, from the hill overlooking Crackington Haven. It was one thing to question a teenaged boy's imagination, it was quite another to ignore the observations of a very skilled and loyal Royal Army officer.

"I shall look into this further," Winston Churchill said to himself.

Clear across England, standing alone in the control tower overlooking the runways at **HMS Vulture**, Tabitha Bixley couldn't control her impassioned sigh of relief. She had the strongest feeling that Sub-lieutenant John Mobley was just fine. The news on the BBC had been a bit dicey, when it looked like **Bismarck** was going to eradicate most of the Royal Navy's finest ships. Then a brave batch of Swordfish pilots took off after the vaunted battleship and at least two torpedoes had made the difference.

Tabitha just knew that John had launched one of them.

She smiled.

Perhaps it was love after all.

However, there was one little secret she would have to share with John Mobley, before Tabitha could think about romance. Biting her bottom lip, the Wren wondered how he would take the news.

"Oh, never mind," she said to herself. "I'll cross that bridge when I come to it."

In Boscastle, after helping her mother hang up all the clean washing, Emily asked if she could go to Crackington Haven until suppertime.

Harriet Scott said, "Why not stay close to home, dearest? I would feel better if I knew you were nearby."

Disappointed, but still obedient, Emily set out to explore the stand of trees across the road. She picked several beautiful flowers along the way and listened to the birds singing in the trees.

"Hello, again," a tiny voice spoke from behind one tree.

To Emily's delight, it was Kitto Bideven. "Oh, hello."

"What are you doing?" the elf asked as she popped out.

"Just enjoying nature," Emily replied. "I'm not supposed to wander far from home, because my mother is worried about my safety."

"Mothers fret," Kitto stated. "So, children must misbehave."

"What?" Emily asked with surprise.

"Oh, you must," the elf insisted. "You must not be dependable, or you will you grow up into an adult and spoil everything."

Emily was shocked, but her resistance didn't last for long. "What should we do?"

"Take me to meet your dragon," Kitto suggested.

"Oh, I don't know," Emily hesitated. "Tintagel Castle is so far away."

Kitto reached out and took Emily's hand. "Hold on."

Poof!

For just a split second, Emily was surrounded by the trees. In but an instant, she was standing before the ancient ruins of Tintagel Castle.

"How did you do that?" she asked.

Kitto merely smiled.

Emily pointed across the coastal road. "Thaddeus actually lives up there."

The elf could only see a little white cottage on the hill.

Emily took Kitto's hand and they walked up the path.

"It is so small," the elf observed. "How does your dragon fit inside?"

"I'll show you," Emily replied as she grasped the rusting handle and pushed, leading the elf inside.

The giant fireplace began to fall apart, as each shaped stone tumbled down, but before hitting the earth, the stones started shifting and moving through the air. Chunks and slabs sailed clear across the room, almost colliding overhead. Kitto ducked, but Emily had seen this fantastic display many times before.

What once had looked like an ordinary stone fireplace was now replaced by the awesome and powerful form of a crouched dragon. His scales glistened and sparkled with radiant colors, including bumblebee yellow, ripe-apple red, autumn-leaves copper, and freshly mined coal black.

"Who's this then?" Thaddeus asked after appearing.

"Sir Osbert," Emily began the introductions. "I would like you to meet my new friend, Kitto Bideven."

Suddenly the elf was faced with a large dragon's head and a long scaly body firmly attached. Kitto cowered a little.

"Hello," said Thaddeus. "It's a pleasure to meet you."

"I didn't know dragons could talk!" stammered the elf.

"Every dragon I know can," replied Thaddeus. "How many have you known?"

"Only a few," Kitto replied reluctantly.

Thaddeus wasn't certain she was telling the truth, but he didn't comment.

Kitto wasn't quite sure what else to say, because she had never actually talked to a dragon before. She had been taught proper manners, though, so she politely said, "It is an honor to meet you, sir. Is this your home?"

Thaddeus smiled at Emily and spread his paws apart in a gesture of welcome. "Yes, indeed, please make yourself comfortable. I'm afraid I don't have many possessions, but Emily and her friends often sit here before me."

The dragon moved the lone stool to the center of the hardened dirt floor.

Kitto was fascinated. "Have you lived here a long time? It has been ages since my people have seen a live dragon."

"I only go out at night," replied Thaddeus. "I must be careful that humans do not see me, for they would surely send someone to investigate."

"Why would people try to hurt you?" Kitto demanded.

"Dragons have been painted as the villains for centuries," Sir Osbert said. "There were dragons in the past that made a mess of our reputation. Some of them actually ate people."

"You're not going to eat me, are you?" asked the elf.

"Oh, no, I would never do that," Thaddeus replied. "You and Emily are friends and Emily is my friend. Friends do not eat other friends. Besides, I don't eat elves or people. Yuck!"

He stuck out his tongue and made a face as if he was gagging.

Both Kitto and Emily burst into laughter, because the dragon was making such a silly face, rolling his eyes and turning his scales different colors. It was quite a sight.

Now back in Boscastle, Emily's mother had been pleased when her daughter hadn't fussed after it was suggested the girl not venture far from home. However, Emily had been gone for quite some time now.

As it turned out, Gavin Kane knocked on the door at the most opportune moment. Bunty waited out on the street, playing with the gravel.

"Oh, Gavin, it's good to see you," Emily's mother greeted him.

"Is Emily home?" the boy asked.

"I haven't seen her for several hours," Harriet replied. "I told her to stay close to home, but I'm afraid she disobeyed me."

Gavin shook his head. "Oh, Mrs. Scott, you know Emmy would never do that. "I'll go find her."

"You're such a dear. Thank you."

Gavin and Bunty headed up to the coast road. They followed their intuition, which clearly directed them towards the little white cottage on the hill.

It hadn't taken long for Emily and Kitto to prove that Thaddeus was a fine playmate. They went for a short flight on the dragon's back, circling over the ruins of Tintagel Castle and swooping down over the village of Boscastle, where Emily pointed out her house. In fact, her mother was out back, tending to the vegetable garden.

"You British were nutty about gardening," the dragon commented. "An entire nation hopelessly addicted to mucking around in the dirt."

Emily puffed up like a peacock and said, "That's right."

When Thaddeus touched back down outside the cottage, Kitto bowed deeply before him. "I am most grateful for your kindness, Sir Osbert. I must return to my people before the sun goes down."

"Fare thee well, Kitto Bideven," the dragon said.

Poof!

The elf vanished.

"How does she do that?" Thaddeus wondered.

He took Emily's hand and as they stepped forward, the cottage walls parted to allow them entrance. The girl knew she should go home, but the dragon was so much fun to be with and she learned so much with every visit.

It turned out Thaddeus also owned a large collection of books, which thoroughly delighted Emily, who immediately sat down on his paw and started reading one volume. Most of his books had dragons in them and Emily especially liked looking at the gorgeous artwork. She read one story aloud, but stopped suddenly when the central dragon character was killed.

"Why do knights always hunt the poor dragons?" Emily asked with tears in her eyes. "Don't they realize you are wonderful creatures?"

"I think humans have always been afraid of anything they don't understand," Thaddeus offered as explanation. "Dragons are very difficult to figure out, unless you do so through the eyes of a child."

Satisfied with that answer, Emily resumed her reading. Later, the girl polished several of his scales, which in some spots were hard for Thaddeus to reach. She used a mixture of motor oil and baking soda, which really brought out the sheen.

The dragon enjoyed the attention. Suddenly a gigantic mirror appeared before them and Thaddeus admired his reflection.

"You are such a handsome beast," Emily said with a smile.

"Do you really think so?" the dragon asked.

"Oh, yes, indeed," she replied.

He flashed a toothy smile. He had terribly unclean teeth.

"Your teeth, on the other hand, are atrocious," the girl announced. "When was the last time you saw a dentist?"

"I don't ever recall seeing one."

"My mother insists I see the ivory snatcher every six months," she lectured the dragon.

"I don't know any dentists who specialize in dragons, do you?" Thaddeus asked.

Emily shook her head. Holding out her hand, she commanded, "Find a big toothbrush and I will look after those bicuspids."

The dragon just happened to have an old brush lying about, so he retrieved it.

Thaddeus opened his mouth wide and with backing soda in one hand and the big bristle brush in the other, the girl sat down on the dragon's extended tongue, to get just the right angle. Emily scrubbed and scrubbed each tooth, until she was satisfied. There were so many teeth, this project took more than an hour to complete.

There was a knock on the door.

"Emily, are you in there?"

It was Gavin.

"Yes, I'm here," she replied.

Bunty and Gavin stepped inside, but came to an abrupt halt when they saw Emily inside the dragon's mouth.

"Oh, my God, he's going to eat her!" Bunty exclaimed, running forward. He picked up the stool to swing at Thaddeus, but was suddenly upended by the dragon's whipping tail.

"Oof," the boy grunted as his rump hit the earthen floor.

"Are you insane?" Emily screamed as she jumped off the dragon's tongue.

Once she was clear, Thaddeus lowered his head to just inches from Bunty's outstretched legs. The beast's nostrils flared and he snorted a little puff of dark smoke.

"Do not trifle with me young man, especially if you are small and crunchy and would taste good with powdered sugar!" the dragon bellowed.

"I'm sorry, Sir Osbert," Bunty trembled with his apology. "I thought ... well ... you know what I thought."

The dragon opened his mouth to flash his sparkling clean razor-sharp teeth and then chuckled, his rumbling laughter echoing through the cottage. "No harm done, actually. I've always wanted to say that to somebody."

Emily shook her head. "Thaddeus, what are we going to do with you?"

The dragon grinned. "Feed me sugar and I'm as sweet as a butterfly."

"If you keep eating sweets like you do, your teeth will rot away with cavities," Emily pointed out. "You really must find a substitute for your sugar craving."

Thaddeus looked disappointed. "Well, I suppose I could try."

Gavin stepped forward and said, "Not if it will spoil your disposition, Thaddeus. We've become attached to your pleasant personality and if sugar makes you happy, then we wouldn't want you to change."

Even Emily had to agree with Gavin's statement. "Yes, I only suggested you cut back a bit, not stop altogether."

The dragon smiled. "All right, then, I'll give it a go, but under no circumstances will I use saccharin."

The teens all laughed.

20

Himmler's Horrors

Reichsführer Himmler secretly met with his twelve handpicked SS generals at Wewelsburg Castle. Himmler informed his trusted officers that the purpose of the coming war with Russia was to reduce the indigenous population by thirty million, to provide living space for German settlers. He then ordered that all "undesirable" people were to be exterminated immediately after German troops had achieved victory in each hamlet, village, or city. After the meeting had adjourned, Himmler met with SS Dr. Horst Schumann, whom Himmler had put in charge of his experimental science department.

"What do you have to report today, *Herr Doktor?*" Himmler asked.

Schumann beamed with satisfaction. "My experiments were a complete success, *Herr Reichsführer.* I have brought to life strange creatures, which were a race of fierce, brown-skinned human-like beings that once ruled the earth. They have been waiting to be set loose, long buried in crypts beneath the great forest. They are not the product of some warped imagination, but truly do exist. I have revived over one thousand of them today alone."

Himmler was stunned by this revelation, but also intrigued by the doctor's ramblings. Rubbing his palms together feverishly, the Reichsführer could barely contain his excitement. "Is this true? How can this be? Let me see them."

Schumann's creatures looked like some form of primitive humans, with brown skin, stooped postures, low foreheads, and protruding lower canines that resembled boar's tusks. They had lupine ears, their eyes were reddish, and when they had hair, it was dark black.

"What do you call these monsters?" Himmler demanded.

"Their species are known as Orcanians, *Herr Reichsführer,*" Schumann replied.

Himmler looked baffled, but he also couldn't hide his fascination. "Where did you say they came from?"

"This castle sits overlooking the mystical Teutoburg Forest," the Doctor replied.

"Do you mean the Niederhagen Forest?" Himmler corrected Schumann, because the Reichsführer had renamed the forest earlier that year.

"Yes, of course, *Herr Reichsführer*," Schumann corrected himself. "Please forgive my oversight."

"Go on," Himmler said.

"I discovered ancient manuscripts hidden inside a secret vault under the main castle staircase," Dr. Schumann continued. "Much of the writing was Nordic Runes, but not difficult to translate. Based on the information revealed, the forest was used to hide these strange creatures, until they were required again by mystical rulers."

The beasts standing before Himmler were generally more than seven feet in height and weighed an average of 250 pounds or more. Their arms and torsos were long, with short, bandy legs. Their eyes were red or black, and they had small pointed ears. From their mouths protruded large, almost tusk-like lower canine teeth.

There were enormous physical differences between orcs and humans. The most immediately noticeable was that orcs were massive when compared to humans, because they stood between six and eight feet tall, and were often twice as wide as a human was. These Orcanians, commonly referred to simply as Orcs, were endowed with massive strength. Even an adolescent could pull a human or elf limb-from-limb, and an adult male could probably tear the roof off a German staff car.

Their mouths jutted from their faces, and they sported two white tusks that curled from their lower jaws up to their noses. Their tongues were dark, almost black. Their eyes had large black pupils. Their arms were a little longer in proportion to their bodies. All parts of an orc were strikingly muscular, and because they needed massive food intact to survive, they were usually lean. Some Orcs painted their faces, while others tanned them to leather-like darkness. Apart from their musculature, and their striking features, the bodies of orcs stood out in comparison.

Orcs seemed to exist only to seek revenge on all other living creatures. They had strong passions for slaughtering elves and an equal amount of hatred towards humans. They believed elves to be the cause of their undesirable life and would take every opportunity to drive any other species to the brink of extinction. Misery and anger kept the Orcs going and their sheer displeasure towards life in general set them apart from any other race.

Orcs tended to have slower reflexes and were often thought to have slower minds. Their German masters soon discovered this wasn't the case at all, because orcs generally thought things over longer than humans, rather than rashly taking action on a whim. They actually had excellent memories, rarely forgetting even the most minor details.

Under the direction of the Third Reich, however, they were rewarded for being evil, brutal, and misshapen. They ate all manner of flesh, including men and horses, so it was unnecessary to provide rations.

Orcs were extremely warlike and geared towards constant warfare. This need to fight was an expression of orc culture, a fact that prevented orcs from forming anything but temporary alliances with each other. In combat, they transformed even the most common object into a lethal killing instrument.

In short, these creatures were perfect for Himmler's subversive plans. They were the oldest and fiercest foes of humanity, perfect in the role of mass exterminator.

During training, the orcs quickly proved to be brutal, fast and deadly, whose only purpose in life was to kill. Orcs became restless quickly and when not in battle, they were only interested in breeding, picking fights with each other, or drinking the strongest, most vile spirits their masters could provide.

Orcs were very effective in close-quarter combat and were typically very loyal to their leader. They lacked general intellectual skills, thereby requiring them to rely on a strong leader to make their decisions for them. If an orc leader issued orders that continually confuse them, the pack would look to someone else for leadership, or abandon the operation.

Orders that usually confused orcs were multi-stage battle tactics, such as flanking movements or timed attacks. Himmler's officers instead concentrated on creating simple orders that relied on frontal assaults.

Orcs were not total idiots and did understand basic covert tactics, such as hiding in a spot to wait to ambush their foes. Beyond that, battle tactics were kept simple, promoting charging and melee.

The species was inherently a pack hunter and preferred to stay with other orcs. After several nasty brawls in Wewelsburg beer gardens, it was obvious that taking an Orc into a civilized area was simply a catastrophe waiting to happen. Therefore, the creatures were confined to their own barracks and alcohol was provided.

Orcs knew only fighting and excelled at killing.

Formed up in sections of 50 each for review, the dark skinned, flat nosed, pointed eared monsters would have looked terrifying, except for the way they were dressed. Try as they might, Himmler's supply officers were unsuccessful in finding any German uniforms that would fit properly. So instead, the sleeves of the tunics barely reached the elbow, buttons were strained or burst apart at the chest, and helmets were many sizes too small, sitting high on their heads.

"They look absolutely ridiculous like that," Himmler protested upon his arrival.

"*Jawohl, Herr Reichsführer*," Schumann said. "But each one can fight with the strength of ten."

"Can you prove that?" Himmler asked.

"Would you care for a demonstration, *Herr Reichsführer*?" Schumann wondered.

"*Ja*, I would like to see them in action," Himmler replied.

"Major Steiner, the *Reichsführer* would like to see what your recruits are capable of," Schumann suggested.

"*Jawohl, Herr Doktor*," the SS Major agreed. "With your permission, *Herr Reichsführer*."

Himmler impatiently motioned for the officer to proceed with his demonstration.

"*Kommen Sie hier und töten Sie diese vier Kameraden*," Steiner shouted at one of the orcs standing at the front. The major had ordered the Orc to kill four of his fellow orcs.

Himmler was surprised, but also pleased by the choice of commands.

"His name is Tulgan, *Herr Reichsführer*," Steiner announced.

As Tulgan lumbered forward, Himmler realized he had never seen anything like him before. The orc towered over even his own kind. Suddenly, without warning, Tulgan spun around and killed the orc nearest him with a single punch.

Wham!

Not hesitating for even a brief second, Tulgan grabbed two other orcs and throttled them by the neck.

Crack … crack.

He broke their necks and cast them aside.

Before their lifeless forms hit the floor, Tulgan had already dispatched yet another orc, making the count exactly four, just as ordered.

Up from the ranks came a mighty roar of admiration and exhilaration. The echo of their cries reverberated throughout the castle, thundering all around them. It was the most primordial chant for blood that Himmler had ever heard.

"Tulgan is the orc clan's leader, *Herr Reichsführer*," Schumann announced.

"I can see why," Himmler observed. "He's gigantic."

Tulgan had broad shoulders and a thick neck common to his ancestry. His large mouth sported sharpened tusks. He rarely spoke, but when he did, it was in a gravelly voice unaccustomed to use, and he only said what he felt needed to be said. Tulgan's outlook was often dour and grim. His movements were as economic as his speech, and he only moved when necessary, and then only as much as needed.

"Tulgan also possesses an inbred hatred for anything that resides in Britain," Steiner added.

"Why is that?" Himmler wondered.

"We are not certain, *Herr Reichsführer*," the SS major replied. "It must have something to do with his ancestors."

"I am impressed and pleased, gentlemen," Himmler announced to the crowd of SS officers and staff. "I will review your orcs now."

The Reichsführer slowly walked up and down the rows of orcs, while realizing he had been handed his own private army of homicidal maniacs. They weren't even human, which made his sordid plans even more tantalizing.

"Tulgan will lead this army into battle, advised and supported by ten of our own SS commanders, including myself," Major Steiner explained. "These brutes will follow Tulgan and he obeys our orders."

Himmler continued reviewing the ranks of orcs, until he spotted an especially ugly monster, whose malformed face made the German leader nauseous with disgust.

"Does that foul beast over there have a name?" Himmler asked, pointing.

"Orgoth is insane with the bloodlust, *Herr Reichsführer*," Steiner answered. "He is perfect for the slaughter, a veritable killing machine."

"*Ja*, this is obvious," Himmler said. "He is the most wretched creature I have ever imagined. His stench permeates the air, even where I am standing."

"He refuses to bathe, *Herr Reichsführer*," Dr. Schumann interjected. "It is some ritual we don't yet understand."

"I have seen enough," Himmler said. "We will commit these orcs to a covert operation I have been planning. You have done well, *Doktor!*"

The German trainers had discovered their orcs were capable of two main tactical skills, which were their raging and their speed. Orcs enjoyed fighting in an enraged state, and were usually quick to invoke this ability, regardless of the anticipated outcome of a battle. They were unlikely to kill just a single enemy, but would enter a rage when seeing more than a dozen of the enemy. Unlikely as it seemed at the time, Major Steiner had also discovered that if elves or dragons were nearby, a greater level of insanity would overtake the orcs. These legendary foes held both fear and contempt for each other and the SS commander almost wished he could locate a few elves to use as motivators.

Most orcs were only mentally capable of fighting with two weapons, and their preference was for dual war-axes. Those that did fight with just one weapon preferred the mobility and opportunity that a double-bladed axe provided. Over fifty orcs had become incredibly deadly fighting with German bayonets in each hand, wielding them with incredible speed and precision. Disappointingly, however, the SS had only been marginally successful in training orcs how to use firearms, as long as the barrels were pointed in the right direction. Several lethal accidents had discouraged their instructors from pursuing continued training with anything as complicated as a rifle or machinegun.

To compensate for that shortfall, however, it was soon discovered that aside from being able to breathe underwater, the orcs had a thin membrane protecting their corneas. Ordinarily, human eyesight becomes blurry under water, because the eye is structured to see through a liquid surface. Orcs, on the other hand, could close off the fluid surface with this thin lining and vision was unhampered.

Once Major Steiner was satisfied that the orc army was as trained as he could make them, he reported to Reichsführer Himmler.

"I am very pleased with the end result, *Herr Major*," Himmler said.

"*Danke, Herr Reichsführer*," Steiner replied.

"Will you require transport?" Himmler asked.

"*Nein, Herr Reichsführer*," Steiner said. "The orcs will march through the night, avoiding all contact with humans, making camp in uninhabited areas until they reach the coast of France."

"How will they cross the Channel?" Himmler asked.

"Underwater, *Herr Reichsführer*."

"Where will they go ashore?"

"Where they're least expected."

"What is the battle plan?"

"The objective is to land at least ten thousand orcs on a deserted stretch of beach on the northeast coast of England, where no one will expect them," Major Steiner outlined the strategy. "The army will move across northern Britain, spreading terror and death, slaughtering everyone they come upon."

Himmler smiled thinly. "Will any of the orcs survive?"

"Probably not, but they will send England into a state of panic, *Herr Reichsführer*."

"You may proceed with the invasion," Himmler said. "*Heil Hitler!*"

Two days later, on a stretch of deserted French coastline, the orc army formed ranks. It was their final review before setting forth into the Channel waters. The crossing would take place at night, bringing the invaders to their landing beaches at dawn of the following day.

German infantry tactics hadn't changed much since the First World War. The orcs were given simple instructions, which translated to following the path of least resistance, inflict as much damage as possible, and spread fear and panic throughout the English countryside.

Unfortunately for the accompanying SS commanders, the orc leaders had their own agenda, which had nothing to do with fighting humans.

At least not right away.

That would come later.

For the orcs had other victims in mind.

Masses of half-naked orcs waded out into the sea, eventually disappearing under the waves, as they marched along the bottom of the Channel. Their German officers boarded a captured fishing trawler, which would make the crossing covertly.

That evening, at Wewelsburg Castle, Himmler was enjoying a splendid dinner with Reinhard Heydrich and his inner-circle of SS officers. The mood was festive and the guests were treated to fine cuisine and expensive French wine. The conversation around the table centered on the eventual victory over England and the subsequent invasion and destruction of Russia.

Himmler stood up and tinked his wine glass with the handle of a spoon. "May I have your attention, gentlemen. I have an announcement to make."

The officers halted their individual conversations and directed their undivided attention to the Reichsführer.

"It is my pleasure to inform you that Reinhard Heydrich has been promoted, by order of the *Führer*, to *Reichprotektor* of Bohemia and Moravia," Himmler stated, lifting his glass. "Congratulations!"

Heydrich stood up, clicked his boots together, and bowed. "Thank you, my fellow comrades. I am deeply honored by this acknowledgement from our *Führer*. This will be a critical opportunity to bring order out of chaos, to subject our enemies to retribution on a grand scale."

There followed polite applause.

Then Heydrich raised his glass. "To the Fatherland, Adolf Hitler, and the glorious Third Reich. *Sieg Heil.*"

"*Sieg Heil,*" everyone around the table repeated.

After the meal was concluded and personal congratulations petered out, Heydrich was ushered into Himmler's private study, high atop one of the castle towers. Two glasses of schnapps were sipped in silence, as the rivals studied each other.

Himmler felt obligated to reiterate the importance of Heydrich's promotion. "You are replacing that fool von Nuerath, who the *Führer* considers insufficiently harsh. I hope you can be exceedingly harsh, *ja?*"

"*Jawohl, Herr Reichsführer,*" Heydrich replied with a tone of impatience. "I will crush Czechoslovakian resistance under my boot, even without the help of sorcery."

Himmler was surprised. "What do you mean by that?"

"Will you lend me some of your witches, warlocks and goblins?" Heydrich replied sarcastically.

"How dare you insult me," Himmler fumed.

Heydrich forced a yawn. "Please, if anyone insults you, it is you alone. Your actions are ridiculous, with rumors of dragons and orcs and witch's brew. Have you completely lost your mind?"

"At least I don't fancy myself as Genghis Khan!" Himmler spat. "Go play with your toy soldiers and leave this war to men with vision."

"*Jawohl, Herr Reichsführer,*" Heydrich said, snapping to attention, lifting his right hand in salute. "*Heil, Hitler!*"

Reinhard turned and marched down the hallway, shoulders thrown back in defiance and arrogance. He would seek his revenge at a more convenient time and location, when Himmler least expected it. When Heydrich was inside his room, he pulled off his boots and stared out the window.

"Have you done as I ordered?" a voice spoke from the shadows.

Heydrich spun around, but there was no one there. Yet the voice was quite familiar to him. "I have done as you demanded, Master."

"I will not reward you with the power you seek, unless I have more souls," the voice spoke again from nowhere. "You must provide me with many more."

Heydrich bowed his head and said, "I have arranged for millions of people to be killed for you, my Master. You will be pleased, I assure you."

"That is good," the eerie voice chuckled with demonic delight. "You have done well. Your reward shall be great indeed."

Reichsführer Himmler often lost patience with Heydrich, berating and abusing him, calling him names, but ultimately found him indispensable, though exasperating. Perhaps Reinhard would be able to straighten things out in Czechoslovakia after all. That would certainly please Hitler and would make Himmler look like a genius.

Several days later, Reichprotektor Heydrich took control of all SS operations in Czechoslovakia, establishing his headquarters in Prague. Reinhard toured the prisons and torture chambers, the concentration camps under construction, and reviewed the elite troops assigned under his command. He bragged about the success of his severe methods in the past and promised even harsher treatment of the Czech population, which he considered inferior. Reinhard stopped to visit all the historical sights and later announced that martial law would be enforced with lethal force.

Then Heydrich entered the Treasure Chamber of Prague Castle, where the Crown Jewels of Bohemia were kept. There he took the Royal Crown out of the display case and placed it on his own head. He posed for the accompanying Nazi cameramen and postured about, making jokes about Czechoslovakia and her conquered people.

Heydrich wasn't aware at the time, nor would he have cared if he knew, that Czech legends claimed that whoever put on the crown, without lawful right, would die within a year.

21

Elven Priorities

Kitto Bideven was a gray elf, probably the most somber and serious of all elven clans. Throughout the ages, this species of elf grew beautiful rocks and precious gems, like others grow plants. They lived in ornate palaces, mighty fortresses, and quaint little villages, which they grew themselves. For unlike other clans, gray elves did not build their homes. Water wasn't a problem for gray elves either, because even in the driest deserts, they grew springs wherever they needed them.

Of course, these fantastic skills with rocks, gems, and water made gray elves much prized in the desert, or anywhere buildings or water was needed. Gray elves not only grew homes, but also things they needed, like tables, food, and even weapons. Their artisanship, however, was easily distinguished from dwarven work, because their creations looked organic in nature. Gray elves often sold raw materials, such as iron, silver, and manganese.

Gray elves were in demand for their services, because of these unusual skills. Kitto's village was renowned for their foundry, arguably equal to or surpassing dwarves with shaping metals. However, at the highest levels of craftsmanship, Kitto admitted that dwarves fashioned the best weapons.

Perhaps because they traveled so often to other places, gray elves were amongst the most tolerant of clans, not unduly disturbed by anyone's customs and usually quite tolerant of them. Gray elves did follow the traditional elven ways, but regarded other shadow creatures as important to the diversity and health of the forests.

However, their relationships with other races also explained their pride. While they weren't often vocal about it, gray elves believed they were superior to everyone else. Kitto acknowledged that other races sought gray elves for the metals and gems they made, but she also admitted stealing items that belonged to other clans, without guilt.

"The most noble and reclusive of the gentle race are gray elves," Kitto told Gavin, Bunty, and Emily. "We are the protectors of good in the world, which is why we have sought humans, because we are faced with great evil."

"Do you think your clan will fight?" Bunty asked.

"The elders are very noble and honorable, doing everything to make sure a promise is kept, or a common enemy is defeated," Kitto replied. "They agreed the threat is real and have sent word to all the other elven clans to gather for war."

Emily touched Kitto's sleeve. "We are grateful for your help."

The elf smiled. "Our wizards will disguise the entrances to our villages and farms with powerful magic, ensuring that only elves are allowed access."

Gavin had been silent up to this point. "Kitto, Sir Thaddeus Osbert cannot participate in this war without permission. Is there any way your clan can send an emissary to the dragon lair on his behalf?"

Kitto quietly considered Gavin's request. Then she shrugged. "I do not know. I am not as important as I pretend. I am only a scout and a thief."

"How do you know the Germans are coming?" Bunty asked.

Kitto frowned. "This invasion will not be conducted by humans."

"What?" the teens all reacted with surprise.

Kitto smiled grimly. "The enemy I speak of is far more dangerous and destructive than any of you humans."

"How is that possible?" Bunty wondered. "Who or what is more dangerous than Germans with artillery, tanks, and dive bombers?"

"Orcs," Kitto replied bluntly.

Emily looked at Bunty, who looked at Gavin.

They didn't know what to say.

Kitto thought she understood their reaction. "Orcs are the sworn enemies of any elf, no matter what the situation. Over the centuries, we have been slaughtered by their kind. Something evil has awakened them from their slumber and freed them from their imprisonment. An army of orcs is amassing and when they come, there will be a battle to remember."

Gavin was deeply concerned. "I don't think Thaddeus knows were dealing with orcs. We just assumed it would be German troops."

"We must go see Sir Osbert and give him this news," Emily insisted. "He must go to Iceland and ask his fellow dragons to come to our aid. Otherwise, the Germans will win this war using orcs."

"Such use of orcs must be a violation of some ancient law," Bunty guessed.

Kitto was impressed. "For a human, you know much."

Bunty beamed.

"Is this true, Kitto?" Gavin asked.

"Yes, the use of orcs for war is forbidden," the elf replied. "Such a violation should free Sir Osbert from any restrictions that currently bind him."

"We must go warn Thaddeus right away!" Bunty exclaimed.

"Take hold of me," Kitto ordered, extending her hands.

Gavin, Emily and Bunty did so, snatching hold of Kitto's fingers.

Poof.

Seconds later, they reappeared inside the little white cottage on the hill.

Thaddeus was already in his dragon form, but had been reading poetry from a book of dragon verse. Startled by their sudden appearance, the creature grumbled with alarm, but reluctantly set the volume aside.

"You really must stop doing that," the dragon said. "It's rude to sneak up on me."

"We're sorry, Thaddeus, but it was vitally important we talked you right away," Emily apologized.

"Very well, then, what's on your minds?" the dragon asked, stifling a yawn.

"The Germans have created an army of orcs, Sir Osbert," Gavin reported. "According to the elves, they intend using these orcs to invade England."

The dragon listened carefully. He didn't immediately respond, nor did his facial features give away any clues as to his true feelings. Then, just like a cat, Thaddeus rose up on his hindquarters and stretched, raking his talons along the dirt floor.

"In that case, I must make ready for war," Thaddeus said.

The dragon started making preparations for battle. His membranous wings were tightly pressed to his broad scaly back, and the claws of his strong legs made deep furrows in the earth. Thaddeus filed each talon, until the points glistened with deadly sharpness. Flexing his massive muscles, the dragon practiced dodging and slashing with his spiked tail.

His audience sat mesmerized by this potentially lethal display of fighting prowess. There was no doubt in their minds that Thaddeus Osbert would be a formidable opponent against any living creature, even an orc.

"He's amazing," Bunty commented.

"Orcs are much less likely to fall to dragons when they have their bloodlust up," Kitto felt obligated to inform the red-haired boy.

The dragon stopped what he was doing and said, "Then I shan't allow them to get that angry."

The elf giggled.

"How will you defeat them, Thaddeus?" Gavin asked. "Kitto estimates the orcs will come in the thousands."

The dragon grinned. "The same way you beat me at chess. Control the center, the high ground, and then do the unexpected."

Gavin also smiled.

"There is always a purpose to my lessons, son," Thaddeus said. "You will have an opportunity to see your tactics in action, for I will use several of your counter-moves throughout the engagement. I have learned from you too."

"I can't wait to see this," Bunty said.

"I forbid you children from participating in the upcoming battle," Thaddeus stated categorically. "I can't afford to keep an eye on the three of you, while conducting the intricacies of fighting orcs."

"But Thaddeus ..." Gavin tried to object.

"There will be no discussion this time, Gavin," the dragon interrupted. "Orcs are wanton killers, with no regard for life, only battle. You may watch events from the safety of the treetops, but be prepared to flee for your lives if things turn out badly."

"When the call to battle is sounded, you can count on me," Kitto volunteered.

"Will they come across the Channel in ships or airplanes?" Gavin wondered.

"Neither," the dragon replied. "They have no need for man's machines. The monsters will suddenly appear in our midst, from somewhere least expected. That is why the elf clans will send scouts in every direction, to give us early warning."

"I must leave you now," Kitto said. "My primary duty is to locate the orcs as soon as they arrive."

"Thank you for bringing this dire news to my human friends, Kitto," Thaddeus said. "Go now and tell the clans to muster arms before the first orcs arrive."

Before Kitto departed, she handed Bunty her elven sword. "Take this in honor of me, that my spirit may protect thee."

"Thank you," the boy said bashfully. "Please, be careful."

She gave him a quick kiss on the cheek, before vanishing into thin air.

"How does she do that?" Bunty wondered, his face beet-red with embarrassment.

"Kitto's an elf, silly," Emily reminded him. "She has magical powers."

"So does Thaddeus and you don't see him going poof," Bunty said. "How rude."

"Sir Osbert can make himself invisible," she pointed out.

"It's not the same," Bunty protested.

The dragon sighed and shook his head, but instead of trying to interfere, he made eye contact with Gavin.

"May I have a moment of your time, Gavin?" Thaddeus requested, motioning for the boy to join him to one side.

"Of course, Thaddeus," Gavin replied.

The dragon stepped to one side and the two of them spoke in low whispers.

"With the coming conflict, I will be hard-pressed to be in two places at the same time," the dragon said.

Gavin grinned. "Oh, I thought dragons could do that."

Thaddeus chuckled. "In the future I shall endeavor mastering that skill, but until I have done so, I would feel better knowing that you have some form of protection."

"What do you have in mind?" Gavin wondered.

"Come with me," the dragon beckoned.

While the others were distracted, Thaddeus motioned for Gavin to climb up on his back and Sir Osbert took flight.

"Where are we going?" the teen asked.

"You'll see soon enough."

Thaddeus flew for a short distance and set down near the village of Helston, which was pleasantly situated on rising ground above the small river Cober, which, a little below the town, expanded into the picturesque estuary named Looe Pool.

This lagoon was separated from Mount's Bay and the open sea, by a thin stretch of stones and sand surrounding the pool. With the ocean so close, it was a unique situation. High winds buffeted the visitors and they could feel the boom of the waves crashing against the shore with all their fury, even up on the hill. Nearby beautiful woodlands whispered of ancient times and quiet creeks trickled past, carrying pure waters to the sparkling deep lake.

As they proceeded on their journey, they drew closer to the water. Gavin looked puzzled as he gazed upon the blue depths. Thaddeus, however, knew what lay ahead. The dragon and boy stopped at the head of the pool and Sir Osbert motioned for Gavin to go on.

Suddenly, up from the middle of the lake protruded a shimmering arm holding aloft a familiar sword. It was a remarkable sight. Gavin looked over at Thaddeus with astonishment, but when he looked again at the lake, the maiden was standing on the water and coming closer.

The teenaged boy bowed his head and spoke to her with deepest admiration, saying, "Lovely maiden, why do you bring *Caladfwlch* once more?"

Vivienne took a step back and looked at Gavin, before she spoke ever so softly, replying, "The sword belongs to the lake, but I am compelled to return the enchanted blade to you until the threat is no more. The forces of evil are not content to admit defeat. You must wield *Caladfwlch* until such time as the enemy is truly vanquished."

"I shall do as you wish," Gavin said.

"In due time, I shall ask for the blade's return, Sir Gavin," she reminded him. "Until then, carry the sword with my blessing."

Vivienne then departed.

Thaddeus felt obligated to comment. "Handing you that sword was not giving you permission to seek combat, but to use it for defense. Vivienne merely wished you to be well-armed, in case you are threatened."

"I understand, Sir Osbert," Gavin said as he reverently held the mighty *Caladfwlch* with both hands.

The sword throbbed with power, as if it recognized who grasped the hilt.

Thaddeus nodded his head with the realization the boy and sword were forever intertwined. "There is no doubt that *Caladfwlch* responds to you, lad."

Gavin didn't reply, for he was far too busy admiring the edged weapon.

They returned to the little white cottage on the hill, where the others hadn't even noticed their departure.

"It is time to join the gathering elven clans as they prepare for war," the dragon announced. "The three of you must travel with me."

"Yes, Sir Osbert, right away," Gavin obeyed, joined by Bunty and Emily.

They climbed up the spines and took their seats on the dragon's shoulders. The hamlet roof parted and as Thaddeus took off, he became invisible.

Far to the north, along an uninhabited stretch of quiet beach in Northumberland, the ocean tides were unusually active. The water changed colors and churned as if stirred by a giant soupspoon.

Something was amiss.

The soft golden sands seemed to retreat from the waves, while the ancient trees, which sat on windswept dunes, shook and bent under the onslaught of wicked winds. A storm was brewing, yet there were no clouds in sight.

The crumbling ramparts of Dunstanburgh Castle overlooked the bay, where once before, many ages long ago, elves and men formed a hasty alliance to battle the forces of darkness. Now only ghosts and legends guarded this place, again strategic in the minds of brutal invaders.

Up from the ocean's depths they emerged, waves of water replaced by waves of hideous orcs. In formations of thirty abreast, for as far as the eye could see, the mighty beasts came marching ashore.

Despite the ruinous state of Dunstanburgh Castle, it presented a formidable and imposing sight from the distance. Beneath those shattered walls, the orcs gathered, preparing for slaughter and mayhem.

Their attempt to come ashore undetected, however, had failed.

For high on the nearby cliffs, one elf had witnessed the feared threat come true. Kitto sighed and turned to face west. Then, with the practiced arm of an expert archer, she launched a magic arrow high into the air. While still in flight, the shaft exploded, filling the sky with fireworks, the likes of which had never been seen before.

In Cornwall, in Devon, in Dorset, and in Kent, up through Essex, Suffolk, Norfolk, and Lincolnshire, the warning signal was seen by the races hidden from human eyes. The word passed quickly, from Yorkshire to Warwickshire, from Leicestershire to Manchester, from Lancashire to Derbyshire, and Staffordshire, Nottinghamshire, Shropshire, Northamptonshire, Herefordshire, Worcestershire, Buckinghamshire, Bedfordshire, Cambridgeshire, and through Hertfordshire, from Scotland and Wales and Ireland as well, until all of the British Isles knew the invader had come.

Trumpets sounded and bugles called, but there were no tanks or machine-guns, no dive-bombers or battleships. The weapons were swords and spears, shields and bucklers, bows and quivers of arrows, yes, and all manner of ancient accouterments for war. The elves left their homes and loved ones behind, to trickle together in small groups, ever expanding in numbers. This long line of mythical warriors headed north, towards their mystical and spiritual birthplace, which the human race had named Kielder Forest.

The forest was densely populated with Sitka Spruce, Norway Spruce, Lodge-pole Pine, Scots Pine, Douglas Fir, and hundreds of other species of trees. This was the largest virgin forest remaining in England, covering over 230 square miles. It was the last remaining refuge for the gentle races, where little people had gathered for centuries. Elves considered the forest their cultural and religious center. For over a thousand years, the forest had thrived, even under the constant onslaught of humans, who cleared great tracts of trees for lumber.

Here the elves gathered, to hear the speeches of their leaders. In the depths of this forest, the elves would pray to their gods, beg forgiveness from those offended in the past, and raise morale for the fight ahead.

It was little wonder then, when surprise raced through their ranks, as a dragon landed in their midst, accompanied by three human teenagers. Word swept through the assembled throng that the mighty Sir Thaddeus Osbert was now in attendance.

The High Elven Circle was a meeting of the tribal leaders from each of the twelve elven clans. Traditionally, the Circle was called together once every 50 years to discuss matters of interest, but generally met to make decisions only in times of mutual need.

Messengers had been sent out as soon as the possibility of an orc invasion was uncovered. The meeting site was vulnerable to attack, of course, so it was heavily guarded by warriors. Elven magicians also protected the members with the strongest possible shielding spells.

The Circle's elected leader was always female. The position was currently held by a striking raven-haired sorceress by the name of Carlina, who had lived for at least 300 years. Yet her age had made no visible impact on the elf's intoxicating beauty. Carlina held the masses spellbound, her mystic power captivating.

"All Elven interests in Briton are threatened by this reported orc invasion," she stated for all to hear. "An evil army has landed upon our sacred shores."

"This isn't our fight," shouted one of the elven ambassadors. "Humans have brought this pestilence upon them, so let them suffer their fate without our help."

Many voices were raised in agreement.

"Senseless wars have become one of the main principles of mankind," another elf emissary offered her opinion. "Our history is filled with stories of elves rushing to man's aid, only to be shunned afterwards. Let the humans rot. Perhaps they will learn a lesson."

"They don't seem to like us very much," Bunty whispered to Emily.

She merely nodded, not yet ready to reach a conclusion.

"At the war's end, we elves must fall back to our reclusive ways and close our borders to alienate all humans forever," stated another elven leader. "History has proven this to be the only recourse."

The opinions were growing more emotional and less forgiving.

"Will they not come to our aid?" Gavin asked Thaddeus.

The dragon shook his head. "No, no, the elves are not that foolish. This ritual allows everyone to publicly voice their inner thoughts and reservations. The clans know they must face the orc threat, or perish."

Gavin couldn't see that Thaddeus had several talons crossed behind *his* back.

"We elves protect the land, while the humans deforest it by cutting down trees and laying waste," spoke yet another elf. "The world would be a far better place with all humans dead. If the orcs do this deed, then perhaps we should thank them."

"Harrumph!" Thaddeus grumbled, startling everyone by clearing his throat.

His unexpected growling instantly silenced the gathered throng.

"Sir Osbert," Carlina recognized their guest. "Do you wish to say something?"

"What, me?" the dragon pretended to act unprepared. "Oh, well, if you insist, I did have a few things on my mind."

"We recognize your right to speak to this gathering, friend," she said, a sly smile adding to her already unnerving and mischievous beauty.

Thaddeus cleared his throat again. "Thank you, Carlina. I only wanted to point out a few details, in case the clans had overlooked anything."

"Please, continue," the female cleric said.

"I would like to remind everyone gathered here that the orcs aren't coming to massacre humans," Thaddeus roared. "They're coming to eradicate all of you. These orcs won't stop until they've destroyed the magical races. After that, humanity will suffer untold pestilence and disease. Once the fairies, dwarves, elves, and pixies are gone, nothing can prevent the forces of darkness from conquering this planet. Therefore, just in case you haven't recently studied your own history, the orcs have only one thing in mind—the death of all elves, everywhere, forever!"

The thousands of elves remained silent. They knew the dragon spoke the truth.

Then one lone elf spoke out. "What chance have we?"

Thaddeus shrugged. "Perhaps no chance at all. Still, I'd rather go down fighting, than surrender my life to an orc!"

Many of the little people cheered, but the mood was still difficult to gauge.

Carina studied the crowd for a moment, looking for something that would convince her there was an inkling of hope. She found that clue, not in the faces of her fellow elves, but in the sparkling eyes of a teenaged human girl. Emily was determined to make a difference and the elven sorceress could clearly sense the impassioned truth in the girl's eyes.

"The Council thanks Sir Osbert for his comments," Carina said. Then she raised her staff high over her head. It was obviously a symbolic gesture of great significance.

All the elves knelt to the forest floor and bowed their heads.

Carina closed her eyes and uttered a blessing in her native Elven tongue. "*Elen sila lumenn omentilmo. Gurth gothrim Tel'Quessir! Lye nuquernuva sen e dagor. Tae shi shi shaeraer shia kyr thyseli. Bolysia eil beroli shor os pandryl eil cestal eilor.*"

"What did she say?" Emily whispered in the dragon's ear.

"She asked that a star shine bright when the battle is done, signifying the righteousness of our cause," Thaddeus replied quietly. "She blessed her fellow elves and spurred them to victory, while thanking the four of us for aiding them during this difficult time."

Carina waved her staff again and as the elves came to their feet, she made an announcement. "The Council has decided to meet the orcs in battle. Everyone report to your respective clan and prepare to partake in the *Thaer-os-Shari* or Feast of War."

"Eat all there is and drink all you can," proclaimed the elven king from his throne. "For tomorrow your lives may be forfeit."

"What a pleasant way to start a party," Thaddeus commented under his breath. "You children may eat whatever you want, but do not drink anything but water."

"Why not?" Bunty asked innocently.

"Elven concoctions are not meant for human consumption, my red-haired adventurer," the dragon replied. "They smell and taste delicious and are made from a mixture of fruits and berries, before being enchanted with the tiniest bit of faerie dust to blend the tastes together. Such refreshment would curdle your brain and make you do things you would regret later. Pay heed to my warning."

A pretty elven maiden passed amongst them, carrying a large tray of food.

"Rationing doesn't seem to be a problem around here," Bunty commented, following the elf girl, his mouth watering.

While suddenly appearing quite jealous of the impact the serving wench had on Bunty, Kitto led Gavin and Emily to a spot reserved for them. Thaddeus joined them and the group willingly sampled the foodstuffs presented. Bunty found his way to where his friends were sitting, but was surprised by Kitto's unexpected standoffishness.

Elves loved eating all types of food. The selection was colorful and varied, which amazed their human guests. Emily had never guessed there were so many unique and heretofore unknown things to eat. She wanted to remember each fruit or vegetable, to supplement the limited diet created by strict rationing. As growing teens, they were always hungry, so the plentiful choices spurred them to taste everything before them.

"Yum," Emily said after biting into something orange and fruitlike. "Delicious."

"Scrummy, indeed," Bunty added, taking another huge bite from a mutton joint.

Gavin's mouth was too full to say anything, but he enthusiastically nodded his head in agreement. The feast was fantastic.

Even Thaddeus was served. While his manners were usually quite proper, he was a dragon after all, so nobody scolded him. Platter after platter of pastries and desserts were placed before Sir Osbert, who usually wolfed it all down in one bite.

"This is how all wars should begin," Bunty stated. "If we were too busy stuffing our faces with scrumptious yummies, we'd have no time to fight."

They all agreed.

Soon, however, they were stuffed.

"I can't eat another bite," Gavin announced, licking his fingertips.

"Me too," Emily said.

Bunty looked disappointed. "I was going to ask if I could taste one of Sir Osbert's desserts."

The dragon chuckled. "What desserts, my boy? I don't think I left even a crumb remaining."

Bunty pouted, but not for long.

As the emerald forest sparkled in the glittering moonlight, a light and mystical elven tune began to float on the wind. A circle of toadstools was formed, creating a ringed area for the elven dancers to perform.

Kitto momentarily forgot her troubles and was quickly swept into the dance, switching partners back and forth, laughing and singing with delight. Emily also danced in-and-out of the frosty moonlight, spinning around the thin saplings at the edge of the forest.

Gavin and Bunty sat clapping to the beat.

They didn't understand, of course, that the elves were performing a ritual funeral dance, as preparation for countless deaths in the morning.

"We must depart, children," Thaddeus suddenly announced. "It's time to take you home, before your mothers fret. We shall return before the sunrise."

The teens were uncharacteristically quiet during the flight to Boscastle, which took less than fifteen minutes with the speeds the dragon was capable of reaching. Once he set down near a stand of trees, Emily hopped off.

"We'll see you before the sun comes up," Gavin reminded her.

"Won't we get in trouble for ditching classes?" Bunty asked.

"Not if our mothers don't find out," Gavin said.

"Oh, they'll find out," Emily interjected. "Mothers always know everything. That's why they're mothers."

"We'll worry about that when and if the time comes, Emmy," Gavin said, avoiding Emily's conclusion. "Let's meet here at the crossroads and Sir Osbert can pick us up together."

"See you in the morning," Emily called out as she scampered towards her village.

The boys waited until she was safely inside her house, before remounting the dragon's back. When settled, Thaddeus took off again. The trip to Crackington Haven only took a few minutes.

As the dragon dropped off his passengers on the beach, he said, "I am tempted to not come back in the morning, you know."

"Why ever not?" Gavin demanded.

"My better judgment," Thaddeus replied. "I sense you boys will get in trouble, no matter what I try to do to prevent it."

Bunty laughed. "Not us."

The dragon scowled. "This is no joking matter, son."

Bunty gulped.

"We'll behave, Thaddeus, I promise," Gavin said, crossing his heart. "I won't let Bunty or Emily out of my sight."

Sir Osbert looked at the Kane boy with a certain amount of suspicion, for he knew the boy's destiny. "Very well. I will come for you before dawn. Be at the crossroads when I arrive, or I will leave without you. England's future rests on defeating these invaders, so I shan't be late, under any circumstances. Understand?"

Gavin and Bunty nodded emphatically.

Thaddeus departed then and only the flapping of his mighty wings could be heard. The boys stood outside the Kane house, wondering what the morning would bring. It all seemed quite fantastic.

"We're home," Gavin called out as the boys entered the house.

"It's about time," Winifred said from the kitchen. "Do you two have any idea how late it is and how worried I was?"

"We're sorry, Mum," her son said.

"Well, this is the fourth time this week you've been late," she added. "Perhaps you would be more mindful if I punished the both of you?"

Bunty looked at Gavin and vice versa.

There was desperation in their eyes.

"We promise to wear our watches, Mrs. Kane," Bunty pleaded.

"Perhaps you have something special planned for tomorrow?" she asked knowingly, quite observant of their reaction. "Then your punishment will have even more impact. You are to come straight home from school. Do you understand?"

"Oh, please Mum, not tomorrow," Gavin whined.

"There will be no discussion, young man," Winifred countered. "Now wash up for supper and then off to bed. I've run out of patience."

Bunty and Gavin trod off to the bathroom, where they washed their hands and faces. The dinner conversation was very subdued and neither boy asked for second helpings, because they had already eaten too much at the elven feast. They even skipped listening to the nightly BBC War Report, but went straight to their bedrooms.

Several hours later, when Gavin was certain his mother was asleep, he snuck into Bunty's room.

"Are you awake?" he whispered.

"Of course."

"I'm still cutting school tomorrow," Gavin said. "Are you with me?"

"Bloody well right," Bunty said. "I wouldn't miss it for the world."

"Mum is going to throw a wobbly over this," Gavin said.

"We're loony, you know," Bunty said in return. "Now go back to sleep. We're off in just a few hours."

Gavin returned to his bed, but he couldn't fall sleep. His head was full of depressing thoughts and his heart filled with doubts. The air around him was charged with energy and it didn't feel positive either. With pillows propped up behind him, the boy closed his eyes and concentrated on his father, praying he was doing the right thing.

It was still pitch black when Thaddeus arrived to pick up Gavin, Bunty and Emily. He was cloaked in invisibility, of course, but the teens were extra vigilant as they climbed up the dragon's back and disappeared. Such unexplained sightings might complicate matters greatly.

Thankfully still undiscovered, Thaddeus flew directly to Kielder Forest, where the elven army had formed ranks, their numbers facing the coast road.

In the distance, the sounds of stomping feet and rattling equipment echoed.

Heavy fog obscured everyone's view, but no one doubted the noise originated from the orcs marching inland up from the beaches.

Thump, thump, thump, rattle, boom, boom, boom!

Thump, thump, thump, rattle, boom, boom, boom!

The trees shook from the thunderous pounding of war drums. The deep guttural chants of the orcs had a rhythm of their own, but the result was unnerving.

The sounds gave Bunty shivers.

"I shall return," Thaddeus informed everyone. "Remember, children, you are forbidden to participate in this conflict."

"Yes, Sir Osbert," the three of them replied dutifully.

The dragon took off again, heading due north.

"I wonder where he's going?" Bunty asked.

Gavin gripped *Caladfwlch* tightly and finally made up his mind. He would use the magical sword to fend off the orcs until Thaddeus returned. It was the least he could do to help the cause.

Just as everyone was getting used to the constantly reverberating drums, the beating suddenly stopped.

There followed only silence.

Complete and utter silence.

22

Invasion

After their non-combatants had fled to the relative safety of distant Wales, the elf warriors formed their war groups into compact battle cells within Kielder Forest. Each unit was effectively independent, able to melt invisibly into the thick undergrowth of their homeland, and possessing a near infinite number of prepared caches of weapons and food. Incredibly mobile, these teams could regroup and coordinate their hit-and-run attacks from an equal number of hidden strongholds, such as caves behind waterfalls, platforms high up among branches, and bunkers among the roots.

The typical elf warrior forewent armor in favor of mobility and stealth, choosing instead camouflaged clothing and body paint. Those few warriors, who departed from this standard, often wore only a flexible breast covering of hardened bones, or one of boiled leather.

Shields were also made of hardened leather stretched across a circular frame of wood and were decorated with black feathers. Weapons, like bows, spears, long-bladed knives, clubs, and hatchets were the most typical arms. Most of the heads of these weapons were of the highest quality, though they were blackened with oils to eliminate glinting. Elves made the most of native materials, both in place of and alongside metals. Obsidian was commonly used to augment clubs and axes, as the edges were often sharper than steel.

The first elf unit to march to battle was the light infantry. These elves, usually younger and nimbler than others, were armed with swords, bucklers, and javelins, with leather armor. They were lightly armed, because they were skirmishers and flankers, darting back and forth along the flanks to reinforce, outmaneuver, and throw their javelins continually into enemy formations. If the battle took place on the coastal road, the light infantry was free to move through the flanking woods, without worrying about bulky armor or weapons.

Then came the light archers, similar in attributes and armor, but armed with short bows as their primary weapon, backed up by short-swords, daggers, and hatchets.

The heavy infantry came next, usually chosen from the more experienced and steady of the elves, dressed in golden chainmail, helmets, and other accoutrements. They marched in phalanx formation, wielding halberds, spears, pikes, glaives, and other pole-arms. The elven halberdiers were renowned throughout the mystic lands. The phalanxes were exceptionally skilled at breaking up the massed charges of orc attackers. Once the enemy ranks were broken, the orcs were easier targets for the archers.

The heavy archers took positions of advantage and were armored with silver chainmail. A heavy oval shield was imbedded in front of the archer for protection. From great distances, these units would launch their arrows into the rear of orc formations, to cause havoc on the supporting units. The heavy archer was armed with a giant longbow, and weighed down with multiple quivers of heavy sheaf arrows. They were unable to move as fast as the lighter archers, but their arrows blackened the sky and punctured orc armor like paper.

In addition, the forest was home to many unusual beings, including treants, fairies, and other magical races. Most of these creatures were well aware that should the elves fail, the earth would not last long in the face of orc conquest, so threw in their lot with the elves. Treants were useful as medics, while fairies were deployed as spies and messengers.

Unlike so many elves, Kitto preferred face-to-face combat. However, her culture insisted she use her stealthy abilities to take advantage of each situation. To this end, she was able to hide in the shadows, which made her invisible for short periods of time. Using this tactic, Kitto was constantly leaping from dark corners, darting behind enemies, and using a backstab motion, which was the elf's signature attack, assuring quick and silent takedowns.

Kitto also had some fancy moves when it came to acrobatics, as she took to flipping up onto the heads of rather surprised orcs and doing them in from the top down. Probably not a pretty sight from afar, but up close it was breath taking.

Kitto once again cursed herself. Exhilarated by her initial success, she had felt invincible as she went after a group of scouting orcs. Of course, even a half dozen orcs would have been more than a match for her abilities, but only because they were so big and ugly and smelled disgusting.

She made an angry noise.

The female elf was exhausted, but she couldn't afford to rest right then, because there were even more orcs roaming the area after coming ashore. Her double blades would have to suffice, if the big slobs were foolish enough to attack her.

Crack.

A noise alerted her.

Reluctantly, Kitto drew her knives. Even with such fine artistry, these sharp instruments were such a crude and primitive way of killing orcs.

Crack.

She jumped.

There it was again, almost as if on purpose.

Kitto started moving again and was thankful that none of her companions could see her now. It was incredibly disgraceful, an elfish thief of her rank picking her way through the shoulder-high grass and startled by every little noise.

Maybe she was even afraid of orcs that might be lurking in the grass around her.

Ridiculous!

Angrily, she started chopping at the grass ahead of her with her knives to speed up her progress. There was no way she would ever be afraid of an orc. After all, orcs were just big stupid brutes.

Kitto's face curled with disgust at the mere thought of orcs. They smelled foul and slobbered, drooling between their hideous tusks.

Another twig cracked nearby.

Kitto whirled around, forcing herself to make a confident smile.

So, she was being followed after all.

She would teach those orcs a thing or two about trying to sneak up on an elf.

Facing the direction of the noise, Kitto took up a desperate stance.

Then she had second thoughts.

It was too late.

Just as she was about to run away, a gigantic orc burst from the undergrowth. The monster let loose a wild scream and slammed headlong into Kitto's exposed left side.

The attack sent both her and the orc sprawling to the ground.

She quickly regained her footing, both knives in hand, but the orc was already back on his feet too. All of a sudden, the monster displayed a large, wicked looking double-headed battleaxe.

Kitto met his gaze and lifted her weapons to defend. Slowly, they started circling each other. It was hard to believe this orc had been able to surprise her, but now the combat would be close-in and even more brutal.

As they gauged each other, waiting for an opening to appear in the other's defense, she was again filled with fear after looking into the orc's red eyes staring back at her. The wind carried the odor of his sweat over to her and she recoiled in disgust.

That was the very moment the orc chose for his attack.

His downward swing of the axe was met by the desperate crossed block of both her long knives. The impact drove all feeling out of Kitto's arms, as she was forced to retreat. She could barely hold her weapons, as waves of pain raced up and down her arms.

With a grunt, the orc pulled back, but he immediately tried to follow up with another blow. This time Kitto managed to evade it, knowing that the orc had the strength and endurance she could not hope to counter.

Trying to take advantage of her superior speed, Kitto responded with a quick slash, scoring a shallow cut on the orc's forearm. The pain of the slash only fueled the beast's anger. Again, Kitto managed to jump aside, but when she tried to counter with another quick attack, the orc simply knocked her knife aside with his free hand.

Too late, Kitto noticed that she had underestimated her opponent again.

With incredible agility for such a big creature, the orc vaulted to one side and brought his battleaxe down to strike.

Kitto tried to spin away, but the flat side of the orc's axe hit her in the head.

The force of the blow sent stars dancing in front of Kitto's eyes. Losing her grip on her knives, she was thrown back and went down to the ground. Her last thought, before losing consciousness, was of the human boy named Bunty.

When Kitto opened her eyes again, she was surprised to discover she was still alive. A groan escaped as the elf tried to move her head. Closing her eyes until the pain became bearable again, she sat up once more, very carefully this time.

In a sitting position, Kitto was able to see that she was a prisoner of the orcs. While unconscious, the elf had been placed in a cage, which was deep within the orc base camp. She recoiled in horror when realizing her prison was actually near the field kitchens.

"You will be my dinner upon my return," one orc said slowly as he passed her cage. The creature seemed to have trouble forming sounds foreign to his throat, but Kitto understood him anyway.

The orc moved closer, so the elf would not be able to miss a word he was saying. Kitto could smell his stinking breath and see his sharp teeth as he continued talking. "I shall return, elf and when I do, you will make a tasty little snack."

Then off he went, lumbering along to join his many comrades.

As the sun peeked over the horizon, Kitto watched the orc army assemble and move ahead towards the thick undergrowth. They appeared to cover the ground like giant insects. Her eyes opened wider as she realized the sheer numbers of orcs milling about. Surely, her fellow elves had no idea how many of the enemy they would be facing.

Kitto studied seven-foot-tall, gray-skinned goblins with pointed ears, fangs and claws, carrying battle-axes and wearing strange black or gray uniforms. Surely, her people had no chance of surviving this day.

For there were literally tens of thousands of orcs forming to attack.

As the sun came up over **RAF Medmenham**, Lieutenant Commander Richard Kane was trying to enjoy a simple cup of black coffee.

There was knocking on his billet door.

"Enter," Kane said.

In stepped Lieutenant Stevens.

"Ah, it's you again, Michael," Kane chuckled.

"Aye, sir, me again," Lt. Stevens said as he came to attention. "You're wanted in photo analysis, sir. It is vitally important, I'm afraid, sir."

Richard stood up, stretched, and grabbed his coat. "No need to apologize, Lieutenant. I'm getting used to being indispensable."

Stevens chuckled. "Yes, sir, I imagine you are."

The two officers strolled over to the main building, sharing chitchat about nothing in particular. It was difficult to talk about family, home, and happiness in the middle of a war.

Kane walked into the photographic interpretation room, where as usual, he was greeted by a mob. He held his hands up before they all started chattering.

"All right, one at a time," the lieutenant commander said. "Let's let Margaret go first."

"Thank you, sir," said Margaret Bromley, a Wren who specialized in German aircraft. "Please take a look at this, sir."

Kane stepped over to Bromley's station, where he peered into her stereoscope. He almost swallowed his tongue. So as to not give his reaction away, Richard kept his forehead pressed down on the rim and studied the details of the photograph.

There was no use trying to deny what he saw this time.

It was clearly the image of a dragon in flight, wings spread wide. However, it was most certainly not Thaddeus Osbert. That was some consolation.

Richard stood straight and turned to look at his staff, one at a time. They all were expectantly waiting for his reaction. Kane shook his head, coughed a little, and said, "Well, it looks like a bloody big dragon!"

The interpreters were amazed by his candor.

To himself, Richard wondered what else could he have said? This way his response was so obviously impossible, that it might deflect them from reaching the right conclusion, no matter how improbable that answer might be.

"But, sir, how can it be a dragon?" Sally Fairborne asked.

Richard smiled. "Well, it can't be, of course. It's obviously a very ingenious attempt to drive us to distraction, which I would say was quite effective, based on how many of my people were baffled by what they saw."

There was some uncomfortable laughter from the group.

"It's possible the Germans have developed a new fighter or bomber that resembles a dragon, which would be pretty frightening," Kane continued. "In that case, we will have to notify our reconnaissance flights to re-photograph this area. Where exactly was this photo taken?"

"Near Wewelsburg again, sir," Miss Fairborne replied. "There seems to be a lot of unusual activity nearby. Our pilot complained of strange atmospheric conditions and electromagnetic interference. Some of the photos turned out blank."

"Overexposed or underexposed?" Kane asked.

"Both."

"Now that is strange."

"We thought so too."

"So, the Germans probably *do* have something to hide, if they would go to all that effort to prevent our air reconnaissance," Kane concluded. "Let's bump up the status on this region to orange. I think Bomber Command should be made aware of the activity and let's prepare a report for the SOE boys too. They may want to send a covert operative to the area to snoop around."

"Yes, sir," Miss Fairborne obeyed. "I'll get right on it, sir."

"Very well," Richard wrapped up the briefing. "Carry on, everyone."

Before returning to his room to continue his five-hour break, Kane decided to visit his commanding officer, Wing Commander Derek Cranwell.

He rapped softly on the door to the wing commander's office.

"Richard, do come in," Cranwell said in a very informal manner.

"Thank you, sir," Kane replied, coming to attention.

"What brings you my direction?" Cranwell asked, rising to shake Richard's hand. "I haven't done something to irritate the Royal Navy now, have I?"

Lt. Cmdr. Kane laughed and shook his head. "No, sir, nothing like that."

"Well, take a seat and let's chat."

"Very good, sir."

Both officers sat down across from each other. Richard knew it was up to him to start the conversation. He really wasn't comfortable with what was on his mind, so it took a moment to screw up the courage to ask.

"Spit it out, lad," Cranwell coached. "I can't say no, until I hear what you've got on your mind." He ended the statement with an exaggerated smile.

"Well, sir, it's like this," Richard said. "I have a hunch."

"Oh, bravo!" the wing commander reacted with delight. "I love bloody hunches, especially from your branch. They usually turn out to be something quite marvelous."

Cranwell's enthusiasm came as something of a relief.

Kane just launched into his theory, saying, "I'm afraid I don't have much to go on, sir, but I think the Germans have built a top-secret experimental base in the Alma Valley, near Wewelsburg."

Cranwell leaned forward with obvious interest. "You don't say?"

"We have some photographic evidence to raise suspicion, but much of it is circumstantial at best," Richard added. "It's just that …"

The wing commander didn't let him finish. "It's just that you've got this feeling that something is amiss, eh?"

"Yes, sir," Kane replied.

"I see," Cranwell said, pondering and evaluating. For what he knew of the lieutenant commander, the Navy officer wasn't given to flights of fantasy and didn't make rash judgments either. If Richard Kane suspected that the Germans were up to something, then they probably were.

"Let me have what you've got and your recommendations," Kane's commanding officer said. "I will push for Bomber Command to assign a recon flight with the next outgoing bombing run near the Alma Valley. Would that be to your liking?"

Kane smiled and came to attention. "Yes, sir."

"Jolly good," Cranwell said. "Carry on."

Richard returned to his room with a new list of worries to add to the ones he already had been balancing.

"A dragon," he mumbled to himself. "I wonder if Thaddeus knows?"

Just then, Richard remembered the suggestion Gavin had made a month before. It was possible Thaddeus Osbert's special visual abilities could make a difference after all. Lt. Cmdr. Kane closed his eyes and willed his thoughts to carry on the wind.

"Thaddeus," he whispered aloud. "I desperately need your help, please."

After awhile, Richard fell asleep, exhausted by the long day and the concentrated effort to make mental contact with Sir Osbert. The lieutenant commander had no idea, of course, that the dragon was actually quite distracted.

For at that very moment, the dragon was flying to Iceland.

Richard's mental transmissions did successfully travel that great distance.

Unfortunately, Thaddeus was not the only one receiving those thoughts.

For deep within the Alma Valley, perched high overlooking the Wewelsburg Castle, a black dragon intercepted Richard Kane's mental telepathy. In so doing, the creature, empowered with a sadistic human mind, had discovered the whereabouts of the dragon realm.

23

The Tide Turns

"It sure is loud," Bunty whispered.

The silence continued, as the fog slowly burned away under the rising sun.

"Alarm!" a single elf scout suddenly cried out.

Near the forest's edge, an enormous orc stepped to the front, raising his sword overhead and flexing his massive muscles. His temples throbbed with the sadistic urge to kill. This was the moment of reckoning, when his orc brothers would slaughter every last elf, before moving on to massacre the entire human race.

"Argh!" Tulgan roared with all his might.

His hideous battle cry was the signal to charge.

A flood of orcs stormed out of the bank of dissipating fog and down the hill, resembling a stone avalanche, rolling ever closer, snarling and howling for blood. On they came, a wall of slathering and mindless creatures, bent on the destruction of all living things before them.

Nothing could stop the densely closed shields and spears of the fearless orcs. Every feature of their faces expressed their single-minded desire to lock in mortal combat. Their pulsating red eyes burned with the lust of easy trophies.

"Never mind, let blood cover the entire battlefield!" shouted the elven general.

The mass of charging brutes barreled headlong into the solid thin line of golden armor. The elven ranks dissolved under the sheer weight of the assault. However, the solid wedge of orcs suddenly encountered the whirling and slicing blades of the finest elf army in the hidden world. It was no human screams of death and pain that echoed up over the valley and nearby British farmers stopped what they were doing, wondering what animals were suffering so, to make such wretched sounds.

Suddenly, detaching from the line and swiftly circling to attack the enemy army's flank, the elven heavy infantry cleaved into the orc formation. At that very moment, the elven archers drew hundreds of bowstrings and a black swarm of piercing arrows fell upon the orcs like lightning bolts, striking again and again.

As the battle developed, Emily and Bunty watched from the relative safety of a series of pixy-stands, erected high in the trees. While orcs fought tooth-and-nail with elves, each side swinging deadly swords and clanking massive shields, the teens cringed at the horrible sounds of impact. Thousands of orcs were still amassing on the beachhead. Along the shattered front lines of the conflict, elven archers were launching wave after wave of magic arrows in the direction of the advancing army, perforating hundreds with long shafts.

"Kitto still hasn't returned," Emily whined worriedly.

"We must go see if we can find her," Bunty suggested.

"It's too dangerous," she protested. "Besides, where is Gavin?"

"But Kitto's my friend," Bunty countered.

"Thaddeus forbid us from getting involved."

"I can't just sit here and do nothing, Emmy."

"What do you think you can do? You're not a soldier."

"I know that, but I must do something."

"We can't leave this spot without Gavin's permission."

"And where is he? Gone off to be a hero, I imagine, and without us."

Emily finally relinquished "All right, let's go, but quietly and quickly."

Carefully they climbed down from the tree-stand and tiptoed from trunk-to-trunk, dodging from left-to-right, easily avoiding columns of assaulting orcs. The duo was able to find a gap through the advancing formations, as many orcs detoured wide to avoid the heaps of their own dead and dying.

Lowering their heads behind the thick underbrush, the teens were passed by dozens of slobbering orcs. Finally, the army of invaders passed by, and Emily took Bunty's hand. Flitting from tree to boulder to bush, the pair came upon what looked like the orc staging area. Several cages were suspended from nearby trees and inside one of them Kitto struggled to break out.

"Hang on, Kitto, I'll set you free," Bunty called up to the elf.

The boy jumped high to grab a branch, and then swung himself up to latch onto another. From there he scooted up the trunk, before inching out onto the limb where Kitto's cage was suspended.

Reaching down, Bunty tried to unfasten the crude rope fastener. He fumbled with it for awhile, but without success.

"Don't move!" Emily whispered harshly from the bushes below. "Someone's coming."

Bunty held perfectly still, hoping his outline would appear to be part of the branch.

Kitto slowly sat down and pretended to be asleep.

Just as Emily had warned, two orcs wandered into the base camp. They seemed to be loitering, as if engaging in the battle was the last thing on their minds. Bunty wondered if perhaps even orcs could be cowards at times.

One of the brutes looked up and saw one of the cages wasn't empty.

"Food," he grunted.

His companion drooled. "Eat."

Together the orcs untied the rope holding the suspended cage and lowered it to the ground. Kitto remained motionless.

"Kill it first," the larger beast instructed the other.

Out slid a wicked looking blade and the wielder aimed for the elf's chest.

"Not bloody likely!" Bunty yelled, just before he jumped from the limb overhead.

"Ugh," one orc grunted, pointing up in surprise.

That was the only sound the orc uttered, for Bunty drove his elven sword straight through the creature's chest. The two of them tumbled to the ground, but unfortunately, the orc's body fell on top of Bunty, pinning him.

"You kill Molkar?" the other orc said after kicking his comrade's lifeless form. "Me kill you."

However, his face was suddenly etched with intense pain and complete surprise.

The orc took one step forward, croaked, and fell over dead.

Two knives jutted from the center of his back.

Elsewhere in the forest, Gavin had completely disregarded Sir Osbert's orders. Instead of sticking close to his friends, the young man had ventured off on his own, hoping to outflank the enemy forces and attack them from the rear. After all, he wielded a powerful weapon and the boy was certain Arthur's sword would tilt the balance in favor of the elves.

Caladfwlch vibrated, emitting an eerie whistle.

"There must be orcs nearby," Gavin whispered to himself.

Swish.

Ducking instinctively, the teen just barely avoided being skewered by an arrow.

Thud.

The shaft imbedded itself in the tree trunk just behind him, the feather still quivering. Gavin sighed and looked in the direction from where the arrow had come.

Standing in plain sight was a monster, with tusks jutting from his mouth.

The creature was clearly evil and clearly not human.

"So, you're an orc," Gavin shouted, hoping to steady his nerves.

The orc roared back in defiance.

Gavin set his eyes on his target and charged, running headlong toward the beast.

This action pleased the orc immensely, for he was convinced his target would be an easy kill. Just as Gavin reached the end of the path, he leapt to one side and engaged in a quick, brutal swordfight with the orc archer that had tried to kill him. *Caladfwlch* struck home with unerring accuracy, instantly severing the orc's head from his shoulders.

Gavin had no time to congratulate himself, for emerging from the surrounding forest, burst a horde of orcs, all converging on the teen. The boy considered running in terror, but it was too late. They quickly surrounded him, jaws drooling and snapping open-and-shut in a disgusting rhythm of doom.

To kill any orc required one savage, well-placed blow.

Gavin knew that *Caladfwlch* would make a noticeable difference, however, because its enchanted blade could slice through any armor, ancient or modern. He pointed the tip of the blade in the direction of the advancing orcs.

"Destroy!" he shouted.

A bolt of searing blue lightning blasted them all to pieces, evaporating orc lives in an instant. Nothing remained except for little piles of gray ash.

Gavin looked down at the sword and shuddered for a moment, feeling the supernatural power of the blade reverberating through his body. Recovering from the initial impact that such a weapon caused, the boy headed towards the rear of the advancing orc army, hoping to inflict more casualties.

Inside the abandoned orc base-camp, Bunty, Emily and Kitto were grateful to be alive. The impromptu rescue has succeeded, but perhaps only by sheer dumb luck.

"You are so brave," Kitto said to Bunty, before she threw her arms around him and planted a huge kiss on his cheek.

Poor Bunty turned several shades of deepening reds, tremendously embarrassed. He staggered and stammered, retreating as best he could

Emily thought it was adorable and said in a childlike voice, "Oh, Bunty, you're our hero!"

"Stop that!" he demanded.

Kitto was confused by Bunty's reaction, but she grabbed his hand and pulled him closer. "You are very smart and courageous, for a human."

Still blushing, Bunty said, "You're pretty brave for a girl ... I mean elf ... to fight orcs all by yourself."

Kitto batted her eyes. "Do you think so?"

Emily couldn't help giggling. "You two are so cute together."

Bunty tried to take control of the situation, before it got out of hand. "It's time to get back to our lines, before Thaddeus finds out we disobeyed him."

They turned to look across the meadow, watching the battle unfold.

"We're losing," Kitto whispered sadly.

"Not yet, we're not," Bunty blurted, pointing up at the sky. "Look!"

Thaddeus Osbert had returned and just in time.

Thundering downward from the clouds, the dragon was a gigantic quadruped reptile, with vast bat-like wings. Armed with razor-sharp teeth and tearing claws, along with his mighty tail, Sir Osbert's most formidable weapon was the white-hot jets of liquid flame shooting from his mouth. His timely intervention instantly lifted the morale of the embattled elves and motivated his young fans to cheer in delight.

Thaddeus was perhaps the most magical of all of God's creations, with powers of shape shifting, self-regeneration, mind reading, and invisibility, all available to him when necessary. He was covered in impenetrable scales and had evolved into the perfect fighting machine, almost impervious to any weapon the orcs had at their disposal.

Out of the sky he came, a flying, fire-breathing, swooping-down-to-obliterate-his-enemy, flesh-incinerating dragon. His mighty roar reverberated throughout the countryside. Any human within a hundred miles knew that something awesome and powerful had arrived, even if they had no idea what exactly it was.

24

Secret of the Dragon's Breath

As waves of orcs swarmed over the scattering elf defenders, Thaddeus had suddenly appeared overhead. The red dragon swooped down over the battlefield and let loose repeated torrents of liquid flame, incinerating hundreds of orcs at every pass. The attack was perfectly timed and executed, much like some of Gavin's finest chess moves.

The dragon's breath came from a distance of over 90 feet, sweeping an arc of thirty degrees in either direction. The liquid flame stuck to anything it touched and burned for several minutes.

The orcs died in droves.

Piles of charred remains slowed the orc advance, giving time for the battered elven army to regroup. Their once majestic ranks of shimmering golden armor now seriously depleted and every last reserve committed, the next stage would be the deciding and perhaps final phase of the conflict.

It was either victory or death.

The orcs regained their courage and as a mass moved forward once again. This time, however, their charge was not as reckless, as the invaders were forced to pick their way around or over piles of their fallen comrades.

Once again, arrows rained down upon them, as every elven archer unloosed the last remaining shafts from their quivers. Scores of orcs fell, but the bulk of the army marched onward, the cries for blood increasing in volume and tenacity.

The clash of steel and cries of combat drowned out every other sound. Battle-hardened elves met slathering vicious orcs, fighting for their very lives, standing toe-to-toe, slaughtering each other in droves. It was horrific, insane, and brutal, but the outcome would decide the future of all elf races, as well as humanity.

The orcs fighting style was nothing more than insane brawling. They waded into the ranks of elves, swinging their axes from left to right, almost without regard to their comrades beside them. Axes fell and swords slashed, shields were shattered and spears broken, lives were taken with little thought to who they had once been.

Orcs poured into the lines of elves all across the battlefield, and so the fight continued in earnest, up and down the hillside. Heavy blows landed and elves died at the hands of their enemies. The battle ebbed and flowed, raging on, until things looked like they would definitely go against the elves.

The left flank was holding, as the heavy infantry managed to limit the number of orcs breaking through, thereby preventing the enemy from getting in behind and surrounding them. With only one or two orcs squared off against one or two elves, the orcs couldn't expand on their initial gains. Still, the fighting was intense and many brave elves died along with their orc victims.

Unfortunately, the right flank was a completely different story.

Tulgan's handpicked orcs, with the aid of his best archers and berserkers, were able to crush the defenders, leaving the right flank broken. Much death and slaughter was brought upon the elves and much feasting was had by the hungry orcs! In fact, if not for the return intervention of Thaddeus, the conflict would have been lost.

Along the front lines of the battle, orcs were launching scores of flaming arrows, which rained down on the elven center. Yet before they could capitalize on their good fortune, the massive red dragon appeared overhead. It was highflying death from above.

Sir Osbert's fiery breath, which was similar to a large flamethrower, was one of the most powerful weapons the dragon possessed.

Not only did Thaddeus use his jet of liquid fire to engulf the charging orcs, but he also hurled red-hot fireballs down upon them, incinerating them to ashes. The dragon had momentarily returned to Iceland to stock up on lava ammunition, which he now tossed into the midst of the orcs, cutting through their ranks like bowling pins.

Thaddeus was not fond of orc as a meal, but neither could he be fussy, so with each pass the dragon inhaled the wafting ash and smoke. His hunger was quickly satiated and after that, the dragon attacked with a renewed sense of vigor.

The orcs could no longer stand by and be defeated by this flying scourge.

Tulgan redirected his remaining orc archers to aim their arrows at Thaddeus. At first, the dragon just swatted aside hundreds of flying shafts coming towards him. Then, as if often the case in war, the unexpected changed the balance yet again.

"Thaddeus, look out!" Gavin shouted as he emerged from the forest.

A giant ballista spear came hurtling upward, heading straight for the dragon's head. Only as a reflex, Sir Osbert avoided taking the deadly missile in his left eye, but in his desperate maneuver to flip away, the twenty-foot-long spike pierced his left wing.

"Grrrrgh!" Thaddeus growled in pain.

The membrane was perforated and with the injury, the dragon lost his ability to fly. Down he came, headlong to the earth.

"Oh, no," Gavin cried out. The boy darted between orcs, stabbing left and right, intent on aiding the dragon in any way he could. He certainly was glad he carried the magical sword *Caladfwlch.*

Thump.

Thaddeus hit the earth, sending shockwaves like a miniature earthquake.

"Kill the dragon!" Tulgan shouted.

Blood lust in their eyes, many orcs broke away from the main battle to seek vengeance on the wounded creature. Whosoever killed the dragon would undeniably prove their courage to the clan.

"We're with you, Gavin," shouted Bunty, who was running forward with Emily and Kitto too.

"Thaddeus has been badly wounded," Gavin informed them. "We must go and protect him."

"What about all the orcs?" Emily naturally asked.

Bunty waved his elven sword before her face. "God help the orc that gets in my way. For God, King, Country, and Thaddeus Osbert!"

Side-by-side, Gavin and Bunty took off on the run, straight towards the mob of orcs converging on the struggling dragon.

Emily and Kitto were right behind them.

The teens could see the downed dragon, who was in a bit of an irritable mood, seeing as how there were orcs trying to slice at his face with blackened swords. With razor-sharp tooth and talon alike, Thaddeus slew every monster that came too close.

Gavin and Bunty continued their headlong charge.

The orcs were firing wildly now, blindly shooting arrows through the trees. Just as the boys started to reconsider their impetuous attack, it was too late. An orc jumped out and shot a poisoned arrow straight at Kitto's head.

"Look out!" Bunty cried, pushing the elf aside.

With a cry of pain, the red-haired boy staggered and fell.

His side had been pierced, the slender shaft protruding.

Horrified, Kitto leapt forward, thrusting both of her sharp knives deep into the orc's heart.

Thaddeus witnessed this tragedy and suddenly reared up on his hind legs. With a titanic roar of sorrow and unbridled rage, the dragon opened his mouth wide. However, instead of molten-hot flames, out came a completely different type of breath. This incredibly magical dragon began spitting a steady stream of freezing blue liquid, filled with puncturing shards of solid ice.

Gavin dropped to his knees and grabbed Bunty's hand. "Hang on, old chum. I'll get you help right away."

Grimacing, Bunty said, "I'll be just fine, sport."

Kitto was sobbing. "He saved my life."

Emily put her arm around the elf and squeezed. "He'll be okay."

"Can you walk?" Gavin asked.

"I think so," Bunty replied, grasping his bleeding side.

Gavin lifted his friend to his feet and draped one arm over his shoulder. They started to hobble away, but both boys stopped to look over their shoulders.

Thaddeus was now unbelievably enormous, growing to such size that he towered over the trees themselves. The dragon was thoroughly enraged and his face was contorted with terrible intent. Unleashing his icy breath in a sweeping arc, the orcs within range were immediately frozen solid. Hundreds of elves regained their courage and charged across the meadow, following right behind the dragon's chilly path, shattering the orcs into a thousand pieces with their hacking swords.

What moments before had been the rout of elven forces, was now reversed into a coordinated counterattack. This, in turn, developed into the slaughter of the remaining orc invaders.

"He sure is something when he gets mad," Bunty commented.

Gavin didn't say anything. In his heart he suddenly felt sorry for the orcs, for they never had a chance. Turning his attention to Bunty once again, he said, "Come on, old chap, I need to get you to the elf wizards, so they can take care of that arrow."

Kitto's face was ashen white.

"What's wrong?" Emily asked her, holding back her tears.

The elf's bottom lip quivered. "Orc arrows are tipped with poison."

"Oh, my God!" Emily exclaimed.

Gavin half-carried the wounded Bunty straight to the elven base camp, where news of the victory over the orcs was just being delivered. Amongst the cheering crowd of little people, Kitto pushed ahead to make a path.

"Clear the way, please," she cried. "A hero is mortally wounded."

"Don't say that!" Emily protested.

With Kitto's pronouncement, however, the elves parted. In the center of the camp, the clan's wizards, sorcerers, and magicians gathered to care for the wounded human. The elven king decreed that Bunty was to receive the best medicine possible.

"It burns," the red-haired boy groaned through clenched teeth.

One wizened old elf carefully snapped the arrow shaft in two and slid the pieces out from either end of the puncture. He cast them into the fire, where they burst into purplish-orange flames.

The sage's face was etched with worry. He dug deep into his embroidered cloth bag of remedies, potions, and cure-alls, searching for just the right concoction. All about him the elves were deathly silent, for this type of work required deep concentration.

For over an hour, the soothsayer worked on Bunty's wound, applying balms and stopping the flow of blood. His strange chants and incantations didn't seem to prevent the boy from slipping into semi-consciousness.

Finally, the sage shook his head in frustration. "Nothing I do is working."

Kitto stepped forward. "How is that possible?"

The wizard shrugged with confusion. "I do not know why our trusted remedies are failing. Our magic does not seem to help this human recover."

Gavin fought back tears of sorrow and took off to find Thaddeus.

He was running along a thick forest trail, a place so dark that the bark of the trees was black and the leaves were silhouettes against the small amount of light that managed to make it through the upper branches. Gavin was breathing heavily and squinting to avoid the wooden fingers that seemed to jump out of the darkness scraping his cheeks and arms. When he finally came upon a patch of bright light, the boy slowed and in an instance of clarity, the shape of a dragon loomed before him.

Thaddeus was plucking hundreds of arrows from between his scales, while nearby lay the gigantic spear that had pierced his wing. There were literally thousands of dead orcs all around the dragon.

"Will you be all right, Sir Osbert?" Gavin asked as he burst out from the trees. He had to pick his way around the bodies.

"I've seen better days, lad, that's for sure," Thaddeus replied. "How is Bunty?"

Gavin's eyes filled with tears once again. "The elf wizard says he will die."

Thaddeus came to his feet in one fluid motion, the rip in his left wing quite noticeable. "What did you say?"

Gavin started to cry. "It's all my fault, Thaddeus. I didn't listen to your warning and now Bunty is going to die!"

"Not as long as I breathe, my boy," the dragon roared. "Follow me."

Lumbering through the forest like a maniacal bull on the loose, Thaddeus pushed aside trees as if they were matchsticks. He was on a mission and pity anyone who got in his way. The mighty beast pulled up just as he entered the elven camp, afraid he might crush some hapless elf.

"Where is the red-haired boy?" Thaddeus called out.

"Here on this cot, Sir Osbert," Carina replied. "Our best sages can do nothing to save him."

"Harrumph!" the dragon growled. "Utter nonsense."

The dragon was actually bluffing, because he new the situation was dire. Yet he had to bolster morale for the children, even if Bunty was too delirious to hear any of it.

"Oh, Thaddeus, what will you do?" Emily asked desperately.

"I'm considering my options, Emmy," Thaddeus replied, thinking hard.

"Would your magical tears help heal him?" Emily wondered.

The dragon shook his great head. "I'm afraid not, lass. Orc poison is impervious to dragon magic. This requires the special skills and spells of a human witch or wizard."

"Do you know any?" Gavin asked.

With a twinkle in his eyes, Thaddeus said, "In fact I do, but first I'll fly you children home, before contacting an old friend."

The dragon flapped his damaged wing and implored the elven wizards to gather. "Help me repair this tear in my wing, please?"

They surrounded Thaddeus and applied elixirs and potions to the nasty gash, holding the membrane in place. Within minutes, the magic worked to repair the wound.

"I'll be sporting a nasty scar from now on," the dragon joked, testing the wing.

Gavin hung his head.

Thaddeus gently lifted his chin with one talon. "This is no time for feelings of guilt, lad. There is no greater waste of emotion. You must have faith. We have work to do. You want to save Bunty, don't you?"

"Of course," Gavin replied.

"Then you must fabricate a story to tell your mother," Thaddeus said. "I hate to ask such a thing of you, but it's for her own good. Do you think you can do so convincingly?"

"Yes, I think so," Gavin replied.

"After I have dropped you off, I will fetch a wizard and return as soon as possible," the dragon said. "Let's go!"

Picking up Bunty as gently as a feather, Thaddeus placed the suffering child on his shoulder. Gavin and Emily climbed up the dragon's tail and held Bunty still, as Sir Osbert prepared to take off.

"I will see you soon," Kitto called out. "Bunty will recover, for his courage will defeat the orc's poison."

Emily waved, but Gavin was too despondent to react.

"Here we go!" Thaddeus announced.

As the dragon jumped into the air, Emily and Gavin looked down upon the battlefield. Thousands of bodies littered the hillsides and many more were hidden by the canopy of trees. Up until that very moment, the teens had no real concept of how vast the scope of the battle had been, nor how many lives had been lost.

Thaddeus wasted no time. He flew like a bullet, invisible and fast, straight for Crackington Haven. Even with his recently injured wing, the dragon made incredible time.

25

Black Wing

Hidden within the darkest chambers of Wewelsburg Castle, Reichsführer Himmler stood scowling before his chosen few. The incoming reports from the German officers leading the orc army, were nothing more than garbled fragments, but by all accounts, the invasion had been a dismal failure. No one was quite certain if the spotty details were accurate, but it was possible the British had been waiting to battle the orcs with their own mythical forces.

"Do they honestly believe I will accept their lame excuses for their bungled attack?" Himmler demanded.

Dr. Schumann bravely attempted to defend the orcs. "There is no other feasible explanation, *Herr Reichsführer*. Your orcs were unstoppable, at least by any British military forces currently in England. The only logical conclusion we can reach, comes from the last radio transmission from Major Steiner."

Himmler flew into a rage. "Elves! You expect me to believe my orcs were defeated by little pointy-eared elves? It is sheer nonsense!"

"Don't forget the dragon, *Herr Reichsführer*," another aide dared to point out.

Himmler gasped and stepped back, his face turning a ghostly white. The very mention of another dragon drained the man of his vitality. He stammered for the right words, but when they failed him, Himmler pulled out his Luger automatic.

The Reichsführer aimed and pulled the trigger.

Blam!

The Reichsführer shot the man stone dead.

The other SS officers froze, afraid of what their leader might do next.

Heinrich Himmler returned the firearm to the holster, straightened his belt and walked away. Partway down the gloomy passageway, he spoke over his shoulder, "Remove his body and bury him in an unmarked grave."

"*Jawohl, Herr Reichsführer*," one of the other Nazis replied. "It will be done immediately."

Himmler had barely regained his poise, but shooting the insolent runt had helped channel his rage. The man in black decided to go visit his fledgling dragon, in hopes the creature would instill in him a renewed sense of confidence.

Schwarzer Flügel was still too young for Reichsführer Himmler to commit to the war effort. It would take a few years for the firedrake to mature to the proper size and strength to make a difference in the outcome. Until then, Himmler intended to raise the dragon to be the most deadly creature imaginable.

Luftwaffe Staffelkapitän Ritter Hahn had been given the duty of teaching the young dragon how to fly in formation with select groups of top-secret German fighters and bombers. *Black Wing* learned fast and soon the creature was performing feats of maneuver, evasion, and blistering attacks from high above. In his zeal to impress his masters, however, several brave pilots were accidentally incinerated by the dragon's fiery breath. Himmler wouldn't allow anyone to punish *Schwarzer Flügel*, insisting that such lessons were necessary to harness the beast's natural tendency to do battle.

Testing that theory, the Reichsführer approved a request to fully arm the airplanes being used to teach the dragon fighter skills. Therefore, each time *Black Wing* went up, he was fired upon with live ammunition. Each time the dragon landed, there were several less returning aircraft.

In just one month, the black dragon had grown to 40 feet long and had a wingspan of 80 feet. Of this length, 1/3 was his head and neck, 1/3 his body and 1/3 his tail. The tail came to a point with a barbed growth, similar to an ancient mace. Black Wing's back was covered with lethal spikes, which made any attack almost pointless.

Several weeks after observing *Schwarzer Flügel's* tactics in action, Himmler called together his elite staff to discuss the progress of the project. The Reichsführer had accepted the defeat of the orc invasion, but was ready to move onto another plan.

"Perhaps we lost the orc battle, because we didn't fully understand their limitations," Himmler stated. "However, once *Black Wing* is more fully grown, we will unleash him upon the hapless British and be done with their little empire."

The black dragon was an androgynous creature, with daylight vision as powerful as that of an eagle, and night vision as acute as that of an owl. His eyes were huge red spheres that protruded half way out of the top of his head. It was soon discovered that *Schwarzer Flügel* had poisonous breath, which he could breathe down upon victims while flying overhead. The gas proved to be poisonous to all mammals, killing by provoking violent convulsions. It smelled like skunk spray, but was far more dangerous. *Black Wing* could expel one cloud of gas on each attack, or ten altogether, before he would be forced to rest.

According to Dr. Schumann's precise calculations, Himmler's dragon could kill thousands of enemy soldiers with each expulsion of poisonous gas. Anyone caught in the cloud would die after a series of horrible convulsions.

Schwarzer Flügel also proved to be an excellent flyer. He could turn on a small radius for his immense size and cruise at incredible speeds. In a steep dive, before emitting his deadly gas, the black dragon was capable of matching the speeds of Germany's fastest experimental jet aircraft.

Nevertheless, *Schwarzer Flügel* had great difficulty taking off from ground level. *Black Wing* much preferred to perch way up high, surveying a large area, before swooping down upon the enemy, in accordance with the simple instructions given to him by Staffelkapitän Ritter Hahn.

Each day the dragon became more and more dangerous, as the creature surpassed everyone's expectations. *Schwarzer Flügel* quickly learned his own capabilities and limitations, capitalizing on either, depending on the situation. With the expert training *Black Wing* received, he soon developed into an incredible weapon.

Now it was up to Himmler to decide where and when the dragon would attack.

It was just a matter of time.

Later that evening, the black dragon sat perched atop one of the castle towers, observing its domain. It hungered for combat and craved death and destruction. The creature also was aware that there were people in England who communicated with dragons. This knowledge tempted *Schwarzer Flügel* to dispense with the shackles placed on him by Heinrich Himmler and seek out these other dragons in combat. Still, he must bide his time, waiting for the right advantage.

At **RAF Medmenham**, Richard Kane was once again studying photographs taken near Wewelsburg, Germany. There was nothing of consequence to be seen and this conclusion was quite disappointing for everyone involved.

"I'm convinced the Germans are up to something," Sally Fairborne spoke up after tossing another photograph into the rejected stack.

"I agree, Miss Fairborne," Richard said after rubbing his tired eyes. "But what?"

"Why don't you take a break, sir," Sally suggested. "You've been at this for almost seventy-two hours straight."

Kane nodded and yawned as a reflex. "I suppose you're right. I was hoping for some conclusive evidence."

Just then, a messenger was given clearance to enter the analysis section, where the young man delivered an important communiqué from one of the other departments. Sally retrieved the envelope and slit it open, quickly perusing the contents. Suddenly her mannerisms changed and she lost color in her face.

"What's wrong, Miss Fairborne?" Richard asked with concern.

"This came from the Radio Interception Team," she informed him. "They picked up several garbled German radio transmissions."

Richard waited for her to say more, because that news, in and of itself, wasn't very startling. There was something about her mannerisms that was quite unsettling.

"The transmissions originated from Northumberland, sir," she said slowly.

Now that piece of information really caught Kane's attention.

Sally nodded as a sign of confirmation. Then she handed over the copy of the decoded and translated transcript.

After reading a few lines, his eyebrows went up and stayed up. Then Richard looked at the Wren in astonishment.

"It isn't possible, is it, sir?" she asked.

Richard shrugged and sighed, before saying, "I've seen a lot of strange things since this war began. I'm not sure I will ever be a skeptic again, after all this is over."

"But orcs, sir?" Sally protested. "Such creatures only exist in fairytales and fantasies. They're big and green, with tusks and red eyes, aren't they?"

"Or so we have come to believe."

"Sir?"

"Please pass this to MI-6," he said, trying to remain professional.

"I'll send a priority message right away, sir."

"Good," Kane said. He scratched his chin.

"What are you thinking, sir?"

"Well, it's possible they don't mean orcs at all, but some new terminology we're not familiar with. ORC might be an acronym for some new weapon or tactic."

Sally was delighted with his line of reasoning. "Oh, sir, I never thought of that. Of course, that must be it. I'm so glad you're here to add a bit of logic. Otherwise we'd be going off in flights of fantasy all the time."

The lieutenant commander laughed. "Oh, I hardly think that. Now I'm going to catch a few hours sleep while I can. You know where to find me."

"Yes, sir," she said. "I'll pass on your thoughts to MI-6 as well."

"Thank you."

Richard quickly went out the door and headed straight for his billet. However, he hadn't taken more than a few steps, when he seriously began to question the conclusion he had reached regarding that intercept. After all, he knew dragons really existed. Why not orcs? Unfortunately, this line of reasoning gave him a king-sized headache in no time.

Once inside his billet, Richard pulled out a bottle of whiskey and poured a splash into a glass. He downed it in one gulp and coughed as it burned.

"Oh, Thaddeus, where are you when I need you most?"

Little did he know that the dragon was actually not that far away, but had other things on his mind. For Thaddeus Osbert was in Piddlehinton, imploring the help from an old friend.

The dragon also needed to find a sizeable supply of sugar, because using his icy breath had seriously depleted his energy reserves. Perhaps he would make a quick detour past one of the London warehouses undamaged during the recent bombings.

26

Turn for the Worse

"Mother!" Gavin screamed as loudly as he could, kicking at the back door. "Please, come quick. Bunty is hurt badly."

Winifred came running from the kitchen. She instantly saw the blood all over Bunty's shirt and his ashen skin.

"Dear God, what happened to him?" she demanded.

"We were playing by some old ruins," Gavin sobbed as he told his fabricated story. "Bunty fell and impaled himself on a sharp branch. Please, Mum, can you make him better?"

Mrs. Kane scooped Bunty up in her arms and carried him to the sitting-room sofa. Then she grabbed the telephone and rang up the exchange in Bude. "Gracie, this is Winifred Kane. I have a seriously injured teenaged boy here at my home. He needs immediate attention from a doctor. Yes, I'll wait."

"Hold his hand and talk to him," Gavin's mother ordered.

Emily stepped into the room, still in a daze, sniffling back her tears. Winifred wanted to soothe the girl's sorrow, but that would have to wait.

"Yes, Dr. Heath, this is Winifred Kane," Mrs. Kane spoke into the mouthpiece. "This is an emergency. The refugee boy billeted with us has been seriously injured. By the looks of him, he's lost a lot of blood and the puncture is quite deep."

The doctor gave Gavin's mother some basic instructions, while he grabbed his medical bag. After hanging up, the doctor headed to his car to make the drive to Crackington Haven.

After placing the telephone back on the hook, Winifred ripped away Bunty's shirt, but was very surprised to discover a crude bandage in place.

"Did you do this?" she marveled.

"No, Emmy did," Gavin embellished his lie.

"It stopped the bleeding, so that's good," his mother said.

217

They made Bunty as comfortable as possible, but he mumbled incoherent nonsense about dancing elves and fire-breathing dragons. It was obvious to Winifred that the red-haired boy was delirious with pain. A shot of morphine would help him sleep. Of course, she had no idea about the orc poison that coursed through his veins.

Less than twenty minutes later, Doctor Heath arrived. With the assistance from some strong local men, Bunty was carried up to his bedroom. Shooing everyone out, except for Mrs. Kane, the doctor examined the wound, gave the boy a shot of morphine, and then cleaned the puncture. He applied a clean dressing and checked the boy's temperature.

The thermometer registered 103 degrees and rising.

"I'm afraid an infection has set in, Winifred," Doctor Heath informed her. "He's in serious danger and we must keep a careful eye on him, to make sure the fever doesn't go any higher."

"Yes, Doctor," Winifred said. "I will go to *Coombe Inn* and see if they can spare some ice."

"That would be splendid, dear," the doctor said. "You go do that, while I sit here with the lad."

Mrs. Kane hurried downstairs and out the front door, up the street to the *Coombe Barton Inn*, where she approached Mr. Chillingsworth, who was tending bar.

"Winifred, whatever brings you here at this time of day?" he asked.

"Oh, Basil, I'm in need of a huge favor," Mrs. Kane replied. "There's a wounded boy at my house, suffering from fever. I wonder if you have any ice to spare?"

"Why, of course," Chillingsworth replied. "Let me scoop some shavings from the ice block."

Several minutes later, Winifred returned to Bunty's bedside carrying a bucket of ice. "Is there any improvement?"

Doctor Heath shook his head.

Bunty's fever continued to worsen, reaching 105 degrees. The poison was firmly entrenched in his system, life threatening as it attacked his heart and lungs. Only his youthful vigor had saved him thus far.

At this stage, Winifred and the doctor packed ice all around the boy, which did prevent his temperature from going any higher, but his life was still endangered. Gavin's mother sent her son to fetch another load, but the ice wouldn't last forever.

Not that it would have made any difference, because Mrs. Kane had no idea what had really happened to Bunty, and Doctor Heath, without that vital piece of information, was acting on an inaccurate diagnosis of the problem. Frustrated by the lack of improvement, the doctor returned to Bude to look through his medical journals, hoping to find some clue. He promised he would come back in the morning.

Realizing that Bunty might not survive through the evening, Winifred went downstairs and gathered Emily and Gavin to her. Their cheeks were stained with the tracks of tears and both looked simply devastated.

"I sent word to Bunty's father hours ago," Winifred informed them.

"Was Dad able to help?" Gavin asked.

She shook her head. "No, your father was tied up in some top-secret meeting and couldn't be disturbed. With the help of his aide, however, we were able to reroute the message directly to **HMS Ark Royal**, which was supposed to drop anchor in Portsmouth today."

Gavin wrung his hands.

His mother fluffed his hair. "Now there's nothing more we can do, my dearest. Bunty's a strong boy, so he'll pull through, you'll see. You have to trust in God now, because Doctor Heath has done everything medical science can do."

Sadly, Mrs. Kane didn't know the truth and probably wouldn't have believed it if told. Gavin and Emily paced back-and-forth, worrying about their friend and hoping Thaddeus would locate the wizard in time.

Rap, rap, rap.

There was confident knocking on the front door.

"I wonder who that could be at such a time?" Winifred asked aloud as she went to open the door.

To her surprise, a kindly looking, white-haired gentleman stood before her.

"May I help you, sir?" Mrs. Kane asked.

"Yes, dear lady, my name is Dymchurch Bixley," he introduced himself. "I hope I haven't come at an inconvenient time."

Winfred sighed. "It's a pleasure to meet you, sir. Is there anything I can do for you?"

The elderly man smiled. "I understand you have a badly injured boy at home."

She nodded sadly. "I'm afraid he's not improving."

"Well, I may be of some assistance," Dymchurch said. "I am a physician, though retired these many years."

Winifred regained a glimmer of hope. "Oh, sir, I would be very appreciative if you could look at our dear Bunty."

Dymchurch stepped inside and immediately smiled at Gavin and Emily. "I don't normally intrude on people's personal affairs, but an old friend of mine asked if I might look in on Bunty. *Uncle Thaddeus* has seen you children playing and heard the boy had been injured."

Then the man winked.

For the first time all day, Gavin's faith was renewed and Emily instantly stopped her whimpering. Their looks of desperation and despair were instantly replaced with hopeful smiles.

"Right this way, Dr. Bixley," Winifred invited him to go upstairs with her.

Gavin and Emily were right behind them.

Dymchurch quietly tiptoed into Bunty's bedroom and sat down beside the bed. The red-haired boy's breathing was labored and he was as white as freshly washed linen. Bunty's lips were blue and green and a discolored froth dribbled from the corners of his mouth.

"I think the lad isn't fighting an infection, exactly, but perhaps some unidentified disease carried on whatever punctured his side," Dymchurch stated after his examination. "The only way to fight such maladies is with meditation and medicine. I'll leave the Psalms up to you, Mrs. Kane, while I pour this elixir into the boy's mouth."

Winifred didn't know exactly how to react, but neither did she object or fuss.

Dymchurch pulled a small vial from his left coat pocket and pulled out the cork. "The lad should really like this, because it tastes like cherry lollies."

The man pried apart Bunty's lips and poured the entire measure onto his tongue.

"There," Dymchurch said with some satisfaction. "We'll wait for that to do some good, while Mrs. Kane makes a pot of tea. Let's not dally around here, but go downstairs and have a nice chat. The boy should sleep."

His bedside manner, while somewhat eccentric, was really quite agreeable and everyone did as he suggested. They filed into the kitchen, where Winifred put the pot on to boil.

Once Thaddeus had successfully sent Dymchurch Bixley in the direction of Crackington Haven, the dragon engaged his invisibility cloaking and flew up to **RAF Medmenham**, where it was clear that Richard Kane was in need of Sir Osbert's many skills. The trip was a bit hazardous, for the skies were filled with German bombers and British fighters vying for air supremacy. The dragon did manage to make an emergency stop, devouring several hundred bags of sugar supposedly stored in a secret cache.

Lieutenant Commander Kane was sleeping, although it was quite restless, filled with disturbing dreams. He tossed and turned, first hot and then cold.

Clink, clink, clink.

Richard sat up with a start. Something was tapping on his billet window, but he couldn't see anyone outside.

That was strange.

Tink, tink, tink.

There it was again.

Richard scooted out of bed and opened up the window.

"Greetings, Richard," spoke a recognizable voice from nowhere.

Richard gulped in surprise. "Thaddeus?"

"Who else?" the dragon reacted with a chuckle.

"Why are you here?"

"I believe it is you who summoned me."

Richard sighed heavily and ran his fingers through his hair. "I did at that. Thank you for coming. I need your help."

"What service may I provide?" the dragon asked politely.

Richard retrieved a batch of photographs from his briefcase. "Please, take a look at these."

Still invisible, Thaddeus carefully held the snapshots between his talons. Flipping through the special magnifying lenses within his eyes, Sir Osbert studied them intently.

Richard was aware the dragon has seen something important, because for just a moment the invisibility flickered and failed. In that brief instant, the dragon's face was etched with worry.

"Is that really a dragon, Thaddeus?" Kane asked quietly.

"I'm afraid it is, Richard," Sir Osbert replied. "However, it's not a species born in the natural order of things. This Black Dragon is a creation of sorcery and dark magic. It is entirely evil and motivated only by the pursuit of death and destruction. Where was this photograph taken?"

"Near Wewelsburg, deep within the Alma Valley in Germany," Kane answered.

"You were wise to seek me out, Richard," Thaddeus said. "I must inform my fellow dragons regarding the location of this vile creature. We may wish to take direct action of our own, for such evil threatens our species as well."

"How would the Germans be able to conjure up such a beast?" Kane asked.

"There are wicked men dabbling with powers they don't understand and can't control, Richard," Thaddeus replied. "In fact, with Gavin's help, we just repelled an invasion of orcs."

The lieutenant commander's mouth dropped open. "Did you just say orcs?"

The dragon nodded. "Thousands of them, sent to spread terror throughout England!"

Richard was dumbfounded.

That meant the translated radio transmission had been accurate after all.

"What else do you know?" Gavin's father finally asked.

"All dragons are the result of magic," Thaddeus replied. "As long as there is magic in the world, there will be dragons, and as long as there are dragons, there will be magic. If either is lost, then the other is gone forever."

"Then the Germans have discovered secrets far more dangerous than anyone could imagine," Richard surmised.

"That is what I fear has happened, yes."

"What do the other dragons propose?"

"No immediate action will be taken to interfere. At least not yet."

"What would change their minds?"

"If England is defeated."

"Then what, God forbid?"

"There would be no room for mercy, Richard. The dragons would fill the skies."

Richard sighed. "Then England better not lose this war."

Thaddeus said, "I couldn't agree more. That is why you must figure out a way to destroy Wewelsburg Castle as soon as possible."

"That won't be easy, my friend. It's outside the range of almost all of our existing bombers and it certainly isn't a primary target."

"Then you will have to convince your leaders to make it so."

The lieutenant commander knew the dragon was right, but to accomplish such a task seemed daunting. After all, the decision for priority bombing targets was decided at the highest level of Bomber Command, usually with the sanction of the Prime Minister.

Thaddeus sensed Kane's concerns and said, "I would take your case directly to the Right Honorable Sir Winston Churchill. You will have more success convincing him of the importance. The Prime Minister will be more sensitive to our plight."

Richard was surprised. "Does he honestly believe in dragons?"

Thaddeus grinned. "Oh, yes, indeed he does. In fact, he is quite jealous that Gavin has actually developed a friendship with me."

"Then perhaps it's time for Winston Churchill to meet you as well," Richard suggested.

"No, no, not yet," the dragon reacted. "Mr. Churchill must act on faith alone, or victory will not be assured. Trust me on this. There will be a time and place for me to make myself known to Mr. Churchill, but not until the time is right."

"Whatever you think is best, Sir Osbert," Kane said. "I bow to your convictions."

"I must be on my way, dear friend," Thaddeus said. "I have three teenagers to admonish for not heeding my council."

"Are they all right?" Richard asked worriedly.

Thaddeus decided to skip Bunty's injury. "They are fine, but children no more. This war is forcing them to grow up too fast, I'm afraid."

"Thank you for guarding over them."

"It is my sworn duty to protect the House of Kane and all those who reside therein," the dragon stated. "That includes Gavin's friends and allies."

Thaddeus Osbert patted Gavin's father on the shoulder, before disappearing yet again, taking flight with the strengthening breeze. Richard waved and then closed the window. He sat down on the end of his bed. It was only then that Kane realized the dragon had not returned the photograph of the unidentified dragon.

HMS Ark Royal had just dropped anchor in Portsmouth's heavily protected harbor, when CPO Charles Digby received word that his son was very ill. However, when the chief requested compassionate leave, it was refused by Captain Ridgeway, the commanding officer. The reason was quite simple, because after emergency repairs were completed, the aircraft carrier was rejoining her battle group out to sea. This was not the time for the chief to be absent and his services were considered critical.

"Look, sir, this is how it's going to be," Bunty's father reacted to the news. "I'm going to walk off *Ark Royal* right now and you'll have to put me behind bars in the rattle, or shoot me, to stop me from going. I must see my dying son and that's that!"

Nobody tried to stop him and neither did Captain Ridgeway put the chief in jail. CPO Digby took the first available train from Portsmouth and after a long rail journey, walked from Launceston to Crackington Haven.

Doctor Heath had also returned from Bude, prepared to fill out a death certificate. Much to his dismay, he wasn't allowed admittance to Bunty's room.

Dymchurch Bixley was administering another dosage of his delicious elixir.

"Who's this bloke, then?" CPO Digby demanded indignantly as he paced around Bunty's bedroom.

"This is Doctor Bixley," Winifred replied. "He's a specialist from Scotland."

"He doesn't look like much of a doctor to me," the chief said.

"Good day to you, my man," Dymchurch said cheerfully, shaking the chief's hand.

"How's my boy?" Digby senior asked.

"His fever has gone down significantly," Dymchurch answered. "He'll recover."

"Dad?" Bunty suddenly croaked after opening one eye.

"Right here, son," his father said. "Now you rest easy."

It was obvious to everyone present that Bunty had passed the crisis point, for the color of his complexion was quickly returning to normal. "Don't go, Dad."

"I'm not going anywhere, lad," CPO Digby said. "Except maybe across the street for a quick pint."

Bunty smiled.

"That's the spirit," his father said.

"Let's let the boy sleep," Bixley said, shooing everybody out.

In the hallway, Dymchurch tapped Dr. Heath on the shoulder. "You can go in now, but the boy won't need the mortician after all."

Dumbfounded, the physician could clearly see that Bunty was greatly improved.

Winifred credited Dymchurch with the cure. "If you hadn't come when you did, I'm not sure Bunty would have pulled through."

"I won't take all the credit, Mrs. Kane," Bixley said. "The boy's father was the perfect medicine."

Chief Digby liked hearing that. He patted Dymchurch on the back and asked, "Don't suppose you'd care to join me at the *Coombe Barton Inn* for a quick one?"

"I'd be honored, Chief," Bixley replied.

The two of them acted like old friends and strolled up the street to the pub.

Very quietly, Gavin and Emily slipped into Bunty's room and sat by his bed. The red-haired boy opened one eye again.

"Hey, chum," Gavin whispered.

"Hello," Bunty whispered in return.

"There's someone here to see you," Emily said, opening the window.

In climbed Kitto.

Bunty smiled broadly.

The elf quickly came to the side of the bed and leaned over to give Bunty a gentle kiss on the forehead. The boy turned bright red again.

"I think he's feeling just fine," Emily stated with a giggle.

Gavin and Kitto laughed too.

Bunty, however, scooted under the covers to hide.

Gavin's mother intercepted her son as he emerged from Bunty's room. "I need to talk to you in private, young man."

Her voice was quite stern.

"Yes, Mum," Gavin said, retreating to his own bedroom.

"I am very disappointed in you," Winifred said as soon as the door was closed behind her. "I told you boys to come straight home from school."

"I know, Mum," Gavin said. "I'm so sorry Bunty was hurt."

"That's not all," she countered.

"It's not?"

"No, I also found out that you and Bunty skipped school today," she said. "What's worse, you convinced Emily to join you."

"Oh, that," Gavin said.

"You will be severely punished," his mother said. "I wrote your father and I'll let him decide what should be done about this, but I want your promise that you'll never cut classes again, unless an air raid interrupts school."

"I promise, Mum," Gavin said.

Winifred had no idea her son had his fingers crossed behind his back. For Gavin knew that circumstance might arise again, which would force him to trade his schooling to help Thaddeus Osbert in time of need.

"All right then," his mother said with relief. "Take Emily home and be polite when you get a scolding from Harriet Scott as well."

"Yes, Mum, I'll be a perfect gentleman," Gavin said.

The next day, Chief Petty Officer Digby returned to Portsmouth and rejoined his mates on *HMS Ark Royal*. The Royal Navy decided there would be no disciplinary action for leaving his duty station without permission, especially when Captain Ridgeway learned Digby's son had recovered fully.

Later that morning, Gavin and Dymchurch Bixley were sitting out by the garden, enjoying a nice cup of tea. It was a beautiful day.

"Thank you for making Bunty well again," Gavin said.

"It was my pleasure, son," Bixley said.

"How long have you known Thaddeus?" Gavin whispered.

"We go way back," Dymchurch replied. "He and I have had our share of adventures."

"He's a wonderful dragon."

"Yes, indeed he is. Someday he'll be the last of his kind."

"No, that's not possible. I've seen hundreds of dragons, in Iceland, their home."

Dymchurch smiled sadly. "What you say is true, but Sir Thaddeus Osbert is the last of his unique species. It's a shame the old boy has no heir apparent, because the world can ill afford to lose such vital dragon secrets."

"What are these secrets you speak of?" Gavin wondered.

"Perhaps you should ask him yourself," Bixley replied.

"Believe me, sir, I plan to," Gavin vowed.

"Well, lad, I must be on my way," Dymchurch said as he stood up.

Gavin escorted him through the village, until they were on the coast road.

"Fare thee well," Bixley said goodbye.

"Thank you," Gavin said, waving.

Dymchurch Bixley wandered down the road, not in any real hurry, while enjoying the scenery and gorgeous weather of an early day in June.

Emily joined Gavin on the outskirts of town.

"How are you?" she asked.

"Still confused," he replied.

The girl took his hand and pulled. "Come on, let's go for a stroll."

He went with her willingly.

"It sure was close," she said.

"It sure was," he agreed. "I thought we were going to lose Bunty for sure."

"Do you think we're in trouble?"

"Oh, there's no doubt of that. I'm just wondering who will punish us more, our mothers or Thaddeus Osbert?"

"Probably our mothers."

They smiled at each other.

"Have you seen Kitto lately?" Gavin asked.

Emily grinned. "She's sitting with Bunty. I think she's in love."

They both laughed this time.

"Oh, he is going to suffer," Gavin commented.

They stopped and looked out to sea.

"What is it about this place?" Emily asked after awhile.

"It's not just about England, home, and beauty," Gavin said. "This spot reminds us of our mums and dads, of Bunty and Thaddeus and all the good friends we know. This is our Cornwall, our Tintagel Castle and our little white cottage on the hill."

Emily took Gavin's hand and squeezed. "Thank you."

He smiled and pointed out a passing British motor torpedo boat. "That's why we're fighting, Emmy. This is our bloody island, nobody else's."

They headed for Boscastle.

Inside the little white cottage on the hill, Thaddeus Osbert was listening to his own wireless set, as Prime Minister Winston Churchill was closing his speech to the Canadian Parliament. Churchill said, "We have not journeyed across the centuries, across the oceans, across the mountains, across the prairies, because we are made of sugar candy."

The Canadians cheered and applauded.

Thaddeus grinned and simply said, "No, but I wish you were made of sugar candy."

Epilogue

The hillside was littered with thousands of bodies, although none of them was human. Ancient weapons, from double-bladed battle-axes to great two-handed swords, lay scattered here and there, many jutting up from lifeless forms. Even more of the unfortunate victims had been shafted with long arrows, their silvery plumes reflecting light from the setting sun. Other bodies were charred beyond recognition, or had been sliced to ribbons as neatly as if by a surgeon. The carnage was difficult to accept, especially to the human eyes presently surveying the battlefield.

Major Traber Vickers stood silently looking at the corpses. Based on the obvious signs before him, some of the casualties had been victims of a fire-breathing dragon. He had seen the end results before, though in far less numbers.

"It doesn't make any sense, sir," commented Royal Marine Sergeant Nigel Smythe, after he returned from a quick tour of the site. "These poor slobs don't even look human. Where did they come from?"

Vickers refrained from answering the inquiry, but instead started walking amongst the dead. He could hazard a guess, of course, but was in no mood for the ridicule that would follow his reply. The major could barely lift one of the battleaxes, the double blades covered in green bloodlike ooze. Looking down at the form who had apparently wielded the weapon, it was obvious to see the creature was anything but human.

"Let's clean up the mess, Sergeant Smythe," Vickers ordered. "I want the graves detail to dig one large mass grave and once it's filled over, it must remain unmarked. Do I make myself perfectly clear?"

"Aye, quite clear, Major," the sergeant replied, saluting. He turned and called out, "All right, you filthy slogs. Let's get the lead out!"

Vickers retreated up the hill and watched two bulldozers carve out a gigantic hole in the valley floor. The same earthmovers were used to push the piles of bodies into the mass grave and cover it once again. In a matter of hours, the grisly job was completed. For the unfortunate men handling this burial detail, no explanation for what they had seen was forthcoming. They were simply reminded of their oath and sent on their way.

Kitto Bideven had watched all this transpire from her hiding place in the fork of a high oak tree. Once the humans had finished their macabre duties and departed, scores of gray elves emerged from hiding and sprinkled magical dust over the mass grave, to prevent anyone from discovering the final resting place ever again.

In the village of St. Merryn, Wren Officer Tabitha Bixley sat down with a hot cup of freshly brewed tea. After taking a few sips, she closed her eyes with a pronounced sigh and smiled. Her thoughts were of Sub-lieutenant John Mobley.

Suddenly there was a knocking sound on the front door. She got up and opened it. An elderly white-haired man stood before her, wheezing a little as if out of breath.

"Oh, Father, you didn't have to come all this way," Tabitha exclaimed.

Dymchurch smiled. "Won't you invite me inside?"

His daughter stepped aside. "Please, do come in."

He entered and nodded approvingly. His daughter had done miracles with the place.

"This is such a pleasant surprise, Daddy," Tabitha said, throwing her arms around her father's waist. She gave him a big kiss on the cheek and then rested her head on his chest.

"It's good to see you in person, lass," Dymchurch said. "Your mother frets so."

"It was my decision to become a Wren, Father," his daughter said with some defensiveness in her voice.

He smiled with pity. "Now, now, child, don't get angry. I think your decision was the best one possible, all things considered."

That statement made Tabitha uneasy. "Will you join me for a spot of tea?"

"I will indeed."

"Sit here, while I brew a fresh pot of water."

Dymchurch found the chair quite comfortable. "How are things?"

"I make do," she replied from the kitchen. "It's a challenge sometimes, if you know what I mean?"

"I do, I do," he said. "Your mother never could get the hang of it. When things were especially tough, she would resort to the old ways."

Tabitha came out from the kitchen carrying a pot.

"I'll play mother," Dymchurch volunteered, plopping a bit of sugar in each cup.

His daughter poured the tea and they sat across from each other.

"Thank you so much for looking after John," she whispered, leaning forward to kiss him on the cheek again.

Her father chuckled. "Oh, it does help to have Thaddeus for a friend, Tabitha. You never know when you might need a dragon."

Later that night, in Crackington Haven, the boys enjoyed another delicious meal, courtesy of Gavin's father, who had arranged for a special care package to be sent all the way from Canada. There were a few advantages to having a father in the Royal Navy after all.

Winifred decided they would go without the BBC War Report that evening. Instead, Bunty made sketches in his new art portfolio, which was a gift from Mrs. Kane, who had actually found it in her husband's radio/photography shop. Gavin, on the other hand, sat curled up in his father's armchair, reading a book.

Soon it was time to turn in, so after washing up and saying their prayers, the boys settled in their beds. Bunty quickly fell asleep, but Gavin was troubled by something. Unable to relax, he opened his bedroom window and pushed aside the blackout curtain, gazing up at the night sky. At first, he saw nothing but stars and a "bombers" full moon.

Without warning, a distinct shape temporarily eclipsed the silvery glow. It was huge, with large flapping wings, a long tail and slender neck. For only a brief moment, the dragon was silhouetted against the moon, casting an ominous dark shadow across the land.

In that instant, Gavin also knew it wasn't Thaddeus Osbert.

Then it was gone.

Is this the End?
No, no, definitely not!

Notes

Are Fire-Breathing Dragons Scientifically Possible?

Methane gas is produced in enormous quantities in the large intestines of mammals and since paleontologists now believe that dinosaurs were probably mammals, it is possible that dragons were mammals too. They would need a molecular filtering system in the intestine, to diffuse methane across the lining of the intestine into a transportation system, just like all other substances are absorbed into the body. Such systems exist in almost all cell and tissue membranes.

The dragon would need tubes to transport the methane gas from the intestine to a storage area in the head or throat. This system would be natural, because there are already all sorts of tubes for transporting fluids, such as blood vessels and the urinary tract. Perhaps there were even backflow valves to more efficiently force the methane towards the head and prevent it from moving backwards.

At the end of the transport tube, where it enters the storage area, a sphincter or muscle was in place to prevent the methane from being forced back down when pressurized. These control valves would be similar to the entrance and exit to the stomach and heart. There would also be one of these control valves at the exit from the storage area, to control the release of methane and prevent the ignited methane from being drawn back into the storage area, when the dragon released pressure from the storage area. This would safeguard the storage area from becoming an internal bomb.

This storage space would be a flexible and contractible bladder, perhaps designed around the poison bladders used by deadly snakes. Most of these are capable of considerable pressure. The dragon's bladder would be able to compress methane gas, enough to expel the gas from 30 feet to 100 or more feet. A great example is the Black or Spitting Cobra, which can spray its poison, with deadly accuracy, up to ten feet. Since gas is much lighter and more compressible, it could easily be projected much further with the same type of existing bladder.

The dragon would require two little tubes in the roof of his mouth, also like the venom tubes in poisonous snakes. These openings would expel the methane when the dragon opened his mouth, which would give the appearance of the creature breathing fire.

Some form of heat would be necessary to ignite the methane gas as it was leaving the mouth. There are a number of electrical-generating animals, such as the Electric Eel and Electric Catfish, which are capable of generating enough voltage to kill an adult human. Not much of a charge would be necessary to ignite the methane gas. To create the spark, the dragon would simply have two nodes hanging from the roof of his mouth, or two well-defined teeth or fangs for the spark to jump across.

About the Author

Secret of the Dragon's Breath is the second book in Derek Hart's dragon series. The characters have grown a little older and as teenagers faced with a prolonged war, they're questioning their place in the world. The transition from child to teen is often a difficult journey of self-discovery, but the rewards can be profound. For Gavin, Bunty and Emily, World War II was not only changing the world around them, it also had a direct impact on their beliefs and assumptions. If it wasn't for the council of a wise old dragon, many of these questions might have produced less favorable answers. Still, the British adolescents of the 1940's had to balance the demands of encroaching adulthood, with the deprivations and shortages caused by the war. It's little wonder these factors produced a future generation of rebelliousness.

Yet during these tumultuous times, the main characters are also able to hold onto the truly important traits of humanity, such as loyalty, love, and sacrifice. There's no doubt that the war adversely affected Britain's society as a whole and altered the Empire forever. Overall, the common citizen rose above the hardships and became richer for it. The three teens in ***Secret of the Dragon's Breath*** are no exceptions. Gavin, Bunty, and Emily discover their friendship can withstand much adversity, while they're also forced to accept a magical world heretofore unknown.

Derek Hart would like to thank all the people who volunteered their services to assist the author in his craft. Without such help, this novel would be missing vital elements that make the story come together.

Derek would like to give a huge hug to **Doreen Turner**, of Launceston, Cornwall, who maintained a steady communication with the author. Without her participation in this process, these novels would not have the sense of setting and place that makes the stories ring true.

To **David Burke**, for the innovative and breathtaking cover art, as well as his loyal friendship and dedication. It is difficult to add anything else to his growing list of skills and attributes, but David is simply amazing. The man continues to break the mold for visual communication and sets a standard of excellence far above the author's expectations.

Finally, what would an author be without readers? Fans and friends do make a difference in the writing process. Derek Hart continues to recognize **Carla Malerba, Michele Desjardins, Harry Schwartz, Alice Simon, Kathy Lenthart, Bill Crist, Gary Jordan, Hannah Fox, Stephen Gilbert, Dave Hilburn, Katie Ashcraft, Ryan Riesenbeck** and **Carol Frey** for their support and input.

The next book in the series—***Secret of the Dragon's Claw***—is coming soon!

(Preview)
Secret of the Dragon's Claw

Drunken Old Fool

Darkness blanketed the city, permeating along the streets and collecting in the alcoves and alleyways. An eerie silence hung heavily over the bombed-out ruins of Plymouth, the shells of buildings swathed in thick smoke-filled fog. Where the *Dingles Department Store* had once stood, there was nothing but rubble, which had been painted white to show people where to walk. Dust permeated everywhere, clouds of grit filling the air with the acrid smell of wet plaster and burnt wood. The city streets were nothing more than an urban desert, abandoned and desolate, ringed by sorrow and despair.

A drunken old man came stumbling down the street just then, avoiding the neatly stacked piles of bricks recovered from the debris and wreckage that once had been people's homes and businesses. Reaching the nearest alley, the inebriated man leaned heavily against the wall, before sliding down to plop on a pile of rubble. Reclining against the building, he violently retched all over himself. Throwing back his head, the wretched old codger began singing some unidentifiable tune and he was badly off key.

Clunk.

A piece of brick fell from a crumbling wall nearby.

"Who's there?" the drunk shouted.

A brief movement further down the narrow lane startled him even more and poised, he peered into the darkness.

"Stay away!" he slurred, trying to focus on anything in the inky blackness.

Nothing happened, however, so after a few seconds the man slumped over.

The dense smoke drifted past, swirling slightly with the faint breezes. Bunty Digby watched from his hiding place, but no other signs of life were evident on the deserted streets. Satisfied he had remained undiscovered, the red-haired boy cautiously stepped out and made his way towards the alley. The teen hugged the rough brick walls of each building and tried to stay hidden in the shadows. Bunty

237

slipped past the wrecked and silent storefronts, carefully closing in on the snoring drunk.

The old coot was a graying gent with a scraggly beard and mustache, who wore filthy tattered clothes and stunk of ale and vomit. In fact, the smell almost made the boy turn away. Still, there was something fascinating about the bum, although Bunty was clueless as to why such a magnetic pull existed. A long, wooden pipe jutted carelessly from the man's coat pocket, but otherwise it appeared as if the vagabond had no other worldly possessions.

Bunty knelt down and reached for the pipe.

"Have you come to rob me?" the man suddenly asked, his eyes still closed.

Startled, Bunty jumped back and said, "No, I wouldn't think of it."

"Then why do you hover over me?"

"I saw you collapse," Bunty replied. "I came to see if you were ill."

"Bah!" the old fart grunted. "Surely you can smell?"

The boy held his nose.

"Indeed," said the man. "I thought so."

His eyes were still shut.

Bunty was amazed. "How do you do that?"

"Do what?"

"See things without opening your eyes."

Suddenly they popped open. The man's eyes were beady-black, like the eyes of a crow. They darted about, clearly focused and not bloodshot, as Bunty had imagined they would be. He certainly didn't act like the drunken old slob he appeared.

"May I be of assistance to you, sir?" Bunty asked.

"Oh, so it's *sir* now, is it?" the man grumbled. "Do I look like someone who deserves to be addressed in such a manner?"

"My father taught me to speak to anyone older than me with due respect, sir," Bunty replied defensively.

The old man started to laugh, but his sharp guffaw was interrupted by a wicked cough. After hacking and wheezing for several minutes, the man slumped back, gasping for breath.

"Perhaps you should see a doctor, sir," Bunty suggested.

"Not bloody likely."

"Well, I can't leave you here in this condition," the boy added.

"Why not?"

"Because it wouldn't be right, sir."

"Do you have a name, lad?" the man asked, his voice suddenly quite kind.

"I go by Bunty, sir, Bunty Digby."

Out stretched a hand.

"Pleased to meet you, Bunty."

The boy shook the man's hand, but immediately noticed several faded tattoos inked into the weathered skin.

"Likewise, sir," Bunty whispered.

"I'm known as Lamken Rune," the man introduced himself.

Bunty sat down on the pile of rubble and took a careful look at the fellow opposite him. Rune wore a wool overcoat several sizes too big for his frame and a rumpled floppy hat that had lost its proper shape long ago.

"Never seen the likes of me before, I venture," Lamken guessed.

Bunty shook his head.

"I could do with a drink," the man stated.

Then he belched noisily.

Bunty cringed and grasped his nose again. "What a foul stench!"

"Pardon me, lad," Rune attempted an apology.

"I don't think you need a drink, sir," Bunty said. "You need a hot bath, new clothes, and some decent food."

Rune grinned. "Sounds lovely. Do you have some place in mind?"

Bunty shrugged. "Perhaps."

Lamken grunted. "If I had my Elizabeth, I could just conjure up those things."

"Who is Elizabeth?" the boy asked.

"She was my staff," Rune replied angrily.

Bunty scooted backwards, afraid the old drunk might turn violent. The red-haired boy vaguely remembered his father sometimes getting physical after drinking too much. His poor mother had been the unfortunate one who felt the brunt, however. Thinking of his mum made Bunty sad.

"I won't hurt you," Lamken tried reassuring the boy. "I just miss my Elizabeth, that's all."

"I'm sorry she's gone, sir," Bunty said.

"Taken from me, she was," Rune said.

"That's awful. Did you report her kidnapping?"

The codger gasped with surprise, and then bellowed with laughter. "Good God, chap, who would care that some old wooden staff was kidnapped, as you said?"

Bunty was befuddled and confused. "Elizabeth isn't a living person, then?"

Rune wiped his eyes. "Alas, she didn't eat or sleep or breathe, as you would know it. Elizabeth was a wooden pole, enchanted and powerful as she was."

Bunty's eyes narrowed. "Do you take me for a fool?"

"Not at all, Bunty," Rune replied.

"Then explain yourself or I'll turn you in to the local old bill."

"Not the police," the old man pretended to protest. "In all respects, they're so immaculately turned out, so immaculately polite, so immaculately trained and so immaculately infuriating!"

"Come clean then, you smudger," Bunty demanded.

"There's nothing to explain, lad," Lamken said. "I'm a man of magic, down on his luck, who had his staff seized from him, while in the company of some questionable fellow wizards."

"You expect me to believe you're a wizard too?" Bunty scoffed.

Rune asked, "What's a wizard, besides a bloke with a big stick and tricks up his sleeve? In fact, most of my fellow sorcerers are exceedingly rude fellows, who possess little, if any, social skills whatsoever."

Bunty sighed. The addled old fool was seriously brain-damaged after years of alchol consumption. What was he to do?

"Help me to my feet, lad," Lamken said, holding out his hand.

Bunty obliged, giving Rune a mighty tug.

The geezer brushed himself off and pointed towards the way out of town.

"As a rule, I avoid large cities," Rune said. "I was only passing through Plymouth, when my thirst overtook me. Let us depart and you can keep me company until you find a nice place to dump me."

"I would never do that, sir," Bunty said.

"We'll see," Rune grumbled.

The two of them ambled away, heading west, but avoiding the dusty rescue squads digging to get trapped people out from smoldering ruins. Soon the strange pair joined a steady parade of people shuffling along in the same direction. It was a mass exodus of the population, as they temporarily departed from the expected target area.

Some carried bundles of blankets. Some carried suitcases. Some carried nothing at all, because they traveled light and were the hardy ones. A long line of lorries waited to shuttle these refugees to the countryside. Kindly policemen had taken the law into their own hands, and urged the drivers to give these poor people a lift. They piled on, with their kiddies, their bundles, and their thermos flasks.

The children dangled their legs over the tailboard and laughed. The boys waved to the pretty girls as they passed. Neighbors crowded together with their bundles and chatted. Bunty thought it was like going to the fair. Now and then, a child stopped laughing and turned to look at her mother for reassurance.

Most of these survivors were homeless.

"Yes, I've lost my house and my furniture is gone," one old woman said to Lamken as they passed. "The only clothes I have are these I'm wearing. But I can do what no German dares do, for I can say what I think."

Many of them were women, women with children, women with bundles of goods. There were few men, and those who left the city were old. Often they had been refused shelter for the night. Yet they hadn't lost their spirit.

Each evening, before nightfall, they vacated Plymouth, without haste, without anxiety. There was no crying, no panic, no clamor, only people moving along the streets, along the highways, towards the countryside, away from the city.

Scrounging one of the last remaining gold sovereigns from his purse, Rune was able to purchase a bottle of spirits from one of the departing proprietors. Lamken had become nothing more than a beggar, living day-to-day as a destitute and inebriated old vagabond.

It was true that he was nothing more than an unemployed wizard, eccentric and easily distracted. He was a strangely erudite bumpkin, which was what he wanted everyone to think.

For in truth, Lamken guarded a dark secret, as well as a legendary past.

Yet in this modern age, wizards kept a very low profile, often journeying as country tinkers, traveling merchants, or wandering has-beens, which wasn't far from the truth in Rune's case. He spoke with a strange accent too, which brought difficulty wherever he went. To his credit, Lamken was well traveled, but he lacked certain cultural refinements. Bunty observed that the man was coarse, gruff, overly blunt and at times even quarrelsome.

Rune, for his part, often created adversity with his rude and ill-mannered ways. Recently, while wandering through Kent, he irritated the locals by expressing drunken profanities and pursuing the affections of a tavern barmaid. Later, Lamken got into a bitter argument with several RAF officers regarding the conduct of the war, when he insolently referred to them as "pitiful brutes who couldn't fly brooms."

The man often engaged in vehement debates with anyone foolish enough to participate. The topics ranged from rationing to theology, but always ended in hostile feelings and physical escorts to the road out of town.

On a more pleasant note, the wizard loved children, which was evident by how quickly he took to Bunty. Perhaps it was in desperation that the old man agreed to accompany the boy to Crackington Haven, but Lamken had seen something unusual in the lad's eyes. As strange as it seemed at the time, Rune spotted a dragon's shape reflected in Bunty's pupils. Such a vision required immediate investigation. Faintly disturbing, however, was the fact that the likeness of the dragon seemed vaguely familiar, which created all sorts of unsettling possibilities.

With Bunty's assistance, Lamken announced his intentions. "Lead on, lad. I shall journey with you to the North Cornish coast. It has been ages since I wandered the hills of Arthurian legend."

They strolled along the country lanes, stopping occasionally to steal an apple or take a short break for the old man to rest. The two of them sat on a hillside, looking up at the moon, when Lamken intently looked over at the boy.

"What?" Bunty asked, suddenly self-conscious.

"What were you doing in Plymouth alone?" Rune asked.

Bunty shrugged. "It was me home, before me mum was killed."

The wizard took pity on the boy. "I'm sorry, lad. I didn't mean to pry."

Bunty said, "I know that, sir. I lived in Plymouth for most of me life and I guess I missed the place, though there not be much left. I live in Crackington Haven now, with me best friend, Gavin Kane."

"Cornwall has a reputation for being a special place," Rune said. "The Cornish villages are different from anywhere in England, because the magic of the earth runs very close to the surface."

Bunty only nodded.

"Let's be on our way," Lamken said, standing up with a groan. "I wish to see your village, for it has been many years since I traveled these parts."

They walked in silence for a distance.

"Is something troubling you, lad?" Rune asked.

"Doesn't anyone ever suspect you're a wizard?" Bunty wondered.

"I attract few questions, due to my gentle nature and dislike of direct interference with other people's internal affairs and policies," the old man tried to explain. "However, I do feel negative human emotions, such as greed, jealousy, and the lust for power."

"How did you become a wizard?"

"Oh, it's a very long story. Let's just say I was born to it."

"I thought wizards used magic wands."

"Not me. My power resided in my enchanted staff."

"I see, I guess."

"When Elizabeth was taken, I lost my power and now I'm worthless."

"Not to me you're not," Bunty said loudly.

"Well, thank you, boy."

"Why did you name your staff Elizabeth?" Bunty started with the questions again.

"Oh, I didn't name her at all," Rune replied. "It's the name she came with. I merely inherited her from another great sage."

"I'm sorry she was taken from you, sir," Bunty said. "Elizabeth sounds wonderful."

The wizard looked at Bunty with sincere regard. He affectionately fluffed the boy's red hair and said, "Perhaps I'll find Elizabeth one day and you can meet her."

"I would like that."

"As I would enjoy having you as a student."

"Did you like being a wizard?" Bunty asked.

"It had its moments."

"If I knew magic, I would make chocolate cream pies every day and stuff myself."

Lamken laughed aloud. "I bet you would."

"I never imagined wizards still existed in this modern age."

"I'm afraid not much has changed in our world," Lamken said. "We still cling to our old and ineffective traditions. This terrible war has uncovered many of our weaknesses and as a result, even the wizard community is divided by petty rivalries and unstable alliances."

"Don't you worry the Germans might win the war?" Bunty asked.

Rune stopped walking and sighed heavily. "I can't imagine anything more terrifying, lad, to be certain. There are strange things going on in Germany, horrific things that defy description. Unearthly powers have combined to seduce the hearts and minds of weak-minded men, who now conspire to plunge this planet into permanent darkness."

Bunty had hung on every word.

The wizard mistook the boy's mesmerized expression for a look of fear.

"I'm sorry, I didn't mean to frighten you," Lamken said.

Bunty shook his head. "No, that's not it at all. I was just thinking how much you sound like someone I know."

"Oh, and who is this great orator?" Rune jokingly inquired.

"A dragon," Bunty replied matter-of-factly.

Lamken gulped, as he inadvertently swallowed his surprise. "You know a real dragon?"

"Oh, yes, indeed I do," Bunty said proudly. "Sir Thaddeus Osbert is his name."

With a jolt, Lamken Rune's face turned ashen-white, all the color leaving his features in a flash. He grabbed his heart and staggered backwards, as if he had seen a ghost. The wizard's mouth opened and out came a pitiful moan, before the man dropped to his knees, eyes shut tight and his body shaking.

Bunty had witnessed all this in a state of shock. He regained his wits and ran forward to throw his arms around the trembling old man, desperately trying to provide comfort.

"Please, sir, don't die," Bunty begged.

The wizard's lips were blue and his eyes were wide with fear.

"Thaddeus won't hurt you, sir," Bunty continued, hoping to reassure the old man. "He is a friendly and generous dragon, unless you're a German soldier, of course. The Jerries would be terrified."

It was then that the old man formed his quivering lips to speak. His words came out as nothing more than a hoarse whisper.

"Or unless your name is Lamken Rune."

Critical Acclaim for
Secret of the Dragon's Eye

Twelve-year-old Gavin Kane lives in Crackington Haven, a small seaside town in North Cornwall. He makes the most of the last gasp of childhood by playing let's pretend games with his best friend Emily Scott, but now the war has come to change everything. Before his father is called up he shares a book with him, a wonderful book all about King Arthur and a dragon called Thaddeus Osbert. But dragons are made up, aren't they? Surely there isn't really one living in Tintagel?

Reading this is a great way to learn a lot about what it was like to live during World War II. It's all here in some considerable detail, including evacuee boy Bunty who witnesses the bombing of Plymouth, air raid shelters, gas masks, rationing, the Home Guard and more. It almost seems a shame to interrupt it with the fantasy, as there is so much here that is so much larger than life, and distant to how we live now. Letting the dragon appear sooner would have been a good plan, as when he does appear it causes a rift between the real world of bombings, people dying and feats of domestic heroism and the other one of talking dragons and magic swords. It certainly puts a new spin on war fiction, and if this is your sort of thing then you will be pleased that it is only book one in a series. This is an extremely difficult sort of novel to pull off, balancing the two extremes of wartime realism with rather cute fantasy, but it works better than many other efforts.

Reviewed by Rachel A. Hyde
MyShelf.com

978-0-595-48095-1
0-595-48095-0

LaVergne, TN USA
07 January 2011
211425LV00003B/11/A